A HARD LIFE

Ronald Wallace

Bloomington, IN  Milton Keynes, UK

AuthorHouse™
1663 Liberty Drive, Suite 200
Bloomington, IN 47403
www.authorhouse.com
Phone: 1-800-839-8640

AuthorHouse™ UK Ltd.
500 Avebury Boulevard
Central Milton Keynes, MK9 2BE
www.authorhouse.co.uk
Phone: 08001974150

This book is a work of fiction. People, places, events, and situations are the product of the author's imagination. Any resemblance to actual persons, living or dead, or historical events, is purely coincidental.

© 2006 Ronald Wallace. All rights reserved.

No part of this book may be reproduced, stored in a retrieval system, or transmitted by any means without the written permission of the author.

First published by AuthorHouse 6/9/2006

ISBN: 1-4259-2907-9 (e)
ISBN: 1-4259-2906-0 (sc)

Printed in the United States of America
Bloomington, Indiana

This book is printed on acid-free paper.

DEDICATION

I dedicate this novel to my beautiful wife Cheryl, who has always supported my craft, my brother Bobby Dave, my mentor and most encouraging reader, and especially to my new granddaughter.

I petitioned, before she was born, to name my only granddaughter, Rosa Kate. Rosa for my sweet sister Rosalie, who sadly has been called from this earth, but lives continually in our hearts, and Kate, for my pretty daughter-in law. Katie.

Katie and Boyd named their new daughter, Macie Rose, and now I can't imagine her name different, but I still liked the name Rosa Kate, so I penned this novel and gave the name to the heroine of the tale.

My only goal in writing is that someday my children and grandchildren might read my words, think about me, and know in their hearts how much I love them.
Author

TABLE OF CONTENTS

DEDICATION v
ABOUT THE COVER ix
PROLOGUE xi
CHAPTER ONE 1
CHAPTER TWO 13
CHAPTER THREE 25
CHAPTER FOUR 32
CHAPTER FIVE 40
CHAPTER SIX 53
CHAPTER SEVEN 61
CHAPTER EIGHT 69
CHAPTER NINE 80
CHAPTER TEN 88
CHAPTER ELEVEN 94
CHAPTER TWELVE 103
CHAPTER THIRTEEN 113
CHAPTER FOURTEEN 124
CHAPTER FIFTEEN 133
CHAPTER SIXTEEN 142
CHAPTER SEVENTEEN 157
CHAPTER EIGHTEEN 164

CHAPTER NINETEEN	173
CHAPTER TWENTY	181
CHAPTER TWENTY-ONE	191
CHAPTER TWENTY-TWO	200
CHAPTER TWENTY-THREE	205
CHAPTER TWENTY-FOUR	215
CHAPTER TWENTY-FIVE	224
CHAPTER TWENTY-SIX	237
CHAPTER TWENTY-SEVEN	246
CHAPTER TWENTY-EIGHT	258
CHAPTER TWENTY-NINE	265
CHAPTER THIRTY	274
CHAPTER THIRTY-ONE	283
CHAPTER THIRTY-TWO	291
CHAPTER THIRTY-THREE	298
CHAPTER THIRTY-FOUR	307
CHAPTER THIRTY-FIVE	316
CHAPTER THIRTY-SIX	322
CHAPTER THIRTY-SEVEN	328
CHAPTER THIRTY-EIGHT	341
EPILOGUE	344
LAW OF THE PROPHET	346

ABOUT THE COVER

It was springtime in 1959 and I was driving my grandfather, Jesse Lea Wallace, to Bloomfield, Missouri, the county seat of Stoddard County. On Crowley's Ridge, west of Bloomfield, Grandpa asked me if I would like to see the place where his grandfather was hung by bushwhackers during the Civil War. Of course, to a seventeen year-old, this was pretty exciting stuff so naturally I said yes.

We pulled over to the side of the rural highway, parked Dad's truck and got out. We crossed a barbed wire fence and made our way to the top of the ridge south of the road. I can still remember the pasture of fescue grass being exceptionally green and nearly waist deep to me, but the grass only came to just above Grandpa's knees. My grandpa was six feet-two inches tall. At the top of the hill he stopped and pointed out a quantity of large stones scattered haphazardly over about a half-acre area. He told me they had been the original foundation of his grandfather's house and barn that had burned years previously.

He also showed me a still-visible depression in the ground where a big white oak tree had stood in front of the house, and he told me it was where his grandfather, Charles Edward, had been hung for the crime of feeding Confederate soldiers in 1865. He went on to say his father, Benjamin, who was fourteen years of age at the time, had been forced to stand on the front porch of the log house, alongside his mother, to watch the hanging.

The picture on the cover is of my great-grandfather Ben. I'm not sure how old he was at the time of the photograph, but he died in Ripley County, Missouri, in 1917.

Author

A HARD LIFE

PROLOGUE

It had been a bad day so far, and from the string of taillights I could see in all three lanes of traffic just ahead of me, it was not about to get better! Usually the so-called five o'clock afternoon rush hour is pretty well over by six, but now it was six-thirty and traffic was still snarled!

My day had begun badly when the incessant alarm clock had awakened my wife and me at 4:30 am. My wife is a registered hospice nurse and normally doesn't have to get up until seven or so.

We're living what my wife and I term as the late term, yuppie, modern lifestyle. Our two boys are grown now with families of their own and my wife and I are trying to put away as much savings as we can to augment our not too distant retirement incomes.

I leave home either on Sunday afternoon, or early Monday morning like today, and drive the hundred and seventy-five odd miles to St. Louis for the week. I lease a two-room apartment above an appliance store five miles or so from my office at St. Angelina Medical Center and commute every day to the hospital.

Sometime after noon on Fridays I leave my office and make the trip back to my home to spend the short weekend, mostly completing and complaining about, all the honey-dos that my honey has jotted down for me during the week.

All three lanes of traffic had come to a dead stop and I noticed the lady in the Mercedes next to me open up the St. Louis Daily Post Dispatch across her steering wheel and lean back to read. I was prepared too, or thought so, and reached for a novel I kept in the console of my new sparkling silver, four-wheel drive, gas guzzling SUV

The book was gone! For a moment I panicked, convinced someone must have been in my truck! I retraced in my mind the last time I remembered seeing the novel and suddenly remembered taking it out at the car wash on Saturday and leaving it on top of the vacuum machine.

Dad Gum it! I hope whoever finds my book enjoys it! Annoyed even further because now I had another reason to whine about the bad day I was having, I leaned back in the soft bucket seat and sighed pitifully.

The day had started badly at home in my bedroom as I've already said. When I arrived at work this morning I had an urgent message on my voicemail to call my admissions supervisor. She had terrible news. On the previous Friday afternoon, after I had left the office to drive home, one of the emergency room admission clerks had gotten into a cursing match with a pediatric patient's mother. My boss, the chief financial officer of the largest hospital in St. Louis County, had to drive back to the hospital from his south St. Louis suburban home to meet with my supervisor and the offending employee.

My supervisor seemed to enjoy informing me the offending employee was the nice little church going lady I had practically insisted on hiring against my supervisor's firm recommendation that we shouldn't! My Supervisor went on to say that she and my boss suspended the employee pending a full investigation by human resource staff.

I could almost swear I detected a barely camouflaged note of glee in my supervisor's voice when she told me that Mr. Wilbanks, the CFO, informed her to tell me to come to his office first thing on Monday morning. I figured I was in for a chewing for leaving early on Friday, therefore creating a situation where he was forced to come back to the hospital to deal with the altercation involving my staff member

I didn't disappoint myself on my prophetic abilities. Carl Wilbanks can chew with the best of administrators and he reamed me out good and proper!

That was my day before nine o'clock this morning! I won't even tell you about the rest of the day for it was too painful for me to try and re-live for you! Just ask any healthcare worker about the Monday following a full moon weekend and they will fill you in. Did I mention the parking lot door ding I just found on the driver's side of my new SUV?

I opened my eyes to check the traffic and all I could see now were red taillights shining brighter as daylight faded along with my hopes of a stress relieving late afternoon run in Forest Park. Only those with a death wish run in Forest Park after dark! The bright red orbs extended as far down the inter-belt as I could see.

"Now all I need is for it to start raining or snowing!" I mumbled aloud to myself, and almost magically big wet snowflakes the size of goose feathers began to plop down on the big import's windshield! I leaned back again in the soft bucket seat and rested my tired, throbbing eyes.

A HARD LIFE

A HARD LIFE

CHAPTER ONE

My name is Ben Branch Walker and I turned seven on January ninth, four months previous to a tragic day in my life. The year was 1864 and my home was in Stoddard County, a mile or so south of Bloomfield, Missouri.

My papa had sent me to the springhouse at the bottom edge of our yard to fetch a bucket of fresh water. Our four-room log house sat atop a large hill that is part of a long series of ridges named Crowley's Ridge. Crowley's Ridge extends all the way from northern Illinois across eastern Missouri, and south halfway across Arkansas, ending at a tall bluff overlooking the wide Mississippi River. I know that now, but back then I probably didn't even know we lived in Missouri!

I was big for my age and stronger than most seven-year olds. That's why Papa trusted me to bring in water for the house. My mama was cooking a meal for a group of Graycoats, which was the only name I knew for confederate soldiers. I had never heard the term confederate at the time. I only knew them as Graycoats.

"Gimme' a dippah o' thet' cool watah', Boy!" a large bearded Graycoat officer said to me as I entered the kitchen where Mama stood stirring a big pot of stew simmering over a bed of coals in the fireplace.

He was standing in the doorway leading from the kitchen to the living room. The officer was wearing a gray, wide-brimmed hat that matched his stained shirt. An ostrich plume was stuck in the brim of the hat, although I didn't recognize it as such then, for I had no idea what an ostrich was. The biggest bird I had ever seen was a wild turkey gobbler my papa had killed the previous summer.

I obeyed the big man wordlessly and shuffled across the wood plank floor holding the heavy bucket by the bail rope with both hands. He was tall and his boots were muddy. When he reached down for the gourd dipper, I could smell chaw tobacco emanating from his dirty beard.

"You strong fer' ye' age, ain't ye, Boy?" he said with a smile that showed ugly yellow teeth.

"Come over here, Branch," my mama said, "you can stir the stew whilst' I slice up some bread." I think my mama wanted me to stay away from the soldiers.

There were three more soldiers sitting in the living room with my papa. My big brother Jon David sat on the floor by the front door. Jon David was fifteen and almost growed up! I couldn't understand why he looked so angry. Jon David never got angry!

"Bonnie Ann!" my papa called from the living room. "Supper cooked for these boys yet?"

"It'll be ready in a jiffy, Eddie," she answered. My mama had always called my papa, Eddie. Everyone else called him Ed, or Edward. I never called him anything

A Hard Life

but Papa, or the seat of my home-sewed britches would have gotten warmed up considerable, to say the least!

Me, Papa, and Jon David sat in the living room while Mama served the soldiers sitting around our big kitchen table like they belonged there. Papa sat where he could keep an eye on Mama, although I really didn't understand why. I was mystified why we had to stay in the living room while my mama served our hard-earned larder of food to rank strangers!

Although I didn't understand what was happening, I was shrewd enough to keep my curiosity to myself. I had never seen my papa act quite this way around strangers and I sensed that all was not right.

I didn't rightly know what was wrong, but I knew Jon David was terrible angry about something! I already told you earlier, Jon David never got angry about anything, and Papa was watching my mama like a rooster watching a june bug crawling across the chicken yard!

The graycoats mounted up and left a cloud of dust swirling in the front yard when they left. Papa watched them until they were nothing but wee specks on the horizon riding toward Bloomfield.

Papa bolted the doors that night and tilted a kitchen chair against both the front and kitchen doors. I had never seen him do that before in my life. It wasn't cold and usually we left the doors open to let the house air out at night.

We heard several horses riding up the ridge toward the house the next morning while we sat at the kitchen table eating breakfast. Mama had arisen early and baked sweet cornbread in a big iron pot over the fireplace coals.

There's nothin' I loved more than sweet cornbread and cold jersey cow milk!

"Charles Edward Walker!" a booming voice said from beyond our front porch. Papa looked at mama across our table then and the look that passed between them I will remember and carry with me until the day someone kicks dirt atop me in my grave!

"Who is it?" Papa shouted through the front door.

"Open in the name of the Union Army, Walker!" the booming voice answered. "There's rifles trained on the house, so come out with your hands empty!"

"Don't open the door, Eddie?" my mama pleaded, but Papa slid back the bolt and opened the door. The morning sunlight streamed through the doorway, practically blinding us so we almost couldn't see who was in the front yard.

"I'm Captain James Asbury, representing the United States Army, Walker." The man speaking was tall, dressed in blue, and sitting stiffly on a white horse. He wore a wide-brimmed hat similar in shape to the graycoat officer's, except the union captain had a big red feather stuck in his hatband.

"Trooper Davis of my platoon said he sat over in that patch of woods yonder and watched you feed and care for confederate soldiers yesterday afternoon! What do you have to say for yourself?" my papa nodded his head.

"They had guns, Captain, just like you," Papa answered. "If we hadn't fed them only the good Lord knows what they might have done to my family."

"Did you try and resist, Walker?" the captain asked, "and do not invoke the name of the Lord again in my

A Hard Life

presence, Sir!" I saw the muscles in Papa's cheek bunch up like they did when I was in deep trouble.

"This is my home, Captain!" my papa retorted, "and your horse is standing in my front yard. If I want to call on the name of the good Lord I'll do so, Sir!"

"You're under arrest, Walker, for aiding and abetting the enemy of the United States of America!" the captain retorted.

I could tell from his tone he was as mad as my papa. I was scared and I felt for my mama's hand behind her long skirt. She gripped my little hand until it hurt, but it felt good at the time.

"You have admitted your guilt, Sir!" the captain continued. "The punishment for aiding the enemy is hanging!"

The captain waved for two of his men to dismount and approach the porch where my papa stood defiantly. He was pale suddenly, but still defiant.

"If I submit without a fight, will you spare my family, Captain?" my father asked before the two soldiers took hold of him. My mama protested, but the captain nodded his head.

"I'll spare your wife and sons, Walker." he said. "but you must hang. I have no choice. If I allow everyone in Missouri to feed the confederate trash without recourse it will prolong this awful war."

"I ain't part of your awful war, Captain!" my papa said, "and neither is Missouri!"

I watched in mortal fear and disbelief of what was happening as my papa's hands were bound behind him and he was lifted to the back of one of the soldier's horses. A rope was thrown over the limb of a big white oak in our front yard and the noose was put around my papa's neck.

Mama caught Jon David as he started off the porch. She wrapped her arms around his chest from behind and held him so tightly I wondered how he could breathe.

"Let me go, Mama!" Jon David cried, but mama held him tight.

"Jon David!" My papa shouted from the back of the Union horse. "Don't fight against your mama, Boy! You've got to be a man and help her, Son. Lord knows she's gonna' need you!"

Papa glared directly at the union captain when he used the name of the Lord again. Jon David quit straining against Mama, but she didn't release her hold on him

"Bonnie Ann!" my papa shouted, "Sell this place and move to Doniphan. Find my brother Clady. He'll take care of you and the boys."

My mama was crying harder than I'd ever seen her before. Something kinda snapped inside me when I saw her crying like that and I jumped off the porch after picking up a piece of stove wood from the pile beside the door. I headed straight toward the union captain brandishing my chunk of wood like a battle-axe!

I got me in a pretty good blow to his leg and then he reached down and grabbed my right arm holding the piece of wood. He hauled me up with my arm bent kinda' backward and everyone in the yard heard as the bone in my elbow snapped like a piece of frozen Dutch elm!

Captain Asbury dropped me back to the ground immediately and then dismounted to come to stand over me. I jumped to my feet with my broken arm dangling. He reached down and folded my afflicted limb across my belly and told me to hold it with my left hand. Then he looked up at my father sitting on the union horse with the rope around his neck.

"I apologize for breaking your son's arm, Walker." he said. "I promise I'll take him back to my camp where a surgeon can attend to him."

"You heartless bastard! Damn you, Captain!" my father said vehemently.

"Eddie don't swear, " my mama cried. "This ain't no time for swearin'!"

Papa looked at her and for the first time in my seven years I saw tears streaming down my papa's cheeks.

I was kinda' in a daze. My arm didn't hurt, but I couldn't even move a finger on my right hand. It was as numb as if it were frozen. I stood there holding it with my left hand and watched as a union soldier slapped the horse my papa was sitting on.

Papa slid off the back of the horse when it jumped from beneath him and he fell until the rope went real taut. I heard his neck snap making the same sound my elbow had made just earlier. I was only seven, but I realized then that my dear papa was gone from me forever!

Captain Asbury wrapped his coat around me and lifted me up to his saddle and then mounted behind me. I was still dazed and I didn't fight him. When we rode away my mama was down on her knees on the front porch crying like she would never stop. Jon David stood beside her with his hand on her back. He glared at Captain Asbury with a look I had never seen in Jon David's eyes before. He stayed glaring like that until we were out of sight of my home.

The union army was camped in a big flat field near Dexter. White tents in neat rows covered the field from fence to fence. Captain Asbury took me directly to a large tent at the edge of the field where a field hospital had been set up.

I don't remember much of what went on after that. I do remember being cold. I heard the surgeon tell Captain Asbury that he couldn't set my arm without operating on it first, but he said the swelling was too bad to operate. He said my arm needed to be kept in ice until the swelling went down enough.

For years I never knew where Captain Asbury came up with ice in Dexter, Missouri in the month of May, 1865, but he did, and that's why I distinctly remember being so cold. I remember being near to freezing day and night for several days and then they put me to sleep and operated on my right elbow.

After my surgery I was put into a tent by myself next to Captain Asbury's. The pain in my splinted arm was severe and when no one was around I cried into my pillow until I was so exhausted I had to sleep. I remember the pain in my elbow being real bad, but I think I cried mostly because I was scared and homesick. I wanted my mama and home, but when I thought about home then the image of my papa's face when he came to the end of that hangman's rope would appear and I had to put all of them out of my mind!

Long after midnight one night, a week or so after my surgery, I had my face buried in my pillow and I heard a strange sound coming from the back of my tent. I raised my tear-streaked fact to see what might be attacking me and was practically paralyzed by fear when I saw the blade

A Hard Life

of a knife stuck through the tent fabric, slitting downward toward the ground.

My eyes must have been as big as saucers when Jon David's face appeared in the opening he had made with papa's pig-stickin' knife. He put his finger to his lips and smiled at me. I was never so glad to see anyone before in my life!

"Are you all right, Branch?" he whispered after he had crawled through the opening and came to stand by my cot. I buried my face in his belly and wept uncontrollably. Jon David held me and let me cry for a little while and then he shook me.

"You got to be strong, Branch." he whispered. "You got to do it for Mama. I know you're scared and you're hurtin, but you got to suck it up and steel yourself agin' it!"

The sound of my big brother's voice shaming me had always had a dramatic effect and when he told me to be strong, suddenly I was.

"Do you know where Asbury's tent is, Branch?" Jon David was holding my face up so he could see my eyes. I nodded and pointed to my left.

"He's in the tent next to yours?" he whispered, and I nodded solemnly. I was done with crying now. He nodded back to me.

"You stay here until I come back for you, Branch." he whispered. He had a funny look in his eyes that I had seen before. It was the same one I remembered from the day Captain Asbury put me on his saddle and rode past the front porch where my mama was grieving.

"Where you goin'?" I whispered, but Jon David put his hand over my mouth and shook his head from side to side.

"Never you mind, Branch!" he whispered emphatically. "You just stay put till' I come back to git you!" He must have recognized the fear and doubt in my expression, for he put his face closer to mine.

"I won't never leave you, Branch." he said. "I promise I'll always come for you when you need me!" Then he was gone.

I stared at the opening in the back of my tent and suddenly I couldn't stay put any longer and I eased off the cot. I had my britches on, for I never took them off anymore, even when I slept. I pulled my homespun wool shirt over my head with only my left arm going into the sleeve. I left my bandaged right arm tight against my skinny belly with the sling around my neck to support it. The heavy wool shirt helped to hold it against me. I dropped to my knees and using my left hand as balance crawled through the opening.

The moon was full, but the sky was cloudy making it dark as a dungeon. At that precise moment however, the moon moved out from behind a cloud and I recognized Jon David's feet sliding through a slotted opening in Captain Asbury's tent.

I eased over silently to the slit and opened it just enough to see inside. The scene from inside chilled my heart!

Captain Asbury was sound asleep and snoring. He was lying on his back, bare-chested with a wool blanket pulled up to his waist. His head was nearer to me and I marveled at how white his skin was and how peaceful he

A Hard Life

appeared. Jon David was standing beside his cot, holding papa's knife and gazing downward at the captain with the cruelest expression I had ever seen on my brother's face.

As I watched in silent horror, Jon David reached down, picked up an extra wool blanket folded beside the captain's cot and held it kinda' bunched in his left hand. Then with a strong quick movement of his right hand he slit Captain Asbury's throat from one side of his neck to the other!

Jon David then quickly placed the folded blanket over the captain's face and upper chest and held it down with all his weight. The captain flounced on the cot with Jon David holding him down for what seemed like an eternity before the spasms of death subsided and Captain Asbury lay still.

Jon David stood erect then and gazed down on the blood-soaked blanket. Jon's hands were glistening with blood that had soaked through the thick wool fabric.

Suddenly the flap of the tent beyond the dead captain's feet was pushed aside and a familiar soldier stepped into the tent with a cocked rifle in his hands. It was the union sergeant that had placed my father on his horse and later slapped him on the rump causing my papa to hang! Jon David stood beside the dead Captain, still holding the knife clutched in his bloody right hand.

The sergeant aimed his rifle at Jon David and I winced and closed my eyes, waiting for the inevitable shot to ring out that would end the life of my big brother, with me probably getting shot with the next bullet! When the shot didn't come after a few moments I opened my eyes slowly, one at a time..

The sergeant was staring at first me and then back to my brother. He slowly eased the rifle down and lowered the hammer on the Springfield. He then spoke the most surprising words we could imagine. Words Jon David and I never expected and will always wonder about.

"Git outta' here, both you boys!" he said in a quiet, but clear voice. His blue eyes above his full mustache shone with a resolve that I had only seen once before in my young life. It was the same resolve I had seen in my papa's eyes when he had looked at my mama from the back of the horse just before he was hung.

"You boys forget about killin'!" he continued. "This'un and the other you had to watch!" He stared directly into each of our eyes. "Take your mother to your uncle's place and watch over her like your daddy tole' you! Now git!"

He didn't have to tell Jon David again. My brother first turned toward me and then back toward the Sergeant. Jon David then lowered his head in an abbreviated bow that said thank you to the union sergeant more than words could ever say.

Then my brother reached down and picked up Captain Asbury's hat and looked at the Sergeant with raised eyebrows. The Sergeant nodded his head to him and then me and Jon David were gone like two foxes out of the chicken coop!

A HARD LIFE

CHAPTER TWO

Mama cried and held me so tight I was afraid she about squeezed the breath outta' me! It felt so good I didn't care though.

"I missed you so bad, Branch." she whispered to me and I closed my eyes to blink back the tears. I felt like I needed to be grown up like Jon David and I didn't want Mama to see me cry.

Jon David and me had ridden back home on one of Papa's draft horses. My brother had ridden it close to the union camp and left him tied in a small grove of trees until we returned.

Our big wagon was sitting by the front of our home and all of our possessions had been moved into it and stored under a white tarp that was tied down securely. Jon David caught the other horse and hitched both of them to the wagon within an hour of us returning home.

We were still afraid the union soldiers would come after us. Mama didn't know what had happened to Captain Asbury and Jon David and I had made a pact that we would never tell her about last night's events.

I looked at the white oak tree in our front yard where my papa had been when I was there last.

"Where's papa's grave, Mama?" I asked and she held me back from her to stare into my face.

"You've figured that out already?" she asked and I nodded.

"I'm so sorry that we've all had to endure this horrible time, Branch." She combed her fingers through my hair as she spoke to me. "You're too young to have to face such tragedy, but it's come upon us and we have to withstand it and go on. Do you understand?" I nodded.

"I'll take him and show him Pop's grave and marker, Mama." Jon David said. "You've already said your goodbyes, so you don't need to go."

"Are you sure you don't want me to go with you, Branch?" she asked me and I shook my head. I didn't trust my voice right then.

"Mama, we're loaded up and ready to go." Jon David said. "Why don't you take one more spin around the inside of the house and make sure we didn't leave nothin'. When Branch and I get back from sayin' our goodbyes to Pop, then we'll head out for Doniphan."

She nodded and turned toward the porch steps. Jon David waited until she was inside and out of sight and then he retrieved Captain Asbury's hat and waved for me to follow him at a trot.

Jon David and Mama had buried Papa under the only apple tree we had managed to make grow in the heavy Stoddard County soil. It was up the hill from the barn and house a hundred yards or so. Jon David told me that Mama had scratched Papa's name and other things on a

A Hard Life

wide cypress plank he had pulled from the floor of the barn loft.

He had buried the plank standing at the head of the mound of fresh dirt. I couldn't read or cipher as yet so Jon David traced the words on the board as he spoke them,

Charles Edward Walker
Beloved Father and Faithful Husband
Born July 17, 1829
Murdered by Captain James Asbury, U.S. Cavalry
May 4, 1865

"See this notch I cut into the top of the board, Branch?" I looked up at the top of the cypress plank through tear-filled eyes and nodded.

"You know what that's for?" he continued and I shook my head.

"For this." he said and placed the union captain's hat into the slot. The hat sat there on Papa's grave marker jauntily, as if placed there temporarily, but until a very strong wind came along, the notch would hold it securely in place. The red feather in the hatband fluttered slightly in the wind and the early morning sun reflected its crimson brightness.

"Long as this hat lasts, everyone who sees it will know that our pop's murder has been avenged." he said.

I nodded, but I didn't really understand and I wondered how anyone else who saw it would know what it meant, but it seemed important to Jon David so it was certainly fine with me.

"Now let's go to Doniphan and see what kind of sonsabitch' Uncle Clady is!" Jon David said this emphatically and started back down the hill toward the house and barn.

I was hesitant to leave Papa's marker for some reason. It didn't seem right somehow, for I had not left Papa anything to remember me by. I looked down at the fresh dirt that Jon David had mounded up on the gravesite. I dropped to my knees and put my good left arm out placing my handprint deeply into the soft soil.

I stood then, surveyed what I had done and turned my eyes to the cypress marker.

"Goodbye, Papa" I said, "I'd have left you both hands, but my right arm hurts real bad." I turned then and ran down the hill trying to catch up with Jon David.

I spent the next ten years trying to catch up with Jon David. So did the law! When I was seventeen, I rode a skinny mule, still wearing his plow harness and blinders to town, to visit my brother in the Ripley County jail in Doniphan.

"Are you all right, Jon David?" I inquired. I was standing outside the jail cell twisting the brim on an old ragged felt hat. My brother was in the back of the cell leaned against the brick wall with three other men and they were telling nasty jokes. At least that's what I figured they were doing judging by their raucous laughter and a few dirty words I had heard as I approached the cell. Jon David looked over at me and frowned in an exaggerated way that told me he didn't mean it.

"You didn't need to dress up in your Sunday best jest' to visit us, Branch!" he said and the three men around him took a better look at me and broke up with laughter.

A Hard Life

I looked down at my dirty homespun shirt and patched wool trousers that were hand-me-downs from Jon David himself. The ragged cuffs of the pants struck me about halfway between my bony knees and skinny ankles that disappeared into old brogan work shoes with no socks. I smiled back at my big brother.

"I actually started out from home in a brand new suit and shined boots, but crossin' them dad-blamed rivers betwixt' here and there is a bitch, Jon David!"

My brother dropped his head to laugh and then crossed the cell, reached through the bars and pulled me up closer with a hand behind my neck and kissed me soundly on the forehead.

"Any of you gents, who can't stand seein' a man kissin' his baby brother can look the other way or kiss the biggest part of me facin' em'!" Jon David stated loudly staring into my eyes affectionately. I flushed red and dropped my eyes from my big brother's.

"How you doin', Branch?" he practically whispered and when I raised my eyes to his, the smile was gone from his face.

"Mama still mad at me?" I shook my head at his question.

"She ain't mad at you, Jon David," I replied, "jest hurt and worried bout' you and all your shenanigans." I could still smell two-day old liquor on his morning breath. He dropped his eyes and head for a moment.

"I know, Son." he said.

Jon David had started calling me that after Papa was killed. Not all the time, but once in a while and it usually made me feel kinda' warm all over. He looked down again for a moment and when he looked back up at me, the seriousness was gone and the old go-to-hell mischievous glint in his eyes that attracted bad women and furious lawmen by the score was back.

"You still kissin' Uncle Clady's ass for Mama's board and keep?" he asked and now it was my turn to frown.

"I work the fields for im', Jon David!" I said as I leaned back from the cell bars, "but it ain't to kiss his ass! I'm tryin' to do right by Mama and repay him for takin' us in and keepin' us outta' the pore' house!"

"They ain't no such thing as a pore' house, Branch!" he said defiantly. "That's a damned ol' wives tale. I wish to hell there had been sometimes! Truth is, if folks don't have somebody takin' care of them, then they starve and die and other folks just kick em' outta' their path, claim their land, and put their profits in a bank vault!"

I stared back at my big brother's sudden angry eyes with mine probably just as angry. I guessed this had to be at least the thousandth time we had debated this subject over the last ten years.

"You ain't never gonna' git over us losin' our Stoddard County land to the carpet-baggers, are you, Jon David?"

"Nope!" he said with a crooked smile, and once again, almost miraculously, the anger was wiped away from his expression and his devil-may-care look was back in his eyes.

"How long you spect' on bein' here this time?" I asked him, deliberately changing the subject.

"We're kinda' at the beck and call of Judge Peters, Branch." Jon David said waving his arm at his buddies. "We figger' he'll get tired of feedin' us in a day or two and turn us out. We got ourselves in a fight with town boys, but we didn't hurt no one real bad."

A Hard Life

"I heard tell one of them town boys didn't come to till' Sunday afternoon, Jon David." I said and my big brother smiled.

"I socked im' pretty good didn't I, Son?" he replied with a crooked smile. I frowned and then looked at the floor.

"You comin' home when you get out?" I asked. He looked at me sharply.

"Our home is in Stoddard County, bein' turned into a hog waller' by some damned ol' politician, Branch." he replied bitterly. "I spect' by now it smells worse than this jail cell. I don't plan on ever goin' back again."

I held my brother's angry eyes for only a moment before I had to look down again. I nodded and put my old hat on again.

"Mama keeps a lamp lit at night for you, Jon David." I said without looking up. "Bad as we need to save kerosene, she leaves it burnin' all night."

"Tell her she best save Uncle Clady's coal oil, Branch!" he replied angrily again. "He might kick both of you offen' his place if he finds out she's wastin' it!"

I nodded and turned to leave the jail without looking at Jon David again.

"Hey, Branch," Deputy Sheriff Brady Foreister spoke to me as I was about to exit the jail. "They's a lawyer from St. Louis here yesterday lookin' for a young man your age named Ben Walker. You know ary' Walkers named Ben?" I looked at him with a puzzled expression.

"My first name is Ben. Everyone always called me by my middle name, Branch." I replied. "What would a St. Louis lawyer want with me?" He shrugged.

"Didn't rightly say," he answered, "jest' said he was searchin'. Seemed right dedicated to findin' im'." I nodded and turned to leave again.

"You could ask im' yourself, Branch." Brady looked up from his paperwork to say. "He's stayin' over at the hotel, leastways he'll be there until the night train comes through headed north."

I had no interest in talking to an attorney from St. Louis, besides I was still smarting some from Jon David's remark about the way I was dressed. He had made it into a joke, but I felt the barb just the same. I didn't appreciate criticism about mine and Mama's poor ways, even from my own brother, and I had no inclination to receive snooty looks from hotel lobby clerks or a city slicker attorney from St. Louis.

I rode Uncle Clady's mule back to the thirty-acre plot we called the horseshoe field, named that because the Little Black River circled it, except for a narrow neck at one end about a hundred yards wide. The little two-room clapboard house Uncle Clady allowed me and Mama to live in was a quarter mile downriver from the horseshoe field.

Every wet year the horseshoe field flooded when the Little Black rose out of its banks. It was the only field where Uncle Clady allowed Mama, Jon David, and me, to keep whatever we could raise there. About every four years, on the average, the field flooded and we lost whatever we had managed to coax into growing.

During those flood years, we had to buy food and rent high land from Uncle Clady. Seemed like about the time we got him paid off from the last flood, it would start raining somewhere up north and we'd be back in debt again.

Jon David used to work all day for Uncle Clady and then was allowed to use one of his mules to farm the horseshoe field at night. My brother had done that from the time we moved from Stoddard County until he had finally gotten fed up, quit, and moved out on his own, two years previously. I was fifteen then and it became my responsibility to work for Uncle Clady.

The only reason I wasn't working for Uncle Clady today was because according to him his fields were too wet and we'd make dirt clods instead of seedbeds. The horseshoe field was wetter than Uncle Clady's high land, but I plowed it anyway because I took advantage of every opportunity to work days instead of at night by lantern light.

A day's work for Uncle Clady began at daylight and ended when it was too dark to see. When there wasn't fieldwork to be done, there were daily backbreaking chores with the livestock, including killing and butchering, usually in the fall and winter. Uncle Clady maintained hogs, cattle, chickens, turkeys, horses, and mules.

By the way, we didn't kill and butcher horses and mules. However, if Uncle Clady or Aunt Imogene could have found someone to have bought the meat we'd probably have done them too!

Mama did washing and ironing for all of Uncle Clady's family, which included himself, his wife Imogene, and their two daughters, Carla and Darlene. We figured the two girls had to change wardrobes at least once every day, judging from the wagonload of clothes that Uncle Clady had me pick up and deliver every week.

I would pick up clothes on Wednesday mornings and they had to be brought back, washed, starched, ironed, and folded to Aunt Imogene's satisfaction, every Friday by noon.

Uncle Clady and Aunt Imogene lived on high land a mile north of our place. Our little house sat way back off the main road on the bank of the river. An all-weather gravel road maintained by Ripley County road crews went by Uncle Clady's house. The dirt road that snaked across his fields back to our house would become impassable, even for a wagon, for the better part of the winter. Mama would have to walk through the mud to Aunt Imogene's on Wednesday's, Thursday's, and most of Friday's to do their washing and ironing during the worst part of the winter, then do her and my clothes washing back at our place on her off days.

Mama wasn't allowed to eat with Uncle Clady's family when she was there doing washing, so she had to carry food with her, or as she did most often, go all day without a bite to eat.

I could smell meat frying long before I got within sight of the dim lantern light shining out from the only window in the back of mine and Mama's little house. Moonlight reflected off the peaceful little river to my left as I rode the harnessed mule toward home. Then when I passed around a small bend in the river road, suddenly I could see the light!

Something about that light glowing out into the darkness always gave me goose bumps and put a lump in my throat that I didn't quite understand. It had become a sign of warmth and security to me when I was out in the dark approaching our house.

A Hard Life

I knew that beyond that dim light and inside that little house were all the things that presently I counted on and valued above any thing else in my life. Warmth from the open fireplace, and belly pleasing food for a hungry boy who never, ever seemed to get enough of his mama's cooking.

But more important than all, I knew there was absolute unconditional love waiting inside, from the only person I had left in the world who really cared a snap whether I lived or died.

Well, maybe that's not entirely true. I know that Jon David loves me, but now he's mostly interested in taking care of Jon David! Uncle Clady and Aunt Imogene would have been distressed at my death, or my leaving, but really only because of what it would cost them in lost labor.

But, I was absolutely convinced that my mama loved me totally, in spite of any spots or blemishes I might have imagined or recognized in myself. That little light shining out on a cold and mostly uncaring world might as well have been a beacon shining down from Heaven as far as I was concerned.

"Hello, Son." Mama said after I had cared for Uncle Clady's mule and washed up in the wash pan sitting on the back steps. Mama had watched from the open back door for me to finish with the mule and when I approached the house, brought out a heated kettle so I wouldn't have to wash my hands and face in cold water.

When I was finished washing, I hugged her tight and kissed her hard on the cheek and then she held my face in her hands for a moment before she hugged me hard again. When I pulled back from her she smiled and pulled off my hat so she could reach up and tousle my dark brown hair.

"I need to cut your hair, come Saturday, Son." she said. I nodded and put my arm around her shoulders. I had grown to be two heads taller than she in just the last year.

"Are you hungry?" she asked. "I've not got nothin but hog jowl, boiled taters', butterbeans with cornbread, and fresh picked greens that's been simmerin' over the fire all afternoon, so's I guess you'll just have to make do."

I turned my eyes toward the sky and spun around on the porch step on the instep of my right foot.

"Thank you, Lord!" I shouted aloud at the stars and the silent dark world surrounding our little home. Then my mama and I laughed at each other as we fought to see who could get in the house first!

A HARD LIFE

CHAPTER THREE

I was by the fireplace taking advantage of the flickering light running a cotton patch down the barrels of Papa's old Belgium made muzzle-loading shotgun. It was the only gun the union soldiers had left us on the day they murdered my father.

Young rabbits were frying sized now and I wanted to go out early the next morning and collect some before the foxes and owls thinned them out. The fields along the river had been lousy with them for the last few days, as I would leave our house to go to Uncle Clady's. Mama's slow fried rabbit was the epitome of fine eating in our world.

Mama was sitting in her rocker by the kerosene lamp darning up heel holes in my only pair of wool socks. I'd glance over at her from time to time to rub my belly and smile. I had eaten man-sized portions of her fabulous supper and didn't quit until I was about ready to pop my buttons!

I heard an unusual sound from far off and my smile turned to a look of unease.

"Somebody's comin' on horseback." I said, somewhat concerned, for no one ever visited Mama and me, especially at night.

"Put the gun away, Branch." Mama said. I considered disobeying her, but thought better of it and hung the old shotgun back up on the hooks above the front door.

"I ain't loaded it yet anyway." I said to her and opened the door to see if I could tell who might be coming to see us at this time of night. The moonlight was bright and I made out two riders trotting their horses down the lane through Uncle Clady's fields.

"It's Jon David and somebody!" I said over my shoulder excitedly, for I would have recognized the way my brother sat his horse as far away as I could see him, even at night.

"Are you sure?" Mama said excitedly and almost pushed me off the front step as she tried to get to where she could see too. She stared at the rider's shapes barely discernible in the moonlight. They were still a half-quarter away across the field.

"I do believe you're right, Son!" she said excitedly. "Maybe your visit to see your brother in jail did some good." Mama had been worrying about Jon David more than usual lately and she had readily agreed when I had suggested that I might take some time off from plowing to go see him today.

"I wonder who's with im'?" she asked. "Can you see to tell?" I shook my head as I strained to see across the field.

"Don't recognize the other rider." I replied. "He rides like a city slicker, but it's probably one of John David's buddies he was in jail with." I replied. "Jon David probably smelled your supper all the way to Doniphan."

Mama slapped me on the shoulder, but in a kidding way. She always got excited when Jon David made one of his infrequent visits.

"Hello, the house!" Jon David shouted from the edge of the yard. "Don't shoot the prodigal son!"

"Hello yourself!" I shouted back. "Come on in, Brother! We didn't kill the fatted calf, but I suspect you'll like what Mama fixed for supper even better!"

I stepped off the front step and tried to avoid the mud puddles, and other things, in the front yard as I walked to the hitching post where Jon David and the other man I didn't recognize, dismounted and tied up their horses. I noticed that the portly man with Jon David was riding a rented horse from the stable in Doniphan. I could tell by the brand on the sorrel.

"You and your friend watch where you step, Jon David." I said. "Mama's chickens ain't trained to always go out back to do their business." I led the way back to the house and held the door for the two men to go in.

"Mama, this here's Reuben Rosenthal. He's a lawyer all the way from St. Louis." Jon David said as he gave Mama a big hug. Mama's face was flushed with excitement from seeing her eldest son for the first time in months.

"Welcome to our home, Mr. Rosenthal." she said and held out her hand to the balding man holding his derby hat that he had removed upon entering the house.

"Thank you, Mrs. Walker." he said as he returned her handshake and even dropped his chin in a respectful bow. "You have a lovely home."

I looked at Jon David as I stepped around the two men and moved over by the fireplace where I could be out of their way. My older brother raised his eyebrows to me as he smiled. We both knew Mama and me didn't have a lovely home. An honest and mostly clean one, but definitely not one that could be described as lovely.

"Would you care for a bite to eat, Mr. Rosenthal?" Mama inquired. "I'm right certain Jon David will want something." she said this with a smile toward her son.

"Maybe a cup of coffee, or tea, Mrs. Walker?" he replied courteously. "I've had my supper at the hotel."

"Mama don't keep tea leaves," Jon David replied frankly, "coffee, she saves for breakfast. How about a pitcher of buttermilk? I spect' when you see and smell Mama's cookin' you'll change your mind about eatin' somethin'."

Attorney Rosenthal nodded and sat down at the kitchen table when Jon David waved him toward a chair as he took one himself at the head of the table.

I smiled to myself. When Jon David came in the house, regardless of how long since his last visit, he automatically took over as the head of the home, but I didn't mind. Since Papa had been gone I had always looked at my big brother as the head of the family too.

For a man who had already had his supper, Mr. Rosenthal accounted for himself quite well at Mama's kitchen table! He had just finished his third plate of butterbeans and cornbread when he finally wiped the buttermilk from his upper lip with the back of his hand and pushed himself back from the table, smiling at Mama as he shook his head.

A Hard Life

"I don't remember when I've ever enjoyed such a fine meal, Mrs. Walker." he said. "Your two sons are quite lucky to have such a fine cook for a mother."

My mama blushed a little and Jon David looked over at me and winked. Jon David had filled his belly some time earlier and the three of us had watched with interest as Reuben Rosenthal ate like it was his last meal on earth.

"I would imagine you folks are wondering why I am here?" he began and his eyes moved around the room until he had included all three of us in his conversation.

"I paid your son Jon to bring me to meet both of you." he continued and Mama looked sharply at Jon David.

"He paid you to bring him here?" she asked my brother

"When someone's foolish enough to offer me money to come eat one of my mama's meals I feel he deserves me accommodatin' him!" Jon David said defensively.

"I was more than happy to pay him for the assistance, I assure you, Mrs. Walker." the attorney said, taking up for Jon David. My mama looked back at the attorney questioningly.

"Why would you pay money to have somebody bring you to see us?" she inquired.

"Because, Madam, a very wealthy family is paying me to find you, or at least to find your son, Ben." he replied and then looked directly at me.

"I'm assuming this is Ben?" he asked.

"His name is Ben Branch, Mister Rosenthal, but we've always called him by his middle name, Branch." Mama replied. Reuben Rosenthal nodded his head.

"I've found that out just today, and I must tell you, tracking you down has been quite an experience for me."

"You still haven't said why." I spoke for the first time and the attorney turned his full attention to me.

"Did you suffer a broken arm when you were seven or so, Son?" he asked and I looked at Mama and Jon David before I replied.

"Why do you want to know?" I asked.

"I need to know for sure you're the Ben Walker I have been searching for?" he replied. "I assure you all that I'm not bearing any bad or disappointing tidings to you or your family. Quite the contrary, if you are the Ben Walker I was hired to find, you will be very pleased with what I have to tell you."

I unbuttoned the sleeve of my right arm and pulled the shirt above my elbow and stretched my arm out toward the attorney. The scar on the underside of my elbow was quite prevalent, even in the dim light of our living room.

My right arm will not straighten out completely either. The surgeon who operated on it had to remove a portion of the elbow socket and he laid the end of the bones side-by-side thinking that when it healed the bones would fuse together and my arm would be permanently in an L shape.

However, the surgeon hadn't counted on my brother Jon David not being satisfied with me not being able to flex my arm. When I was finally able to remove the splints and bandages after my wound had healed, I could flex my arm only a few inches. Jon David had immediately

A Hard Life

forced me to toss a ball of Mama's yarn to him for hours on end.

As my arm healed further and the pain receded some, he made me start throwing things. Rocks, walnuts, clods, whatever I could pick up and throw, he made me do it until it hurt so bad I couldn't hide my tears from him and then he would let me stop.

Until the next day! Then the entire process would be repeated. Day after day, for weeks and months on end, he stayed after me until finally the pain went away and I could extend my arm much further than anyone had ever imagined I might be able to.

And could I throw! By the time I was a teen-ager I could take a pocket full of round rocks and kill more squirrels and rabbits than most men could bring in with a rifle! I had grown used to not being able to completely straighten my arm by the time I was fifteen and I hardly paid any attention to it anymore. I was never handicapped by it or allowed it to keep me from doing anything I wanted to do.

"Do you know the date your arm was broken, Branch?" Reuben Rosenthal asked and I nodded.

"The same day my papa was murdered, Mister Rosenthal." I replied. "The morning of May 4, 1865 in Stoddard County, Missouri." The attorney nodded his head.

"You're obviously the young man I've spent the last five years searching for, Son." he replied.

A HARD LIFE

CHAPTER FOUR

Reuben Rosenthal proceeded to tell us an amazing story in mine and Mama's little warm house. He told us that he had been hired five years previously to go to Stoddard County to locate a twelve year old boy named Ben Walker. The woman who had hired him was the wife of Captain James Clifton Asbury.

Jon David and I kept looking at one another without letting Mama see us as Reuben Rosenthal relayed his amazing story. He said that Captain Asbury, the man that had hung my papa and had broken my arm, had written to his wife while I was recovering from surgery in his camp. He had told his wife what he had done to my father, and to me, and told her that he had to find some way to try and repay me for the pain and loss that he had caused me.

Rosenthal went on to say that Katherine Asbury had put her husband's letter away and disregarded it for five years after she was informed of his death! What the attorney told us next would alter my, and my family's, entire future life!

A Hard Life

"Mrs. Asbury began to think about her husband's last wish before he was killed." he said reflectively. "She lives in Colorado, near Denver, and she came to St. Louis to find an investigating attorney which turned out to be me. The letter from her dead husband had instructed her to include Ben Walker in his estate as an heir equal to his only living child at the time. A daughter named Rosa Kate."

I held up my hand and Rosenthal halted his narration so I could speak.

"When Captain Asbury was taking me back to his camp, he asked me my name, my given name." I said reflectively. "I told him my name was Ben Walker. I felt as if I had to answer him truthfully, but I didn't want my papa's killer to call me what my papa had called me. That's why he only knew me as Ben Walker and not Branch Walker."

The attorney nodded his head and my mama walked over to take my hand and stand by me. Jon David was looking down at the table and he listened, but never said a word.

"What does that mean, Mister Rosenthal?" my mama asked. "I'm referrin' to the part about Branch bein' an heir to Captain Asbury's estate?"

"An excellent question, Mrs. Walker." he replied. "It means that your son, Ben Branch Walker is one of three heirs to an estate worth close to twenty million dollars give or take a million or so. When you factor in the ranch land, and its future worth, the Colorado business properties and their future value, and the gold mines, and what the price of gold may become, it might be double, or even triple, that figure. It would take a Philadelphia tax attorney years to come up with an exact amount!"

I'd like to say that Mama, Jon David, and I were stunned by the magnitude of what Reuben Rosenthal had communicated to us, but the truth of the matter is, we didn't comprehend numbers like what the attorney had described. I had no idea how much money a million dollars was! Neither did Mama or even Jon David! We didn't believe anyone could count that much money, much less own it!

"What do we do, Mister Rosenthal?" Mama asked, mirroring my thoughts also.

"Well, Madam Walker," he replied courteously, "you need to start by accompanying me back to St. Louis. I suggest we catch the midnight train out of Doniphan tonight! I have a thousand dollars in cash with me that I am authorized to give to you, or spend on your behalf, to pay for your expenses and transportation to Colorado."

He reached in his vest pocket, withdrew a wallet and showed us more money than either of the three of us had ever seen before.

"We will wire Mrs. Asbury from St. Louis and let her know that Ben has been found. I suspect then, you and your two sons should go to Colorado and meet Mrs. Asbury and her daughter. Ben Branch will need to start learning about what it's like to be responsible for running and maintaining an empire. That, Madam is my professional, as well as my personal recommendation!"

Now we were stunned! We couldn't pull up stakes in the middle of the night and leave everything we had known for ten years!

A Hard Life

"I ain't goin' to St. Louis or Colorado, or anywhere, except maybe I would spend a few nights in a Poplar Bluff hotel. That is if you'll spare me fifty dollars or so, outta' the thousand, Branch?" Jon David spoke from his seat at the table. I looked at him puzzled.

"Me and Mama ain't goin' to St. Louis tonight either, Jon David!" I exclaimed and then turned to face the attorney.

"Mister Rosenthal, I normally wouldn't hurt a man's feelins' if someone held a gun on me, but I'm bound to tell you that I can't believe what you're sayin' is true! I ain't callin' you a liar, but there has to be some mistake! This can't be happenin' to us and me and Mama ain't goin' nowhere with you!"

"Yes you are, Branch!" Jon David had arisen from his seat at the table and turned to face me. His eyes were dark and cold.

"This Rosenthal feller' is for real and so is that money, Branch! Take Mama tonight and get out of Ripley County while you can! If you can't do it for yourself, then do it for Mama. If what this man's sayin' is only partly true, maybe Mama won't have to wash anybody's nasty underwear again to pay for a shack and a handout!"

Jon David paused for a moment to glance from mine to Mama's eyes and then back to mine.

"You're gonna' do it, Branch, or so help me, Hannah, I'll take you outside and use your head to blade the yard so bare a sprig of grass won't grow for years!"

Jon David had never spoken to me like that in all my seventeen years! I knew by the set of his jaw that he meant every word and I was about an inch from being beat to a bloody pulp!

"But you and me know the truth, Jon David!" I protested and he grabbed me by the front of my shirt and pulled my face to within an inch of his. His eyes were frightening to me.

"We don't know nothin', Branch!" he said in a low tone, but in a way that communicated to me that what he was sayin' was only for my ears and my ears alone!

"You and me don't know nothin' that everyone else in this room don't already know! You remember that and do what I tell you, Son!"

"All right, Jon David." I said and pulled away from his grip and his frightening eyes. 'I'll see if this really works." I turned to Reuben Rosenthal.

"Mister Rosenthal, would you give Jon David fifty dollars if I told you to?"

"Yes Sir, I surely would." he replied and counted out five tens from his wallet and handed them to my brother.

"Dad Gum it! I shoulda' asked for a hunnerd'!" Jon David said as he fingered the bills and smiled at me.

I was relieved to see that look in his eyes that had scared me to my core was gone now. I turned then to Mama.

"Tell me what to do, Mama?" I said. "I'm confused and my head's kinda' spinnin'!"

"To tell the truth, I've always secretly kinda' wanted to see St. Louis, Son." she said. "I think it's excitin' to think about catchin' a midnight train and goin' to the big city! Branch, if it all turns out to be nothin' but a fairy tale we can always come back home, can't we, Jon David?"

"This ain't our home, Mama." he said sadly. "We lost that a long time ago!"

A Hard Life

Uncle Clady started to throw a hissy fit when we told him that we was leaving that night from Doniphan, bound for St. Louis. It got worse when Jon David told him we needed to borrow a team and wagon for Mama and what few things she was going to take with her.

However, when Reuben Rosenthal offered him thirty dollars for his trouble, Aunt Imogene grabbed that money so fast it near burned a blister on the attorney's fingers! Uncle Clady shut up and went to the barn with me and Jon David to catch up a team. Me and Mama had ridden Uncle Clady's old mule to his house and I handed the reins to Uncle Clady. There wasn't anyone in the barn but him and me and Jon David.

"You took us in when we needed help, Uncle Clady," I said, "and for that, you'll always have my gratitude, bit I'm bound to say that you ain't never been or never will be the man my papa was! Where he was sweet and kind, you're mean and selfish. It's been hard for me to believe that you and him came from the same two folks, but I suppose we have to accept it."

I stepped closer to Uncle Clady then and Jon David was watching me with a surprised expression in his eyes.

"I'm only seventeen, Uncle Clady and you're a growed man! You're bigger, meaner and probably stronger than me, but I'm tellin' you right now that because of the injustices you have heaped on our mama, I aim to kick your sorry ass all over this barn if you're a mind to take a swing at me!"

I kept edging closer to him and my voice was raising some in pitch as my anger came boiling out after so many years of his abuse.

"I'd surely appreciate it if you'd oblige me, Uncle Clady!" I continued. My hands were doubled into fists and held at my sides "I promise that Jon David will stand back and wait his turn until you're finished with me, that is if you're the one still standin' when we're done fightin'!"

By then my face was within a foot of Uncle Clady's and I watched the sweat running off his forehead, down to his nose, and dropping on to the dirty floor of his barn.

"I don't want no trouble with you boys!" he said gruffly. "You best leave me alone or I'll call the sheriff on you!"

He was saying what I expected in the appropriate tone, but I recognized stark fear in Uncle Clady's eyes for the first time in my young life. I knew then he wasn't going to fight with me, or especially with Jon David.

I wouldn't move out of his way and I was standing between him and the barn door. We locked eyes as he edged sideways along the wall of the barn until he was past me and then he started for the door.

"Stand right there, Uncle Clady!" I said. "I ain't lettin' you go to the house for a shotgun! You stand right there until me and Jon David git' the team harnessed and hitched to the wagon. We'll leave your team at the livery with the attorney's rented horse. It'll be there when you go after it!" Uncle Clady nodded his head to me and dropped his eyes to the floor.

Jon David walked one of Uncle Clady's horses around to stand beside the wagon tongue while I hooked up the trace chain. He glanced over at Uncle Clady still studying the dirt on the barn floor, then reached over, grabbed me by the shoulder, pulled me close and kissed me soundly on the cheek!

"I love you! You skinny little shit!" he said quietly with his crooked smile showing his even white teeth. "I've always admired you, Son, but never no more than tonight! I think you made Uncle Clady mess his britches! Since when did you eat bark offen' the grit tree anyhow?"

I stared back at him and he could still see the angry resolve reflected in my blue eyes. He shook his head and continued to grin at me. His last question wasn't asked with an expectation of being answered.

A HARD LIFE

CHAPTER FIVE

Jon David waved goodbye to us from the train depot as the steam engine hissed a cloud of steam the size of a house, and the engineer's shrill whistle reverberated throughout the Ozark hills surrounding Doniphan. The image of my brother's crooked smile and his big ten-gallon hat set at a jaunty angle on his dark head, standing on the railroad freight landing would sear itself in my memory for years to come.

Mama and I watched the morning sun come up somewhere between Poplar Bluff and Union Station in downtown St. Louis. Neither of us could sleep, or even tried, although we had been assigned sleeping berths on the train. We were both too excited to waste time sleeping!

We arrived in the big city mid-morning and Reuben Rosenthal arranged a carriage to take us to the Planter's Hotel near Laclede's Landing.

"Here's three hundred dollars, Mrs. Walker." he said as he handed a wad of bills to my mother at the hotel.

A Hard Life

He arranged for a suite with separate bedrooms for Mama and me and told us that he needed to visit the telegraph office to send word to Mrs. Asbury telling her we would be arriving in Denver within a week.

"After the two of you have rested I suggest you go shopping and buy yourself new clothes. I've alerted the hotel and they will arrange transportation for you and suggest some reputable clothing stores near the hotel. Branch needs at least two new suits, shirts, shoes, socks and underwear, and I won't even presume to tell you what you may need, Madam, but I suggest you don't skimp. I'll be by in the morning to check on you before I go in to my office to catch up on any paperwork that has accumulated since I have been gone. If you need more money for clothes, or other expenses, I'm authorized to let you spend whatever you deem necessary."

"I'm sure this will be more than sufficient, Mister Rosenthal." Mama answered still holding the bills in her hand. "I'm not a spendthrift and I didn't raise Branch to be one either." He touched his hat brim to Mama and left the two of us alone in the grand hotel.

A bellhop escorted us to our suite of rooms and Mama and I stood poker-faced until he had deposited our one skinny little suitcase on Mama's canopied bed that looked as big as a flatbed freight car to the two of us. When the bellhop was gone and we glanced sideways at each other, we both broke into peals of laughter.

Mama walked around through all three rooms we had been assigned. Each room had its own crackling wood-burning fireplace and the floors were covered in thick red carpets neither of us had imagined in our wildest dreams!

"Oh My!" Mama kept exclaiming as she moved from room to room with her hand over her open mouth.

"Mama, if I'm dreamin', please don't pinch me and wake me up! If I wake up and discovered Uncle Clady's mule switchin' his tail in my face I think I'd just have to throw up!" When I said this Mama covered her mouth and giggled like a schoolgirl.

A table of food was set up in the main drawing room in front of the fireplace. Mama and I suddenly remembered that we hadn't eaten since breakfast on the train before daylight. I pulled out a chair for Mama and she thanked me with a smile as I took a seat opposite her. The food tasted delicious and we ate like someone was about to take it away from both of us!

"Let's go shopping for new clothes, Branch." she said when our appetites were finally slated. "You first and then you can come back to the hotel and have a nap while your mama finds a few things for herself."

Our passenger train approached Denver on the third day of June 1875. Mama and I had been nearly hypnotized for the last fifty miles by the sheer grandeur of the great Rocky Mountains rising into the clouds just west of the dusty burgeoning metropolis.

Railroad construction crews were busy all along the last hundred miles of railroad track before we arrived in Denver. Mama said they reminded her of ants as we watched hundreds of men of every race and description working alongside the rail line our passenger train traveled on. Along with the men were seemingly uncountable teams of horses and mules carrying crossties, lumber, steel rail, crushed rock, tools, and all the other essentials needed to build railroad spurs further west toward the mountains.

It appeared to us that all the industry in America was concentrated here in eastern Colorado, getting ready to assault the impending mountainous west.

"Appears to be a good place to make a fortune." Mister Rosenthal said as he looked out the window from his seat across the isle from us. "Doesn't surprise me that men like the Asbury's came here to establish themselves." He continued as all three of us continued to stare out the window of the moving train.

"Tell us about the Asbury's, Mister Rosenthal?" Mama inquired. "Are they a large family?" He shook his head.

"Just three that I know of." he replied and then continued to tell Mama and me the history of the Asbury family.

"Katherine and Rosa Kate are, of course the widow and daughter of James Clifton Asbury. Then there's Grayson Lawrence Asbury, the older brother of Mrs. Asbury's late husband. James and Grayson came west from Indiana in fifty-eight when gold was discovered in Cherry Creek and the South Platte Rivers. They took their gold profits and began to buy up land and invest in businesses to supply the gold miners. In just a few short years they were very powerful businessmen and owned thousands of acres of timberland, ranches, and farmland."

Reuben Rosenthal hesitated for a few minutes as he removed a cigar from his breast pocket and lit it, emitting a cloud of aromatic smoke in the passenger car.

"In sixty-one they were the men who put enough pressure on Washington to have Colorado declared a territory. The educated rumor was that they needed

Colorado to be a territory so they could call on the Army to run off the Cheyenne and the Arapaho Indians, giving them access to the tribal lands. They wanted and campaigned for Colorado statehood and when the war broke out between the states, James went east and volunteered to fight for the Union. I've been told it was a strictly business decision on the two brother's part and had nothing to do with keeping the country united."

Reuben hesitated to take a deep draw from the cigar and glance outside, then he continued his narration.

"Grayson Asbury, who is single and has never been married, stayed in Colorado during the war to watch over James' wife and daughter, and their combined financial empire. A lot of people wondered why James went to fight in the war because according to everyone who knew them, Grayson was the more ruthless of the two, and the one more proficient with guns and knives. Rumor has it he has killed many a man in his pursuit of wealth and influence."

"If he's more ruthless than his brother, then he truly must be a hard man." I said thoughtfully and Reuben Rosenthal, as well as my mother, studied me and my response without replying.

The passenger train came to a stop on the outskirts of Denver, which appeared to be a bustling mining town with most businesses being either bars and brothels or hardware stores.

Katherine Asbury and her driver, a dark-skinned man with long coal black hair, met us at the depot. Mrs. Asbury was a handsome blonde woman in her mid-forties, about the same age as my mama. Her driver was a quiet, sinewy fellow appearing about thirty, named McCloud.

A Hard Life

He carried a Winchester rifle with a custom made action lever that looped wide around his right-handed grip.

I would be told that he was a full-blooded Cherokee and had been James Asbury's near constant companion until James had gone off to war. I didn't know it then, but I would observe later that the Winchester he carried was a constant companion. I would never see McCloud without the rifle either in his hands or cradled over his left forearm.

Katherine was a gracious lady with honest and direct blue-green eyes. I immediately admired her, not just because of the kind way she greeted and treated me, but for the cordiality she expressed to my mama. I predicted after observing them together for only five minutes that she and my mama were going to be great friends. That thought made my heart sing for my mama had desperately long needed a friend of her own gender and temperament.

McCloud, the Cherokee regarded me with piercing eyes so dark brown they appeared black. I met his eyes with my blue ones and I discerned no malice or suspicion reflected in his.

Reuben Rosenthal shook mine and Mama's hand and bid us farewell, then asked to be dropped off at the largest hotel in town after making arrangements to meet with Mrs. Asbury the following day. McCloud offered to let me sit up in the front of the double-seated buggy alongside him as he drove us away from the hotel and the dusty town of Denver, toward the mountains and the western sun.

We entered a wide valley a mile from town and crossed and re-crossed a rushing trout stream as we roughly followed its route northwest, feeling very diminished by the tall peaks rising on either side of us. We must have gone another three miles or so up the valley, passing through several stands of virgin pines before we approached a stately multi-storied log and rock home sitting amongst a stand of enormous pines. Each tree in the immense yard was large enough to have driven a wagon through if a hole had been tunneled though their bases.

A tall snow-capped peak rose majestically behind the house that sat on a plateau well above the approaching gravel road. I watched a bald eagle soaring above the house and as we pulled to a stop on a crushed rock circle drive in front of the house, the eagle screamed from his circling position high above the pines. I looked up at the great bird and smiled. I noticed that McCloud was watching the eagle too, and when his eyes caught mine, he smiled at me.

"The eagle's spirit is welcoming you to the mountain. It's a good omen." he said solemnly and nodded toward the bird.

I smiled back at McCloud. I had never seen an Indian before, but if they were all as stately and admirable as McCloud seemed to be, I figured I could do well to get to know them better.

"My daughter and my brother-in-law, Grayson, are waiting inside to meet you." Mrs. Asbury said as she and Mama were helped down from the buggy by McCloud and me.

The stark differences between Colorado's grandeurs and my native Missouri home should have prepared me and fortified me for what was coming next. I had been feeling nearly overwhelmed by the startling beauty of the

A Hard Life

mountains, sparkling cascading streams, and immense green pines that seemed to reach into the heavens.

However, nothing I had observed today hit me with the force of the lightning strike I experienced when I first saw Rosa Kate Asbury!

She was standing above us on a landing overlooking the entrance of the immense home. Stairways on both sides of the giant room spiraled up to each end of the landing. She wore a simple white blouse with an upturned collar above a navy blue skirt that reached to the floor, hiding her ankles.

Dark thick curls framed her face and fell to her waist. A red ribbon held her pretty hair back from the sides of her face and was tied in a bow atop her head. Her lips were stained the same color as the crimson ribbon. When she smiled her teeth were as dazzling white as billowing clouds on a bight sunshiny day.

Even my mother was struck silent by the sight of the gorgeous girl standing above us.

"Rosa Kate! Whatever are you doing with your face painted up like McCloud's cousins riding on the warpath?" Mrs. Asbury admonished her daughter, but Rosa Kate's smile never diminished.

"If McCloud's cousins ever looked like Rosa Kate does today, I'd refrain from shooting them!" An extremely tall man said this as he rose from an over-stuffed leather couch sitting in front of the largest fireplace I had ever seen.

He was wearing heavy riding pants and a fringed leather jacket. A necklace of bear claws hung around his neck beneath the jacket's lapels. I noticed a bone-handled pistol in a holster on his right side.

He strode toward us and bowed to my mama as Mrs. Asbury introduced us to Grayson Lawrence Asbury. He shook my hand firmly and met my eyes with his. His eyes were the strangest shade of steel gray I had ever seen. He had the kind of eyes that let you know he was hiding his inner feelings. They appeared friendly, but there seemed to be a mysterious quality within them that could have conveyed different meanings.

I made the judgment that Grayson Asbury was not an easily approachable man, nor one to be readily understood.

However, Mrs. Asbury's brother-in-law was not the center of my attention at the time. My mama was looking at me sharply and I discovered that my mouth was as open as if I was trying to catch flies! I closed it with a gulp and had to swallow twice to keep from strangling on my own spit! Rosa Kate was watching me with a look of interest. I took it for the same look a youngster gives the first grasshopper he ever catches and holds in his hand.

"Why don't you come down and show Branch around our place?" Mrs. Asbury said to her daughter. "Supper's not due for an hour and Grayson and I want to talk to Mrs. Walker alone for a little while."

I felt a tad funny about leaving my mother alone with strangers, but when Rosa Kate turned her smile toward me I knew that if she had asked me right then to climb the steps and jump off the railing on my head, I would have complied without any argument.

"How old are you?" she asked when we were outside the house and alone. Her voice was kind of low pitched and different. Not different in a bad way, for I liked the

A Hard Life

way she sounded, but different from any girl I had heard before.

"Seventeen," I replied, "how bout' you, Rosie?"

She glanced sideways at me and her eyes were the softest shade of brown I could imagine.

"Please call me Rosa Kate or just Rosa." she said emphatically and I nodded my agreement, although her request struck me as being a little uppity.

"You're not supposed to ask a girl her age." she continued. "It's not considered polite."

"Is that a Colorado rule, for I've never heard tell of a rule like that back in Missouri?"

"Heard tell?" she teased. "You talk funny. I'm almost sixteen, by the way."

I must have blushed for she changed the subject suddenly.

"Do you fish in Missouri?" she asked. I looked up from the spot on the ground I had been studying. It seemed a strange question from the prettiest girl I had ever seen.

"Mostly noodlin'." I replied. She stopped walking and looked suspiciously at me.

"I've never heard of….how did you say it, noodling?" she said with her pretty eyebrows arched. I shook my head.

"Not noodling." I replied. "Noodlin'. Leave off the "g" at the end."

"How do you noodle for fish?" she asked with a sly smile. I shook my head again.

"We don't noodle for fish." I replied. "We catch fish with our hands and we call it, noodlin'" She looked at me suspiciously.

"How do you catch fish with your hands?" she asked. "We use poles with fishing lines and hooks baited with grasshoppers or worms."

I nodded and replied. "We do that too, but my brother Jon David taught me to catch fish with my hands and I hardly ever use a fishin' pole no more." She regarded me with suspicion and I almost got lost in her big brown eyes.

"I want you to show me how you do it." she said.

"Sure, I'll show you some day." I replied.

"Not someday." she replied. "I want to see you do it now!"

It was my turn to look at her strangely now, but she turned and walked across the road and I followed her through the woods until we heard the sound of the stream in front of us. She stopped at the edge of the rushing creek and tilted her pretty head at me.

"Show me how you can catch a trout with your hands." she challenged me.

"I've never caught a trout." I admitted. "We mostly catch perch or bass, sometimes a catfish in still water." She smiled at me triumphantly.

"I thought you were just trying to make fun of me." she said in a way that let me know she thought I had been lying to her.

I frowned at her, took off my coat and handed it to her, rolled up my sleeves, and sat down on a rock to remove my new shoes and socks. Before I stood up I rolled my new britches up above my knees. She continued to smile suspiciously at me as I waded into the water and almost screamed aloud! It was so cold it nearly took my breath away.

"Dad Gum it, that's cold!" I shouted and her hand went to her mouth as she laughed at me. I frowned at her in an exaggerated way and then steeled myself against the frigid water and made my way to a large coffin-sized rock in the center of the creek, which the current was spilling around. The water piled up against my legs and soaked my rolled up britches legs, but I ignored it and began to feel very carefully around the down-stream side of the rock.

It took a few minutes, but after a few misses, my hands closed around a slippery fish and I held it's wiggling body above my head. Her eyes went from suspicion to amazement as the pound sized brookie suddenly wiggled from my grasp and fell back into the current.

"How did you do that?" she demanded and I grinned at her.

"Come on out here and I'll show you." I said. "It ain't somethin' you can tell someone how to do. You have to be showed! That is, unless the water's too cold for a girl?"

I think it must have been the girl remark that got to her because to my amazement she sat down on the rock and began to remove her shoes and stockings. With them on the ground she stood up, hiked up her long skirt and waded into the fast current to where I was standing behind the big rock. The hem of her skirt got soaked and she stuck it in her belt so her hands were free.

"Now show me how you did that." she demanded. I moved back and let her stand in my spot right behind the rock.

"Ease your hands down close to the bottom behind the rock where the current is slack." I instructed. "Move your hands very slowly until you feel a fish. Don't flinch when you touch them or they'll skedaddle."

I watched her move her hands as I had instructed. Suddenly she felt one and she squealed and jerked her hand away.

"Don't flinch when you touch them!" I coached her.

"I can't help it!" she replied in an exasperated way. "They feel like a snake!"

"No they don't." I said. "This is how a snake feels." I reached down and pinched her on the tender part of the back of her bare arm. She screamed and turned trying to swing at me, her feet slipped on the slick bottom and she sat down flat in the frigid water!

Her big brown eyes were as wide as saucers as I reached for her hands and pulled her erect again. She fell against me laughing and held to me as we both stood in the cold water laughing so hard we could hardly keep from falling down!

Suddenly our laughter subsided as we realized what we were doing and I gently released her and stepped back a little. Her pretty eyes were serious now and she was looking up at me like I had never been looked at before. We stood that way staring into each other's eyes until we heard something that demanded our full attention.

"If you're going to fish, then fish! If you're going to play in the water I suggest you stop now before your mothers catch you!"

It was McCloud. He was standing on the stream bank with his ever-present Winchester draped across the crook of his left arm.

A HARD LIFE

CHAPTER SIX

When Rosa Kate and I walked into the house the adults stared at us in amazement. Rosa Kate was soaked to the bone with her clothes clinging to her and she left little puddles on the hardwood floor with every step. She walked directly to the stairs and started up, her face flushed.

"Rosa Kate!" her mother said to her back. "How in the world did you get soaking wet?"

"Fishing." Rosa said without turning her head. She continued up the stairs and disappeared into one of the rooms at the top of the landing leaving me alone to face the wide eyes and suspicious stares from our mamas.

My mama's eyes were glued to my wet britches. I had rolled them down after putting my shoes and socks back on, but they were soaked to my thighs. McCloud spoke up then and I silently vowed an allegiance to the tall Cherokee for the rest of my life.

"Mister Walker catches eating sized brook trout with his hands." he said solemnly. "Rosa was so amazed she slipped and fell into the creek."

That wasn't exactly the truth, but it was near enough I could live with it and it seemed to ease the suspicion in my mama's and Rosa Kate's mama's expressions.

"You can catch trout using nothing but your hands?" Grayson asked me with an admiring tone. I shrugged.

"I caught one." I said quietly, not wanting to appear a braggart. Mama read my thoughts and spoke up then.

"Branch and I lived alone next to the Little Black River in Missouri and he kept us supplied with all the fish we wanted to eat. There were times when if it had not been for the fish and game he was able to bring in, the two of us would have gone hungry." I noticed a look between Mrs. Asbury and her brother-in-law before Grayson spoke.

"You and Branch will never have to live without necessities again, Mrs. Walker." he said. "In fact, if you will accept the proposals Katherine and I have offered, you can both live very comfortably from now on."

I looked at my mother questioningly and she gave me a look that told me that she would explain his meaning later when the two of us could be alone. During the years we had lived alone Mama and I had developed an uncanny ability to read each other's thoughts and communicate with one another without speaking.

Rosa Kate joined us for supper wearing a very pretty light blue dress with a high neck. The red ribbon she had worn earlier was replaced with a yellow one that coordinated with the lacy trim on her dress.

"You look lovely, Dear." My mother had said to her as we were seated in the dining room. I wondered if Mama knew that was what I wanted to say and said it for me.

After supper Grayson told us good night and left to return to his home a short distance further up the valley.

A Hard Life

McCloud left also, but I had the feeling the Cherokee was never far from Katherine Asbury and her daughter. Mrs. Asbury and Rosa Kate went to their rooms soon afterward leaving Mama and me alone in the living room with the large fireplace.

"What did Mrs. Asbury and her brother-in-law want to talk to you alone for, Mama?" I asked.

"Well," she began, "it's pretty much what Mister Rosenthal has already told us, Son. They want to comply with Captain Asbury's final request before he was killed. They have offered for you and I to live in Grayson Asbury's home, which they told me was even more spacious that this one, although it's hard for me to imagine."

Mama looked around at Mrs. Asbury's grand home.

"Grayson has offered to bring a teacher to his home to tutor you and finish your education. He says he thinks it would be good for you to study your lessons three days a week and then work with him in the family businesses three days a week, until you are ready to assume responsibility for what the Captain requested for you to have. They both told me that although they are not legally bound to follow the Captain's instructions, because his letter does not really constitute a will, they both will honor his wishes." Mama stopped to look deep into my eyes then.

"A lot of what they will do depends on you, Son." she said. "Grayson, especially is very concerned with the future of what he and his brother have accumulated and he told me directly that he will not allow you to squander what you have been offered."

"I suppose I can understand that." I said. Mama nodded.

"I told them that you would understand and not be offended, Branch." she replied. I could tell she wanted to say more and I waited.

"Branch, this is a wonderful opportunity they are offering you, however you should realize that if you accept this offer it will be a drastic change to mine and your lives and the way we have lived since your father has been gone. I believe in you Branch, and I have faith that you are mature enough to make this decision yourself. I also want you to know that if you do not want to do this, then we will go back to Missouri and go on living the way we were."

Mama reached and took my hand then.

"Branch, I know we thought we had a hard life working for your Uncle Clady. However we both know that you and I were very happy most of the time, because we had each other to depend upon, and we brought one another through the hard times. I was happy with our life, Son, and I just want you to know that I will support your decision, whatever road you decide to take."

I studied a spot on the hardwood floor for several moments before I replied.

"Mama, I probably don't need to tell you, but I will say that it scares me some, this decision to live in a world that you and I have only dreamed about before. I think you will understand when I say that sometimes I think it's better to dream about something than to have it for a while, only to have it snatched away!" I looked deeply into my mama's intelligent eyes.

"Regardless of my fears though, Mama, I want to try it!" I said. "Like you told me before we started this trip, if it turns out to be a fairy tale, then we'll go back home and live the way we did before."

Mama smiled and nodded. "I was confident you would say that, Branch. Especially after you seeing Rosa Kate!"

I frowned and tried to look away, but Mama touched my cheek and held my eyes to hers.

"Don't be ashamed of what you're feelin', Branch. She's about the loveliest young lady I have ever seen, so don't feel bad about admirin' her. Someday I'll lose you to a woman like Rosa Kate and that'll be all right. That's the way things should be." Mama smiled at me.

"So, it's decided." she said. "We'll try this life for a while and if we decide we're not cut out for it, then we'll simply go back home." Mama hugged me then.

"Mama, you won't ever lose me to Rosa Kate, or anyone else." I said into her ear as I hugged her close. "I won't ever allow that to happen."

I pulled back and wiped a tear from my mama's cheek with my thumb as she smiled at me in a way that made me wonder if she knew something that I didn't know yet.

The next day Grayson brought his carriage when he came to visit and Mama and I rode back with him to his house. We followed the same road that brought us to Katherine's, but we traveled north about a mile further up the valley. It was obvious when we got there why he had chosen this particular spot to build his home.

His house was some larger than Katherine's and it too was built on a relatively flat shelf above the valley floor on the west side. Snow-capped mountain peaks surrounded his home site, but the reason he had chosen this particular place was the scene across the valley in the front of his home.

Across the gorge from the front of his house a river plunged two hundred feet or more from the mountain east of the valley and created the river where Rosa Kate and I had gotten wet the day before. Mist from the waterfall enveloped the eastern side of the valley, and rainbows danced through the mist as the sun moved across the sky. The soothing sound of the waterfall could be heard easily, even from this distance.

"How do you make yourself leave this place, Mister Asbury?" Mama asked as Grayson stopped the team in the front yard and we surveyed the valley and the waterfall.

"Please call me Grayson, Mrs. Walker." he replied and looked at me then. "You too, Branch. I've never been too high on formalities."

"I will if you will call me Bonnie." Mama answered and he nodded.

"To answer your question, Bonnie, it is very hard for me to leave this place at times. My brother and I found this valley when we were prospecting back in fifty-eight, and before we found the gold vein over by Denver that made owning all this possible. I will always believe in my heart that the dreams we shared of owning this some day and building our homes here was the driving force behind what James and I have accomplished." He hesitated for a moment as he looked out over the valley.

"This was the first land purchase we made after our gold strike. It saddens me each time I think that my brother didn't live to see his home completed. When he went east to fight in the war he only planned to be gone a year or so, and I had promised to finish his house before he returned. That was the reason he went instead of me. I was the better architect and builder of the two of us." Grayson stopped talking and Mama and I looked at one another. I observed then, maybe for the first time, that money and possessions did not insulate anyone from the pain of losing a loved one.

"Bonnie, how do you feel about the use of firearms?" Grayson asked. It seemed to be a drastic change of subjects, but Mama answered the seemingly strange question.

"Guns have been a part of my homes since I was a little girl, Grayson." she replied. "I look upon them as a necessary tool for frontier folk." Grayson nodded in agreement.

"Well said, Bonnie." he replied. "I suppose you won't mind if I make the use and handling of firearms a part of Branch's education?" Mama looked at me and shook her head.

"I don't mind." She replied. "Branch has used a shotgun since he was big enough to load and hold it up." The big man nodded and turned to look at me then.

"Did you talk to your mama about our plans for you, Branch?" I nodded.

"She told me, Sir, but I'm not sure I understand all your expectations."

"Wouldn't expect you to, Branch." he replied. "I appreciate your courtesy, but you don't have to call me Sir. I told you I didn't put much stock in formalities."

"All right, Grayson." I replied and he held my eyes as he nodded.

"Let's go in and introduce you to my housekeeper." he said. "While she and Bonnie are thrashing out their future relationship I want to give you something and let you try it out." I nodded back to him and we went inside the house that would be my home for the next few years.

A HARD LIFE

CHAPTER SEVEN

Grayson's housekeeper and cook was a pleasant Mexican lady named Maria Ortega. She was about my mama's age and the two women eyed each other quietly while Grayson made the introduction. He motioned to me and we left the two women to, as he had stated earlier, "thrash out their future relationship."

Grayson led me to a large room off the living area with a heavy polished wood door, which he unlocked with a key from his pocket, and closed behind us, separating us from the two chatting ladies. Inside the room on three walls were ceiling high cabinets, filled with practically every pistol, rifle, and shotgun known to the modern world.

Grayson opened up the cabinet containing pistols of every size, shape, caliber, and age, and retrieved a new Army Colt Peacemaker in forty-five caliber.

"I purchased two of these recently and they bear consecutive serial numbers. One I kept for myself, the other I want to give to you, Branch."

He handed the gun to me. It had a shiny blued barrel, casehardened frame, and sported polished bone grips that I would learn later were carved from bison bone.

I had never handled a handgun before and it felt heavier than I expected. I had been taught by Jon David to never point any gun, loaded or unloaded, at myself or anyone else and I held the weapon, barrel toward the ceiling, in both hands admiring it.

"It's a man's weapon, Branch," Grayson said, "and one you will need to be schooled in thoroughly before you carry it loaded. I will teach you how to draw and shoot the Colt, if you will allow me?"

I nodded to him enthusiastically and he reached behind him and retrieved two boxes of forty-five ammunition from the cabinet.

"All the rifles and shotguns in this room are for you to use whenever you choose, Branch. I will give you a key and you can come and take any of them at your leisure. I would prefer you ask either me or McCloud, if he is available, to acquaint you with the proper use and care for the weapons, before and after you use them." I nodded to him as he spoke

"Thank you, Grayson." I said. "I've never shot nothin' but an old Belgium muzzleloader, so I will need instructions. Do you hunt game?"

"Yes, I do." he replied. "I will take you with me on hunting trips into the mountains when I go. However, McCloud is a master tracker and when he is available, he will share some of his knowledge with you, but you must ask him yourself."

That seemed a strange statement from the man I had considered to be McCloud's employer up to that time.

A Hard Life

There were many things going on at the Asbury ranches that I did not fully understand.

"Let's go outside where I have a range set up and you can shoot the Colt." Grayson said to me as he reached for a holstered Colt identical to the one I was holding and buckled the cartridge filled belt around his waist. I watched with interest as he tied the holster down to his right leg.

We exited the gunroom through a back door that led into a hallway leading to the back of the big house. Once outside, we walked a winding, ascending trail through the trees that led to a small box canyon with forested ridges on either side. A heavy wooden table with benches sat in the middle entrance to the canyon that ran for two hundred yards back into the mountain before ending at a vertical dirt wall.

Grayson sat the cartridge boxes on the bench and showed me how to load the Colt.

"The only time you load all six chamber, Branch, is when you intend to fire the pistol without holstering it. I have made it a habit for myself, and I will insist that you follow the same guideline, of never holstering a Colt Peacemaker without an empty cylinder beneath the hammer." He watched my face closely as he gave me the instructions.

"Do you have any idea why, Branch?" he asked and I studied his question.

"Maybe because it could go off in your holster?" I offered and he nodded.

"That is precisely what can happen, Branch." he replied. "Any sharp blow to the Colt's hammer over a loaded cylinder and you could be a cripple for the rest of your life!"

The recoil and the deafening roar of the Colt was more than I anticipated. I fired all six shots and Grayson watched me reload the Colt carefully. He reached to the ground and retrieved two of the spent shell casings.

"Put these into your ears, Branch." he said. "It'll help with the noise until you get used to it." After three cylinders of cartridges had been fired I was able to hold the Colt fairly steady and squeeze the trigger as Grayson stood behind coaching me.

I was firing at a two-foot high stump only ten yards away and after the first few errant shots, I could consistently keep a shot pattern the size of my head. Grayson nodded appreciatively and eventually stepped back, allowing me to load and fire the Colt without his assistance.

When the last box of cartridges was empty and I had practically blown the middle out of the stump, he congratulated me.

"You appear to have a knack for shooting, Branch." he said. "Next time we'll shoot at a more distant target."

"Show me how well you shoot." I asked him as he turned to lead me back to the house. He turned back and held my eyes for a moment.

"Take the empty cartridge boxes and place them on the ground." he instructed. I picked them up and began to walk, going past the stump I had been shooting.

"How far?" I asked over my shoulder.

"I'll tell you when to stop." he replied. I estimated I was twenty to twenty-five yards down range when he called.

A Hard Life

"That will do." he said. I lay the boxes on the ground a couple of feet apart and sprinted back to where he stood beside the table. His Colt was still holstered and he was facing the boxes that looked very small and far away to me.

I don't think I even saw him draw! The Colt appeared suddenly in his right hand and I flinched from the unexpected blast. The first cartridge box went flying further down range and his second shot sent the second box flying. His next three shots were fired with his right hand holding the Colt's grip and his left thumb working the hammer back after each shot. The explosive display probably didn't last more than three seconds! Both cartridge boxes were destroyed when the smoke cleared from in front of him.

I stared at his exhibition in awe as he spun the Colt on his right index finger a full revolution before the barrel slid smoothly back into the holster at his side. He smiled at my open mouth as he drew the pistol again and reloaded it, sliding five cartridges from his belt and inserting them into the revolver.

"I don't want to see you attempt a fast draw like that with a loaded weapon, Branch." he said emphatically. "Not for quite a while and not until you have mastered drawing and cocking the Colt effortlessly."

I nodded. I wondered if I would ever be that fast or that accurate.

My tutor arrived two days later and I began my studies of mathematics, English literature, history, science, and philosophy. My teacher's name was Hiram McDougall. He was a slight, balding, Irish man in his early fifties and he carried himself in a very dignified manner, always wearing wool plaid trousers, a starched white shirt, and a green woolen vest.

The only time I saw him without a crooked-stemmed pipe in the corner of his mouth was when he was eating. When he had finished his meal, and after he had wiped his mouth with the corner of a napkin, the pipe was re-inserted back into the corner of his lip. I assumed he removed it to sleep, but I never had verified evidence of that fact, because he always retired early and alone.

Around three o'clock each afternoon he would remove a plug of tobacco from his pocket along with a small penknife. He would shave pieces of the strong tobacco from the plug into the bowl of the pipe and light it, usually when he was lecturing me in either science or philosophy. He smoked the pipe vigorously until the tobacco was gone, then he would empty the ashes into a trash bowl and reinsert the empty pipe into his mouth.

Mister McDougall lived alone in Denver and rode an old swaybacked mare to the ranch on Sunday afternoons and back to Denver after my studies were completed on Wednesday.

I began my schooling at six o'clock each morning and worked non-stop until precisely six in the evening, with a half-hour for our lunch provided in the study room by either my mama or Maria Ortega.

On Thursdays, Fridays, and Saturday's, I practiced shooting my Colt, various Winchester and Sharps rifles, a lever action Winchester ten-gauge shotgun, and to please McCloud, a Cherokee hunting bow and arrows. McCloud said shooting the bow would make me a better rifle and pistol shot. I'm not sure I ever understood his logic, but

A Hard Life

drawing the powerful longbow surely developed strong arms and back muscles.

My shooting masters were both Grayson Asbury and the native Cherokee, McCloud, and they shared my lessons fairly equally

Grayson was the more adept pistol shooter of the two, but McCloud *is* the best rifle shot I have ever seen. He can hit small things consistently at extreme ranges where I can barely see the target, and I have exceptional eyesight.

Every night in my room after supper I spend from one to three hours standing in front of a mirror practicing my fast draw with an empty Colt. The nights I can only spend an hour are the nights when I have written assignments to hand to Mister McDougall the next morning.

I have discovered that my crooked right arm seems to be an advantage to me for fast-drawing my Colt. Because of the unusual angle of my elbow my hand falls naturally to the butt of my Colt, and the distance I have to draw the pistol is less than anyone with a normally straight arm. I haven't discussed this with Grayson or McCloud, but I plan to some day when they are confident I can fast-draw a loaded gun without blowing off my right foot.

My study days seem to drag sometimes when Mister McDougall and I are working on tedious projects, but the days of re-loading ammunition and practicing with various firearms fly by.

Soon it was September and Grayson appeared in our study room one Wednesday afternoon when I had heard southern-bound geese honking overhead. Grayson told Mister McDougall that he needn't come the next week for I would be going on a hunting trip with he and McCloud.

I was ecstatic at the declaration, but Mister McDougall frowned a bit and even removed his crooked stemmed pipe from his mouth. I was certain it surely meant that he was going to protest, but he jammed the pipe back in the corner of his mouth and said nothing. Grayson gave him a questioning look, then turned and left the room.

The next morning McCloud appeared with three riding horses and three pack mules. The mules were laden with canvas-covered supply packs lashed down. Each riding horse had one or two hunting rifles in scabbards hanging from the saddles.

Mama hugged me right in front of the stoic Cherokee and Grayson Asbury sitting their horses waiting for me to join them.

"Mama, I'm getting too old for you to hug and kiss like a little boy every time I'm going to be gone for a while." I protested. She stared hard into my blue eyes.

"Mister McDougall is having an improving influence over your use of the King's English, Son." she said. "I appreciate Grayson for that and I realize you are getting older and more educated, but as long as you're my boy Branch, I'll hug and kiss you when you're leaving for a spell until you're eighty, if I live that long!" I smiled back at her

"Yes Ma'am." I said with a smile. "I guess I know who's still in charge around here, but if you'll give me another little kiss I won't tell Maria that you think it's you!"

Mama grabbed me by the ear and twisted it a little then pulled me down and kissed me soundly on the lips! It made a good smack and she looked defiantly at McCloud and Grayson as she turned and walked back into the house.

A HARD LIFE

CHAPTER EIGHT

It was a glorious early fall day in the mountains. I rode behind Grayson, who led our hunting expedition, followed by McCloud and the pack mules. I kept glancing upward at the unbelievably blue sky and each time I would notice McCloud looking up also to see what I might be looking at. I'd glance back at him and smile and he would glance upward again, his face frozen in its familiar expressionless appearance.

"I've never seen a bluer sky." I explained and again McCloud looked upward as if trying to discern what could possibly make this sky, that he had observed all his life, so interesting to me.

"Bluer than a blind carpenter's thumb." I announced, quoting one of Jon David's old jokes. Grayson looked back at me and chuckled and I turned to see if McCloud appreciated my humor. He was staring at me with the same expressionless look on his features so I turned my face forward. I had to assume the Cherokee either did not appreciate or did not understand my sense of humor.

We followed an old trail higher and higher into the mountains, following a mostly northwestern direction. I marveled at the expanse of the country we were traveling through. Most of my life I had heard older Missouri people talk about how crowded the country had become and they wondered if over-crowding continued how folks would have enough land to support themselves.

When I looked around at the miles of pristine wilderness surrounding me that appeared to have never seen a human before, I wondered what those old folks back in Missouri would think if they could see what I was seeing.

We crossed over a snow-covered pass and I was grateful for the warm sheepskin coat and felt hat Grayson had given me. The valley that opened up on the west side of the pass was expansive.

As we began to descend into it, we rode through stands of ghostly white-barked aspen trees with their yellow leaves fluttering in the warming breeze flowing up from the valley below us. I had heard somewhere that a person could hear his ancestors whispering to him in the rustling aspen leaves, and I tried in vain to distinguish words and phrases as the leaves whispered to me.

From time to time as we traveled through the aspen groves Grayson would point out wrist-sized saplings that had been stripped of their bark nearly as high as our horse's backs.

"Elk rubs." he would announce quietly and then we would move on. On a wind-swept grassy slope that covered more acres than Uncle Clady's entire farm multiplied by ten, he reined up and stared at the ground. He glanced back at McCloud and raised his eyebrows. I glanced back

A Hard Life

at the Cherokee, but could not read any difference in his expression.

When I rode by what Grayson had stopped to observe I saw a big pile of scat and tracks with enormous claw marks clearly imprinted in the softer trail soil. As I moved on behind Grayson, I continued looking back watching McCloud to see his reaction to the sign. He looked down at it and I swear I saw a sadness like a shadow come over his face. Not much of a change to his normal expression, but one I would wonder about for a while.

We reached the valley floor in the afternoon and followed a small chuckling stream north up the valley. Grayson stopped there and we established a base camp at the source of the little stream we had been following. An all-weather spring creek rushed out of a small cave on the west side of the valley and provided fresh water for the horses as well as we humans. I could see signs in a nearby aspen grove of a previous campsite.

"Have you camped here before?" I asked nodding toward a blackened depression that appeared to be an old fire pit. McCloud nodded his head.

"This was Cherokee hunting ground until we white men came and took it from them." he replied. "The Asbury brothers and I have camped here many times before."

I noticed Grayson give McCloud a sharp look at his comment, but he didn't say anything. I also noticed that McCloud had included himself as a white man in his comment, but I didn't say anything about it for I supposed the Cherokee had simply misspoke and it would have appeared impolite for me to point it out.

"Tomorrow, Branch," Grayson said, "you and I will leave McCloud here at the base camp and the two of us will take a pack mule to climb the west slope and hunt a big lake on the other side. I only care about killing bears and I thought you might enjoy killing a grizzly yourself?" I nodded enthusiastically.

"Was that grizzly sign we saw in the big meadow on the way down the mountain?" I asked and Grayson nodded in agreement.

"Why aren't you going with us to hunt grizzlies, McCloud?" I asked the Cherokee. He didn't look up from his chore of lighting a fire in the depression.

"McCloud would prefer to stay here and scout for bull elk." Grayson replied for the Cherokee. "After you and I have killed a grizzly or two I'll bring you back to the base camp and you and McCloud can hunt elk and mule deer while I take the bear meat and hides back to the ranch."

I had not been told the hunt would be split into two segments and I wondered why it would be, but I kept my curiosity to myself for the moment.

Spruce grouse were plentiful on the hillside above camp and I took the Cherokee hunting bow and arrows that McCloud had brought and collected four of the plump birds before sundown. McCloud helped me dress the birds and he skewered them on green poles and suspended them over a bed of coals in the fire pit.

We had the roast grouse along with boiled eggs and fresh tea made from the nearby spring water.

"You say you killed these birds with that bow?" Grayson asked as he pulled his bird apart and devoured the white breast meat. I nodded to him, for I was busy eating my own tasty grouse.

Grayson had been setting up a rope corral for the horses fairly close to our campsite while I had gone on my short hunting trip up the mountainside. I had thought to myself that he had placed the corral much closer to the camp than necessary, for the odor of a total of six horses and mules could get pretty rank after a few days.

"The grouse are practically tame." I said in response to his question after I had wiped some of the grease from my fingers and face. "They let me slip up to ten feet or so of them before they would run. When they did spook some when I killed one of them the others wouldn't go twenty yards before they'd stop again."

"Damned stupid behavior I'd say." Grayson commented and McCloud and I exchanged glances, but neither of us said anything about his statement.

McCloud had erected a canvas lean-to to catch some of the reflected heat from the campfire. We spread out oilcloths on the ground and rolled up in blankets to sleep. I could see at least a million stars twinkling in the autumn night as I lay there between two men I had known upwards of a year, but still considered strangers to me.

I thought about Jon David and the times he and I had lay together on campouts and watched the stars until sleep claimed us. I missed my brother and wondered where he might be tonight and what he might be doing. I thought about how secure I had always felt when Jon David was near and suddenly I was very lonesome and homesick for him.

I was awakened with a start the next morning when McCloud rolled out of his bedroll and pulled on his high top boots. As soon as he had moved away to rekindle the fire I threw back my own blanket and shivered some as I stuck my stocking feet into my cold boots. I could see my breath in the fresh mountain air.

McCloud warmed up the tea and he and I were sipping it from tin cups when Grayson emerged from the lean-to and joined us by the fire.

"You ready to kill a grizzly, Branch?" he asked.

"I suppose so." I replied. "I hope I don't mess my britches when I see my first one. How will I tell it's a grizzly and not just a large black bear?" McCloud looked at me as if I had asked a dumb question, poured out his tea, and walked away into the darkness toward the horse corral.

"When you saw your first rattlesnake, did anyone have to tell you what it was, Branch?" Grayson asked and I shook my head.

"It'll be the same with a grizzly." he replied simply.

McCloud saddled horses for Grayson and me and slid a Sharp's 45-70 rifle in the scabbard beneath my right stirrup. It was a rifle I was familiar with shooting, for I had practiced with it often back at the range. He handed me a box of cartridges for the big rifle and I slid them into my coat pocket. McCloud was not a talkative man at any time, but I noticed a tension in him now that was unusual.

Grayson spurred his horse and I followed behind him and the pack mule. We followed a dim trail zigzagging up the ridge stopping occasionally to let the horses recover from the steep climb. As soon as the horses began to catch their breath Grayson would put a spur to his mount and we would continue to climb.

It took us an hour or longer to break over the top and begin the ascent down the other side. Occasionally through the tall pines I would catch a reflection of sun off water in the distant basin. It took us until about nine o'clock to reach a bench on the side of the mountain a few hundred feet above the shore of a lake that appeared to be a half-mile wide and four times that long.

"Grizzlies should be in the access creek catching fish." Grayson said as he dismounted then reached into his saddlebag to remove a spyglass. He used his saddle as a rest to steady the glass and looked through the instrument several minutes before he spoke again.

"There's a big boar working a shoal about two miles upstream from the lake." he announced. I had dismounted and held the reins of my horse and the pack mule.

"Here take a look for yourself." I had never looked through a magnifying glass and had no idea what to expect. It was amazing to me how much closer objects appeared when I pressed my right eye to the lens. It took a few seconds for me to adjust to the magnification and be able to identify objects. With Grayson's help I was finally able to spot the bear he had told me about. The enormous hump-backed bear was chasing fish in the shallow water. I could see the spray glisten in the sun from his charges and once I was able to identify a shiny fish in his mouth as he raised it after one of his mad rushes.

"I see him, and you're right." I said. "There would be no way to mistake him for an ordinary black bear."

"We need to decide now who is going to shoot this one, Branch." he said as he took the spyglass from me and settled it back on his saddle to continue to observe the large carnivore.

"You shoot him, Grayson." I replied. "I'll watch how you do it. Then if we can find another one I'll know what to do."

"You sure?" he asked without looking away from the glass.

"I'm sure." I replied. Grayson started moving the glass away from the bear and picking a route for us to take to get near the animal.

"It'll take us an hour or more to get close." he said. "I hope he's not already getting full of fish." He collapsed the glass and put it back into his saddlebag. We mounted and began to skirt the slope going toward the head of the lake and downward at the same time.

We rode to within a quarter-mile, down-wind of the bear, and tied the horses and pack mule securely in a scope of aspen near the small river rushing toward the lake.

"Bring your rifle and load it now." Grayson said quietly. I noticed a nervous tension in his voice and his hand shook some as he loaded his custom built Sharp's 45-110 caliber rifle. I did as he said and kept my rifle pointed to the side as I followed his quick steps toward where we had last seen the big bruin.

Thick brush lined the creek and we had to wind our way through it until we could sneak to the edge of the river and peek through the last screen of brush between us and where the bear should be.

Sure enough the bear was about seventy-five yards away eating a large fish on a little dry island in the center of the river with the current flowing past the bear on both sides. Heavy muscles rippled beneath the shiny brown coat of the big bear. I could even hear his teeth tearing out great chunks of the fish, chewing briefly and swallowing, most of it in bloody chunks. The bear's great paws and maw was covered in bright red blood.

A Hard Life

Suddenly the wind shifted and the bear must have gotten a whiff of our scent. He dropped the remaining piece of fish and stood erect looking across the river directly toward us. I expected to see him break and run to get away from us, but to my surprise the bear didn't seem to be alarmed at all. He didn't seem angry at our scent either. To me he appeared curious.

That's the way he died also, because Grayson's large rifle roared and I saw blood spurt from the back of the bear as the big bullet entered his chest and exited leaving a ragged cavity. He fell as dead as a stone and never moved again!

"I got him!" Grayson screamed and literally ran across the shallow rapids toward the still form lying on the little island. I took my time and navigated around the deeper water, trying in vain to keep from going over my leather boots. Finally I gave up that venture and let the frigid water fill my boots as I slogged the remaining distance to within a few feet of Grayson, who was standing triumphantly over the big bear, pumping his rifle into the air with his right arm.

The bear was indeed larger than I could have imagined. Grayson could barely hold the big head off the ground in order for me to see the two-inch teeth still stained with fish blood.

"He's the largest grizzly I've ever seen!" Grayson said in an excited voice I had never heard before. The man usually seemed so restrained and sober it was curious for me to observe him acting the way he was now.

"Go get the horses and mule, Branch." he ordered. "I'll start the cleaning and skinning, but you'll need to help me. This thing is huge!" I looked the great bear over and something about the death of such a magnificent creature did not inspire me to be as happy as Grayson seemed to be. He noticed the way I was looking at the bear.

"Aren't you happy to be a part of this?" he inquired curiously. "This is a real trophy, Branch! Maybe a once in a lifetime kill! Why aren't you excited?"

"I don't know." I said honestly. I had killed before and I had watched other animals killed and it had never bothered me much. However, all of the killing I had done was to put meat on mine and Mama's table and seemed very important from that stand point, but to kill an animal this magnificent just as a trophy didn't seem right to me for some reason.

"I think I would have liked to see him angry, or frightened even." I said. "He acted as if he was happy to see us." Grayson looked at me like I was crazy.

"Angry!" he practically shouted. "You'd rather see him angry?" he continued derisively. "What's wrong with you, Branch? Have you lost your mind? This thing could have killed either of us with one swipe of one of these monstrous paws!" He picked up one of the bear's front feet and showed me the six inch long claws!

"I'll go get the horses." I said and left Grayson Asbury staring after me like he didn't even know me. I felt he was angry with me for some reason and as I thought about it I realized I was angry with him! Why? I asked myself, and for the life of me I could not fathom a reason for my strange emotion.

I had to tie the horses upwind from the bear for the smell of blood and the smell of the bear made them roll their eyes and lay their ears back. I was afraid they might break their lead ropes and run away so I moved them to where they couldn't see or smell the bruin.

The mule seemed to realize the bear was dead and presented no further danger to him, for he followed me out to the island and stood obediently while Grayson and I finished the skinning operation.

I had no previous experience in skinning and butchering a bear, therefore I was astonished to see how much a bear looks like a man when he is skinned and lying prone on his back! His paws became hands and feet, and other than his elongated mouth full of teeth, his torso looks very much like a man also.

It bothered me more than I wanted to admit and Grayson kept glancing at me and even mentioned that I appeared pale to him. I told him I was all right, but when he asked if I wanted to hunt the next morning for a bear I could kill myself, I declined. I told him that watching him kill this one was enough of a hunt experience for me. He sort of smiled as he studied me and my answer, but he had no further comments.

We camped on the shore of the lake and loaded the heavy hide and bags of meat on the mule just after daylight. Before nightfall we had retraced our trail back over the mountain and rode into McCloud's base camp in time for supper.

A HARD LIFE

CHAPTER NINE

McCloud seemed to recognize a subtle change in mine and Grayson's relationship when we returned from the bear hunt. He didn't inquire as to what had transpired while Grayson was present, and as for me I probably could not have given him a truthful explanation. I don't really know what Grayson would have said if he had been asked, and quite frankly I didn't care at the time.

Grayson saddled his own horse and left camp with the loaded pack mule the next morning after breakfast. He wasn't unpleasant to me or McCloud, but all three of us knew that something had changed.

"There are elk bugling in a valley north of here." McCloud told me a little while later. "I think we should harvest two of them, plus two or three mule deer for meat back at the ranches." I nodded to the Cherokee and met his eyes for a moment. I thought he was going to ask me something else, but he didn't. We saddled our horses and took both pack mules with us.

McCloud bugled up a big herd bull in a green meadow high on the side of a tall peak a mile or so above our camp.

A Hard Life

He had positioned me with the Sharp's rifle a few yards in front of him and the bull ran into the small alpine meadow and stopped broadside about eighty yards from me.

I placed the front sight just behind the animal's front shoulder and touched the sensitive trigger. At the blast the bull spun and ran away from us as if I might have missed him, but fell after only running a few yards.

We approached the elk with rifles held ready, but he was stone dead and didn't move when I touched him with the rifle barrel.

McCloud was watching me to see how I would react to killing the magnificent animal.

"When I kill an animal I always take time to say a prayer of thanks." McCloud said to me as we stood observing the slain elk. "Would you like for me to say the prayer for you?" I nodded, more curious than anything else. McCloud removed his hat and I did likewise as I stood with my head bowed.

"Our Father who art in Heaven." the Cherokee began and I opened my eyes and looked over at the Cherokee standing with his head bowed deeply.

"Hallowed be thy name." he continued. "I come to you in prayer, Father, on behalf of my young friend, Ben Branch Walker. We thank thee Father, for the gift of life and we thank thee for the gift of this animal that will sustain us to further our life on this earth." By this time I was staring in amazement at the Cherokee with my mouth beginning to open involuntarily.

"Forgive us for the taking of one life to sustain another and forgive us of all our sins we commit daily. Be with us, Father, and keep this young man, Ben Branch

Walker, safe in his walk on earth, and honor this humble servant by hearing my prayer that is offered through, and in the name of your Son and our Redeemer, Jesus Christ. Amen."

McCloud opened his eyes and reset his black hat on his head, then turned to return my stare and my look of utter fascination!

"What?" he questioned me. "Why are you staring at me?"

"I apologize, McCloud." I replied. "I guess I figured you were going to pray to some great spirit of the wind, or the mountain, or maybe this dead bull elk's spirit or something! I didn't realize you were a Christian!"

"This valley would not hold what you don't know about me, Ben Branch." he replied. "By the way, I was very amused at your joke about the blind carpenter. I will think of it now every time I happen to notice the blue sky" McCloud then pulled his skinning knife and went to work to field dress the elk.

After the night's wonderful meal of elk tenderloin McCloud and I were lying under the lean-to watching the myriad of stars above us. McCloud slept with his black hat pulled over his face.

"In your prayer today you referred to me as your friend, McCloud." I began. "I must admit that I didn't know you felt that way?"

"Do you not want to be my friend, Ben Branch?" he asked and I raised up on my elbow.

"I've always wanted you to be my friend, McCloud!" I replied. "I just didn't know you considered me one." He didn't reply which I had begun to understand meant that

A Hard Life

oftentimes my statement really didn't solicit a response, therefore he didn't give one. I lay my head back down.

"Would you be insulted if I asked you some questions? Questions about yourself?" I asked.

"Ask, Ben Branch." he replied.

"For starters, why do you call me Ben Branch, and everyone else just calls me Branch?"

"Isn't your name, Ben Branch?" he asked. "Would you prefer me to call you a half name?"

"No, I think I like that you address me different than others. I just wondered why." I replied and again my statement didn't need a response and I smiled a little to myself when I didn't get one.

"How did you get an Irish name, McCloud?" I asked and this time he raised up and pushed his hat back away from his face. I sat up also and we scooted back and leaned against our saddles behind us.

"I've never known my real name." he began. "An Irishman named Tom McCloud lived in these mountains trapping beaver and hunting wolves and bears for their skins. I never knew how I came to live with him, for I had no memory of my parents or their tribe. I grew up thinking that McCloud was both a mother and father to me. He never called me anything but Boy, so that was the only name I knew." He glanced over at me before he continued.

"When the beaver became scarce he started to work for the Asbury brothers killing meat for their mine workers. I was about twelve or so by then and I was a big help to him, although he never made me do anything. He taught me how to track and read sign and I cared for his horses and pack animals. I also did most of the skinning and butchering of the animals he hunted and killed. That spring Tom McCloud and I were camped on the lake where you and Grayson were yesterday. I was in camp scraping elk hides and I heard his rifle shot a mile or so up the valley. He didn't come into camp that night and I began to look for him the next morning. I found what was left of him that afternoon. I chased a grizzly away from his remains and buried what was left of him on the bank of the lake." He stopped talking then and I remained silent until he started to speak again.

"Tom McCloud had been a gospel preacher at some time in his life, but when he lost his wife and daughter to smallpox he came west to live in the mountains. He called himself a Campbellite preacher sometimes, but he always smiled when he said that. I never asked him what it meant. He taught me to pray and he taught me about Jesus. He would preach to me practically every night from his old Bible and the night before he was killed I asked him to baptize me. He took me down into the lake and immersed me in it that very night. I buried Tom McCloud where he led me to Christ." Again he hesitated for a few minutes before he began again.

"James and Grayson Asbury were our only friends and they took me to live with them. When they asked me what I wanted to be called, I told them McCloud, and that has been my name since. I was a boy then, but not too long afterwards I became a man."

His last sentence intrigued me and my curiosity overcame my hesitance to ask him any more questions.

"How did you become a man?" I asked. He turned his head toward me and I could see his dark eyes in the light of the stars.

"That happened in this very place." he replied. "I continued to hunt game for James and Grayson and oftentimes when they could get away from their work they would come and camp with me. I was about your age and I had made a corral on the other side of this grove of aspen, downwind so the smell wasn't so bad. The next morning our horses were missing. I had told Grayson the night before that I had discovered a Cherokee hunting party camped a few miles north of here. Further north than where you and I killed the elk today. Our missing horse's tracks seemed to lead in that direction and Grayson was convinced the Cherokees had slipped in during the night and stolen them. We walked directly to their camp and caught all four of them getting ready to break camp with their meat and hides on travois'. We didn't see our horses, but that didn't seem to deter Grayson. We began firing and we killed all four of them. One of the braves was younger than me at the time." He stopped talking as he had done before and I waited patiently.

"I found our horses eating grass a half-mile from this camp. One of them had a fresh wound where a bear had clawed him. We figured the bear had frightened them so badly they had broken down the corral and ran blindly away without making enough noise to awaken us. We never told anyone about the Cherokee braves we murdered without cause. We buried them where they fell and later shot their horses. After that I never felt like a boy. I became a man that day." There was another silence where I sensed the Cherokee had more to say so I remained silent.

"I've never attended a regular church service." McCloud spoke quieter now. "But a day never passes that I don't ask McCloud's God to forgive me for my part in those killings. I believe James Asbury felt so much guilt he later went to fight in the war not caring whether he lived or died. Grayson blamed the grizzly instead of accepting responsibility for what he did. He's killed every bear he finds since then and revels in their death, thinking that will absolve him of his guilt."

We sat there in silence for several minutes without speaking again.

"I wonder if I sensed his unreasonable hatred for the grizzly, which might explain why I began to hate Grayson Asbury for killing the bear?" I asked, the question more to myself than to McCloud beside me. I'm not sure he understood my meaning, but this time he waited patiently for me to speak again.

I began to relay what had happened beginning when Grayson and I had left camp two days before, and I told McCloud about the experience of watching Grayson kill the monster grizzly and about his celebration afterwards. I told him how something about the killing had fostered an anger in me toward the man that bordered on hate. I told him I didn't understand it at the time and that the feeling had not diminished a bit since.

He thought about what I had told him and then without saying a word to me, slid back down and lay prone with his hat over his face again.

"We all have grizzlies we fear in our lives, Branch. Grayson has not learned yet that killing them will not make them go away." It was quiet after that and in a few minutes McCloud was snoring very quietly.

McCloud and I continued to hunt for three more days. We killed another elk and three mule deer. We sat our horses one warm afternoon and watched a grizzly on

A Hard Life

a hillside three hundred yards away turning over rocks and logs searching for grubs. Neither of us reached for our rifles and after a while we backed our horses away from the bluff and left the bear in peace.

McCloud and I never again talked about what had happened on that hunting trip and the revelations we had shared with one another. After that trip I always felt that other than my mama and my brother Jon David, I would never have a more trusted friend on this earth.

A HARD LIFE

CHAPTER TEN

Hiram McDougall came back to Grayson's on the Sunday afternoon following McCloud's and my return from the hunting trip. He appeared to be perturbed with me about something and was critical of the fact that I had gotten behind in my studies. By Monday afternoon however, he seemed better satisfied with me, notwithstanding the fact he gave me enough extra school work that I knew my nightly gun handling practice would have to be put off for a while.

Winter set in by the middle of October and snow was on the ground, and would be until the following March. I was secretly looking forward to Christmas because McCloud had told me that Rosa Kate came home from her boarding school back east every Christmas.

Grayson and Mrs. Asbury had opened an account in mine and Mama's name at the Bank of Denver when we had arrived in Colorado. They had made regular deposits to the account based on the family company's profits every month since then. The accumulated balance in the

A Hard Life

account already amounted to more money than Mama and I had ever imagined having in our lifetimes.

The last Sunday in November at Katherine Asbury's, where we nearly always had dinner on Sundays, I asked if Mama and I might go to Denver and purchase Christmas presents. Katherine appeared embarrassed and looked at Grayson. He put down his fork and wiped his mouth with his napkin.

"We stopped celebrating Christmas the year James was killed." he said quietly. "It had always been his favorite holiday and it has been too painful for Katherine, Rosa Kate, and for me, to join in any festivities." Mama and I looked at one another sadly. It was McCloud that broke the silence.

"Maybe ten years is long enough to mourn James and forget the birth of Christ." Grayson looked sharply at the Cherokee and I detected a flash of anger in his steely gray eyes.

"I believe McCloud is right!" Katherine said, coming to the Cherokee's defense. "Rosa Kate has begged me to let her put up a tree for the last two Christmases, and I refused to allow it. I believe I will wire her and tell her that this year we will have an old fashioned Christmas. I've been thinking about it and I believe James would approve."

I smiled at Mama and McCloud. Grayson appeared angry, but he nodded to his sister-in-law.

"As you wish, Katherine." he said. He excused himself and left the table. It was apparent he was upset at the decision, but Katherine didn't seem to mind his poutiness and she smiled more that afternoon than I had observed her since Mama and I had arrived to live in Colorado.

McCloud harnessed a four-horse team and pulled an enclosed buggy on sled runners to the front of the house the following Saturday morning. Mama and Katherine sat inside and I joined the Cherokee up on top for the ride into Denver. McCloud and I could hear the two ladies chatting and giggling like two schoolgirls on the trip into town.

McCloud had tied small silver bells to the harness on each horse and as we plowed through the new snow the sled runners hissed in time to the bells, creating music specific to Christmas time.

Snow covered the giant ponderosa pines and ice crystals glistened along the edges of the spring creek the road paralleled. I couldn't remember a time when I had been happier. The only dark place in my heart was a yearning to see Jon David. When I thought about him I actually felt a dart of pain in my gut. I missed him terribly and the thought of having Christmas out here and not knowing that he was all right put a short damper on my otherwise happy mood.

I bought a pair of fur-lined gloves for McCloud and then bought a second pair for Jon David. I reasoned that I could always give them to him later and tell him they were a belated Christmas present.

I spied and purchased a silver brandy flask for Grayson in the same store. He had complained about not being able to find one and did without his brandy on our hunting trip back in September.

I met up with McCloud on the street and pulled him into a store established to equip men headed into the mountains. There I found a three piece split bamboo fly rod with two extra tip sections all encased in a polished mahogany satin lined case. A brass reel spooled with silk fly line fit inside the case with the rod.

"The finest fly rod in the world outside Scotland, Laddie." the Scottish salesman had said. "You'll be the envy of every mon' on any stream you fish." he added.

"This isn't for me." I replied. "This is for Rosa Kate Asbury." McCloud came as near to laughter as I ever saw him and the Scottish salesman looked at me as if I was wasting a lot of money on a girl. McCloud actually just smiled some broader than usual, but for him that was a laugh."

Katherine Asbury spied me and McCloud coming out of the outfitter's store and asked me if I had purchased anything for my mother yet. I told her no, and she took me by the hand and marched me into an exclusive lady's store and showed me a blue wool coat with a mink collar. She said that Mama had tried it on and loved it, but thought it much too expensive for her.

I counted out enough gold coins to the sales lady, from what Mama and I had withdrawn from our bank account, to have fed us for a year back in Missouri.

"Your mother is well worth it, Branch." Mrs. Asbury said as she smilingly instructed the saleslady to gift-wrap the coat.

Between the lady's store and where McCloud had parked our team was a tavern and as Katherine and I walked past, three young men in miner's clothes pushed open the door almost blocking the wooden sidewalk.

Katherine and I stopped for the men to move out of our way. One of the three, the larger of the trio, stumbled some and his friends supported him until he jerked away from them and cursed.

"Watch your language, Friend." I said to him. "I'm escorting a lady to her carriage." He stared at me and Katherine through alcohol bleared eyes and then grabbed his dirty hat from his head and performed an awkward bow.

"Well, excuse me, Madam'!" he said with a toothy grin that wasn't really a smile. "I best move my ass outta' the rich folk's way?"

His friends grabbed him by the arms for they recognized he was acting ignorant and in danger of being arrested if a deputy came along. He cursed them again and jerked away, almost falling down on the sidewalk. I took Katherine's arm and guided her off the sidewalk and around the trio.

McCloud was at the carriage a block down the street and recognized what was happening. He came running with his Winchester held in both hands. He took Katherine's arm and escorted her back to where my mama had followed and was waiting. I turned then and faced the drunk who wasn't smiling any longer.

"You wearin' a gun, you rich asshole?" he practically screamed at me.

"A Missourian doesn't need a gun to handle a drunk Coloradoan." I answered, and the man cursed and ran toward me, or maybe stumbled toward me is a better description.

Jon David had taught me how to fight and we practiced on one another all my life. My right arm won't completely straighten and since Jon David was a good fighter he had recognized that I might be some handicapped unless I planned and trained to make allowances for it. My left arm was always stronger than my right and he taught me how to use it to jab and hook with power. Once I had somebody close I used my right fist like a hammer.

I felt a little ashamed to punch a drunk, but if I had allowed him to get his hands on me he would have taken me to the ground and not only would we both have gotten terribly muddy, he might have turned out to be a stronger wrestler than me. I ducked his wild haymaker right and caught him flush on the nose with a solid left hook. He went down like a sack of potatoes, his nose broken and bleeding profusely.

McCloud's Winchester made a deadly sound behind me as he levered a round into the chamber. That noise alone froze the downed man's friends in their tracks.

"Drag your friend back into the bar and buy him a drink." the Cherokee said as he flipped two silver dollars to the sidewalk. "When he wakes up tell him my name is McCloud, and then tell him how lucky he is to be alive to see Christmas!"

A HARD LIFE

CHAPTER ELEVEN

It was a Wednesday, the second week of December, and Rosa Kate was due to arrive in Denver today on her Christmas vacation. McCloud had told me on Sunday that he was going to pick her up at the train station and she would be home until after New Years. All week I had racked my brain trying to find an excuse to skip class and ride to Denver with McCloud, but I had been unsuccessful in coming up with anything inspired or reasonable that my tutor, Hiram McDougall, would accept.

The Irishman had been observing my inattentiveness and about three o'clock announced that he would cut today's lessons short and give himself time to ride back to Denver before darkness completely set in.

"I have been appreciative of the progress you have made this year, Branch." He told me as he donned his overcoat and hat. "If you will continue to work as hard next year as you have the past few months, by this time next December you will be ready for graduation."

"Thank you, Mister McDougall." I replied and he nodded to me.

A Hard Life

"I was wondering, Branch?" he said thoughtfully, holding his crooked-stemmed pipe in the corner of his mouth clenched between his teeth.

"Might I impose on you to accompany me as far as the main road at the mouth of the valley? My old mare, Josephine, almost slipped on the ice as I rode in last Sunday, and I am certain I recognized a fresh panther track at the last river crossing. I would be most comforted by your company until I am beyond the river road." He hesitated and I noticed a distinctive twinkle in his eye before I could answer.

"It would also be a most appropriate excuse for you to stop by Katherine Asbury's for a hot sustaining drink before your return trip home. Besides, It would only be gentlemanly for you to pay your respects and welcome her daughter back from finishing school, since you would have business in the neighborhood." He smiled as it dawned on me what his intentions were. I probably reddened some, for I felt my face heat up, but I sheepishly met his eyes and smiled back at him. No further comments were necessary.

McCloud answered the door and stepped back to allow me to enter Katherine's home. He appeared curious about why I was there.

"I saw a fresh cougar track between here and the main road, McCloud." I explained. "I wondered if you might want to put the dogs on it come mornin'?" He stared at me. McCloud had a pen of trained lion dogs he used to control the number of lions on the two ranches.

"I wasn't aware that finding cougar tracks was one of your school lessons, Ben Branch?" he countered and I glanced downward from his probing dark eyes.

"Mister McDougall was worried his old mare might slip and fall and make the two of them panther bait, so he asked me to accompany him out to the main road." I explained.

"I found the lion track crossing our road and it appears to be only a few hours old so, I thought I'd stop and tell you about it, just in case you wanted to go huntin' tomorrow." He nodded his understanding of what I had said, but his eyes were still suspicious. When I thought he wasn't looking I was stealing glances up the stairs to the landing above.

"Any other reason for you to stop by, Ben Branch?" he asked. "You keep looking around as if you might think the lion came inside the house to warm up." I frowned and turned back toward the door.

"Sorry I bothered you, McCloud." I said.

"Rosa Kate's in the kitchen teaching her mother how to cook." McCloud said and I stopped in mid-stride

"Katherine would probably appreciate an interruption about now." he continued. "Rosa Kate's made a hot drink from something that looks like elk droppings to me. She calls it chocolate and says it comes from somewhere beyond the great sea. Her mother and I are afraid to try it, but maybe since you are younger and not as intelligent as the two of us, you will not be frightened. I think it would please Rosa Kate if you tried it and liked it."

Katherine smiled at me as I entered her big kitchen. A heavenly smell was coming from a steaming pot Rosa Kate had lifted from the cooking grate and placed on the table.

Rosa Kate was more beautiful than I even remembered. Her dark hair was down extending past her waist and she wore a red blouse with an upturned collar. A wide black belt was around her tiny waist over the blouse and she wore a black skirt that didn't quite hide her shapely ankles.

I believe her lips primarily account for why her face is so appealing to me. She has full rounded lips that for some reason make me think of blooming red tulips. As I remembered from our first meeting her lips were stained the same shade of scarlet as her shirt and her face appeared flush with color. Her big brown eyes were wide, and she seemed to be literally bubbling with enthusiasm.

"Hi Branch!" she said with a big smile. I was glad I had taken time the night before to polish up my boots and stopped to slick back my hair before McCloud had answered the door. Before classes this morning I had selected a new shirt and trousers that had been pressed by my mother until the seams were nearly sharp enough to cut a finger.

"Hello yourself." I said. "Been fishin' lately?" Her smile widened and I think my knees began to sag just a little. McCloud was watching me closely and he slid out a kitchen chair for me.

"Maybe you better sit, Ben Branch." he said. "You're getting too big for me to pick up if you fall down." I glared at the Cherokee, but his deadpan expression never seemed to change.

Rosa Kate was still smiling, but her eyes were questioning his remark.

"Ben Branch would like to try your drink, Miss Rosa." he said. 'He may be so overcome he faints from the pleasure." I wasn't sure his explanation was absolutely truthful but it covered his remark of why I needed to sit.

I watched as Rosa Kate poured a muddy looking liquid into a cup and handed it to me. They were watching me as I steeled myself and brought the cup toward my lips to try a taste of the ugly mixture.

I frowned in spite of myself for I remembered a time years before when Jon David had pushed my face into soft mud during one of our perpetual wrestling matches. Unfortunately I had my mouth open at the time screaming for Mama to come and rescue me and got a whopping good taste of Missouri swamp! It had not been a pleasant experience to say the least!

With that in the back of my mind, yet determined to please Rosa Kate, whom if she simply asked I would have most assuredly have kissed a cottonmouth, I closed my eyes and took a small sip.

My eyes widened as I experienced my first taste of milk, sugar and melted chocolate. All three sets of eyes in the room were studying me closely as I took a more healthy drink, closed my eyes again, raised my face toward the ceiling and swallowed I lowered my chin and opened my eyes trying to maintain an expressionless look on my face as the three others watched me in fascinated anticipation.

I remembered an expression my Papa had said to Mama one time that for some reason had embedded itself in my adolescent mind.

"This is dangerous stuff, Rosa Kate." I said. "It'd make a man slap his mama away from the table for wantin' some!"

Rosa Kate and her mother laughed as I gulped the remainder of the warm mixture and licked the rim of the cup with my tongue.

A Hard Life

"I read about chocolate in one of Mister McDougall's world geography books." I said. "It stated that down through history wars have been fought over the control of chocolate, and now I understand why."

"Why aren't you in class studying one of those damned books instead of being the center of attention here in Katherine's kitchen?" All four eyes in the room shifted to the doorway where Grayson stood glaring. He shifted his attention from me to McCloud.

"The front door was unlocked and I was able to walk in and catch all of you completely unaware, McCloud. What if I had been Clifton McCarty looking to revenge his broken nose, or a Cherokee war party bent on kidnapping Katherine and Rosa Kate?" His tone was accusatory and his steely gray eyes bordered on being frightening.

"Do you really want to discuss Cherokee war parties, Grayson?" McCloud asked. I saw color drain from Grayson's face and I watched as his eyes narrowed at McCloud's question. The Cherokee hesitated and then continued.

"Branch came by on his way back from escorting his teacher out to the main road to tell me about a lion track he found. I'm the one who invited him to the kitchen."

McCloud picked up his rifle then and pushed past Grayson, who was almost blocking the doorway. The two men glared into each other's eyes as McCloud stepped past him.

"Who put you in such a horrible mood, Grayson?" Katherine asked. "We are so happy to have Rosa Kate back home we were in a festive mood and you act as if the world is coming to an end." Her brother-in-law dropped his eyes to the floor and when he raised them again it was as if we were looking into the face of a different man.

He began to smile and walked across the kitchen to Rosa Kate, taking her in his arms even though she was not returning his smile. It seemed obvious to me that although she submitted to his hug I detected a stiffness in her toward her uncle.

"Forgive me, Rosa." he said gently. "I am very happy to see you and I apologize to you and your mother for disrupting what was probably a little welcoming get-together." He glanced over at me then.

"I didn't mean to snap at you, Branch. We are having labor problems at both mines and I suppose I let outside influences affect the way I spoke. When the holidays are over I will begin taking you with me when I visit the mines and a few of our other businesses. You'll be eighteen soon and you need to become more familiar with our companies and our enterprises."

"Yes, Sir." I said, emphasizing the "Sir", and he caught my eyes again. He had told me once not to be formal and to call him by his first name. It had been difficult for me for a while, but for the last few months I had willed myself to call him by his first name. My deviance from that now had significance and he recognized it. He nodded to me and left the kitchen without saying anything about it. We could hear him talking low to McCloud in the next room, although we could not actually hear their conversation. I would remember how hateful Grayson had appeared and the unveiled evil glint in his eyes that I had observed for the first time when he had surprised the four of us in the kitchen.

A Hard Life

"Thank you for the chocolate, Rosa Kate." I said. "I best get back to Grayson's and check on Mama." She smiled then and for me the tenseness of the previous few minutes vanished as if they had not occurred. Katherine caught me by the hand as I turned and a new uneasiness came over me.

"Branch, don't let Grayson's sometimes brusque manner affect you." she began. "His intentions are good and I know he admires you as we all do. I haven't told you before, but I understand now why my husband was so affected by you, even though the time he spent with you was short and...." She hesitated for a moment before she continued.

"I suppose the time you spent with James was horrible for both of you, but it would mean a great deal to Rosa Kate and me if you could find it in your heart to forgive him for what happened to you? Branch, do you remember having your arm packed in ice for several days before your surgery?"

I glanced at her in surprise. I had not told anyone about that. I guessed that James must have included it in his letter. I nodded my head and she continued.

"There was a physician in Dexter who had installed an icehouse cellar. James bought the ice for your arm from him and went himself every day to pick it up for you."

I couldn't meet Katherine's eyes then, so I fixed them on a spot on the toe of my boot. She waited for a moment hoping I would raise my head and meet her eyes. I was struggling to control emotions within myself for reasons I couldn't possibly explain to her, so I kept my head down.

"I know it was a hard time in your life when you were so young and I realize I am putting undue pressure on you too soon. Please forgive me for that, Branch, it's just that Rosa Kate and I have come to care for you and your mother and we would so much like for the two of you to think of us as part of your family."

I nodded my head, but I could not meet her eyes, for if I had I'm afraid I would have blurted out what Jon David and I had done to James Asbury!

If the truth of that long ago night was made known I was certain the fairy tale life that Mama and I had been living for nearly all the past year would come to an abrupt halt! I could foresee that the two of us would immediately be on our way back to Missouri to beg to work for Uncle Clady again.

I couldn't do that to Mama, so I clamped my mouth shut and kept it that way, while my eyes were kept glued to the toe of my boot. Katherine released my hand and I turned and walked from the kitchen without looking at either of them.

"Saddle your horse and meet me here at daylight tomorrow, Branch." McCloud said as I was exiting the house. "Bring a Winchester and your Colt and we'll see if we can tree your lion." I nodded to the Cherokee without meeting his eyes and closed the heavy door behind me.

A HARD LIFE

CHAPTER TWELVE

It was so cold my fingers hurt as I saddled up Rascal before daylight the next morning. A kerosene lantern barely illuminated the wide hallway where I led him to a rack where saddles were stored. I had left Rascal in a stall in Grayson's barn the previous evening and had given him a generous portion of grain to better sustain him for today's hunt.

The big roan gelding was one of a half-dozen riding horses that Grayson had told me I could use as my own. He had become my favored mount for he always appeared eager to greet me and would stand patiently to be haltered and saddled. He had proven himself to be sure-footed and could make steep climbs all day without giving out on me.

Mama had a worried look on her face the night before when I told her that I would be lion hunting with McCloud today. I had kissed her forehead and told her not to worry, that I would be careful. My assurance had not erased the worry lines on her face, but she had not argued with me. Grayson had merely grunted when I informed him that I would be using one of his Winchesters and my Colt sidearm for today's hunt. I had removed the weapons from the gunroom the night before and taken both of them to my room so I would not disturb anyone with my early morning departure.

I slid the loaded Winchester into a leather scabbard beneath the saddle and mounted Rascal, then reached to turn out the lantern before riding out into the darkness. Mine and Rascal's breathing made clouds of vapor in the early morning high country chill.

The moon was receding over the mountain leaving starlight to illuminate the snow packed road down toward Katherine's ranch. The morning was crisp and still and Rascal's hooves seemed to make unusually loud crunching sounds in the frozen snow.

I felt an almost unrelenting urge to be looking behind me as we moved down the dark roadway and I involuntarily reached down with my right hand to loosen the Winchester in its scabbard. It seemed to be one of those mornings when predators would feel urged to be out hunting and I didn't want Rascal and me to end up on the breakfast menu of a hungry mountain lion. A worse and more dangerous threat could be a marauding grizzly that sometimes came down from the peaks to try and catch a fat calf.

I guess my uneasiness was being communicated to Rascal for I had to hold constant pressure on his halter bit to keep him from breaking into a gallop until Katherine's house came into view on our right. I could see lantern light glowing from the barn up the ridge behind her house and I allowed Rascal to step up his already fast pace toward the welcome light.

A Hard Life

"You must be in a hurry, Branch." McCloud said as I bent my head over to ride inside the barn's alleyway. "We could hear your horse coming like the barn was on fire!" I pulled Rascal up short and noticed McCloud wasn't alone in the barn. Rosa Kate was cinching up the bellyband on a paint mare, and she looked up at me and smiled. She was wearing blue denim jeans, a heavy sheepskin lined coat that fit her loosely and appeared more suitable for a man. Her pretty hair was tucked inside a wide-brimmed felt hat with a chinstrap.

I must have appeared surprised enough to elicit a query from her.

"Did you think you were the only one McCloud invited to go along today?" she asked, just a tad sarcastically.

"No, it's not that." I replied. "It's just I didn't know we were settin' lion traps today." When her expression turned questioning I continued.

"McCloud must be bringin' you along for bait." She frowned and her big brown eyes narrowed. McCloud, however shot me one of his rare smiles before he disappeared into a tack room, then reappeared with a Winchester in each hand. One was his customary rifle, which he slid into his saddle scabbard and the other he put into a scabbard on the paint mare that Rosa Kate stepped up on.

She mounted her spotted horse effortlessly, which indicated to me that she was probably an accomplished rider. I hoped so, for McCloud had once told me that following hounds on a lion track in the mountains was dangerous business.

The sun had not yet appeared over the mountain, but it was getting light when McCloud rode around to the back of the barn, while Rosa Kate and I followed on our horses. He opened a pen and released five noisy hounds, all whining and bawling in anticipation of the day's hunt. He remounted his black stallion and gave an order to the dogs that must have been in Cherokee, for it was not a phrase I understood. The dogs fanned out behind his stallion with Rosa Kate and me following in single file.

McCloud rode down the road toward the river with the dogs following obediently. Before we got to the first river crossing he stopped his horse and leaned over to examine a set of tracks crossing the road. Rosa Kate and I watched as one of the lead hounds stuck her nose in the snow and raised her head to bawl excitedly. McCloud looked back at us and nodded and gave another command to the dog and then the whole pack was off in full chase, their bawling music reverberating and filling the entire valley with a sound exhilarating to a hunter.

We followed the hounds, trying to stay as close as possible, however the pack was soon out of sight. Once they crossed a ridge a half-mile or so above us, they went out of hearing also. When we topped the same ridge we stopped to listen and could barely hear the dogs for they had already crossed the gorge and were headed up the other side of the ridge. Our horses were blowing hard from the initial climb and McCloud sat for a while to allow them to rest.

"The lion is headed for the rocks above the timber." the Cherokee said as he listened to the far off music of his hounds. "He's been trailed by dogs before, I think. I believe this ridge bears east around the head of the valley, so we will follow it and maybe we can cut them off."

We followed the spine of the ridge that curved around the valley and soon we were headed in the general

A Hard Life

direction the lion and dogs had gone. As we climbed higher the timber became sparse and the snow-covered ground changed to solid rock with large boulders strewn about that had to be skirted.

We began hearing the dogs again and McCloud stopped to listen.

"He's gone to tree." he said. "We'll leave the horses and go on foot from here." We dismounted, took our rifles and Rosa Kate and I followed McCloud in a zigzag path down the slope toward the baying hounds.

We descended the snow-slick incline without mishap and moved further east a half-mile until we could see the tree the lion had chosen to climb to get away from the pack of hounds. The lead dog was looking up the tree and her baying had changed to a choppy bark with every breath she took. The other dogs were milling around the base of the tree, occasionally rearing up on it to bark excitedly. We couldn't make out the lion yet for the pine tree the cougar had chosen was thick with vegetation, especially near the top.

"Don't walk directly toward the tree." McCloud informed Rosa Kate and me. "Stay behind the boulders as much as you can and move from one to the other in a circular approach, else he'll bail out. If he reaches the boulders at the top of the mountain the dogs will probably lose his scent and he'll escape."

"Do we have to kill him, McCloud?" Rosa Kate asked and the Cherokee glanced sideways at her.

"It's Branch's lion." he said. "He found his sign first so he gets to make the kill." Rosa Kate looked seriously at me, but I avoided her eyes as I followed McCloud in a circuitous route toward the big pine tree.

The lion was crouched next to the main trunk in the very top of the big pine. His yellow eyes glared down at us and the tip of his tail twitched from side to side. The dogs were going crazy with excitement now that we were near. They knew what was coming next.

I raised my Winchester and put the front sight on the lion's face.

"Don't do it, Branch." Rosa Kate said as she stood to my left. I moved my face from the rifle stock to look at her and saw a pleading expression in her big brown eyes.

"He's not hurting anyone way up here away from the ranches. I believe he's learned his lesson now and will stay away from civilization."

I glanced back toward McCloud who had deliberately fallen behind as Rosa Kate and I had slipped up beneath the tree. The Cherokee had his rifle over his left arm and his expressionless eyes met mine. I looked back at Rosa Kate and her soft pleading eyes.

"Please Branch." she repeated and my resolve dissolved. I lowered the rifle and let the hammer down to the safety position.

"All right." I said to her. "I won't shoot him." She smiled and the two of us turned to walk away from the tree and the excited hounds. We were glancing at one another and didn't see McCloud raise his rifle and take quick aim.

His rifle cracked and both Rosa Kate and I flinched from the unexpected blast. We heard limbs breaking above us and suddenly the lion plummeted to the ground in a shower of broken limbs and dislodged snow behind us, dead as a stone from a well-placed bullet through the heart.

A Hard Life

Rosa Kate gasped and put her hand to her open mouth. We both looked at McCloud in astonishment and surprise.

"When something needs to be killed, then kill it. Don't walk away from it." he said, seemingly without emotion.

"But, I didn't want the lion killed, McCloud! There was no need to kill it!" Rosa Kate said loudly and emphatically, and I noticed that her face was flushed with anger and her usually soft brown eyes were flashing with emotion.

"It wasn't your lion, or your hunt, nor was the kill your decision, Rosa." McCloud said to her plainly. "My dogs worked hard doing their job and deserved the kill."

He ignored her angry stare and walked past her to pull the dogs away from the dead carcass. He patted each dog as he pulled them away individually and spoke to them in Cherokee. The dogs seemed to understand him and quieted down as he grabbed the dead lion by the front legs and pulled him up out of the snow and over a waist high boulder that he had brushed bare.

"Do you want me to fetch the horses?" I asked. He nodded to me and pulled his skinning knife from its scabbard.

"Take Rosa with you" he said, "for she might not want to see this."

"I'll stay!" Rosa Kate said emphatically and McCloud and I both looked at her and noticed that her eyes were still blazing. The Cherokee shrugged.

"As you wish, Rosa." he said and turned toward the lion to begin the skinning operation. I saw her resolve begin to fade as his sharp knife made the first cut.

"No, on second thought, I've changed my mind." she spoke again more calmly now. "Branch might need my help with the horses." she continued. McCloud never even acknowledged her response this time and continued on with his gory chore.

By the time we returned with the horses, McCloud had completed the skinning job. He rolled up the skin and placed it along with chunks of de-boned meat from the carcass into canvas bags behind the saddle of his black stallion. The dogs had fed well on scraps from the lion carcass and were ready to follow us when McCloud mounted his stallion. What remained of the lion's carcass was still draped over the blood-drenched boulder. I figured we would retrace our path up the slope and take the same ridge back toward the ranch. McCloud had a different plan however.

"I've been smelling smoke coming up from the valley." he said as he faced down toward the bottom of the canyon. "Let's go that way instead of the way we came." He led the way and Rosa Kate and I followed. I tried to catch a whiff of the smoke the Cherokee had mentioned, but for the life of me I could not detect what he had smelled.

However, before we had gone very far I not only could smell smoke, but we could see a thin column of it coming from the far side of the valley. We eased through the thick timber toward the source of the smoke and began to see signs where someone had felled pine trees. The stumps and piles of snow-covered brush the axe had left looked to be only a few weeks old.

On the far side of a little stream at the base of the valley someone had built a crude one-room log house. The smoke was coming from a fire pit just outside the cabin's single front door. We sat on the ridge watching the cabin for several minutes before we detected any movement. A girl who looked younger than Rosa Kate came outside the cabin to stir a pot of food cooking over the open fire. The faint cry of a baby got her attention and she left the fire to go back inside. She reemerged a minute or so later carrying an infant and returned through the snow to tend to the cook pot.

"Is this valley on our land, McCloud?" Rosa Kate asked quietly and McCloud only nodded.

"Do you know who she is?" I asked and the Cherokee shook his head to indicate that he didn't.

"How in the world did they find this place?" Rosa Kate asked.

"The main road to Denver is not far down the valley." he replied as he pointed to our left.

"She appears to be alone, but she must have people nearby. She looks too young to be married, but she carries the baby like it is her own. I wonder where her husband could be?"

"Probably a miner who doesn't want to pay rent to Grayson." McCloud said. "Others have built cabins on our land and when Grayson finds out about it he has the law from Denver run them out." Rosa Kate stared at the Cherokee as if she was surprised.

"Does Mother know he runs off families from her land?" she asked. "If I'm not completely turned around this would be Mother's land and not Grayson's."

"I doubt she knows." McCloud replied. "Grayson takes care of the property as if he owns it all."

"Would he have the law evict a young girl with a baby like the one down there?" Rosa Kate asked and the Cherokee nodded an affirmation.

"Mother would not approve of that if she knew it was happening." she said flatly. "I want to go down and meet this girl." Rosa Kate kicked her horse in the flank and turned her toward the cabin. I looked over at McCloud and he shook his head and frowned.

"I wish I had not invited her to come with us today." he said to me and then followed Rosa Kate's paint horse.

A HARD LIFE

CHAPTER THIRTEEN

The girl saw us riding down the ridge toward her cabin and she ran inside with her baby. I imagined she was frightened and I felt bad for her. She probably knew she wasn't supposed to be living there and had been dreading the day she might be caught.

I could identify with what she was probably feeling. Mama, Jon David, and I had lived under the threat of losing our home at the whim of Uncle Clady back in Missouri. Although Papa's brother never directly threatened us with eviction if we had not met his expectations, he hinted at it enough that we thought it could happen. I will always believe that was why Jon David had to leave Mama and me and go out on his own. His pride would not allow him to be beholding to Uncle Clady for our livelihood.

Suddenly McCloud spurred his black stallion to Rosa Kate's side and grabbed the paint's reins to pull her to a stop.

"Don't ride up to the front of the house, Rosa!" he ordered sternly. "We don't know who might be inside or what their intentions are. You let me check things out and if there's no danger, you can meet this girl!"

It was obvious to both me and Rosa Kate that McCloud was not asking permission. He was taking charge of her safety and making sure she complied. He had his rifle in his right hand and Rosa Kate nodded her agreement without argument.

"You inside the house!" he shouted. "We mean you no harm! My name is McCloud and I have Rosa Kate Asbury and Ben Branch Walker with me! Rosa Kate wants to meet you and your child!" We waited for a reply.

"What do you want with me?" The voice wasn't very loud and sounded more like a child. It was high-pitched and did not hide the fear the girl must have been feeling.

"Don't be frightened of us!" Rosa Kate shouted. "I just want to meet you and your baby."

"My husband ain't home." the voice replied. "I'm alone and I ain't prepared for no company." McCloud motioned for Rosa Kate to stay behind and he walked his horse around the corner of the cabin. He held his rifle pointed down toward the snow-covered ground, but I noticed his thumb was on the hammer and he was ready to bring it into action quickly if he felt threatened.

"We don't mean to bother you, Girl." he said as he stopped his horse in front of the cabin. "What's your name?"

"Beulah." The voice replied. "Beulah McCarty, Sir."

"Come on outside, Beulah." McCloud said as he dismounted. "Bring your baby out so Rosa Kate can meet the two of you." He motioned for Rosa Kate to come to join him and I followed.

A Hard Life

Beulah McCarty couldn't have been more than fourteen. She was big-eyed and thin with straggly red hair and her childish gaunt face was streaked with black soot. Her clothes were worn, dirty, and much too thin for the outside temperature. The baby was wrapped in a piece of an old stained quilt.

"Hello Beulah." Rosa Kate said with a reassuring smile and she stepped toward the frightened girl. Beulah McCarty was shaking visibly and I had the feeling it was more from fear than from being chilled.

"May I see your baby? Is it a boy or a girl?" Rosa Kate asked.

"It be a boy." the girl replied shyly. "My husband named im' Angus, after his daddy."

"Hello, Angus." Rosa Kate said and took the baby from the thin girl. I saw Rosa Kate's face pinch in anxiety as she looked down at the little boy.

"Beulah, he is so thin! Are you able to nurse him?" Beulah McCarty broke into sobs and tears streaked down her face making visible tracks in the soot and dirt on her cheeks.

"I ain't got much milk, Missy." she said between sobs. "Clifton ain't been home in over a week and I ran out of food three days ago. I've been livin' on soup I can make from boilin' water and bacon grease. I been afraid Angus was goin' to die. He don't even cry much no more!" She broke into sobs again and Rosa Kate held the baby in her left arm and put her right arm around the frail girl.

Rosa Kate looked at McCloud to see the Cherokee's jaw was clenched and his dark brooding eyes were narrowed.

"We've got food, Beulah." he said. "You and Rosa take the baby inside and try to keep him warm while Ben Branch and I pour out your soup and fix you something more substantial."

We buried little Angus McCarty at the foot of a giant ponderosa pine on the ridge overlooking the log cabin and the meandering little creek that flowed beside it.

The only tools Clifton McCarty had left at his cabin consisted of a dull single-bitted axe and a broken-handled spade. The ground was frozen several inches deep beneath the snow and McCloud and I had to take turns chopping out chunks of frozen soil with the axe until we could dig with the spade.

Rosa Kate held Beulah McCarty with both arms to keep the sobbing girl from throwing herself into the shallow grave where I laid the quilt-covered form. I had to lie on my belly reaching down as far as I could to avoid dropping the little baby boy.

When the baby was settled to the bottom of the hole, McCloud clasped my hand and helped me back to my feet. He stooped over and grabbed a handful of the moist soil and put it into Beulah's shaking hand.

"You should throw the first soil over your child, Girl." McCloud told her gently. "I know it's hard, Beulah, but you should be comforted to know that your little boy is in Heaven now. He's being comforted and tended to by Angels at the throne of Jesus, where there's no snow or cold winds, no hunger, or any other discomfort for him forever. He'll never again have to know how hard life is for some of us."

A Hard Life

I felt hot tears streaking my face and through the blurring of my tears I could see that Rosa Kate was crying also as she held a sobbing Beulah McCarty in her arms. McCloud prayed for the child and afterwards Rosa Kate and the grieving mother went back inside the cabin while the Cherokee and I completed the burying.

Beulah McCarty rode behind Rosa Kate and I carried all her worldly possessions in one little cotton sack tied behind my saddle. McCloud took a piece of charcoal from the fire pit and scribed a message on the front door of the cabin.

"Beulah McCarty at Katherine Asbury's ranch
Angus McCarty buried under big pine above cabin."

We took Beulah to Katherine Asbury's home where Rosa Kate, Katherine, and my mother did their best to comfort the pitiful little girl.

On Sunday, a week before Christmas, we were gathered at Katherine's for our weekly dinner and Rosa Kate brought Beulah downstairs from her room. I was astonished to see what a difference the women had made in Beulah in only three days!

Beulah's skin was fresh and clear and her reddish, auburn hair had been washed, trimmed, and brushed out to fan across her shoulders. She was wearing one of Rosa Kate's pretty blue dresses that my mother had altered to fit her. She was still thin and fragile appearing, but her big blue eyes weren't nearly so shrunken into her face as they had appeared the first day we had seen her.

I stood up from the dinner table and Grayson and McCloud did likewise when the two girls descended the stairs. Beulah still appeared a tad frightened, but when she saw me and the adults smiling encouragingly at her, she glanced over at Rosa Kate and a tiny smile crossed her face, transforming her into a pretty young woman.

McCloud began to bring his hands together in gentle applause and when Grayson and I joined him the two girls began to laugh. It was a touching scene and one I would not soon forget. My mother's face was wet with tears when we took our seats and bowed for McCloud's prayer of thanksgiving.

The meal was soon finished and we were all sitting comfortably, chatting and smiling at one another, and truly enjoying each other's company. Most Sunday meals at Katherine's house were enjoyable, but previous to today, there always seemed to be a tension between Grayson and McCloud and Grayson and me.

Today was different and all I could account for it was the fact that we all had a part in bringing a little civility and pleasure into Beulah's life that she had probably never experienced before. Something about doing a righteous act for someone who really needed it brought us closer and made us forget our differences.

We were finishing our deserts when we heard a shout from the front of the house. Beulah's hand flew to her mouth and we all heard her say his name.

"Clifton." she murmured and her eyes became troubled again and a shadow seemed to descend over her pretty face.

McCloud reached for his rifle and Grayson buckled on his gun belt and settled his big black hat on his head. I followed the two men as they went to the front door and opened it.

A Hard Life

Clifton McCarty stood in the front yard holding the reins of the thinnest, most uncared for horse I ever remembered seeing. McCarty's eyes were red from drinking and his face was gaunt and mean looking. He was the same young man that I had poked in the nose in Denver the day McCloud and I had taken the women shopping.

He carried no weapons that we could detect and I wondered to myself if he was courageous enough to brace armed men, or was he so drunk he didn't know what a dangerous situation he was really in. Grayson Asbury or McCloud could have shot him dead where he stood and been acquitted by any judge or jury in Colorado.

"I understand me wife is bein' held here!" he practically shouted, although we were only standing ten yards or so from him.

"Is that a fact?" he continued in an accusatory tone.

"We're not holding anyone against their will, McCarty." Grayson replied. "Beulah is here and she is being fed and cared for. If these two men had not rescued her when they did she would have starved the same as your son!"

"My son couldn't of starved!" McCarty shouted back, his face contorted in misery and he seemed almost in tears. "Beulah was nursin' im!"

"Your wife was starving, McCarty! Starving mothers don't produce milk, you moronic bastard!"

Grayson's voice had changed. He wasn't shouting, but his deep voice was distinctively clear and the barrel of McCloud's rifle held in the Cherokee's right hand moved upward a few inches.

It was a dramatic gesture and not one that Clifton missed, even if he was as drunk as he appeared. He took an involuntary half step backward and his face paled perceptibly.

The door was open behind me and Beulah McCarty stepped out on the front porch. She had the cotton sack in her hand containing her belongings that she had brought with us when we came to Katherine's.

"I'll be leavin' with my husband, Mister McCloud." she said in a timid voice. "I thank ye' kindly for bringin' me here and savin' me, but I'm bound to obey my husband's wishes. I especially thank ye' for the kind words you said over my baby boy."

"You don't have to leave with him, Mrs. McCarty." Grayson said. "Just say the word and I'll run him off this ranch and completely out of Colorado. You won't have to see his drunken face ever again!"

"No Sir!" she replied quickly. "Clifton be my husband and I'm duty bound to go with im'."

"All right, Child." Grayson said. "We won't hold you against your will, but you've not recovered yet. I advise you to stay a few more days until you're stronger?" Beulah shook her head.

"I best leave, Sir." she said timidly.

I couldn't believe what I was hearing and seeing happen. I knew Clifton McCarty could not properly feed or care for Beulah and I feared she would probably not live a month if she left with him. I stepped out from behind McCloud and gently took Beulah's thin little arm.

"Don't do it, Beulah?" I pleaded. "Stay here where you can be safe? At least for a few more days?" She raised her eyes to mine for an instant and then averted them downward again.

"Thank ye, Sir." she said. "I appreciate what you're tryin' to do, but I have to obey my husband."

I could see that she was not going to relent so I stepped past her and walked toward Clifton McCarty until my face was not two feet from his, and then I spoke only loud enough for him to hear me clearly. His bloodshot eyes defiantly met mine, but he didn't try to interrupt me until I had finished speaking to him.

"Listen closely, you miserable sonsabitch! You don't seem too worried about these two older men, which I can assure you is a damn foolish attitude, but you and I are near the same age and you would be wise to pay attention to me! If you take Beulah away from here today, and I find out that she comes to any harm! I mean, any harm! If Beulah trips and twists an ankle, and I hear about it, I'll come find you and when I'm finished your own mother won't recognize what's left of you! You best believe what I'm telling you!"

I held his eyes with mine until his finally wavered first and he looked away. I stepped back then and stood in the yard while Beulah made her way to the hapless old mare. Clifton helped her up on the horse and then he turned and led the old swayback out of the yard and down the river road. I stood and watched them go until they were out of sight. My arms were stiff at either side and my hands were balled into fists so tightly that my fingernails dug into my palms until they drew blood.

I noticed my hands feeling sticky and I raised them up to look curiously at the blood on them. I had not felt even the smallest stab of pain in my hands!

Christmas day came on Sunday and we gathered at Katherine's for dinner and to exchange gifts afterward. The situation surrounding Beulah and the death of her baby had served to dampen all our spirits some and the holiday was not as festive as we had planned for it to be.

The memory of James Asbury and his admiration for Christmas time was on Katherine's, Rosa Kate's, and Grayson's mind, and Mama and I were thinking about Jon David. Neither of us had mentioned his name, but when we would exchange glances we both knew what the other was thinking about. We had not heard a word from my older brother since we had arrived in Colorado.

Jon David had not appreciated Christmas the way Mama and I had. Mama always said that he took that after Papa. She had told me that the celebration of Christmas had been one of the few things that she and Papa had not agreed on. He believed it to be a Roman Catholic inspired holiday. He had argued with her that no one really knew the exact day when Jesus had been born and picking just one day of the year to celebrate lessened the significance of it. Papa had believed that we should celebrate Jesus every day and not just on Christmas.

I had always doubted that Jon David had put that much thought into why he had never been as excited about Christmas as Mama and me. Jon David had never really accepted Christianity, or religion of any kind. I suspected he felt as if snubbing Christmas was a small way to continue a loyalty to Papa.

It had never been a secret that Jon David had maintained more bitterness than I about Papa's murder. Not that I didn't remember the sad day, but maybe because

A Hard Life

I had been younger it seemed that I had accepted it more easily and it didn't eat at me all the time like it seemed to torment my older brother.

I took Mama aside after dinner and handed her the gloves that I had purchased in Denver.

"These are for Jon David." I said. "Don't let me forget to give them to him the first chance we get." Mama teared up a little, even though she smiled at me. She knew for certain now that her oldest had not been forgotten by either of us on this Christmas day. We both smiled then because we instinctively knew, without putting it into words to one another, that Jon David would be frowning at us, and probably saying a curse word or two if he was beyond reach of Mama's quick little left hand!

Grayson and McCloud thanked me for the gifts I had picked out for them and Rosa Kate laughed aloud when she opened up her package and discovered the fly rod I had purchased for her. My mother cried over the coat Katherine had helped me choose and she hugged and kissed me soundly in front of everyone!

A HARD LIFE

CHAPTER FOURTEEN

A sheriff's deputy from Denver rode into Katherine's yard just before Mama, Grayson, and I were getting ready to leave to make the short trip back to Grayson's ranch.

It wasn't unusual for one of the Denver lawmen to come to have private talks with Grayson except for the fact that it was Sunday, and even more significantly, it was Christmas. Grayson went outside to greet the man while I watched from one of the front windows. McCloud noticed me paying attention to the curious visit although, as usual, he didn't make a comment. Mama, Katherine, and Rosa Kate were busy chatting and ignored what was going on outside.

I watched as Grayson turned to look back at the house and then motioned for the deputy to accompany him to the barn. Normally who Grayson talked to, and what he talked about, did not interest me, but there was something about the visit from the deputy today that intrigued me. I wanted to know the reason for the visit so I carried my cup of punch toward Katherine's kitchen as if I wanted

A Hard Life

a refill. McCloud regarded me curiously, but the ladies didn't even seem to notice I had left the room.

I slipped out the back door and crossed the yard quickly to the back of the barn. The afternoon shadows at the barn's back doorway helped camouflage my entrance. I could hear Grayson's deep voice from the front of the barn, although I couldn't quite make out the words. I eased forward silently down the hallway until I was close enough to hear better and then eased into one of the empty darkened stalls.

"The girl keeps asking for Rosa Kate, Mister Asbury." The deputy's voice could be overheard from my vantage point.

"How bad sick is she?" Grayson asked.

"Bad, according to Doc Simpkins." was the reply.

"Will she live?" Grayson asked.

"Not likely." the deputy replied. "She's been beat up some, but Doc Simpkins says she's bleeding from her privates and that's what's made her so weak."

"Where is she?" Grayson inquired.

"The Harris Hotel on the east side of town." came the reply. "It has to be one of the nastiest in Denver. Miners and down-on-their luck cowpokes are the only customers. Word is, her husband put her up there and has been charging any man in town six or eight bits for a go at her. He's had a lot of customers, according to Doc Simpkins."

"I'm glad you came to tell me, Frank." Grayson replied. "I won't say anything to Katherine or Rosa Kate. It would just upset them for no reason. I would appreciate it if you would keep it under your hat that she was asking for Rosa Kate. The same goes for the Sheriff and the other deputies. If the girl dies, see that she has a decent burial and send the bill to me."

"You can count on it, Mister Asbury." the deputy replied.

I waited until they had left the barn and then I hurried out the back and sprinted across the yard to the back door. Grayson was just entering the front door of the house when I emerged from the kitchen with a fresh cup of punch.

"You and your mother ready to go, Branch?" Grayson asked and I nodded. When we arrived at Grayson's house I immediately went up to my room. I strapped on my Colt, picked up the Winchester, and stuck a box of cartridges for each in my coat pocket.

When I went downstairs Mama glanced at me and I casually said that I was going hunting for a while. She nodded and I went to the barn, saddled up Rascal and rode back to Katherine's. I was relieved when I got there and discovered that McCloud was gone. The housekeeper who answered the door told me he had saddled up and rode to one of the higher pastures to check on the cattle. Katherine and Rosa Kate had retired to their individual rooms

I knocked on Rosa Kate's door and when she answered it I told her in hushed tones about the conversation I had overheard between the deputy and Grayson. Her big brown eyes filled with tears when I repeated that the deputy had said Beulah might not live.

"What can we do, Branch?" she whispered.

"I'm goin' to the hotel and check on her." I said.

"I'm going with you." she responded.

"Maybe you better not." I replied. "If I run into Clifton there'll likely be trouble and I don't want you to be involved in that. Grayson doesn't want you and your mother to know what has happened to Beulah. He would have a fit if he knew I had told you what I overheard. No tellin' what he'd do if I took you with me and got you into trouble." She bit her bottom lip as she thought about what I had said.

"Beulah needs me, Branch." she said. "You heard the deputy say she's asking for me. Let's take a wagon and if she's able to travel, we'll bring her back here to the ranch where I can take care of her."

"Your mother may not like that and I'm right sure Grayson wouldn't." I observed. Rosa Kate's eyebrows arched as she thought about what I had said.

"Mother probably wouldn't give me permission to go to Denver, or bring Beulah back here, but once she's here, Mother won't throw her out and she won't allow Uncle Grayson to do it either."

"Are you sure?" I asked and held her brown eyes with mine as she nodded.

"Go hitch up a wagon, Branch." she responded. "I'll slip out of the house and meet you at the barn. If we're lucky, Mother and McCloud won't know until it's too late to stop us. I will tell Felicia, the housekeeper what we're doing, but I'll ask her not to tell either of them until we're well on our way to Denver. I can trust Felicia." I nodded my agreement.

"I'll be waiting in the barn." I said. "Give me fifteen minutes to harness the team."

Rosa Kate closed the door and I tiptoed down the stairs and headed for the barn. She was dressed in jeans and her sheepskin coat when she climbed up beside me on the wagon's spring seat. I had put some blankets in the back of the wagon and I pulled one up for her to put across her legs. The mountain air was already cold and the sun would be down by the time we got to Denver.

I found the Harris Hotel and left the team and wagon in the alleyway behind the hotel. The desk clerk looked us over suspiciously when I inquired about Beulah, but he gave us the room number when I laid two silver dollars in front of him. He was a thin, balding man with the big puffy nose of a habitual drunkard.

"Doc Simpkins jest' went up to her room." he said. "You'll have to knock for him to let ye' in. He gave me orders this mornin' not to be lettin' anybody go up, but I don't think he was referrin' to women folk or boys." The man smiled and showed his yellowed rotten teeth. I glared back at him and when I shifted the Winchester rifle from my right hand to let it rest over my left forearm, his smile disappeared.

I tapped on the door with the rifle barrel and after a short delay an old man with white hair opened the door.

"My name is Branch Walker and this is Rosa Kate Asbury." I said to him. "I think Beulah has been asking for Miss Asbury." He nodded and stepped back to let us in. The room was dark, dingy, and smelled bad. Beulah was curled up like a child in an old iron bed with dirty blankets. There were darkened areas on the covers that appeared to be bloodstains.

"Is she awake?" Rosa Kate asked and the old man shook his head.

"She's unconscious." he replied in a raspy voice. "I've done all I can do. I doubt now she'll ever wake up. She's lost a lot of blood and she was weak to begin with. I tried to get her to eat this morning, but she refused anything. Now I'm afraid it's too late. I was getting ready to leave and check back on her at daylight."

"Could we move her to a hospital, or maybe take her home with us?" I asked and the old doctor eyed me coldly.

"There is no hospital in Denver, Son, and moving her now would kill her sure. All we can do is wait to see if she wakes up and has the will to live. We'll know by morning."

Rosa Kate and I looked at one another.

"We'll sit up with her." I said. "What should we do if she wakes up?" He motioned to a napkin-covered bowl sitting on a table beside the bed

"Try and get her to eat some broth soup." he said. "It's freshly made today. I know because I brought it from home. There's a chamber pot beneath the bed for other uses. My name is Doctor Lemuel Simpkins and I'll be back at daylight like I said."

"Do you know if her husband will come to check on her?" I asked and the old doctor eyed me and then glanced down at my rifle and my Colt in its tied-down holster.

"If he does, Son, you have my express permission to shoot him on sight!" Lemuel Simpkin's blue eyes practically blazed with anger.

"He could be the poorest excuse for a human I've ever encountered, and believe me I've seen some bad ones in my time. Word is, he's vamoosed with the money he earned selling off the last of that poor little girl's virtue. With any luck maybe he'll end up on the point of some man's knife, or fall off a cliff somewhere!"

Beulah McCarty never awakened in this world. About three in the morning Beulah's breathing had changed. It would slow down, speed up, and then slow again. Eventually it just stopped, and the little form that had once been a pretty young girl lay still and cold.

Rosa Kate had held Beulah's hand all night and began to cry when she felt it go cold. I got up and walked out into the hallway so Rosa Kate could be alone with her grief.

I was surprised to find McCloud standing by a window at the end of the hotel hallway, a few feet from Beulah's room. I had the impression he had been there a long time. His rifle was in its accustomed place over his left arm and he dropped his eyes to the floor and then lowered his head allowing his big black hat to cover his face when he saw tears streaming down my cheeks.

We buried Beulah underneath the big pine beside her baby boy, Angus. McCloud stood on the ridge above us and read verses from his Bible and prayed for Beulah's soul. Fresh snow had fallen the night before and the Cherokee's bare head was framed by the dazzlingly white mountains and azure blue sky above and behind him as he spoke over her final resting place.

I hoped that what McCloud said about Beulah and Angus being in Heaven now was really true. In my own mind I couldn't imagine Heaven being much prettier than where we had buried the both of them. I silently prayed Heaven would not be so lonely.

Mama and Katherine comforted Rosa Kate while McCloud and I shoveled dirt over the quilt-covered form. When we had mounded up the grave McCloud pounded

A Hard Life

in a cedar cross with Beulah's name on one arm and her son's on the other.

We burned the rough log shack that had been Beulah's last home. We didn't want anyone else to take up residence there, and we especially didn't want Clifton McCarty to ever have reason to set foot on the property again.

Grayson wouldn't attend Beulah's burial service. He was furious with me when he heard that I had taken Rosa Kate into Denver without telling anyone. He and I had locked eyes in a silent challenge that would forever change the relationship between the two of us. The matter was never mentioned from that day forward and for the most part we treated each other cordially and respectfully in public, but we both knew there would never be any true footing for any affectionate feelings between us again.

Mama, Katherine, McCloud, Grayson, and I rode to the train station with Rosa Kate the next week to see her off to go back east to finishing school. When Rosa Kate had said her goodbyes to everyone else she asked me if I would walk her to the steps leading up to the railcar.

I had no idea why she wanted me to go alone with her and apparently her mother and the others were just as clueless. When we got to the steps leading up to the passenger car she took one step up and turned toward me, our faces level now.

"I've never allowed anyone to call me anything but Rosa Kate or Rosa before in my life, Branch. I've been very narrow minded about it." She said this very seriously and I remained silent, lost in her big brown eyes.

"I'm going to make an exception for you and for you alone. I want to thank you for bringing Christmas back to me and Mother. Besides that I want to thank you for being with me and helping me through some very sobering moments in my life in the last month. I want for you, and you alone, to feel free to call me Rosie from now on. That is, if you would like to." I smiled at her.

"I'd really like that, Rosie." I replied, whereupon she reached out and pulled me close and kissed me. Not a brief, goodbye kiss from an adolescent, but a long, passionate, wet kiss that left me speechless with my ears ringing and my knees weakened considerable!

Then she waved at the others behind me and was gone up the steps and into the passenger car before I could say another word!

I stood there until the train was out of sight and my breathing had returned to normal before I turned and joined with the others waiting in the carriage. Mama and Katherine were smiling slightly at me when I stepped up to sit beside the stoic McCloud. I glanced at Grayson and recognized more open hatred reflected back at me in his eyes than I had ever experienced in anyone else's in my young life!

A HARD LIFE

CHAPTER FIFTEEN

Life in Colorado returned somewhat to what it had been before Rosa Kate's Christmas vacation. I say somewhat, because in April, when the spring thaws had begun, I took my first trip with Grayson to visit one of the family's gold mine operations east of Denver.

Asbury Mining Company plant number three was a hydraulic mining operation along the Platte River. The company owned a thousand acres on the northern bank of the river and employed several hundred miners.

It was dangerous, backbreaking work. Water was pumped from the river by powerful steam powered pumps and directed under high pressure to the sides of the ridges, washing gold ore downward through giant sluice boxes and then back into the river.

Mining had to be suspended in late fall and during the long winter months, not to resume until the spring thaw. Grayson and I rode into the camp about a week after operations had recommenced and it appeared to me to be a muddy mess.

Wet and cold miners stared over their shoulders at us from their positions along the sluice boxes. A heavy mist from the hydraulic nozzles spraying high-pressure jets on the slopes above us practically obscured the bright morning sunshine.

Grayson's driver stopped in front of a wooden structure on the riverbank a few feet from where at least a dozen sluice boxes emptied into the river. I would learn later that specially constructed baffles built along the bottom of the sluice boxes caught the heavier gold particles and held it while the lighter material flowed past. The longer the sluice box, the better chance of capturing all the gold in the ore and water flowing through it. Grayson told me that Asbury Mining had the longest sluice boxes in the industry.

A big redheaded man with a full beard came out of the building and reached up to the carriage to shake Grayson's hand.

"Welcome to Number Three, Mister Asbury." the man said. "I'm glad you're here. I've got a problem employee inside that maybe you can help me out with." Grayson nodded to the man.

"Glen Shanahan, meet Branch Walker." Grayson said. "Branch may be in charge of the company someday and I thought it time for him to begin to learn how things get done." The big man shook my hand and I noticed more pressure in his grip than necessary so I returned the pressure. I had milked cows most of my life and strong hands ran in my family. I continued to smile at Shanahan as he finally pulled his hand away from me. I didn't miss the challenge in his stare before his eyes left mine and turned back to Grayson.

"A man named Lonny Mossberg has been stirrin' up trouble in the camp, Mister Asbury." Shanahan said.

"What kind of trouble, Glen?" Grayson asked.

"Union talk." the redheaded man replied. "Mossberg claims to represent most of the workers here. He says they want better food and permanent housing instead of tents. Says he'll talk the others into a strike if he don't get what he wants." Grayson looked troubled.

"We'll talk to him, Glen." he said and we both stepped out of the carriage and followed Glen Shanahan back inside the building.

Two armed men stood inside the building beside the entrance. A third man about thirty years old sat in a chair beside a crude desk and looked up as we entered the room. Lonny Mossberg held his hat in his hands and kept twisting it nervously. Grayson went around and sat down at the desk and Glen Shanahan stood beside him facing Mossberg. I moved across the room to stand beside the only window in the building. I noticed that the window was streaked with dirt, not allowing much sunshine to come through the panes.

"Mister Shanahan tells me you're unhappy working here, Mossberg." Grayson said in his deep voice.

"Well Sir, he lied about that, the same as he does about most things, but at least he told you my name." the man replied and Glen Shanahan's face flushed in anger.

"If you're not happy working here, why don't you just leave and find another job somewhere else?" Grayson continued ignoring the man's remark about the lies.

"Because you and Shanahan will blackball me with the other mines and they won't hire me." Mossberg replied. He held Grayson's eyes bravely even though I saw Glen

Shanahan's eyes narrow with renewed anger at his remark. Grayson held his eyes and began to smile slightly.

"That's what happens with someone who brings up union talk, Mossberg." Grayson said and his eyes weren't smiling. "We don't need unions in Colorado. All a union does is make trouble for everyone, including the miners. I'll let this pass if you promise to keep your mouth shut about a union from now on." Lonny Mossberg shook his head and a determined look came over his face.

"That ain't right, Mister Asbury!" he said hotly. "Men have a right to organize to better themselves and their workin' conditions!" Grayson sat back in his chair and studied Lonny Mossberg and then turned his attention toward me.

"What do you think, Branch?" he asked. "How would you handle a man like Mister Mossberg here, who wants to establish a union so the workers can tell us what we can and cannot do?" All eyes in the room turned toward me.

"I'd probably ask what the men wanted." I replied. "If their demands are not unreasonable I would consider giving them what they want." Lonny Mossberg smiled at me and Grayson frowned. I had the distinct impression he had not intended for me to give him an answer at all. He probably wanted me to say I didn't know what to do in a situation like this. He looked up at Glen Shanahan who was staring at me like I had just gone crazy.

"Did you ask Mister Mossberg what the men wanted, Glen?" Grayson asked with a sarcastic tone. Shanahan shook his head.

A Hard Life

"If they take our wages then they'll damn sure do what we tell them to do, Mister Asbury." he replied and Grayson nodded his head.

"Shanahan's right, Branch." Grayson said. "You need to learn that we are the ones in charge, not the men who work for us. I'll show you how to handle a man like Mister Lonny Mossberg here."

He motioned to the men standing beside the door and they stepped over quickly, each man grabbing one of Mossberg's arms and pulling him to his feet. Lonny's eyes held mine for an instant. I recognized an appeal for help, but there was no fear reflected in his gaze. Glen Shanahan came around the table and he and the other two men escorted Mossberg outside. Grayson followed them out and I stood in the open doorway.

Shanahan waved to a man on the steam engine and when the man looked at him, Shanahan pulled his finger across his throat in a cutting motion. The worker then pulled a lever shutting off the pump sucking water from the river.

When the main valves shut down and the jet streams above us stopped, it suddenly got very quiet in the river valley. All the miners standing along the now empty sluice boxes stood erect and gazed down toward the building and the five men standing out in the open.

"All you men listen to me!" Grayson shouted. "I want you to see what happens to men who think they can take over the running of my gold mine! If any of you don't want to work for Asbury Mining all you have to do is draw your wages and leave. No one will blame you for quitting. However, I'm going to show you what happens to men who stir up trouble and slow down production! I want you to understand that I will not tolerate it!"

Grayson turned then and nodded to Glen Shanahan, who had pulled on heavy leather gloves. The two hired thugs held Lonny up and Shanahan began to pound him in the face and abdomen until his face was nothing but a bloody mess. Mossberg finally sagged unconsciously between the two men.

The beating lasted for a full five minutes and I wondered if Mossberg could live over such a savage attack. He fell to the ground in a heap when Shanahan finally ceased his punching and the two men let go of his arms. Mossberg rolled to his back groaning, his face bleeding profusely. I could see his chest moving as he breathed and bloody bubbles emerged from his mouth and nose. At least he was still alive, I thought to myself. Grayson turned back to address the miners.

"Three of you men come down here and carry this man back to his tent. Tell him when he wakes up that he better be gone by tomorrow. Tell him if I ever see him around one of my mines, I'll shoot him on sight!" Grayson looked up at me then. I was still standing in the open doorway.

"Help them carry him, Branch." he ordered. "You might as well get a little blood on you too."

I realized this was a defining moment in my relationship with Grayson. We had not been friendly toward one another since the day Rosa Kate had gone back to school, but he had never actually ordered me to do anything before. I wondered what he would have done if I had refused, but I decided not to test him today. I wanted

A Hard Life

to see how badly Lonny Mossberg was hurt anyway and this would give me an opportunity.

Three young miners came down off the ridge and I joined them where their fallen friend lay bleeding. Two men took his legs while a husky blond headed boy, about my age, gripped my hands and we supported Lonny's upper body between us.

"I hear you're from Ripley County, Missouri?" he said to me as we carried Mossberg's limp body toward a cluster of tents spread out in a field downstream from the strip mining operation. I nodded to him and met his honest blue eyes.

"Spent the better part of my life on the Little Black River east of Doniphan." I replied. He gave me a crooked smile.

"I'm from Poplar Bluff." he said. "My family's all back on Cane Creek in Butler County. Name's Griffin, Alton's my given name, but everyone always called me Curly. I came out to Colorado with Lonny Mossberg here. He's from Butler County too. He grew up on the Black River south of Poplar Bluff."

"I might have known." I replied. "We Missouri boys tend toward talkin' when we should be listenin'. I hope he's not hurt bad."

"Lonny?" Curly asked. "Hell, these Colorado boys couldn't hurt him with an axe handle! He'll be all right. I've seen him stove up worse after a Saturday night fun fight back in Poplar Bluff! I just hate he's let his big mouth cause him to lose his job! That means both of us will probably have to go back to Missouri without any gold and with our tails between our legs."

We deposited Lonny on a bunk in one of the tents and an older man brought in a wash pan to begin cleaning up his wounds and checking to see if he needed stitches. Lonny was awake and talking to Curly Griffin before I left. I was walking back toward the mining area when I heard Curly behind me.

"Hey Missouri!" he shouted and I stopped and turned as he approached.

"My name's Branch Walker, Curly." I said as he approached.

"Yeah, we know." he replied with his crooked smile. "Word is the Asbury's brought you out here because they owe you for somethin'. Somethin' goin' back to the Civil War's what we've been told. Important thing is you ain't one of them. At least that's the word?" He studied me carefully to see what my response would be and I nodded to him.

"Me and mama came out here over a year ago." I replied. "We're not part of the Asbury family, although I have to tell you they've been very generous to both of us."

"Folks say that Katherine Asbury is a fine woman and we hear she's got a highbred daughter so purty' she makes the boys howl at the moon!" Curly said with his quick smile.

"Grayson's a different story though." he continued more seriously. "We just had a demonstration of what he thinks of the common man." I nodded in agreement to what he said, but I withheld any comments regarding Grayson.

"I hope Lonny heals up all right." I said.

A Hard Life

"Don't be worryin' about Lonny." Curly replied. "The boys will be havin' a little goin' away shindig for him tonight. Why don't you slip off and join us?" I studied Curly wondering if he was trying to lure me into more than just a little fun. He noticed my hesitance.

"Don't be worryin' about any of the boys blamin' you for what happened to him." he said. "Lonny's already spread the word that you had nothin' to do with his beatin'. In fact, he thought you might have even agreed with him?"

"I don't know enough about the situation to take sides, Curly." I replied. "I can say that I don't think giving someone a beatin' is the way to handle working men's complaints." Curly regarded my answer and nodded.

"You just might make a good straw boss some day, Walker." he said. "Come back tonight if you can. Me and Lonny won't let nobody bother you. Besides, you might learn a thing or two."

"I'll see, Curly." I replied. "I can't make any promises."

"Fair enough." he replied and turned to go back toward Lonny's tent.

A HARD LIFE

CHAPTER SIXTEEN

The Number Three mining camp was close to ten miles from Denver and Grayson said we would be staying a couple of days, so we would be spending the nights in the camp. I was shown a small room in the supervisor's building where Glen Shanahan had his office. I was told I could sleep there and either eat in the cook tent with the miners or have the cook send meals to my room.

I wasn't told where Grayson's quarters were, but I assumed it was somewhere near and probably where Shanahan and his two companions usually spent their nights. The little bedroom in the supervisor's building was fine with me for I didn't care to spend any more time than necessary around Grayson, Shanahan, or their hired thug buddies.

I spent the rest of the day following around one of those buddies of Shanahan's. His name was Sartain and Shanahan told him to show me around the mining operations. I wasn't told if Sartain was his first name or his last and it was pretty obvious that the man wasn't any more thrilled about having to show me around than I was to follow him. We both did as we were told and kept our mouths shut.

When we returned to the supervisor's office I had not learned much more about gold mining than I had known before. I did notice that most of the miners minding the sluice boxes would look up and nod or smile at me while nearly all of them ignored Sartain, or glared at him when they didn't think he was looking. Sartain carried a sawed-off shotgun, plus a shiny new revolver in a holster around his waist, and none of the miners appeared to be armed, which seemed a tad odd to me. After all this was rugged backcountry replete with mountain lions, bears, and an occasional Indian war party. There had to be some significance to the fact that the only armed men in the mining camp were the supervisors. If I did accept Curly's invitation to visit the miner's tent camp tonight, I resolved to ask about the absence of visible weapons amongst the miners.

As for me I had begun to routinely wear my Colt in its tied-down holster anytime I was away from the ranch. I had continued my practicing at night in front of the mirror back in my room, and I spent several hours each week on Grayson's practice range. McCloud was my only shooting instructor now for Grayson had stopped offering me any advice, and didn't accompany me to the range any longer.

McCloud didn't hide the fact that he had little regard for handguns, and complements about anything from him were rare, but he had grudgingly acknowledged to me that I had developed quite an aptitude with the Colt. He had reminded me however, that drawing and shooting at a fixed target was quite different from shooting at a man.

Especially one that most probably would be shooting back!

As I had practiced I kept remembering watching Grayson draw and empty his Colt in scant seconds without once missing the empty cartridge case I had put down the range a considerable distance. My goal as I practiced was to duplicate what I had seen him do. My honest evaluation of myself at this point was that I might have already developed the ability to draw and shoot with a speed equal to his, but my accuracy wasn't there yet. That's why I continued to practice.

I had grown physically in the last year too. I was over six feet tall now and my previously skinny frame had begun to fill out. Mama said I reminded her of Papa and that I had inherited his sturdy build. She told me something then that had seemed ridiculous when she first said it, but after reflection I had to admit she might be right. She had told me that now I was physically larger than Jon David had been when we saw him last.

I was thinking of Jon David as I walked the short distance from the Supervisor's building to the tent city where the miners spent their nights. Lonny Mossberg's face was red and swollen, plus he had stitches above both eyes, but he tried his best to smile at me as I approached his tent. He was standing outside with Curly Griffin and a couple of other miners, all about my same age. The warm sunny day was giving over to the late afternoon mountain air and the buckskin jacket I had put on felt right comfortable.

"Boys, I was thinkin' of enterin' the beauty contest, but if this is the waitin' line I don't think I'd stand a

A Hard Life

chance. Especially against you." I said as I smiled back at Lonny.

"Well Son, this is the girl's line anyhow." he replied quickly. "You'd be lookin' for the hairy legged boy's crowd. They're gatherin' up by the cook shack yonder."

Everyone laughed and the suspicion I had noticed in the eyes of the two other men seemed to ease up as Curly and Lonny accepted me into their little group. Curly introduced me to Jack Rivers and Tad Johnson, the two men I had not met. Curly told me they were both from Tennessee.

"What's that bulgin' out the front of your fancy coat, Branch?" Curly commented as he nodded toward my right hand inside my jacket lapel. "Did you come armed?"

"I have to admit I did, Boys." I replied as I opened up my jacket. "I'm packin' double tonight." Their eyes fell on the full bottle of bonded whiskey I had been hiding beneath my coat.

"This bottle is compliments of the straw boss Glen Shanahan." I said soberly. "I found it kinda' hidin' in one of his desk drawers, and I'm right sure he'd want Lonny to have it."

Lonny tried to laugh, but it must have hurt for he had to put his right hand to his mouth. Curly grinned, reached for the bottle, uncorked it and took a long pull.

"I'm the certified whiskey tester for the camp, Branch." he said afterwards. "Iffen' it don't kill me then the rest of the boys ain't afraid of it." He handed the bottle to Lonny and it was passed from one to the other until it came back to me. They were all watching to see if I would drink with them.

I put the bottle to my mouth and took a health drink of the fiery liquid. It burned all the way down my throat, but I didn't let the pain show. It wasn't my first drink of whiskey. Jon David had seen to that before I was twelve.

The bottle was passed around several more times, but my swallows became smaller and I even passed it on once without taking a drink.

"What'd you leave the bosses doin', Branch?" Tad Johnson asked and before I could answer I noticed Curly frown and shake his head from side to side as he stared at the ground. Tad was watching me closely as if he was wondering how I would respond.

"They all left earlier in the afternoon." I replied. "They didn't tell me where they were goin' and I didn't ask." I noticed the group looking at one another and I got the definite impression they knew something that I didn't.

"You boys know more about Grayson and his cohorts and their business up here than I do." I said. "This is my first trip out to see how the business is run."

"You don't know about the bunkhouse?" Curly asked. I looked blankly at him and shook my head. Again they all looked at each other.

"I'll take you up there after good dark." Curly said. "You can see and judge for yourself." I nodded to him and declined to drink any more when the nearly empty whiskey bottle was passed to me again. I was intrigued by the implied mystery of the place they called, the bunkhouse, but I assumed I would have to wait to have answers to my curiosity.

The effects of the whiskey, plus the stress of the morning's beating, soon put Lonny back into his tent for some much-needed rest. I wondered if he would

A Hard Life

follow Grayson's orders to get out of the camp before dark tomorrow? I certainly hoped he would. I thought about what I would do if Lonny weren't able to leave and Grayson was determined to keep his word about shooting him on sight. I didn't rightly know what I would do. I couldn't imagine standing aside and allowing that to happen. I felt bad enough about his beating I had witnessed without trying to stop it.

The bottle was empty now and Tad Johnson and Jack Rivers drifted off to their own tents to get some sleep before the next day's hard work. Curly led me to a corral where I caught my gelding, Rascal, and saddled him while Curly saddled his mare.

We rode west from the camp keeping to the timber and avoiding the main road. About a mile from camp Curly led me up a steep incline utilizing an old dim trail, probably left by prospectors from an earlier era. We broke out on a steep ridge above the main road and rode parallel to it for another mile or so. Soon, I could make out lights from a distant building in the valley below us and oddly began also to hear unmistakable strains of piano music coming from the lighted building.

Curly and I dismounted and left our horses in a copse of timber and made our way on foot to a bluff overlooking the lighted building. Several expensive looking buggies and teams were tied up in front and I could see Sartain patrolling the area, apparently keeping a watch over them. Both female and male voices could be heard from inside the building mixed with laughter and the distinctive clink of glasses. Curly and I were not fifty yards from the roof of the building.

"What kind of gathering is this?" I asked Curly, who was lying on his belly beside me observing the activities below us.

"The miners refer to it as a bunkhouse tea party." he replied with a sly grin. "They usually have one every time Grayson visits the mine."

"Who's down there and what are they doing?" I asked and Curly glanced sideways at me with a curious expression on his face.

"You tellin' me you don't know what happens when men and women get together to party and drink? Men and women who ain't married to one another?" he asked in a quiet voice. I frowned at him.

"That's not what I mean." I said defensively. "It just seems like a strange, far-out place for a bunch of town people to get together for a party."

"Not when you know everythin' that's goin' on." he replied, the smile gone from his face.

"What do you mean?" I asked directly.

"Grayson and some of his rich buddies down there like their women young. I'm talkin' teenage young, most of em'." he replied. "Grayson is particular to Indian girls and a couple of the madams that run cat houses in Denver supply a few of them up here for the rich men parties."

I looked at Curly in stunned disbelief. In all the time I had spent around Grayson he had never indicated his interest in woman at all, much less young Indian girls. It just didn't seem to fit his image. Curly was watching me with interest to read my reaction.

"You didn't know?" he said and I shook my head and frowned as I stared down at the building below us.

A Hard Life

"Who do you think owns the cat houses?" he inquired and I looked at him with a blank expression.

"Grayson Asbury." he replied evenly. "The man you live with owns or controls all the gambling and whore houses in Denver. You'd likely find most of the bankers, lawyers, judges, and even the Sheriff and his select deputies down there."

"Where do they find young girls that would come up here and submit themselves to a bunch of old, mostly married men?" I asked and Curly turned a little so he could see my face clearer.

"You ain't been around much, have you, Branch?" he asked with just a hint of a smile. I lowered my eyes toward the ground.

"I've heard of such things." I admitted. "I've never participated, nor been this close to anything like this before." Curly stopped smiling and turned back to gaze down at the bunkhouse.

"Me neither." he confessed. "Lonny brought me up here once and we watched and listened. We couldn't see much and we had to imagine most of what we figured was happenin'. Neither of us got much enjoyment from the knowin'." He hesitated a few moments before he continued.

"Lonny told me that most of the white women are miner's wives and daughters. Some of them down there right now probably belong to men we work with every day. They do it for the money. Miners don't get paid enough to even properly feed their families. Rumor has it that the Indian girls are kidnapped from the local tribes and sold to the madams owning the cathouses. The Indian leaders complain to the agents in charge of em, but nothin' ever comes of it. The agency boss could be one of the buggy owners we're lookin' at right now."

"Why do the miners put up with such abuse?" I asked.

"No guts and no guns." he replied. "Why do you think none of us are armed?"

"I had wondered about that." I admitted.

"One of the first rules we learned when we got out here is that all miners have to give up their weapons to the bosses before they can get hired. If anyone is found with so much as a bowie knife, they first get a beatin', then they're fired and blackballed with all the other mines. There's spies in all the camps to keep the bosses informed of any hideaways. Grayson and the other mine owners won't allow any armed employees, except for their own thugs."

"Like that one down there?" I pointed at Glen Shanahan, the boss of the Number Three mine. He had come out on an upper landing of the two-story building below us. He waved to Sartain standing among the parked buggies and teams. Sartain waved back at him and then walked out of sight around to the other side of the building where I assumed other teams were tied up.

Shanahan looked all around, but never once glanced up at the bluff overlooking the bunkhouse. If he had he might have seen the two pairs of eyes staring down at him. He turned to leave, then stopped to stare down toward the back of the house below him. When Curly and I looked where he was staring I caught a momentary blur of movement in the darkened area and then I noticed an open doorway leading to the back of the building. I was certain that before our attention was drawn to Shanahan the door had been closed.

"They's somebody slipped outta' the house and hidin' in the back." Curly whispered and I nodded without commenting.

Curly and I both saw the slight figure move again at the same time that Shanahan spied it. He ran to the door he had emerged from and disappeared back inside. The small figure ran across the yard straight toward the base of the steep bluff where Curly and I lay hidden. We watched as the young girl attacked the slope and nimbly clambered upward headed almost directly toward where Curly and I were observing. Before she gained the top of the bluff Shanahan emerged from a side door and ran after her. Curly and I crawled backward from the edge so we could not be seen from below.

Curly and I had a quick decision to make and when I looked over at him I could see from his expression that the decision was expressly mine to make. I considered the alternatives and spoke to him just before the young girl pulled herself over the crest of the hill.

"Grab her when she comes over the edge and hold her." I said quietly. "Try and keep her quiet and I'll deal with Shanahan." Curly frowned at me and gave me a look that said he hoped I knew what I was doing. I hoped I did too.

The lithe figure topped the ridge without noticing Curly or me before it was too late for her to change her course. I figured she would assume the worst when she saw us and be as afraid of the two of us as she seemed to be of the man pursuing her.

I was right in my assumption, for her eyes flew wide with fright when she saw us crouched in her path. Curly and I both tackled her and he wrapped one arm around her arms and slender body while he put his other hand over her mouth in case she screamed. I grabbed her lower legs and held on until Curl shifted his weight above her and held her pinned helpless to the damp ground.

I could hear Shanahan's labored breathing as he climbed the steep slope. I thought about what I was going to do when the man came over the edge and I remembered an old trick I used on Jon David one time when we were playing king of the hill.

It was really steep at the crest of the hill where the Indian girl had come over and I hoped that Shanahan would take the same path. If he did the first thing I should see of him would be his head and face. I sat down facing the edge with my feet out in front of me. I could hear Shanahan climbing quickly as he came closer and closer.

The instant I could see his hat I drew back both feet and a split-second later when his face was visible all he could see were the soles of my boots, which wasn't for very long!

I kicked him flush in the face as hard as I could kick with both feet, which caused him to catapult backwards a long way before he hit the slope on his back, headed downward much faster than he had come up! I could hear him grunting and cursing as he rolled head over teakettle all the way to the base of the slope, which had to have been fifty-feet or more.

I sincerely hoped I had not broken his neck with my kick, or caused him to break his back in the rough and tumble fall. I glanced over the edge just long enough to see him lying flat on his back, but moving his legs around and trying to raise his head. He was cursing loudly however, which made me believe he wasn't mortally wounded!

I turned back and motioned for Curly to get up with the girl. He still had his hand over her mouth and I moved to where I could see her dark frightened eyes.

"We want to help you escape!" I whispered loudly with my face only inches from hers. "We aren't going to hurt you so keep quiet and let us get you away from here!" What I said did not erase the terror in her eyes, but when Curly slowly moved his hand from her mouth she didn't scream.

"We have horses hidden in the woods!" I continued as quiet as I could. "We'll get you away from here if you won't fight us!"

She didn't reply and I couldn't tell in the low light if she understood a word I was saying, but when we started moving away she didn't resist. I took her by one wrist and Curly kept a firm grip on the other as we hurried to where we had left the horses.

She was small and young. I would have guessed her not to be over fifteen and she was slight of build. When we got to the horses we could hear voices from over the ridge and we figured Shanahan had alerted the party that one of their guests had escaped. We didn't know then if Shanahan knew if she had help or not. I guessed he probably did. As quickly as it had happened I doubted if he saw enough of me to recognize who I was, but he was probably smart enough to know the boots that had practically caved in his face didn't belong to a young Indian girl!

Curly stepped up on his horse while I held her wrist. I picked her up like a child and she slung her leg over the horse behind his saddle and put her arms around him to hold on. He had already turned his horse and was riding away when I got Rascal untied and mounted. I followed Curly as he rode along the ridge that formed a bowl above the mining camp.

We rode for a mile before we stopped to listen. The woods behind us seemed silent without any present indications of pursuit. Neither Curly nor I doubted that it would come soon enough. The Indian girl sat quietly although I noticed that Curly still had a firm grip on her wrist. The moonlight here permitted me a better look at her face. She was pretty, but someone had applied rouge and lipstick to her face. I moved my hand slowly toward her face and she withdrew some, not knowing what my intention was. I wiped my gloved hand across her cheek and showed her the color that I removed. She blinked at the rouge and then began to wipe her face with her hands, smearing the make-up on the horse's rump.

"What is your name?" I asked and she stopped wiping at the make-up long enough to meet my gaze. "My name is Branch Walker." I continued and then pointed at Curly.

"This man's name is Curly Griffin. What is your name?" I repeated. She looked helplessly at me and shook her head. It was apparent that she could not understand me. I put my hand on my chest.

"Branch Walker." I repeated it twice as I touched my chest with my palm, then I pointed to her. I recognized understanding in her dark eyes.

"Ăătōn'yăh." She repeated it twice also, with an emphasis on the last three letters. I pointed at her and

A Hard Life

repeated, "Aatonyah", and she nodded. At least we knew each other's name.

"What do we do now, Boss?" Curly asked me and I looked sharply at him.

"I'm not your boss, Curly." I said. "I'm just a Missouri farm boy like you." He dropped his eyes and frowned.

"Yeah I know." I continued quietly. "We're two farm boys that have ourselves in a tight situation now. Probably a downright dangerous one." He nodded and gave me a look as if waiting for instructions. I reached into my saddlebag and removed a scrap of paper and the stub of a pencil. I scribbled a note, tore the paper in half, and then wrote on the second piece and handed both notes to Curly.

"You better get yourself and Lonny out of camp tonight. You've already told me that there are spies amongst the miners who will report that you and I were out of camp tonight. Grayson's smart enough to guess that one or both of us were involved in the little escapade with Aatonyah here." I nodded toward the Indian girl.

"The first note is to a man named Hiram McDougall." I continued. "He's a schoolteacher who lives in Denver. I suspect practically anyone there can direct you to his home. I'm right sure he will put you and Lonny up for a few days without telling anyone. The second note is for a man named McCloud and you will find him at Katherine Asbury's home. Watch from cover and try to catch McCloud alone. I'd rather Katherine not know anything about what happened up here. Be careful around McCloud though, for he's a dangerous man and he protects Katherine and her ranch. When you're sure he's alone ride straight up to him and keep both your hands in the open."

"Where will you be, Branch?" he asked.

"McCloud can find me after he sees the note." I replied. "He'll know how to get Aatonyah back to her people." The Indian girl looked at me when she heard her name.

"What's Grayson goin' to think about you bein' gone from camp?" I nodded to his question.

"Start a rumor in camp that I'm meeting up with you and Lonny and we're riding together." I said. "Say that the three of us are going to start our own business that has nothing to do with gold mining." Curly gave me a questioning look.

"Is that true, Branch?" he asked and I shrugged.

"Maybe." I replied. "This trip has taught me two things. I don't care to have anything to do with gold mining and I want to work at something that Grayson has absolutely nothing to do with."

Curly stepped down and indicated to Aatonyah that she should ride with me. The young girl glanced suspiciously into my eyes before she let Curly help her up behind me. I could understand what she might be thinking. She had no idea what my intentions were and I didn't know how to try and reassure her that I meant her no harm. I simply met her eyes and reached down to take her hand. She shook her head and instead let Curly help her up.

"So long, Curly." I said to the blond Missourian. "Be careful how you approach McCloud." He nodded.

"You be careful yourself, Branch." he replied and glanced up at Aatonyah.

A HARD LIFE

CHAPTER SEVENTEEN

Rascal carried mine and Aatonyah's weight without apparent effort. I stayed in the big timber hoping the thick carpet of pine needles would absorb our tracks. I had no idea if anyone was following me or not, but I chose to assume that they were.

Jon David had taught me a few tricks to throw trackers off a trail and I used as many of them as I could remember. I changed my course several times and when I changed directions I chose places where my sign was hardest to see, and hopefully more difficult to follow.

My general direction of travel was northwest, and after a few miles of twisting and turning maneuvers the sun started to come up and the darkness gave way to daylight. I abandoned my evasive maneuvers and rode in a direct line to put as much distance between us and the mining camp as possible.

As I rode I took mental inventory of my supplies. We had no food, which could be a big problem if I weren't able to shoot something. I did have a canteen of water and I had my rifle and pistol with an adequate supply of ammunition. I had a bedroll, with an extra blanket rolled inside, plus my heavy sheepskin jacket. I always carried matches in my saddlebags in a watertight container and I kept both a skinning and boning knife stored there also. After reflection I decided that I had spent considerable time in the outdoors back in Missouri with less, so I wasn't much worried about our ability to survive for a few days in the Colorado mountains.

Since I didn't know how Aatonyah would react to spending time in the wilderness with a complete stranger, I simply chose not to worry about it. After all she was an Indian and I assumed she must know how to live in the outdoors. As far as her being afraid of me, I could only hope she would recognize my intentions were more honorable than her last captors had been.

My destination was the base camp where McCloud and I had camped during our elk and bear hunt the previous fall. I knew there would be a plentiful water supply and hopefully enough available game to keep Aatonyah and me from starving. It was also practically inaccessible to anyone but those very familiar with the area. I hoped that Grayson would not think of it and I knew McCloud would have no trouble in locating us.

We rode hard all day with only a few stops to rest Rascal and share a few sips of water from the canteen. At one of these stops I attempted to communicate to Aatonyah that I wanted to take her home, but we would have to wait on McCloud.

I tried to use sign language, which I had a very rudimentary knowledge of, so I ended up drawing pictures on the ground with a stick. I didn't really know if she understood me completely or not, but after that stop she seemed more relaxed and less afraid of me. When we stopped again she indicated to me that she wanted to go off alone. I understood her need, for I needed some time away from her too. As she walked away into the brush I wondered if I would ever see her again.

After a few minutes however, she reappeared. I had hurriedly finished my business and remounted so I held down my hand to help her up behind me. She took my hand this time and let me assist her up.

We camped high on a dry plateau that night where the only thing we had to eat was a few pieces of jerky I happened to have in my saddlebag. We shared the inadequate meal and I let her have the bedroll and the blanket. I lay by the fire with my sheepskin-lined jacket and my head supported on my saddle.

Rascal awakened me at daylight with a snort and I glanced over at the bedroll to find it deserted. I glanced around quickly and Aatonyah was nowhere to be seen. My rifle and pistol were beside me along with the canteen and saddlebags. I jumped up as if to give chase, but then thought better and resigned myself that she would either return on her own or she wouldn't. There wasn't much I could do if she didn't.

I heard a slight noise as I added wood to the fire and turned to see Aatonyah coming out of the woods carrying a young porcupine carefully by one of its hind legs. The porcupine's head had been bludgeoned with what I guessed to be a sizable rock. She dropped the animal beside the fire and pointed to the sheathed skinning knife in my belt. I handed the knife to her handle first and she immediately began to work on the animal's soft underside. In just a few minutes she skinned and dressed the porcupine and skillfully skewered it over the fire on a sharpened green pole.

I have never eaten porcupine before, but I have to admit it isn't bad. Given, neither of us had eaten much in over a day, so anything barely edible would have been palatable, but I discovered that seared porcupine meat is quite tasty.

I handed her the canteen when the most of the animal was gone and I pointed at my last portion in my hand, dropped my head in a slight bow, and smiled as I put the last of it in my mouth to chew. She understood my thanks, and I saw the first smile on her dark complexioned face as she raised the canteen to drink. I noticed a small mole on the high cheekbone of the left side of her face that seemed to add something to her natural beauty. I had to admit she was quite pretty when she smiled, even with porcupine grease still smeared on her chin.

We arrived at the hunting camp around noon the following day. I had been watching for human tracks as we rode closer and had found nothing but the tracks of animals. I shot a mule deer yearling an hour after we had made camp, hoping the sound of the shot would not carry to any hostile ears.

Aatonyah gathered herbs and wild vegetables from around the spring and that night we had a satisfying meal. I neither recognized nor complained about the unidentified shoots and tubers she had dug up with a sharp stick, but ate them with relish. I would have preferred some salt for seasoning, but since Aatonyah would not have understood my complaining anyhow, I kept quiet.

On the third day after our arrival in the valley I was sitting beside the campfire and began to have the feeling

A Hard Life

we were being watched. Acting on impulse I glanced up the south ridge and then spoke in a loud voice.

"I know you're watching us, McCloud! You might as well ride on in!"

Aatonyah stopped what she was doing and looked at me strangely. I was still studying the ridge, but I did not detect any movement or sounds. I was beginning to think that my instincts had been wrong when McCloud suddenly materialized from behind a screen of brush beyond the spring.

"You surprise me, Ben Branch!" he said. "How did you know I was up there?" Aatonyah looked alarmed at the sound of his voice, but I held up both palms, smiled and nodded to her.

"It's McCloud." I said in a reassuring tone "Nothing for you to worry about now." I didn't think she could understand a word I spoke, but I hoped my tone might diminish her apprehension.

McCloud rode into the camp and dismounted. He and Aatonyah studied one another and he began to speak to her in Cherokee. She responded with a few sentences to him and he nodded before he turned to me.

"You've caused quite a stir back at the ranch." he said and hunkered down by the fire to extend his hands toward it. The sun had gone behind the mountain and in the thin air the temperature had dropped quickly. I didn't know how to respond to his statement so I remained quiet.

"Grayson took most of his clothes and personals and moved into one of his hotels in Denver." he continued as I glanced at him in surprise.

"He didn't go into any details of his reasons, but he left your mother in charge of his house for the time being."

McCloud continued. "She appeared some confused at first, but she didn't argue with him and seemed to me to accept the responsibility without much hesitance. Your mother is a strong woman." I nodded, but continued to listen rather than question the Cherokee.

"Your friend, Curly Griffin told me what happened at the mine." He hesitated, supposedly to see if I would respond, and when I didn't he continued.

"It was a foolish thing for the two of you to do. If Grayson had caught up with either of you I'm not sure what he would have done. He likes to keep details of his private life from Katherine and now you've become a threat to him." I caught the Cherokee's eyes and held them.

"You've always made me believe that you are loyal to Grayson, McCloud." I said evenly. "Am I a threat to you too?"

The question was simple, but the implications were substantial. My hand was not far from the Colt on my hip and McCloud's rifle was across his knees, pointed away from me. The Cherokee returned my gaze and then his eyes went to my right hand a few inches away from the bone handle of my peacemaker. When his eyes returned to mine we both knew that my implied challenge had been recognized.

"Your problems with Grayson are between the two of you, Ben Branch." he said evenly. I tried to read what lay hidden in his dark eyes, but they remained expressionless. I believed the Cherokee would defend the Asbury's with his life if necessary. What I didn't know was whether the stoic Indian considered my mother and I to be part of the family that held his allegiance.

"You and I will take this girl back to her people and return to the ranch." he said evenly. "You should then return to your studies and finish your education. Katherine will determine what your responsibilities toward the businesses will be from now on. I don't think Grayson will be a danger to you unless you talk about things you should keep to yourself."

It was settled then. The message had been made clear to me that if I kept my mouth shut about what I knew about Grayson, life could go on somewhat as before. The thing that was different was that Grayson and I would never be friends again, if we had ever been?

What I still didn't know was whether McCloud had been told to communicate this to me, or was he telling me this because he knew it would assuage the situation.

Whichever scenario was true was important because what I didn't know was whether McCloud truly cared for my well being, and wanted me to be safe, or was he simply following Grayson's orders. His dark eyes and expressionless face did not give me a clue as to which was truth.

A HARD LIFE

CHAPTER EIGHTEEN
"Three Years Later"

It's the middle of March and at the moment I am at my desk in the corner office of the Western Territorial Bank building in downtown Denver. I completed my advanced school studies with Hiram McDougall back in December and presently I'm immersed in paperwork. Accounting is the least enjoyable part of my responsibilities as an employed principal of Asbury Industries. I work directly for Katherine Asbury, but she has put me in charge of all the lumber and agricultural responsibilities of her holdings.

I tried again to concentrate my thoughts on the lumber inventory sheets and invoices in front of me, but for some reason this morning my mind kept wandering outside the confining walls of my office. Finally I gave up and leaned back in my padded chair to stare out the window to the dusty streets of Denver. I reflected on how things had changed in mine and Mama's life in the last three years.

A Hard Life

Katherine is the principal stockholder of the Western Territorial Bank and owns fifty-one percent of the bank's holdings, while Asbury Industries owns the remainder. She and Grayson had set up all the Asbury holdings in a similar fashion. He maintains a majority stock interest in the varied Asbury mining operations, the two hotels, and the three restaurants in Denver. He also owns a majority interest in the ranch property where his home was built, even though for the past three years he had abandoned the ranch to my mama and me to be used as our residence.

Katherine has majority interest in the bank, as I mentioned earlier, plus all the farmland east of Denver, the stockyards, and the timber rights on over forty-thousand acres of the surrounding mountain forests, including the timber on Grayson's ranch.

I take my directions from Katherine and hardly see Grayson anymore. He spends his time either at the mining operations, or he's in his permanently reserved suite of rooms in the Mountain Top Hotel, the largest and finest of its kind in Colorado.

The proceeds from the entire operations funnel into the Asbury Industry's Accounting office, also housed in the Western Territorial Bank building, three doors down the hall from my rather sparsely furnished corner office.

Once a year, on the last Saturday of May, a general board meeting and financial report of Asbury Industries is held in the bank's ornate walnut paneled boardroom. There Grayson, Katherine, Mama, and me, sit in to hear details of the financial picture of the corporation from the secretary/treasurer of the company, a slight balding man named Harley S. LaMarr.

Katherine and Grayson share the chairmanship position of the corporation and they and LaMarr comprise the voting board of directors. Katherine had nominated me to become a voting board member the previous year, but Grayson and LaMarr had objected to my appointment. They based their objections on the grounds that the board of directors needed to be an uneven number of members so a majority vote could be reached on issues presented before the board. Katherine had countered by nominating Rosa Kate as the fifth member, but Harley LaMarr pointed out that she wouldn't be the legal age of twenty-one until this year, and besides she had never attended a yearly board meeting.

Katherine was visibly perplexed by the two men, because Harley always sided with Grayson on issues when Katherine and her brother-in-law disagreed. It seemed apparent to Mama and me that Grayson had maneuvered things exactly to the way he wanted them and my or Rosa Kate's appointment to the board this year would be met with stiff opposition.

Katherine was adamant about our appointments however, and had pointed out that lawfully Rosa Kate and I would both be eligible to become board members this year. She reminded Grayson and LaMarr that since the two of us were heirs of her husband's estate, according to the company's charter we could not be denied board assignments when we were both of legal age.

Grayson had started to object again, but Harley had interrupted him to state that Katherine was accurate in her interpretation of the company charter's rules. If looks could have killed that day, the withering stare the balding man received from Grayson Asbury would have rendered him dead on the spot, not unlike a moth impaled on a hatpin!

Harley LaMarr would not even look at Grayson however, but I, Katherine, and Mama, were convinced he received a blistering cursing, or worse, after the three of us left the boardroom and the bank building that day.

Therefore, the brightest spot in my life today, as I tussle with the board feet totals in front of me, is the knowledge that in less than a month Rosa Kate will be back home in Colorado for the first time in three years. I have not seen or talked to the pretty girl since that faraway January day at the train station when she had kissed me so passionately in plain sight of her family and all the other departing passengers

Rosa Kate was coming back to attend the board meeting at her mother's insistence. Grayson wasn't happy with how the company was structured now, because the mining operations had fallen on bad times and Katherine's timber operations and farming enterprises were booming. His and Katherine's individual profit sharing agreements were based on the particular businesses each held a controlling interest in. Because of the continuing decline in the mining operations, Grayson's private earnings were falling far short of Katherine's.

The gold rush that had sparked the interest of thousands of adventurers to flock to the mountains of Colorado, and created the city of Denver, was giving way to more stable and elementary commerce, namely timber and farming operations.

Therefore, Grayson and Harley had been working on a new profit distribution plan to remedy his income shortfalls at Katherine's personal expense, and they had put the plan on the agenda for a vote at the May board meeting. We all knew that unless Rosa Kate and I were installed as board members before that proposal, he and Harley LaMarr's votes would outweigh Katherine's. With that victory Grayson would again be in complete control of the net assets of Asbury Industries.

Curly Griffin and Lonny Mossberg had become managers working for me after they were fired from Grayson's Number Three mine. Curly was familiar with the timber industry from his family's trade back in the Missouri Ozarks, and Lonny had evolved from generations in farming backgrounds. I had some experience in both trades and Katherine had allowed me the freedom and responsibility of trying to make her businesses flourish here in Colorado.

Flourish is not an adequate word to describe how well those operations had performed, especially for the last two years. Curly and I had logging operations ongoing in the mountains and we were shipping over a hundred thousand board feet of lumber east every week on the busy St. Louis and St. Francisco Railway.

Hiram McDougall had been my mentor, as well as my teacher, and had advised me on the finer aspects of managing companies that are dependent upon workers for their success. Hiram retained an immense wisdom in how to deal with people, especially working class people, and he drilled that knowledge into me at the same time he taught me higher mathematics, science, grammar, and history.

Upon Hiram's advice, and Mama's permission, I had invested a majority of she and my personal cash into St. Louis and San Francisco Railway stock. As our share of

A Hard Life

Asbury Industries profits accumulated each quarter in Katherine's bank, I would purchase more Frisco Railroad stock certificates.

Based on the upswing of lumber freight and the millions of tons of grain and produce that were shipped east from Colorado yearly, my Frisco stock was doubling in value once or twice a year. Mama's personal net assets added to mine now exceeded our wildest dreams when we were working for Uncle Clady back in Missouri.

I finished reconciling the ledgers I kept on Asbury Industry's present inventory of lumber, then closed and locked my office door. I saw Harley LaMarr pull his watch from his vest pocket as I strolled past his busy accounting department. I smiled a little to myself, for I had realized some time ago that Harley had little respect for my office hour schedules, or, as he would have put it, my lack of scheduled work hours!

I really didn't care much what Harley LaMarr thought of my work hours today in particular, because I was worried about Hiram McDougall, and I was in a hurry to go see how my former teacher was doing. Hiram had been feeling poorly for the last day or so, and I was remembering several times over the past year when he had not felt well. I often kidded him about his weight, which seemed to be steadily declining, but he would clamp down on his crooked stemmed pipe and tell me to mind my own business!

As I rode up the street and stopped to drop Rascal's reins over the hitching post in front of his house I observed Hiram in his little front yard pulling weeds from his garden. He always planted a combination vegetable and flower garden that he took great pride in keeping clean and well watered. His back was to me and he didn't appear to know that I was about.

"I'd hire one of the farmhands to do that for you if you would allow it." I said as I walked up the path toward the small man. He rose to face me and I became concerned as I noticed how swollen his face, and especially his lower lip, appeared to be. I frowned as he brought up his right hand to cover his mouth and the swollen area.

"What's wrong with your face?" I asked and he shook his head defiantly. He didn't take his hand away however, in order to give me a better look at the affected area.

"Nothing for you to be concerned with!" he replied gruffly. "What are you doing all the way over here this time of day?"

"I came to see how you are doing." I replied. "Have you been to a doctor to look at your face?"

"I have," he replied curtly, "and my conversations with my physician are confidential between he and I. Suffice to say I'm going to be fine and my health should not be of any concern to you."

Hiram had a way of making me feel that I was intruding into his life if I asked him anything personal. He had always been that way in relation to his privacy, although he highly encouraged me to talk about my problems and myself. He always listened to me and if he felt it appropriate, he wouldn't hesitate to give me his opinion on what I should or shouldn't do in certain situations.

"Can't you accept the fact that I care about your welfare?" I asked. His eyes caught mine and what I saw there frightened me and made the muscles in my stomach involuntarily tighten. He quickly looked away and when

A Hard Life

his eyes returned to mine there was a softness that I had not seen before.

"Thank you, Branch," he said quietly, "I didn't mean to speak sharply. You have become my only good friend and I care a great deal about our friendship. I just don't want you to fuss over me and I can't accept pity from anyone."

"I can understand that." I replied. "Have you had anything to eat? I would love to treat you to a fine meal at one of Grayson's fancy restaurants."

I smiled then for the softness in his eyes was suddenly replaced with a cold fury. Hiram hated Grayson Asbury with a passion, and anytime I wanted to get a rise out of him, all I had to do was mention Grayson's name. Hiram knew my feelings of the man too, and although we had never discussed it directly, we shared a common low opinion of Grayson Asbury.

"I would rather make a meal of these weeds I've pulled," he replied bitterly, "but if you're in such a generous mood, and since you're much wealthier than me, how would you like to accompany and buy me a wee drink of Irish whiskey over at O'Reilly's Bar?"

To say the least, I was amazed, bewildered, and astounded! In the nearly four years I had known Hiram McDougall he had never before mentioned his desire to have a drink of whiskey, Irish or otherwise!

I had assumed he had never touched a drop of anything intoxicating in his entire life! I was recalling the many times he had lectured me on the derogatory effects alcohol could have on a young man if it was allowed to become a habit. I recovered from the shock of his query quickly however.

"I am just the man who will buy you as many shots of Irish whiskey as you can stand, Mr. McDougall." I said with a smile. "I've always had me a hankerin' to see you loosen up a bit."

"Had me a hankerin'!" he repeated my axiom with a grimace. "I thought I had expunged all those horrible homespun words and phrases from your diction forever, Branch? Did I really give you a passing grade in English? Should I reconsider your graduation diploma?" I smiled at my former teacher's derision.

"All you taught me were new words to use when you thought it proper." I replied. "I haven't forgotten anything I learned before I met you. Especially words like "hankerin", that conveys a meaning your proper English words cannot duplicate!'"

We did indeed go to O'Reilly's Bar, but Hiram only managed to get down one shot of whiskey, which I thought for a while was going to make him throw up. He continued to keep his hand over his swollen lip most of the time we were there, but he laughed heartily along with me at the jokes and antics of the mostly Irish patrons in the darkened tavern.

I took him back home after a while and when I left him at his front door Hiram uncharacteristically took my hand to shake it firmly. The look was back in his eyes that had frightened me earlier. He was standing alone in his doorway as I walked away and he presented a pitiful image in my mind that seemed to take up a permanent residence there.

Something about his image struck me as different than I remembered. It occurred to me that before today I had not spent fifteen minutes around Hiram without him having that smelly old crooked stemmed pipe dangling from the corner of his mouth!

A HARD LIFE

CHAPTER NINETEEN

I was worried about Hiram McDougall as I rode back up the street. I had no intention of going back to my office today, but I had to ride past there on my way home. When I saw McCloud standing on the wooden walkway beside the bank I could tell he had been searching for me, because as soon as he spotted me he started toward me in a trot. Before he was near enough for me to read his face, an intuition gripped me and fear pierced through me like a sharp knife! Although my last hope was shattered, and my most hideous suspicions were confirmed by McCloud's first words, remarkably I wasn't completely surprised.

"I brought your mother to the infirmary," he said and before I could form a question, he continued, "she's been shot and she's unconscious. The doctor and nurses are attending to her." He hesitated only a moment. "She's in bad shape, Ben Branch."

The doctor's infirmary was down the street several blocks from the bank. I kick-spurred Rascal into a gallop and ignored the alarmed looks from the bystanders along the busy street. I jerked the frightened horse to a sliding stop in front of the single-story building and left him unattended, his bridle hanging, as I vaulted from the saddle and practically crashed through the front door of the infirmary into a small waiting room.

Katherine Asbury was there alone, her blue dress blood soaked, her face pale, with grief embedded into her face and eyes. When she recognized me she flew to her feet and grabbed me by both my hands

"You can't go in, Branch!" she cried. "The doctor has forbidden anyone to enter!" I ignored her, jerked my hand away and reached for the doorknob.

"She's in surgery, Branch! You might cause her more injury!"

That stopped me and I lowered my head and closed my eyes with my hand still on the handle. Katherine put her arms around my waist and clung to my back. She was weeping openly now, but I was barely aware. McCloud entered the room and pulled Katherine away from me over to a chair and they both sat down. I continued to face the door, beyond which I was painfully mortified to imagine that a complete stranger was making incisions into my mama's sweet body.

Sometime in the next two hours I finally left my post at the door and sat down in a chair across from Katherine and McCloud. I kept my head lowered without looking at either of them and without a word passing between us. A half hour later the surgeon entered the waiting room. He was wiping blood from his hands on the once white gown he had been wearing.

"I'm sorry, Sir." he said to me softly with genuine sorrow reflected in his big brown eyes. "Unfortunately your mother did not survive the operation, Mister

Walker." He hesitated to let that horrible statement sink in and then continued softly..

"We, did everything we could for her under the circumstances."

"May I see her?" I asked with more control in my voice and my actions than I would ever have dreamed possible. He nodded.

"The nurses are attending to her." he said. "They will be finished in a few minutes and you can go in to see your mother."

Katherine took a room at one of our hotels and offered to take the ominous responsibility of making arrangements with the best undertaker in the city. I felt numb and confused and barely nodded my thanks for her offer.

Word of the tragedy had spread and Lonny Mossberg and Curly Griffin had rushed in from their respective jobs to offer any assistance that I needed. The two men and I had become close friends in the time since they were fired by Grayson and employed by me.

I told both of them to load shotguns and stay as close to Katherine as she would allow, never more than a doorway away. Katherine heard my instructions and started to protest, but a look from McCloud silenced her and she acquiesced without further comment. McCloud told me what he knew about my mother's murder as he and I rode back to the ranch late that night

"Your mother had hitched up the horse and buggy herself to ride down and spend the day with Katherine." he began in his deep voice.

"I had no idea she wanted to go see Katherine, or I would have taken her myself." I replied bitterly. The Cherokee nodded.

"She said she had decided to visit us after you left for work. Katherine was thrilled to see her and both women were in the house chatting about women things, so I had gone to the barn to attend to the horses. I heard a distant rifle shot and stepped out to see where it had come from. That's when I saw your mother collapsed on the front porch. Katherine told me later that Bonnie Ann had left something outside in the buggy and had gone to fetch it. I believe the shot must have come from the timber across the road. If there had been time I could have tracked the shooter, but Katherine and I did our best to stop Bonnie Ann's bleeding before we made the dash into the doctor's office." The Cherokee hesitated before he spoke again.

"I am truly sorry I allowed this to happen to your mother, Ben Branch."

I couldn't look at the solemn Cherokee at the moment, but he was aware of my churning emotions. A little later down the trail I was able to speak again.

"You did all you could at the time, McCloud." I said quietly. "We'll find the shooter together." My eyes found his in the moonlight and our gazes locked for several moments. He nodded to me and the cooling mountain breezes caused his long black hair to swirl around his face accentuating the Cherokee's dark complexion and chiseled features.

We arrived at Katherine's ranch, and after feeding and taking care of our horses at the barn we went to the house. Felicia Doran, Katherine's housekeeper, met us at the door. I was somewhat surprised to see Maria Ortega, mine and Mama's housekeeper, standing beside Felicia. McCloud told me that he had sent Samuel Workman, one of the cowboys that worked for Katherine, to tell Maria what had happened to Mama. Maria began to weep as McCloud was speaking, her head down, her shoulders shaking.

It's probably best for you to stay here and help Felicia for the next few days, Maria." I said. "We'll decide later about returning to Grayson's ranch." She nodded her agreement and Felicia smiled reassuringly at her.

"Sheriff Young and his deputy Frank Albright were here before dark today, Mister McCloud." Felicia told McCloud. The Cherokee frowned and looked at me.

"What did they want?" McCloud asked.

"They heard about the shooting and wanted to investigate." she answered. "When I told them you were not here they said they would return in the morning."

"Did they look around, Maria?" McCloud inquired and the housekeeper shook her head.

"No Senor. They said they would wait and talk to you or Mrs. Asbury first." she replied.

"Good." McCloud muttered. "They would only mess up any sign the shooter might have left." McCloud looked at me directly.

"We better do our looking at first light, Ben Branch." he said. "After Kennard and his flunkies get finished thrashing around any tracks or evidence will be practically useless." I nodded to the Cherokee.

"I'll meet you down here before daylight." McCloud nodded to me and we both left to go to our respective rooms.

I knew trying to sleep now would be fruitless for me, so I sat on the edge of the bed in the guest room until all activity in the house subsided and I knew everyone had retired. I tried to keep my mind clear and not think about what had happened on this horrible day. I had not been alone until now to begin the process of dealing with Mama's sudden death and I felt the need to be outside and not cooped up inside a strange room. I silently descended the stairway and slipped out the back door into the starlit night.

Looking up at the sky full of stars it occurred to me that nothing appeared to have changed in the universe. It seemed puzzling to me for as far as I was concerned the single most spectacular and tragic event in the world had taken place today and the world outside the ranch house seemed oblivious to it. How was that possible?

I wondered where Mama was? Was she among those stars now? Those stars that twinkled with a light that appeared to rise and fell in intensity? Was she watching me at this precise moment from some distant location where we the living cannot see, but only imagine?

I remembered how she had looked in the infirmary when I was finally able to go in to see her. She was lying on an examination table, her pretty head inclined on a pillow and her hands folded together at her waist. A clean white sheet was folded neatly just below her chin with her bare arms outside. Her eyes were closed and she was so pale as to appear almost translucent. The nurses had tried to make her appear as asleep, but they had failed.

It had occurred to me instantly that what I was seeing on the exam table was not my mama any longer! The vibrant life that had loved me and was loved back with

A Hard Life

a depth beyond measurement was gone. Simply gone! Removed forever from the still lifeless form lying so peaceful in that hospital room.

I wondered now to myself why tears were not enveloping me? Before today when I had even allowed the thought of losing Mama to enter my mind, I had always imagined that I would be so consumed by grief that I could not contemplate going on without her.

Yet, here I was only a few hours after the unthinkable had occurred and the grief I had expected was not consuming me. I didn't even seem terribly angry. I could think logically, even strategically Although I was sad, I was very much aware that I wasn't absolutely paralyzed by the anguish of Mama's death, and for the life of me I couldn't imagine why?

As I continued to gaze at the stars it occurred to me that maybe love such as that which existed between Mama and me sustains and continues even when one, or possibly both of us, are beyond death's gate? Maybe love is all that's left when people leave this life and maybe it's the one thing that cannot be destroyed?

"Is that possible?" I asked myself aloud in the darkness. Then I wondered if maybe I was still in shock and the full realization of what I had lost had not dawned on me yet?

"How do I tell Jon David about this?" A chill traveled up and down my spine as that thought materialized as words, unbidden from within me.

I could imagine that Jon David might even hold me responsible, and the thought of his anger at something this tragic wasn't a pleasant one! Then it dawned on me that I was no longer a little boy. I had no logical reason to fear my older brother any longer! Until tonight I had never even realized I feared him!

Suddenly another realization materialized. My mother has to be buried! Where and how in the world do I do that? After a short contemplation I realized there was only one place where she would want to be. That realization and the process it involved brought a completely new dimension to my immediate future.

A thought came to me that also begged to be put into audible words.

"After today I can never be a little boy again!" As I muttered these words I realized how ancient I felt!

I knew deep inside me that the privilege of feeling like a little boy, who relied privately a great deal on his mother, evaporated when the bullet fired from an unknown assailant's gun took away my mama's beautiful life, as well as my surreptitious youth!"

I thought about that for a long time and finally made my way back inside the house, to a strange bed, and eventually to a restless, dream-ridden sleep.

Remember I said earlier that I wasn't feeling any anger? Well, that was then and this is now! Primal anger has begun boiling up inside me like lava within an awakening volcano!

My last conscious thought before I fell asleep concerned the shooter. I wondered if he were lying awake tonight contemplating the terrible act he had committed today? I wondered if he felt even the smallest pang of remorse for taking mama's life? I wondered if he was as afraid as he should be?

"Doesn't really matter." I thought to myself. "If he's not afraid now, he will be!"

A HARD LIFE

CHAPTER TWENTY

I awoke with a start in the darkness and the events of the previous day and night flooded back over me. I shook my head hoping to discover that I had dreamed it all, but now I could dimly recognize where I was and the full realization of what had happened hit me again like a runaway train.

I met McCloud in the barn before daylight. He had already caught up both horses and was saddling them in the lighted hallway of the barn. A faint hint of dawn was showing above the eastern mountains.

"I need to show you something." McCloud said quietly as he reached under Rascal to retrieve the far belly strap. He stood upright and reached in his jeans pocket, extracted something and reached toward me. He deposited it in my open hand and I stared down at the flattened chunk of lead. He didn't have to tell me what it was.

"The surgeon gave me that yesterday.," he said simply. "Looks like a forty-five caliber to me." I shuddered when

I thought about the damage the large bullet must have done to my mama's slender body.

Before we left the house I steeled myself and walked to the front porch where Mama had fallen. Maria and Felicia had cleaned up as much of the blood as they could, but a pinkish stain on the wood was still visible at the top of the steps leading down to the driveway. I removed a white handkerchief from my pocket and tied it to the porch railing above the stain.

McCloud was watching me curiously and then I recognized understanding in his eyes. We crossed the road in front of Katherine's house and entered the timber where I could hear the rushing river ahead of us.

"It might be easier to find where he tied his horse and then we can follow his tracks to his ambush spot." McCloud said as we sat on the bank of the noisy stream. I nodded and we crossed the creek. On the far side McCloud turned right and I turned left.

"If you find sign give it a wide berth, stay put, and give me a whistle." McCloud said as he rode away. Anger flared in me instantly, but I held it in check and remained silent. The Cherokee didn't have to tell me he was better at reading sign than me, nor remind me not to mess it up with my own tracks!

I realized I was overreacting to his comment and made an effort to calm myself down. It was hard for me to do considering the emotions stirring inside me, but I realized that if I wanted to find the man who murdered Mama I needed to calm down and make certain I didn't miss any clues. I also needed to accept the fact that McCloud was better at this than me and it would be best to let him take charge right now.

A Hard Life

Later when the sign was deciphered and tracks were filled with the boots of the killer, then it would be my time to take the lead. I hoped no one, including McCloud, tried to get in my way when that time came.

I was riding within a few feet of the stream's eastern bank and guiding Rascal around a sharp bend where the point of a ridge came down almost to the riverbank. In the soft earth I could see pony tracks leading both to and from the river. I reined up Rascal and followed the tracks with my eyes as they led upward toward the ascending ridge and disappeared into the thick brush. I rode parallel to the tracks a good ten feet away and entered the screen of brush. I had to lean low over Rascal's back to clear the overhanging branches and when we were through the worst of them I rose back up and I could see where the tracks both ended and restarted.

Someone had ridden from the creek up the point of the ridge to where tracks all around a small greasewood bush told me the horse was left for a considerable time. Then the horse was untied and the tracks leading back to the stream were deeper and wider apart.

"I bet I know why he was in a big hurry when he left." I said silently to myself. I was certain I had found the killer's sign. I whistled loudly and in a few minutes I could hear McCloud approaching on foot leading his horse.

"This looks interesting, dependent upon your assessment. " I said. I was still astride Rascal a good ten feet from the sign I had found. McCloud nodded as he carefully approached the area where the sign was heaviest around the small tree. The Cherokee dropped carefully to his haunches a few feet from the tree and his eyes swept the entire area for several minutes. Eventually he rose back to his full height and looked up where the point ascended toward the mountains beyond.

"We should find his ambush spot somewhere up there." he said quietly.

"That's kinda' what I thought too." I said with just a hint of sarcasm in my tone. The Cherokee looked up sharply at me.

"I meant no disrespect when I told you to be careful around the sign, Ben Branch." he said.

"None taken, McCloud!" I lied, my voice just a tad too loud. He knew better, but he let it pass. I felt bad now for I knew that I was being immature and I dropped my eyes toward the ground.

"Remember," the words from last night sang silently in my mind, "you're not a little boy any longer!"

"Do you want to take the lead?" The Cherokee asked and I shook my head from side to side.

"You're doin' fine, McCloud." I said quietly without looking at him. "Ignore my ignorance. I'm workin' hard to be the man I have to be now." I didn't even notice that my accent had reverted back to my Missouri upbringing.

A hundred yards or so up the slope the large timber gave way to oak brush and boulders. On a relatively bare part of the slope a single giant ponderosa pine shaded a jumble of boulders. McCloud and I stood amongst the boulders and looked westward. Katherine's house was plainly visible and the white handkerchief I had tied to the porch railing fluttered plainly in the early morning breeze.

"How far is it?" I asked. "Three hundred yards or four?"

"Closer to four." he replied. "Not an easy shot to make." I nodded my agreement, not allowing my mind to settle on the fact that we were talking about my mama as a target.

"The man's a shooter." I said. "Wonder if he learned that in the Army?"

"Maybe." was McCloud's reply. We began to carefully comb the area looking for anything of interest.

"Here." McCloud said and I joined him behind a round boulder just beneath the giant Ponderosa pine

"See this depression?" I looked where he was pointing and saw a freshly made shallow hole that appeared to be a few inches into the soil. I nodded, but didn't understand. McCloud stepped up on the boulder and stared hard at the ground on the lower side.

"Walk around and look for a forked stick about the size of your wrist." he said and I followed his instructions without question. A stone's throw below the boulder I found a discarded forked stick, three feet long, sharpened to a point. Sap was still oozing from the severed end. I carried it back up the ridge and handed it to McCloud. He inspected it carefully.

"The man carries a sharp heavy knife too." he said. "Probably is, or has been a buffalo hunter. He prefers to shoot off a forked stick instead of taking rest off a rock."

The Cherokee was talking as much to himself as to me as his eyes swept the area around us. "Let's try and find where this came from."

I found it before McCloud and I whistled softly. I saw something lying near the severed sapling stump and I reached for it as McCloud joined me. He looked at the object in my hand and then at the fresh-cut stump standing a few inches above the ground. He held the forked stick down to it and it fit the cut perfectly.

"The shooter wears buckskin." he said as his eyes returned to the short piece of fringe in my hand. "He could have clipped off that piece by accident when he sheathed his knife after cutting down this sapling. Damned careless of him seems to me."

He looked around us and then reached down to retrieve two green branches that fit both sides of the forked stick in his hand.

McCloud slowly broke the two branches into smaller pieces, laid them beside the stump, and carried a large rock from its resting place a few feet away. He covered the stump and the branches with the rock.

"I don't want Kennard Young to know what we know, Ben Branch." he said by way of explanation and I nodded at his logic. We wiped away the sign we had found all the way back down the slope, from around the greasewood tree where the shooter had tied up his horse, and the short distance from the tree down to the river

"The shooter wears old worn army cavalry boots, Ben Branch." McCloud said as we worked together to wipe out the sign. "His horse has a new shoe on the left rear that has a single notch filed on the inside froe."

The Cherokee pointed to a well-defined horse track in the soft soil by the creek and I studied it closely. I wanted to embed its picture into my mind so I would recognize it when I saw it later.

"If we can track him down before he re-shoes his horse we can prove he's the shooter. At least to ourselves," he added, as if talking to himself again, "it might not hold up in a court of law since a peace officer can't testify to the sign we've destroyed."

"I'm not much worried about bringin' him before the law, McCloud." I said and the Cherokee recognized a different glint in my eyes than he had seen before. He only nodded as a response.

Sheriff Kennard Young and his deputy Frank Albright were waiting for us at the ranch house. Sheriff Young was fifty or so with almost white hair. He appeared pale as if he rarely ventured outside his office in Denver. He wasn't a big man, but he had a bulging belly that hid his belt buckle. He wore a large revolver high on his hip in a brown holster with a buttoned-down flap over the butt of the gun. I wondered how he would draw the pistol quickly if he needed to.

Frank Albright was the man I had seen talking to Grayson three years previously, telling him about Beulah McCarty. Thinking of her untimely death brought back more bad memories adding to the depressed mood I was in because of Mama's murder.

"We would like to talk to both of you about the shooting, McCloud." Sheriff Young said as we dismounted. "You two haven't been interfering with my investigation have you?" McCloud looked at the sheriff sharply.

"Interfering how?" McCloud replied.

"You haven't been out investigating on your own, have you?" he repeated.

"Are you trying to tell us that we can't ride on Katherine's land without your permission, Kennard?" McCloud demanded. The sheriff flushed red.

"Have you found anything, McCloud?" If you have I'm demanding you turn over any collected evidence to me right now!" The sheriff was getting redder by the minute. McCloud continued to glare at the uncomfortable looking lawman.

"You're in charge of murder investigations around here, Kennard. Ben Branch and I are only interested in seeing that the murderer is found."

"I'm not convinced it was a murder yet, McCloud." Kennard declared. His statement infuriated me and I stepped toward the man.

"Then how do you explain my mother's sudden death, Sheriff? Do you think she caught a bad cold?" My voice was cold and distinct. He stepped back a little and took stock of my posture. I had stepped closer than he felt comfortable with.

"Calm down, Son." The sheriff began and I cut him off

"I'm not your son, Sheriff, and right now I'm damned proud of that fact! I understand stupidity is an inherited trait!" The redness in his face deepened.

Frank Albright took a step toward me and McCloud stepped in front of him with his rifle held in both hands. The lawman and the Cherokee eyed each other.

"Stay out of this, Deputy." the Cherokee said plainly. "The boy has the right and the reasons to be edgy." Kennard Young put out his hand toward the deputy with his palm open.

"All I meant was that it's possible it could have been a hunting accident." Sheriff Young said in a quieter and friendlier tone. "There's deer hunters everywhere and bullets do stray. We won't know for sure until after we've investigated, now will we? There's no reason for the two of you and the sheriff's department to have differences."

A Hard Life

"You're not the one who had your mother shot dead are you, Sheriff?" I said and Kennard lowered his head before he replied.

"No, Mr. Walker, I'm not. You're right about that. Why don't you let us look around and we'll stop back by the ranch house to let you know what we've found. I have to ask you again. Did either of you find anything that you should tell me about, or pick up anything that you should turn over to me?"

"We didn't find anything you need, Kennard." McCloud answered for me and I continued to stare down the red-faced sheriff. I could tell he didn't like McCloud's answer, but he let it pass. The two lawmen went to their horses and mounted up. They headed down the road a short distance and veered off east toward the river.

"Deer hunting accident, my ass!" McCloud muttered. "I enjoyed that stupidity remark you put on Kennard, Ben Branch, but you need to be careful how you talk to him. He's not as stupid as he acts sometimes. He dances to Grayson's fiddle most of the time, but something has always told me that he has ambitions of his own, and he could be a dangerous man to cross.

"What kind of ambitions, McCloud?" I asked and the Cherokee only shook his head as he stared at where the sheriff and his deputy disappeared into the forest. Something had been nagging at the back of my mind.

"Do you remember if my mother was wearing her blue dress yesterday?" The Cherokee turned his gaze away from the road and to mine. He nodded.

"Why, Ben Branch?" he asked. I shrugged.

"Probably nothing," I replied, "but Katherine was also wearing blue yesterday." McCloud regarded me closely and then a shadow seemed to cross his face.

"I'm going back to town and check on Katherine." The Cherokee said resolutely.

"You can trust Curly and Lonny to keep their eyes on her, McCloud." I replied. "They would give up their lives to protect hers." The Cherokee nodded, but continued walking toward his horse.

"I'll see you back in town, Ben Branch." he said over his shoulder.

A HARD LIFE

CHAPTER TWENTY-ONE

I had two things that I needed to do at Grayson's ranch before I returned to Denver. One was because I was curious and the other I dreaded with all my heart. I wanted to check out the rifles in Grayson's gun room and determine if any of them were missing, or if any appeared to have been fired in the last day or two.

The second thing I had to do that I dreaded so badly was go into my mama's room and choose a dress, accessories, and other clothing to take to the undertaker in Denver. I would have asked Maria Ortega to pick out the appropriate clothing, but I had already told her to stay with Felicia for a few days. I hated to ask her to make a special trip for something that I should do myself anyway.

I unlocked Grayson's gunroom and checked all the rifles. They appeared to be undisturbed and none of them showed signs of either being fired or cleaned since I had checked them before. That didn't surprise me, but neither did it erase my guarded suspicions.

I made my way to Mama's room and opened the door with a tremendous lump thick in my throat. The first thing I noticed was Mama's nightgown laid carefully on her meticulously made bed. I knew that Maria had not done this for her because laying out her bedclothes in the morning had been my mama's practice for as long as I could remember.

Mama always kept our home clean and neat and she made her bed as soon as she got out of it each morning. Even when we barely had enough to eat and she worked like a man in the fields, or at Uncle Clady's house washing and ironing clothes, she always kept a neat organized house for the two of us.

I went to Mama's closet and chose two dresses that I had seen her wear lately and ones I liked. I would leave the final decision to Katherine as to which would be more appropriate. Then I went to her dresser and opened up the small jewelry box I had bought her the previous Christmas.

The first thing I noticed was a simple gold necklace that she wore nearly every day. There were more expensive necklaces in the jewelry box, but I knew the one I held in my hand was special to her. I had bought it for her birthday back in Doniphan when she and I barely had enough money to buy food. She had tried to get me to take it back, but I had refused and we had not starved because of it. Fond memories of the times I had reminded her of that flooded my mind and my eyes.

I changed my mind, put the simple little necklace in my shirt pocket and chose a chain and locket she had bought for herself. I knew the locket contained a picture of me, but I couldn't bring myself to open it. I think it would be the one she would have chosen to take with her.

I had a terrible urge to bury my face in her nightgown and cry like the little boy I was feeling inside at the moment. I fought against it however, and jerked one of her bottom dresser drawers open more as a diversion than for a planned purpose. I rummaged almost angrily through the scarves and handkerchiefs and was just before closing the drawer when my hand struck something unusual at the very bottom.

I pulled an oblong object from the bottom of the drawer. I recognized the covering, although I had not seen it since I was a small boy. It was a woolen scarf that my mama had knitted for my papa and one he wore every cold winter day thereafter.

Tears spilled unashamedly from my eyes now. An object that both of my deceased parents had held dear was practically too much for me to bear. I turned the wrapped object in both hands and almost absent-mindedly unwrapped the mystery object inside. My tears stopped as I stared at what I held in my hand.

I was holding Papa's pig-sticking knife! It was the very knife that Jon David had used to kill James Asbury so many years ago!

I was astounded for several reasons, not the least of which was how my mama had managed to have it in her possession! Memories of the summer and fall following my papa's hanging flooded back to me.

I was seven and Jon David was fifteen the summer of the tragedy. Jon David had replaced Papa's knife in Mama's boxed kitchenwares, where he had taken it from the night he came to rescue me from the Union encampment. Mama had kept the knife with her most prized possessions when we moved to live with Uncle Clady. Uncle Clady had discovered the knife that fall when he saw Mama using it to trim a ham.

"That's my great granddaddy's knife he carried in the Revolutionary War!" he had declared and grabbed it from my mama's grasp. "How in holy hell did you git' yore' hands on it?"

Uncle Clady ignored my mama's pleading that it was one of the few things she had left that had belonged to Papa. He simply took it and told her to shut up!

The next Saturday Uncle Clady had planned to kill hogs and had ordered Mama, me, and Jon David to be up at daylight to help. Mama was sleeping in the wagon and Jon David and me were sleeping under it, parked under a white oak tree in Uncle Clady's back yard. Later on in the fall we moved to the little house at the back of his field.

Uncle Clady had built a table that morning by laying boards over two sawhorses, and had arranged all the knives, meat saws, bowls, and pans that would be needed that day. Papa's knife was there among the other knives on the table. I had slipped up when I thought no one was looking and snatched Papa's knife away.

A big fire was burning under the scalding pot and I stuck Papa's knife in the hot burning embers. I hated to do it, but I was determined that if Mama could not keep it, then I wasn't going to let Uncle Clady have it either. I would rather it melt down to nothing in the hot coals!

A Hard Life

That was the last time I had seen the knife and for all these years I had been convinced it was destroyed and gone forever. Now here it was resting in my hand again.

The original wooden handles had burned away leaving the brass rivets loose in the steel handle section. The blade was blackened, but when I touched the edge it was still razor sharp.

"How in the world did it get in Mama's scarf drawer out here in Colorado?" I said aloud to myself. I had to believe that Mama must have seen me take it those many years ago and somehow had retrieved it and hidden it away. I remember the fit Uncle Clady had thrown when he missed it. He accused Mama of taking it, but I remember her telling him outright she had no idea what had happened to it.

"Mama," I said aloud to her room, "did you lie to Uncle Clady?" I received no answer from the silent walls.

I carefully refolded papa's neck scarf and placed it back in Mama's drawer and stuck the knife in my belt. An idea was forming in my mind and as I rode toward Denver the idea became a plan.

Solingen of Denver was a small foundry and blacksmith shop that specialized in knives and resided on a back street in the city. The owner was originally from Austria and had brought his business west from Connecticut during the gold rush a few years back. He manufactured all kinds of knives, kitchen knives, skinning and scraping knives for the butchering industry, plus a small number of hunting and fighting knives. The owners name was Fritz Solingen.

Mr. Solingen turned the heavy blade over in his hands and viewed it from every angle. It was obvious the knife had originally been forged and beaten into shape on someone's anvil. The blade was a good three-eighths of an inch thick where the blade and the handle section met and it tapered both ways toward the tip of the blade and also to the end of the handle section. The blade was over two and one-half inches wide, and eleven inches long, in front of the guard area and tapered to a semi-spear point sharpened on top and bottom.

"A very unique blade Mr. Walker." he said admiringly. "Do you know who crafted it and when?" I shook my head.

"It belonged to my father." I replied. "Family records say it was carried by his grandfather in the Revolutionary War." Mr. Solingen nodded.

"I would have guessed it to be quite old." he said admiringly. "It might have come from Europe. I have seen similar blades from Ireland and Scotland."

"Would you consider polishing the blade and installing a guard and handles, Mister Soligen?" I asked. "Maybe have a scabbard made for it too?"

"It would be an honor, Mister Walker." he replied. "I can carve the handle from bone, antler, or wood, whichever you would prefer. The guard I prefer to make from yellow brass.

"Antler for the handle." I replied. "Do you have antler that would match my Colt's grip?" He studied the grip on my Peacemaker in its holster and nodded his head.

"No problem." he replied, "How about the scabbard? Do you want it tooled and stained to match your gun belt?" I nodded.

"I would like to carry the knife here." I said, and I turned and put the blade horizontally across my back even with my gun belt. "I will draw it with my right hand." He nodded his understanding and measured the width of my gun belt as I stood with my back to him.

"How soon do you need it, Mister Walker?" I would guess it would take two weeks or longer to complete the project."

"That would be fine, Mister Solingen. I will pay now if you know what it will cost. He thought about it for a moment and gave me a figure that seemed more than reasonable. I paid him in gold and he shook my hand firmly as I left his shop.

I went from the knife shop to the telegraph office. I sent a long message to Reuben Rosenthal, the attorney in St, Louis, and then sent another one to the sheriff's office in Doniphan. From there I rode to the railroad depot, went inside and talked to the dispatcher for nearly an hour.

I couldn't avoid the inevitable any longer so I walked from the livery stable to the hotel where Katherine was staying.

Curly Griffin was sitting in the hallway outside her suite with a shotgun across his lap. He stood when I approached.

"Any problems, Curly?" I asked.

"Everything has been real quiet, Branch." he replied. "Lonny took a break to get something to eat. Have you seen McCloud today?" I shook my head negatively. "He's been here twice looking for you." Curly continued

I had the box of clothes I had brought from the ranch and I tapped on Katherine's door lightly. She answered the door herself and gave me a hug after I put the box down.

"I know this is going to be hard for you, Branch." she said seriously to me "The undertaker will have your mother ready for viewing this evening, but we have to take these clothes over immediately." She regarded me closely as dismay must have filled my face.

"Do you want me to take care of it for you, Branch?" she asked

"Would you, Katherine?" My eyes were pleading and she nodded as her eyes moistened.

"I need to find McCloud." I said. "I understand he's looking for me?" She nodded again.

"He's been by several times, but he didn't tell me what he needs of you, but I have the impression from his insistence that it must be important."

"Curly will accompany you to the undertaker, Katherine." I said. "Promise me that you will not go anywhere without a guard."

"I promise, Branch." she replied.

"Branch," she asked, as an afterthought, "may we place your mother in our family plot on the ranch?" I already had my hand on the doorknob and I turned to look at Katherine.

"I appreciate the offer, Katherine, I really do, but I have decided to take mama home to Missouri. I've already begun to make the arrangements." Katherine appeared amazed at my statement.

"By yourself, Branch?" she asked incredulously. I nodded sadly.

"That's the way I prefer, Katherine. We could have a small funeral service here if you would like?" I said. I could tell she wanted to argue with me about taking Mama back to Missouri, but she restrained herself.

A Hard Life

"I won't interfere if that is what you have decided, Branch. The preacher from the little Church of Christ where your mother had begun to attend came by today." she replied. "I could ask him to do a service at their church if you approve." I nodded my approval and Katherine continued.

"Branch, will you return to Colorado in time for the company's annual board meeting?"

"Yes Ma'am." I replied. "I won't let you down, Katherine, but I believe taking Mama back home to Missouri is what she would have wanted."

A HARD LIFE

CHAPTER TWENTY-TWO

I found McCloud at the livery stables. When the Cherokee had to spend more than a day in Denver it was one of the few places where he felt comfortable. It was also where he slept, for he refused to take a room at one of our hotels. He was brushing down Rascal when I walked into the livery.

"Curly and Katherine both said you were looking for me." I stated and McCloud kept brushing my horse as he nodded. His rifle was leaned against the stable wall, barely an arms length away.

"A Cherokee brave came to see me last night." McCloud said, as he worked the brush down Rascal's back. "Aatonyah was taken from her village again. A hunting party followed her tracks and were ambushed. The leader and another warrior were killed and the remainder returned to the village.

"Where is Grayson?" I asked.

A Hard Life

"He just returned from a business trip today." he replied. He arrived by train from the west. That's all I could find out."

"Does he know about Mama?" I asked and the Cherokee nodded.

"He appeared genuinely distressed about the news, Ben Branch." McCloud said as he studied my reaction.

"He wants you to come to see him at his hotel." he continued. "He told me he wants to express his condolences to you and he wants to be included in your mother's funeral plans. By the way, what are your plans?"

"Katherine is arranging a service at the little church where Mama had started attending." I replied. "I've made arrangements to take Mama's body back to Missouri for burial." McCloud stopped what he was doing, laid down the brush and stepped forward to face me in the hallway.

"Are you sure that's what she would have wanted, Ben Branch?" he inquired. I nodded my head.

"I believe so, McCloud." I replied, holding his eyes with mine.

"Then you should do what your heart tells you." The Cherokee said. "Do you want me to accompany you and your mother to Missouri?" I was a little surprised at McCloud's offer.

"No, I want to do it myself, McCloud," I replied, "but I certainly appreciate the thought. I would rather you stay here and make sure nothing happens to Katherine."

"I'll see to that, Ben Branch."

I left McCloud at the stable and walked to the Mountain Top Hotel. Grayson's suite of rooms was on the second floor at the top of a marble staircase. The second floor had a balcony that overlooked the lavish lobby of the grand hotel.

Grayson answered the door himself when I knocked.

"Branch, I can't tell you how grieved I was to hear about your mother." Grayson said as he ushered me into his extravagantly furnished apartment "You and I have had our differences in the past," he continued, as he waved me to a seat on an imported couch that must have cost a fortune. He took a seat in a matching chair that faced me.

"I hope you know that I always admired your mother immensely and I will not rest until her killer is apprehended."

I was watching Grayson's eyes and expression to try to determine if he was lying to me or not. I had to admit silently to myself that if he was not honestly sincere in his concern I was not able to detect it. I was somewhat guarded in my responses to him, but I had to admit he was making me feel like he really cared about what had happened to Mama. We discussed the arrangements that Katherine was making and he listened as I told him that I wanted to take Mama home to Missouri for burial.

"I had the impression that your mother had adjusted well to living here in Colorado, and might have wanted to be buried here, but the decision is yours, Branch. If you want to take her back to Missouri, then that is exactly what you should do. If I can offer any assistance all you need do is ask."

"Thanks, Grayson." I replied. "I believe I have things in hand." I stood then. "I'll see you at the memorial service?"

A Hard Life

"Yes you will, Branch. I wouldn't miss your mother's memorial." I started to leave and then hesitated at the door.

"Will you be returning to live in your house now that Mama's gone?" I asked.

"No, I think not." he replied. "I like being here in town closer to the businesses."

"You don't mind if I stay on there?"

"You're welcome to stay as long as you like, Branch." He met my eyes and held them as he continued.

"Let me tell you again how sorry I am about what happened to Bonnie. It would appear that your association with the Asbury family has now cost you both your parents."

His remark shook me, but as I held his eyes with mine I realized that what he said was true and he had said it without any discernable malicious intent. I could read nothing in his eyes but genuine sorrow and concern.

I shook hands with Grayson and left his hotel room not a little baffled by the man's apparent turn-around in his attitude toward me. I had no idea then what I would discover in the hotel lobby on my way out!

As I descended the stairs I saw a small group of people gathered around a display in the grand lobby. Curious about what was going on, I turned at the landing and took a few steps nearer to where I was stunned to hear a familiar voice that took me back to my troubled childhood.

"Ladies and Gentlemen," the voice was saying, "what you see in this display cabinet was the favorite jacket worn by Captain James Clifton Asbury during his famous and meritorious exploits in the great war between the states. The jacket was made from elk hides he and his brother had collected before Captain Asbury left Colorado and joined the Union forces to wage a gloriously successful war against the southern rebels."

"The rifle displayed with the coat is the very rifle I carried as I loyally followed Captain Asbury until he was tragically killed in battle in Missouri at the hands of murdering guerrilla scavengers. I recently contacted Mister Grayson Asbury and Katherine Asbury, Captain Asbury's widow, to ask them if I might donate these items for a display to be maintained here in Denver."

The speaker turned toward me then and confirmed what my ears had already told me. Standing before me was the very same union sergeant that had carried out the actual hanging of my papa. The very same man who had a week later came into the tent with his gun raised to confront my brother and I after Jon David had killed Captain James Asbury in his sleep!

I read full recognition in those blue eyes and I saw a small smile form at the corners of his mouth that was almost hidden behind the full, but now graying, mustache. Then his eyes went beyond and above me to the staircase.

"Ladies and Gentlemen, we are now honored by the presence of Captain Asbury's brother, Grayson Lawrence Asbury, at this very moment. Join me in a round of applause in recognition of the tremendous sacrifice this family has experienced in defense of these great United States of America!"

The small gathering of people, mostly dignitaries and the wealthiest folks in Denver, turned their eyes toward the marble staircase and applauded courteously. I turned myself then to see Grayson standing above me on the staircase staring directly at me and smiling broadly.

A HARD LIFE

CHAPTER TWENTY-THREE

I slid open the heavy door of the moving freight car and breathed deeply as cool fresh air rushed in replacing the staleness that had gathered inside overnight. It was early morning and the flat Kansas plains seemed to stretch on for miles on either side of the railway line.

My mama's coffin rested on a wooden pallet in the middle of the boxcar, lashed down to keep it from sliding on the rough wooden floorboards. I had chosen to ride in the fright car with Mama instead of up forward in a passenger car. I had a bedroll along with a small valise filled with extra clothes.

I was confident the Irish born conductor would be making his way up to me in a little while with a pot of coffee. He rode in the caboose two cars back where he maintained a small woodstove with a cook top. The conductor accepted my generous tips and in exchange kept me well supplied with food, water, and hot coffee every morning.

Fifteen miles an hour makes for a long trip from Denver Colorado, across the Kansas plains, into Missouri and finally in eight or nine days to my destination in the southeast part of the state. This was my third day out from Denver and according to the conductor, Shamus Fitzpatrick, we would make Topeka in the late afternoon. I had made arrangements for this freight car to be side-railed for the night in Topeka, to be joined up the next day with a different eastbound train.

As I waited for Shamus and my morning coffee I stood in the open doorway and stared out as Kansas countryside passed by. My mind went back to the days just before I had departed Denver.

A small crowd of folks had crowded into the little Church of Christ for my mama's memorial service. Grayson, Katherine, McCloud, and I sat on the front pew along with Felicia Doran and Maria Ortega, our housekeepers. Just before the service was to begin Hiram McDougall came in and took a seat directly behind me. He reached forward and put his hand on my shoulder so I turned to acknowledge the gesture. My former schoolteacher appeared so emaciated I must have looked alarmed. He shook his head and then turned his eyes downward to the floor. His lower face was swollen and he looked terribly ill.

The service that followed was blurry in my mind now for I had not paid much attention to the songs or the preacher's sermon. My mind at the time had been occupied with how I was going to survive without Mama and how in the world I was going to explain her death to Jon David. I was also thinking about Grayson Asbury and Logan Ryan.

A Hard Life

Logan Ryan was the Union sergeant that I had discovered in the lobby of Grayson's hotel. I had never known his name previous to that day, although his image had been burned into my memory since I was seven years old. Grayson had introduced me to Ryan that day in the hotel and the sergeant had told me that he remembered me from my time in the Union camp after my surgery. He never mentioned anything about that night James Asbury was killed, and of course, neither did I.

At the time my brain had been spinning with the possibilities that his current emergence into my life might mean. Had he told Grayson about James Asbury's death and the two of them were baiting me, watching and waiting to see what my reaction would be? Had Ryan been the one who killed my mother? The piece of fringe in my pocket at the time, and which I now held in my hand as the drab Kansas landscape slid by, had definitely come from the jacket in the display case. I had confirmed that fact the next day when I visited the display when no one was paying attention to me. The jacket had a piece of fringe missing on the right side and the severed end matched the one I held in my hand.

"What kind of game are Grayson and Ryan trying to play?" I kept asking myself for at least the thousandth time in the last week. A tapping on the boxcar roof above me interrupted my thoughts. It was the Irish conductor and he lowered a covered wooden box by a rope from the roof down to the door opening. I reached out and snagged the rope, brought in the box, and removed a hot pot of coffee and a clean tin cup.

"Thanks a heap, Shamus!" I shouted above the noise of the wheels singing on the track.

"You're welcome, Mon! I'll be bringin' lunch by eleven." came the Irish brogue reply and then the conductor continued on his way forward toward the passenger cars and the engine compartment.

I sipped the hot coffee and thought about what I had to do in Topeka. McCloud had taken me aside just before my train had departed the Denver depot. He told me he had heard that Clifton McCarty was in Topeka, Kansas with an Indian girl. McCloud had said that the young woman was Cherokee and by her description McCloud thought it might be Aatonyah.

"Why would possess Clifton McCarty to kidnap Aatonyah and take her to Topeka?" I had asked and the sober McCloud only shook his head. He had no answers, only rumors. I found out the train went through Topeka on its way east and I made a deal with Shamus Fitzpatrick for the layover there.

We arrived in Topeka just before five o'clock in the afternoon. The brakeman unhitched the cars behind ours and the engineer backed me on to a side rail, leaving my boxcar between two large wooden grain elevators. I used a large padlock that belonged to the railroad and locked the door of the railcar securely. I hated to leave Mama's coffin seemingly abandoned, but it was shady here and I doubted that the lone boxcar would be disturbed. I put the padlock key into my jeans pocket, balanced a short, double-barreled ten-gauge shotgun over my shoulder and walked the short distance into Topeka, Kansas.

I stopped at the edge of town and stepped inside a livery stable. An older weather-beaten gentleman looked up at me from his seat behind a stitching vise where he was mending a bridle.

A Hard Life

"Afternoon." I said with a friendly smile. He looked me over with intelligent appearing blue eyes. He wasn't smiling, but he didn't look belligerent either. His eyes lingered on my tied-down Colt and then on the ten gauge.

"You the fool takin' his mama back to bury her in Missouri?" His words could have provoked a challenge, but I noticed a mischievous glint in his steely blue eyes.

"The fool part hasn't been completely established yet." I replied, still smiling slightly.

"Don't get me wrong, Son," he said, a tiny smile crinkling the corners of his mouth. "I somewhat admire what you're doin'. I just can't imagine why anyone would want to bury their mama in such a miserable place as Missouri."

"There's worse places." I replied and his eyes held mine eyes a little and his smile broadened. "My name's Branch Walker." I said simply.

The old cowboy reached up a bony, but strong hand to shake mine firmly.

"Luke Peerman, Son." he said. "Folks around here always pinned the handle of Romy on me. Short for Romeo I'm told. Understand some old-time British writer dreamed up Romeo and made him out to be quite a lady's man." he continued. "I liked the ladies back when I was a colt, Branch Walker."

"Shakespeare." I told him and Romy Peerman's expression turned questioning.

"The English writer was named Shakespeare. William Shakespeare." I told him and Romy nodded his head and continued to smile.

"You're damned smart to originate from Missouri, Branch." he said still smiling slyly. "Spect you might even be educated? Thet' right?"

"Just enough education to know how dumb I am, Romy." I replied and he nodded intelligently.

"Takes a smart man to know how much he don't know, Branch Walker. What can an old broke-down cowboy do for a smart man like you?"

"You might be able to help me, Romy." I replied. "I'm looking for a man from Colorado. He might be traveling with a girl. A Cherokee Indian girl and a pretty one." I added. Romey regarded me closely and he wasn't smiling now.

"You be the law, Branch?" I shook my head.

"Nope, I'm not, Romy." I replied. "It's personal." Romy looked directly at the shotgun I had leaned against the stable wall then looked back up at me.

"Man from Colorado have a name?" he asked and I nodded.

"Clifton McCarty." I replied and Romy frowned.

"I heard tell of im'." Romy said. "The Indian girl important to you, Son?" he asked.

"Just a friend, nothing more." I said, and then as Romy pointedly held my eyes I added. "Yeah, she's important to me, Romy." The old cowboy pointed up the street toward the north.

"They's onliest' one bawdy house on main street, Branch." he said soberly. "It's named the Western Gentlemen's Club and you'll see a big sign on the front. Ask for Mamie Rosebottom, she's the owner and she can tell you more about the little Cherokee girl. The news ain't good, Branch." he added. "I could tell you part of the

A Hard Life

story, but Mamie knows more about it than I do. She's a tolerable woman and when she understands you're a friend of the girl she'll be accomodatin' to you."

"Rosebottom's an apt name for a whore house owner, Romy." I said and the old cowboy's expression turned from serious to humorous again.

"I swear it's her real name too, Branch." he replied almost laughing now. "I do believe the good Lord has somewhat of a sense of humor when he picks names for folks." We both grinned at his remark and then Romy turned serious again.

"You best leave the scattergun here, Branch, and hide your sidearm under a coat. The law here don't cotton to men carryin' guns out in the open much. After you learn what you can from Mamie you can come back and pick it up. I'll keep it safe until you need it."

It wasn't difficult finding The Western Gentlemen's Club and the pretty girl that answered the door smiled provocatively at me. When I told her I needed to talk to Ms. Rosebottom, she seemed disappointed.

"What can I do for you, Handsome?" A middle-aged woman with bleached blonde hair asked. She was buxom and somewhat overweight, but I noticed her waist was small compared to the rest of her. She had big brown eyes set wide on her attractive face.

"You know Romy over at the livery stable?" I asked and she smiled in a knowing way.

"Everybody knows Romy," she replied, "some better than others." There was a twinkle in her eyes that said she could have told me more if she was so inclined.

"He told me you might be able to help me find a young Cherokee woman from Colorado." I said. "She has a small beauty mark here," I touched the left side of my face, "and she was traveling with a man named McCarty. Clifton McCarty." Mamie's face turned serious and her eyes became very suspicious.

"Are you the law, because you don't appear to be a relative of hers?" She replied slowly eyeing me up and down again. Her eyes stopped at the bulge at my side where my coat covered my Colt revolver.

"Like I told Romy, I'm not a lawman." I replied. "My name is Branch Walker." Her pretty eyes lit up with recognition of my name.

"You're the Walker taking your mother back to Missouri for burying!" I frowned a little this time. I wondered how word had spread so fast.

"I stopped in Topeka because I heard that McCarty had kidnapped the girl I knew and might be holding her here. Did I hear correctly?" I wanted to get her back on the subject that had brought me here.

"You heard right, Mister Walker," she replied sadly, "but you're too late. At least too late to save the girl." My disappointment must have shown, for I saw compassion in her brown eyes.

"McCarty brought her to town over a month ago." she began quietly. "He put her up in a rundown hotel and started charging any man that would, or could, pay to use her. I heard that she fought every man like a wildcat and McCarty finally trussed her up to the bed like some wild animal!" Anger was showing itself in her eyes as she spoke now.

"I have some influence with the law in Topeka and I used that influence when I heard what was happening. My first inclination was to put down the competition, but

A Hard Life

when I found out she was being abused, I felt sorry for the poor woman. The city marshals took her away from McCarty and brought her here to me, but it was too late, Mister Walker. I tried to befriend her. I fed her personally, and paid a doctor to tend to her wounds, but I couldn't take away her melancholies. The second night she was here she cut her own throat with a steak knife. We found her the next morning stone dead." Mamie stopped talking momentarily as she saw my pained expression

"My…business tends to be a dangerous one for me and my ladies, Mister Walker. I don't allow any physical abuse of my girls, but I can't defend them against the diseases, not only of the body, but unfortunately diseases of the minds of some too. What I'm trying to say is that I lose one of my girls from time to time. The good citizens of Topeka have a problem with my ladies being buried with the, so-called, good people, so I maintain my own cemetery plot set apart from the rest of the dearly departed folks of Topeka. I order granite headstones for my ladies too, Mister Walker. What I'm taking a long time to tell you is that I buried your friend in my own burial plot. The headstone is blank right now because I never knew her name. Could you tell me her name?"

"Her name was Aatonyah. I can write it down if you have a pen and paper?" I replied and Mamie Rosebottom nodded.

"I'll go to see the undertaker tomorrow and place an order to have the name carved." she replied.

"What about McCarty?" I asked. The buxom woman stared directly into my face.

"I hear he's still in Topeka." she replied slowly. "What do you intend to do to him?" I tried to read her eyes to interpret her meaning.

"I'd just like to give him Aatonyah's regards." I said plainly, wondering how she would take my hidden reference.

"I was hoping you would tell me you were going to kill the worthless bastard!" she replied hotly. "He plays cards nearly every night over at Pedro's Tavern, but I have to warn you, Mister Walker, Pedro's is a bad, bad place. There are men that hang out there the city marshals are terrified of. The law will not protect you in Pedro's. What happens there stays there and the local lawmen do not interfere or even go near the place!" I smiled at Mamie Rosebottom.

"Sounds like a good place to meet up with McCarty." I replied and she frowned at me.

A HARD LIFE

CHAPTER TWENTY-FOUR

"I need my shotgun back and I would like to rent a ridin' horse, Mister Peerman." I said as I entered the livery stable. Romy glanced up at me and then hooked his thumb toward a stall behind him.

"I saddled one what can run, Son." he said. "Your scattergun's already in the scabbard." I smiled at the older cowboy.

"How did you know I'd need a horse, Romy?" I asked.

"'Figgered' you'd be headin' for Pedro's," he replied. "knowed you'd need a fast horse if you're able to walk outta' thet' hellhole."

"Many thanks, Romy." I said to him as I opened the stall door and admired the slick black horse standing saddled, waiting for me.

"Thank me later, Branch. I've just begun to take a likin' to you, so's I'd appreciate you takin' care of yourself, as well as my horse, Blacky."

"Tell me how to find Pedro's, Romy?"

"Ride north past Mamie's place to the last street in town." Romy replied. "Street don't have a name, but if you find yourself in prairie grass you know you passed it up. Turn west and go to the end of the road. Pedro's will be on the right. Just throw Blackie's reins over the hitchin' post. He'll stand until mornin' feed time, then he'll come back here. I spect' if you take that long to come outta' Pedro's you won't be needin' a horse to ride "

"I suspect you're right, Romy" I replied. "Any good place to eat on the way?" He nodded and directed me to a family restaurant a few doors down from the stable. There weren't many folks in the place and the waitress was friendly. I was in no hurry for I wanted Pedro's to liven up some before I ventured there. The meal was good and I spent a couple of hours enjoying my food. The rest of the evening I rode around Topeka admiring the city and enjoying riding the great horse Romy had rented me.

Pedro's was a dumpy looking adobe building sitting alone on the darkened street. One single lantern swung in the night breeze and lighted the front entrance. The windows in front and on the east side were blacked out and there were about a dozen ponies tied up to three hitching posts in front of the place.

I could hear voices coming from the building. Drinking sounds as I had heard back in Missouri from some of the places Jon David favored. I removed the shotgun from the saddle scabbard and dropped Blackie's reins over the hitching rail as I had been instructed. I walked up to the door and cocking both hammers of the shotgun, I held the short barrels pointed downward beside my left leg as I turned the knob and entered Pedro's Tavern.

A Hard Life

All the voices hushed in the smoke-filled cavern of a room when I stepped inside. It was obvious that I was not a regular patron and any one not a regular in Pedro's elicited lots of attention. Eight or ten lanterns hung from scattered support posts that held up the low ceiling. The bar was nothing but boards supported on whiskey barrels standing on end down the left side of the room. The place reeked of stale beer, rotgut whiskey, body odor, and other smells too vile to mention.

A burly bartender stood behind the bar wiping out glasses with a dirty rag. He regarded me with an expression more fitting a mortal enemy than a prospective client. Several eyes in the room were riveted on the shotgun held at my side. I had removed my coat and left it tied to Blacky's saddle outside and my right hand hovered above the bone grip of my Colt forty-five.

Clifton McCarty was sitting at a card table facing the door and he saw me when I entered. Instant recognition showed on his face and he blanched noticeably. I stepped toward him and I caught movement from the bartender. I had the impression he was reaching down for something and I suspected I knew what it was. I raised the cocked shotgun with my left hand and pointed it directly at him without taking my eyes from McCarty's.

"Back away from the bar and fold your arms, Barkeep!" I said loudly enough for everyone in the room to hear distinctly. He eyed the two big barrels pointed at him and slowly raised up, folded his arms and leaned back against a shelf holding up bottles of various brands of whiskey. Suddenly my right hand was level and my cocked Peacemaker was aimed directly at McCarty's face while the shotgun in my left hand swung around, covering the whole left side of the tavern.

"I have business with the man in front of my Colt and nobody else in this room!" I said in the same tone and volume. "However, if anyone wants to get involved in business that don't pertain to them, they can take it up with this ten-gauge!"

All the men in the room were hard, mean looking individuals, but one man sitting to my right at the card table stood out more than any of the rest. He was dressed all in black with black wool trousers and a matching short coat, over a black leather vest. He also wore a big black hat. He had a full thick beard that was also as dark as the hat. It was his eyes that really caught my attention and made him stand out above all the rest in the room. Those eyes were black also and appeared almost reflective in the lantern light. Like a wolves eyes, I thought to myself.

There was not a smidgen of expression in those black eyes, no fear, no anger, no resentment of being interrupted, no discernible emotion at all. He appeared mildly interested in me, but only as a wolf might be interested in watching a hummingbird sip nectar from a flower. He appeared as if personally there was nothing to be gained, lost, or feared, from the experience at hand. He was the first man to speak.

"You're holding up the game, Stranger." he said in a low-pitched, but calm, clear voice. "Either shoot the son-of-a-bitch you came to shoot or state your business."

"I'd like to tell you a story about your gamblin' partner." I replied. "I won't take long." I hesitated to see if he would interrupt and when he remained quiet I continued.

A Hard Life

"I was hunting lions one day a few years back and I ran across a run-down cabin hid back deep in the woods. There I found a young starvin' woman and her child. Her baby had already starved to death and the woman wasn't far behind. Her husband was lyin' drunk in Denver." I could see that everyone in the room was paying attention to my story.

"The young lady was married to the piece of garbage in front of my Colt. I dug a grave and buried their baby and then I carried her back to our ranch where my mother and some friends fed her, clothed her, and brought her back from the brink of death. A few days later this bastard came and took her away again."

"This time he took her to Denver where he put her in a cheap hotel room and invited any man in town to have a go at her for a few coins! They abused her so badly she eventually bled to death." I saw some movement to my left and I swung the shotgun toward it and then everything became quiet again.

"When this man took her from my mama's care that day, I told him what I would do to him if his wife came to any harm. I've been looking for him since, but that's not the end of the story."

"A little over a month ago this same man stole a young Cherokee Indian girl from her village. She was also a friend of mine that I had helped through a bad time previously. He brought her here to Topeka and I suspect most of you know what happened to her. Now she's dead too! I came here to carry out my promise to this worthless tub of guts and I guess now is the time for me to find out if anyone in this room wants to try and stop me?"

"Is your name, Walker?" The man in black asked and then continued. "Would you be the man taking his mama back to Missouri for her burial?" This time I swung the shotgun barrels to cover the card table's inhabitants and there was an immediate shuffling to move back out of the line of fire. The man in black sat where he was, but he did slowly hold up his hands and then gently laid them palms down on the table..

"I'm getting a little tired of having to answer that question!" I said and the man in black shrugged. Clifton McCarty had not moved a muscle during the entire episode.

"Do you have a brother named Jon David?" the man in black asked and I stared at him in near disbelief and then nodded slightly.

"How in hell do you know my brother Jon David?" I asked in amazement.

"Your brother and I spent some time together incarcerated in northern Arkansas a couple of years back." he replied. "I believe public drunkenness was the charge and quite honestly, we were as guilty as sin. My name is John Wesley Hardin."

"You're… Wesley Hardin?" I asked amazed, and a couple of the men at the card table swallowed hard and blinked as they stared at him too, including Clifton McCarty.

There wasn't a man in the western United States that had not heard of John Wesley Hardin. He was the most feared killer anywhere and here I was holding a Colt Peacemaker and a shotgun on him and his card-playing partner!

A Hard Life

"I'm afraid so," Hardin said, "and you must be the Ben Branch Walker your brother rattled on about all night long in that Arkansas jail. I'm pleased to make your acquaintance, Ben Branch, and now that we've heard your story about this scoundrel I suspect we all hate Mister McCarty nearly as bad as you. Truth be told, I was seriously considering killing him myself just before you showed up, for I am morally convinced he has been dealing from the bottom of the deck during this card game." Hardin turned and stared at McCarty and spoke directly toward him, but to me.

"I hate card cheats worse than you hate women molesters, Mister Walker!"

"I doubt that." I replied. "Not this particular molester anyhow." .

"Well, tell us how you want to resolve your vengeance against this man, Ben Branch?" Hardin asked.

"I intend to kill him!" I replied coldly and turned toward McCarty again.

"Are you packin' a gun, McCarty?" I asked and Clifton shook his head violently.

"No I'm not, Mister Walker, and you should know that Grayson Asbury paid me to steal the Cherokee girl away from her village!" McCarty's voice was high-pitched and whiny and Hardin turned in his seat to face the trembling coward

"You're not only a derelict drunk, a child abandoner, a kidnapper, a card cheat, and a woman molester, you're also a liar, Sir!"

John Wesley Hardin made this statement to McCarty and suddenly, somehow, a knife materialized in his right hand! Before I, or anyone else in the room could react, he reached across the table and slit Clifton McCarty's throat as effortlessly and as unemotionally as a normal man would reach to slap a mosquito, or poke his fork at a biscuit!

Here I am holding two cocked guns at the time and the grisly deed was done before I could have pulled either of the triggers, even if I wanted to!

Clifton McCarty grabbed his ruined throat with both hands and the others at the table slid their chairs even further back to keep from getting sprayed with the fine crimson mist that was escaping from between his fingers! Meanwhile, Wesley Hardin was carefully wiping the blade of his thin-bladed knife on his pants leg without even looking at McCarty, or me!

Suddenly Clifton tried to rise up from his chair. His face was contorted in mortal fear and his eyes were wide and crazy looking! Then as I, and the others nearby watched, life faded from his eyes, and he and his chair made a horrible crash as he pitched over backwards to the wood floor, dead as a stone!

He lay there wide-eyed, blood flowing from the horrible gash in his throat, staring up at absolutely nothing! Pedro's Tavern suddenly became as quiet and still as a Monday morning church.

"I do believe I have assuaged your problem situation for you, Ben Branch." Wesley said to me softly. "I believe your brother Jon David would have approved of me taking care of this business without you having to bloody your hands. Would you do me an intense favor and kindly lower the hammers on your weapons before someone, preferably not me, gets their head blown off accidentally?"

A Hard Life

I stared at the cold-blooded killer and slowly holstered my Colt, then raised the shotgun's barrels toward the ceiling while I lowered the double hammers.

"What made you think he was lyin' about Grayson Asbury?" I asked the grim-faced killer. My voice sounded a tad thin and strained. Hardin looked at me with an expression of shocked surprise.

"I wouldn't know Grayson Asbury from Jack Sprat's pig!" he replied quickly. "I only meant McCarty was lying about having a gun. I'm rather certain you'll find one in a holster beneath his left arm!"

And sure enough we did.

A HARD LIFE

CHAPTER TWENTY-FIVE

I returned Blacky to the livery and gave Romy Peerman a twenty-dollar gold piece for all his trouble. He tried to protest that it was too much, but I stopped him and told him it had been well worth it to me. I shook Romy's hand, bid him thanks and farewell, then walked back to the waiting boxcar and slept rather fitfully the rest of the night. I half expected to be awakened at any hour by one of the lawmen from Topeka. Even while I slept my dreams were filled with ghoulish nightmares of knives and bloody throats.

At ten o'clock the next morning the eastern bound train stopped on the main track, uncoupled, and backed up the side rail to the boxcar holding my mama's coffin and me. A half-hour later here we are clattering along headed east again across the flat Kansas prairie toward Missouri.

The St. Louis San Francisco Railway line ends in Cape Girardeau, Missouri. Before I had left Denver,

A Hard Life

utilizing the telegraph wires, I had made arrangements through Reuben Rosenthal, mine and Mama's attorney in St. Louis, with the Abernathy Tie and Lumber Company. A couple of years before, Abernathy's workmen had built a spur line from Cape Girardeau to just north of Bloomfield, Missouri. The Abernathy company owned their own steam locomotive and used it to haul timber from Crowley's ridge to Cape Girardeau where they ran a large sawmill.

Attorney Rosenthal had contracted with Abernathy to pick up my boxcar in Cape Girardeau and take me as near Bloomfield as their line went. Rosenthal had also contacted the Stoddard County Undertaker Company in Bloomfield to meet me at the end of the spur line with a horse-drawn hearse to convey Mama's coffin the rest of the way to my destination.

My destination was our old farmstead just south of Bloomfield. A year previously I had asked Reuben Rosenthal to find the then current owner of the property and make an offer to purchase it. Reuben had been successful in both finding the owner and purchasing the property for us. Mama and I had received the deed to our old farm only three months before she was murdered.

The undertaker company had kept their word and a driver and two workmen were waiting at the end of the spur line. We transferred the coffin to the hearse, bypassed Bloomfield by taking a shortcut through the country and arrived at our farm about noon on Friday, the twentieth of April.

As we approached our old homestead from the east a wave of emotion flowed over me as scenes of my childhood flashed through my mind. The house and barn were still standing, although they looked much more forlorn and abandoned now. The grass around the house had grown up and Mama's garden plot was overgrown in weeds and brush. The old trail that went from the road up the steep incline to the house and barn beyond it was barely visible through the tall grass.

The undertaker company had sent men to the house the day before and a grave had been opened beside Papa's. The dark fresh earth contrasted sharply with the green grass that grew over Papa's grave and out to the downed corral fence in front of the barn. The once small apple tree had grown to a surprising height and girth and was fully leaved out, shading Papa's and Mama's final resting places.

I looked around hoping and expecting to see someone, but the farm appeared completely deserted. The workmen and I carried Mama's coffin from the hearse and sat it on the lip of the grave until ropes could be secured to the handles.

Tears flowed unashamedly down my face and dripped from my chin as the four of us lowered the coffin into the ground. The fresh earth smell reminded me of planting time when I was young and all my family was still around me, sheltering, guiding, and protecting me.

"I could say a few words if you wanted, Mister Walker?" The undertaker offered and I shook my head.

"No offense, Sir," I replied, "but you didn't really know my mama and she wouldn't want a stranger saying nice things that he didn't know for sure was the truth."

"I'm certain your mother was a fine lady…" He started to say and I raised my hand to stop him.

A Hard Life

"No thank you!" I said plainly and he looked down at his black shoes that had been polished when he left Bloomfield, but were now covered in the red clay that comprised most of the Stoddard County soil.

I told the undertaker and the workmen that they could leave now, that I would finish the job of filling the grave myself. They had brought me a rented horse and saddle and they untied the roan gelding from the back of the hearse and tied him up to the porch post of the house, then the three of them departed and headed back toward Bloomfield.

I was completely alone now with only my memories of my dead parents for company as I slowly shoveled the fresh earth over Mama's coffin. I removed my coat and unbuttoned my collar as sweat from the labor beaded up on my forehead.

I mounded the earth up atop Mama's gravesite and was packing down the dirt with the blat side of the shovel when suddenly I became aware that I wasn't alone. I stood erect and looked around, and then spotted Jon David riding down a far-away ridge toward where I was working.

He was still a half-quarter away, but I would have recognized the way my brother sat his horse from as far away as I could have seen him. Jon David rode slowly and I stood patiently waiting until he was only a few feet away.

I was overjoyed to see my brother, especially right now! Tears welled up again in my eyes as I smiled up at Jon David. Jon David, however, was not smiling back.

"You been sittin' up there watchin' this?" I inquired and he nodded slightly. His lips were drawn into a straight line.

"I wasn't sure you would get word, Jon David." I said. "I'm right glad you did. If you'll climb down from that swayback I'll hug your neck."

"If I climb down from this horse right now, little brother, it won't be to hug your damn neck!" His voice was like a rasp on a wagon wheel. "I'm so mad that you let this happen to our mama I'm inclined to beat you black and blue, Ben Branch!"

Jon David's eyes were mere slits in his face. I had seen him like that before. I remembered it was usually just before someone got hurt! The smile vanished now from my face and the tears suddenly dried completely from my eyes.

"Get your ass down and take your best shot, brother!" I replied coldly. "I believe either knockin' hell out of you, or gettin' it knocked out of me would bring me a huge relief right now! It don't really matter, either way would suit me just fine!"

Jon David dismounted, dropped the reins to the ground and walked slowly toward me. I wasn't sure that I wasn't soon to be involved in a horrible fistfight with my brother that I had not seen in over three years!

He stepped within striking distance, but I kept my hands balled at my sides. I watched as the cold fury in his eyes faded and was replaced with a softer expression. Jon David then reached out his hand awkwardly as if to shake mine, but I reached for him and locked my arms around his neck, pulling him close.

A Hard Life

"I'm so sorry, Jon David!" I whispered quietly as I held him.

Jon David's muscled body was taut at first as I embraced him, but as I continued to hug him hard, slowly his inflexibility relaxed, his arms went around me and we hugged each other fiercely! I tried hard to hold back sobs as I buried my face in his shoulder and I felt shudders go through him also. We held each other tightly for a long time until the suppressed sobs in both our chests subsided.

Jon David then released his grip, pulled away and turned from me to stare out across the green pasture. I stepped over the abandoned shovel, walked to the base of the apple tree, and sat down in the thick grass. In a few minutes he joined me and we sat side by side for several minutes without saying a word to one another.

He was the first to speak. "You really think you're man enough to knock hell outta' me, Son?" Jon David asked without looking directly at me. I turned my head and stared at my brother.

"Maybe." I replied quietly. "I've growed some since you saw me last."

He turned and met my eyes with his, then smiled slightly and nodded.

"That you have, Son!" he replied. "You're surely not a skinny little shit anymore, but I'd bet I could still spin you upside down and drive you in the ground like a fencepost! You really know I could, deep inside, don't you?" I met Jon David's eyes and suddenly it was like it had always been before. I would forever be Jon David's little brother. I nodded and smiled slightly back at him.

"Yeah, I suppose you could." I admitted and we sat together quietly again.

"I notice you're well armed." he said. "Anybody teach you more than me?" I nodded without looking at him, but kept silent about the gun lessons from Grayson Asbury and McCloud.

"Are you good?" he asked and I instinctively knew he meant at drawing and shooting a pistol.

"Tolerable." I replied.

"Better'n' me?"

"We'll never know, brother." I replied flatly and he smiled slightly as he gazed at me from the corner of his eyes.

"I met a fiend of yours." I said, more to change the subject than anything else. Jon David gave me a questioning look.

"John Wesley Hardin." I replied and Jon David's eyes opened wide with astonishment.

"I spent a whole night in a Arkansas jail with him once!" Jon David declared. "Deputy told me the next day who I was in with and I damned near pissed my pants! When the realization finally hit me my bowels twisted up and I spent the better part of the next two days in the crapper!"

I smiled at my older brother as I nodded my understanding, then I relayed to him what had happened in Topeka. Jon David listened with utter amazement and even more so when I told him that Hardin had said that he killed McCarty so I wouldn't have to; as a favor to his old friend, Jon David Walker!

"Well I'll be damned." Jon David said as he reflected on my story, then his face hardened again.

A Hard Life

"Tell me about Mama's killer?" His eyes burned with the fury from before. I told him everything I knew, beginning with mine and Mama's arrival in Colorado, and ending when I had boarded the Frisco train with her coffin. It took the better part of an hour and Jon David never stopped me or interrupted me a single time.

His expression changed from time to time as I revealed the events of the last three plus years and became furious again as I told him about Logan Ryan, the Union Sergeant who had hung Papa and then let the two of us leave the Union camp after James Asbury's killing so many years ago.

"You figure Ryan for her murder?" Jon David asked and I nodded slowly. I reached in my pocket and retrieved the short piece of fringe McCloud had found on the ground where the shooter had cut his forked shooting stick

"This came from an elk jacket Ryan presented to the Asbury family." I said. "According to him the jacket had belonged to James Asbury, and Grayson and Katherine affirmed it. McCloud found it close to where the shot was fired."

"Damned careless, don't you think? Unless' he left it on purpose, just so you'd personally know he did it, but not be able to prove it." Jon David commented and then continued. "This Cherokee fellow named McCloud, does he agree with your conclusion?"

"McCloud's not a man to concur with someone else's judgment." I replied. "He's a self-thinkin' man and expects everyone else to be the same." Jon David nodded.

"Probably a man I'd get along with." he commented and I nodded my agreement. to my brother's statement.

"How'd you get permission to bury Mama beside Pop?" Jon David inquired. I reached inside my vest and produced the deed to the property.

"From the new owner of the farm." I replied, then added quickly. "Well, I haven't really asked him yet, but I'm sure he won't object." Jon David stared at me.

"Who might that be?" he inquired.

"You, Jon David." I replied. "Me and Mama bought the place for you. We received the bill of sale, and this deed, a few weeks before she was killed. I was plannin' to come find you and give you this." I handed my brother the paper and he studied it, then handed it back.

"I don't want this damned ol' place, Branch. You're the land ownin' type, not me! It's too late for me to change." It was my turn to stare at him now.

"What's your plan with Ryan?" Jon David inquired and held my eyes with his.

"You remember that old revolutionary war knife of Papa's?" I asked as a response. I was still thinking about his refusal to accept the farm as his. Jon David looked down at the ground before he spoke

"I suppose Mama finally admitted to you that I told her what I had done with that old knife?" he asked rather sheepishly. "I assume she did or you wouldn't know about its whereabouts." I shook my head at Jon David and frowned.

"No, she never shared that conversation with me, Jon David." I replied in a quieter tone. "I found it at the bottom of one of her dresser drawers after she was shot. I concluded she must have known what we had done or she wouldn't have felt the need to hide it from me."

A Hard Life

"You didn't do nothin' back then, Branch!" he declared. "I'm the murderin' black sheep of this family. What you plannin' on doin' with the ol' pigsticker?" Jon David asked as his eyes found mine again.

"I plan to use it on Ryan." I replied. Jon David stared deep into my eyes.

"You might need some help with that, Branch." Jon said. "We both know I've had more experience in that class of action than you. Maybe I better trail back with you to Colorado."

"I'd like that, Jon David." I admitted. "I honestly could handle his killin' myself, but Ryan owes both of us." My older brother studied my face and read the resolve in my eyes.

"Killin' him won't bring you satisfaction, Branch." Jon said. "I know you think it will, but believe me, it won't."

"You're not tryin' to talk me out of it are you, Jon David?" I asked. He shook his head sadly.

"No, nothin' like that." he said. "I just want you to know that killin' someone won't stop the pain, that's all. Not even when it's someone that deserves and begs to be killed!" I studied Jon David. I had the feeling he had more to tell me so I asked him.

"Is there anything else I don't know that I should, Jon David?" I asked. He dropped his head and stayed silent, but it was the kind of silence that I knew would end.

"About a month ago, I killed Uncle Clady." he said quietly and then glanced over at me to read my reaction. I was stunned, but I held my tongue knowing he would tell me more.

"I ran into his youngest daughter, Carla, a time back." he began. "It wasn't in no church neither, Branch" he added. "She's a workin' girl, if you catch my drift? Both girls left home as soon as they was old enough. Darlene left first, a couple of years ago, and she's dead now. Accordin' to Carla, her sister died of consumption, but the word was she had one of the diseases whores usually end up with." I was amazed at what my brother had just told me.

"Carla and Darlene both became whores?" I asked and Jon David nodded.

"Carla confided to me over a bottle of scotch whiskey that Uncle Clady had molested both of them from the time they were teenagers until they ran away from home. That was bad enough, but she also told me that Uncle Clady tried it with our Mama, but she fought him off and told him that she would tell me if he kept it up. Uncle Clady knew I'd kill him for sure. Carla said he left Mama alone after that, but he didn't slack up on either of his daughters."

"What did you do?" I asked.

"I watched his house for upwards of a week until I caught him in the field plowin' corn by himself. He begged and blubbered like a baby when I told him what I knew and what I was goin' to do. I shot him low in the belly and watched him writhe around in his own blood for a while, then I shot his eye out and left him in the cornfield between the cultivator handles."

"Does anyone know who did it?" I inquired.

"They ain't for sure, but there's paper circulatin' on me. Reward's up to a thousand if you want to turn me in to face trial?"

A Hard Life

"Does Brady Foreister know about it?" I asked. Brady was the Ripley County deputy I had wired to get word to Jon David about Mama's burial.

"Fact is, Brady was with me that night in the whorehouse when we ran into Carla. He was also the first one to find Uncle Clady's body. He recognized my nag's tracks and used a cornstalk to wipe out any recognizable sign. Brady won't participate in my capture or trial, but Aunt Imogene was left a piss pot full of money and she ain't bein' stingy in tryin' to find out who killed Uncle Clady. Most folks in Ripley County know the truth. It's just a matter of time until Aunt Imogene's money catches up with me."

"That's why you don't want the deed to this farm isn't it?" I asked.

"Ownin' property don't make much sense to a man on the run." Jon replied.

"We can beat this, Jon David." I said. "Uncle Clady deserved what he got and the Ripley County folks know that too. You can come out to Colorado with me until this matter quiets down some and then I'll contact Reuben Rosenthal, the attorney from St. Louis. He's proven to be quite resourceful for me and I'm sure he can find a way to clear this up without you havin' to go to trial." Jon David nodded his head, then stared up the incline to the two graves of our parents.

"You think they're together now, Branch?" Jon asked and my eyes joined his on the fresh mound of earth and the grass-covered one beside it.

"I don't know, brother." I replied. "I certainly hope so."

Just then while our attentions were riveted on our parent's gravesite, Jon David and I heard a muffled footstep close behind us. We both turned as one, each with a handful of Colt Peacemaker cocked and pointed menacingly toward the sound. I wondered at the time which of us was quicker?

A HARD LIFE

CHAPTER TWENTY-SIX

I don't know which of the three of us was the most startled and confused. I do know that mine and Jon David's Colt pistol barrels were instantly averted upward with the hammers lowered.

Rosa Kate Asbury stood with her hand to her face in astonished surprise, and some fear, though the fear faded from her wide eyes when we averted our pistols She was dressed in a dark blue full-length dress with a fashionable matching hat. The dress, though modest with a high neck, fit her curvy figure well, making it prominent to two attentive observers.

The hat had a mesh veil that covered her face down to the middle of her pretty nose. Rosa Kate was holding the hem of her dress above the grass and her shapely ankles were visible, especially from mine and Jon David's position sitting on our butts in the tall grass!

I had not seen Rosa Kate in three years and let me assure you she had filled out, and if possible, had became even more lovely than I remembered. I holstered my Colt, removed my hat, and smiled up at Rosa Kate, even though she had caught us completely by surprise and my mind was a tad befuddled.

I pulled my legs beneath me in order to stand up, but Jon David was a second quicker and he put his hand on my head to assist himself up. When he was nearly erect and still had his hand on my bare head, he gave me a push backwards that caused me to sprawl awkwardly back to my backside. Meanwhile Jon David removed his big hat and strode toward Rosa Kate with his hand extended and his face split by his winning smile.

"I'm Jon David Walker, Ma'am." he said, taking her hand and holding it softly. "The clumsy one over there is my little brother Ben Branch." I was still sitting on my backside and I watched as Rosa Kate extended her hand to my brother and matched his smile with one not quite as broad, but much prettier, at least to me.

"I'm pleased to meet you, Mister Walker." She replied with her strong sweet voice "I'm Rosa Kate Asbury and I've met your brother before. I came to offer my condolences to both of you for the loss of your sweet mother. I knew her well and I can honestly tell you I admired her immensely. I will surely miss her."

"Thank you Rosa Kate, please call me Jon, or Jon David, as you please." My brother's voice sounded much softer and more soothing than usual. "I really don't care what you call my baby brother over there." he continued, while hooking his thumb toward me "You realize I'm sure that he's still too wet behind the ears to fully appreciate what a lovely and sweet little lady you are to come so far out of your way to pay respects to our mama." I was standing erect now walking toward the two.

A Hard Life

"Just how far out of your way did you go, Rosie?" I asked. Rosa Kate met my eyes as I approached her and I could see that her smile was gone now and her eyes were filled with grief and something else I couldn't quite decipher for sure. Suddenly tears spilled out of her pretty eyes and she moved away from Jon David toward me. I instinctively opened my arms and she pressed herself against me as I folded my arms around her holding her tightly.

"I'm so sorry, Branch." She whispered hoarsely and I could feel sobs wracking her soft body. I held her close as Jon David stood aside and regarded us closely. Her sobs subsided after a short while and as I gently released my embrace she moved back in my arms to stare up at my face.

"How did you know, Rosie?" I asked softly.

"McCloud wired me to tell me what had happened to your mother and where I could find you." She replied. "I was coming home to Colorado in a week anyway so I moved up my plans and got off the train in Poplar Bluff. The stage brought me to Bloomfield two days ago. I didn't know exactly what your plans were and wasn't sure when to meet you here. The undertaker was supposed to come to the hotel in Bloomfield and let me know, but he must have forgotten. I rented a buggy and came out on my own."

All the while Rosa Kate was staring up into my eyes and as I held her I was oblivious to anyone else in the world. Jon David cleared his throat and Rosa Kate released her hold around my waist and moved back a little.

"Are you hungry?" she asked the two of us. "I didn't know who would be here so I brought enough food for a dozen people. It's down where I left my horse and buggy."

"We're starved, little darlin'!" Jon David replied and reached for Rosie's arm and put it under and over his right arm to escort her down the hill. I walked behind the two as Jon David kept looking down at Rosie and smiling his big smile. It was like my older brother to end his grieving as soon as possible. Not only for himself either, for if I didn't miss my guess, I suspected he would be doing his best to liven up mine and Rosa Kate's moods also.

Not that Jon David was not grieving inside as much as me, but it was just not his nature to let it show too much. Especially around someone like Rosa Kate! My thoughts made me smile to myself, because I knew that if Mama was there somewhere, observing her eldest son's overt flirting with Rosa Kate, she would be smiling too.

We spent the better part of the remaining afternoon under the giant white oak tree in our old front yard. I'm sure Jon David was just as conscious as I as to what had taken place there some thirteen years previous, but it was not mentioned to Rosa Kate. Within minutes Jon David was entertaining the both of us with funny stories about himself and escapades of his free and sometimes wild life. He had Rosa Kate laughing so hard at times she had tears in her eyes again, but not for the same reason as before.

As I watched and listened to my brother I realized just how much I had always admired him, sometimes to the point of envy, I had to admit, but not envious for long. Jon David is absolutely unique and trying to copy his behavior would have been fruitless. I could never be exactly like him and really didn't want to be. To try to be like him would have taken something away from his uniqueness, and I didn't want that to ever happen.

"Let's ride back to town and see if there's a place to buy something stronger to drink than this sweet tea you brought, Rosa Kate." Jon David said. "It's gonna' get dark on us out here in a little while and we need to find someplace with lots of bright lights to show you off to the folks in Bloomfield."

There weren't many bright lights in the small town of Bloomfield, Missouri on a weeknight. The hotel had a small bar with only two customers, both drummers, who sat together comparing their wares and probably trying to sell their lines to one another.

Jon David kept Rosa Kate and me up past midnight regaling us with more of his adventures. At the end of one of his narratives, Rosa Kate yawned and announced that she had to retire to her bedroom leaving my brother and me alone in the barroom. The drummers had given up on selling anything to one another an hour earlier and went up to their rooms.

I had a feeling the bartender wanted to close up, but Jon David had been tipping him handsomely every time he ordered a round of drinks. Rosa Kate drank only sweet soda water and I had nursed two mugs of beer all night long. Jon David had been ordering whiskey shots with his beer and I was astounded that he still showed no signs of being drunk.

A few minutes after Rosa Kate had gone up to her room the outside door to the bar opened and two hard looking men came in, separated, and took places standing with their backs to the wall on either side of the door. Jon David's eyes narrowed as he watched the two men's strange actions. His expression changed as a big friendly smile spread across his face.

"You gents want a drink if I'm buyin'?" he announced to them and I began to feel even more suspicious as they both shook their heads to his offer, but neither spoke. It wasn't just their hard looks that alarmed me; it was the two double-barreled shotguns they cradled over their left arms. Bulges under their long dusters told me they were also wearing sidearms.

The strangers didn't appear to be Bloomfield residents. I chanced a sideways glance at the bartender and his puzzled expression told me he neither recognized the two men, nor had any more clue as to who they were than me or Jon David.

Just before the door had opened and the two strangers had come in, Jon David had ordered two more beers for us and now the bartender placed the full mugs on the bar. My brother nodded to me and we both got up from our chairs slowly and approached the bar as if to save the bartender the trip over to our table. Neither of us took our eyes completely off the two armed strangers as we moved to the bar.

When we got to the bar we stepped apart placing some distance between us, leaned our backs against it, and turned to face the two strangers. Jon David hooked his left boot heel over the brass foot rail and smiled again at the two men. I was pretty certain his right hand was over his Colt's grip, just like mine.

The door opened again and Logan Ryan stepped inside, looked hard at Jon David and me facing him and then shot a sideways glance at the two men on either side of the door. He was wearing his blue army hat with the left side of the brim fastened to the crown of the hat. He was also wearing a tan duster like the two men's and it seemed obvious the trio knew one another.

The fact that the last time I had seen Ryan was in Colorado, and now he and some hard looking strangers were in the same room as Jon David and me in Missouri, was too much of a coincidence not to have been planned.

"Hello again, Branch.," he said to me and then his glance took in Jon David. My brother's smile had evaporated and his eyes were cold as he regarded the man that both of us suspected had killed our mama. We had both watched him hang our papa so that crime was a fact and not merely suspected..

"Hello, Walker," he continued as he met my brother's eyes. "It's been a long time." Jon David said nothing in reply and for a few moments there was a deadly quiet in the tension filled barroom.

"What do you want with us Walkers, Ryan?" Jon David asked in a controlled tone. "You must want somethin' other than killin' us or the air in here would already be full of gun smoke!"

"Money, Boys." Ryan replied with a small crooked grin behind his bushy mustache. "These boys," he waved his hand toward the two men with him, "and me stuck together after the war tryin' to find a way to make money without workin' too hard, but we couldn't find any easy way. Then a couple of years ago we began to hear rumors about how our old dead Captain's family had taken a Rebel boy in to share all their money with him. We began to piece things together and then we remembered you two. That's when things started fallin' in place and we come up with a plan."

"A plan to do what?" I interjected and Ryan turned his attention toward me.

"First off, we're gonna' turn Jon David over to the Ripley County sheriff and collect the reward, but that's nothin' but pocket change. You're gonna' make us full partners of yours, Branch." he replied confidently. "Full partners in your portion of the Asbury estate."

"It's a far piece from here to Ripley County, Ryan." I replied, "and just why would I make you partners of mine, even if you could accomplish takin' Jon David to Doniphan?" I asked and his small smile expanded.

"If you don't I'm gonna' tell Katherine Asbury what you boys did and she'll drop you outta' her dead husband's estate quicker'n she'd drop a wet turd!" Ryan's eyes were glistening now with renewed confidence. "That's why, Smartass!" he concluded.

"I see." I replied and then continued. "There's a big flaw in your plan, Ryan, actually there's two big flaws. First off, you'd have to kill both of us to take Jon David, and I might as well warn you now that if you make any quick moves, or if those shotguns move an inch toward either of us, you and your two friends will be stone dead an instant later, simple as that."

"And second?" Ryan quipped, still smiling. My threat seemed not to impress or frighten him at all.

"Second, you may have heard that Katherine Asbury went looking for me because of a letter she received from her husband drafted the week before he was killed?" Ryan nodded his head.

"We heard that." he replied.

A Hard Life

"I'd bet you don't know what else was in that letter, Ryan?" My query caused the first hint of doubt to creep into his eyes.

A HARD LIFE

CHAPTER TWENTY-SEVEN

The two hard cases on either side of the barroom door stared at Logan Ryan. I don't think things were going quite as well as their leader had led them to believe it would. Jon David and I welcomed some doubt in their minds for we needed an edge. Those shotguns they were holding were deadly at the range we were standing from them and both Jon David and I knew it.

"Katherine allowed me to read that letter from her husband, plus a second letter from General Stuart, his commanding officer." I continued. "James Asbury told his wife that he was resigning his commission from the Army and he also told her he was turning you in for war crimes and grand larceny.He called you by name in the letter, Ryan! I figure you suspected he was about to jump out from under you and that's why you didn't turn me and Jon David in for murder."

I was watching Ryan's eyes carefully and I could see that what I was saying was having somewhat of an affect on him. He was becoming pale and his eyes were darting around as if to find an escape. I continued to talk to him.

"The letter from General Stuart was to extend his condolences to Katherine and the rest of the Asbury family for James' bravery and his death in battle. That had to be a battle you and your men staged so Asbury could be found dead afterwards. You were smart enough to know if you allowed any type of investigation into the murder of your captain, all of your platoon's crimes would be uncovered and you would either be hung, or you and your cronies would spend the rest of your lives in a military stockade."

"When you goin' to quit listenin' to this crap and get to the killin', Sergeant?" The man on the left of the door, straight in front of me, was the one that spoke. I thought it odd that he still addressed Ryan as his "Sergeant" after so many years out of the Army.

The man was as tall as me, but much heavier. His hair was long and stringy and he wore a thick beard. Obviously he believed for some reason that the three of them had me and Jon David at a severe disadvantage. I glanced over at the bartender again wondering if he could be part of their gang. With him being behind us, that might give the three assailants the confidence they seemed to have.

The bartender was backed up against the whiskey shelves sweating and as pale as a ghost. I couldn't believe he was going to be of any help to them, or to me or Jon David either!

Just then a shadow passed over the table in front of me and I glanced upward. Jon David and I were standing beneath an overhanging second floor balcony. The balcony extended out over the bar and a gunman could simply lean over and shoot directly down at us. I was convinced now that at least a third member of Ryan's gang was directly above us, maybe more than one!

When the action started it was sudden and the barroom was instantly turned into a fierce raging battleground! The man across from me that had spoken to Ryan suddenly swung his shotgun around to bring it to bear on us. I drew, aimed at the middle of him and fired. He staggered backward at the impact of my slug, but the shotgun was still swinging toward me. I thumbed the Colt quickly and put two more slugs directly into his chest. His shotgun blasted and tore a hole in the floor between us big enough to drop a hat through, but all I felt were a few wood splinters that hit me in the legs.

Jon David had drawn his Colt and shot the second man holding a shotgun. His assailant also got off a blast with the scattergun, but Jon David dove to his left toward me and the blast tore a big hole through the bar where my brother had been standing a half-second before.

Both of the shotgunners were down now. The one I had shot was on his face in a pool of blood and Jon David's man was slumped against the wall groaning from two forty-five slugs in his belly.

Logan Ryan had upturned a table and dove behind it when the first shots sounded. He had not fired a shot yet, but I had seen him digging for his pistol as he dove behind the table. Just then Jon David looked up and suddenly dove into me knocking me backwards against the bar.

A blast from a Winchester directly above us sent a bullet whistling harmlessly past both of us and on through

A Hard Life

the floor. Jon David aimed his Colt upward at the balcony above us and fanned the Colt's hammer with the heel of his left hand. Three shots tore through the balcony's ceiling and apparently up through the thin flooring, then into the body of the man above us.

I surmised that because the dead man's body toppled over the railing and crashed heavily to the barroom floor, literally destroying a table that happened to be in his fall path.

Jon David had his back to the door when he was firing upward. I looked beyond my brother and saw Logan Ryan framed in the open doorway. His Army Colt was leveled at my face and then slowly, or so it seemed to me at the time, he moved the long barrel to the left and deliberately shot Jon David directly in the middle of the back. Ryan grinned at me and I jerked my Colt up to send two quick shots through the now empty doorway!

The entire battle probably didn't last more than twenty seconds, but it seemed hours to me at the time. I ran to the doorway with my empty Colt and saw and heard Ryan on horseback galloping down the alley and out into the darkness. He was gone in an instant, swallowed up into the forest and farmland outside Bloomfield. I stood for a moment cocking and pulling the trigger of my empty Colt at Ryan's fading hoof beats.

I rushed back to Jon David, who was lying deathly still, flat on his face in front of the bar. I turned him over and lay his head in my lap. His eyes were closed, but they opened now and my brother stared upward at me with his patented crooked smile. A trickle of blood ran from the corner of his mouth and I wiped it away with my index finger.

Jon David's eyes were examining my face as if he might be looking at me for the first time! Then the thought hit me that maybe he was looking at me for the last time!

"Hang on, Jon David! Don't you die! Don't you die, damn you!" I literally screamed into his face!

"You promised you'd never leave me!" I pleaded in vain! "You promised you'd always be there when I needed you, Jon David!" I continued shouting into his face..

"We'll get you a doctor damn it, just hang on! I can't lose you too!" I begged, but my brother put his right hand up to touch my face and I watched as his life drained from his eyes and his hand fell away from my face to make a smacking sound as it hit the barroom floor! I buried my face in Jon David's chest and wept like the child I suddenly became again!

Bloomfield's town marshal and two deputies arrived at the hotel a few minutes later while acrid smelling gun smoke still hung heavily in the still air of the barroom. They checked the three assailants for signs of life, shaking their heads at one another at their findings, then the marshal spent some time talking to the bartender in hushed tones across the room while I continued to hold Jon David's limp body in my lap. I had stopped my crying and I seemed extremely calm for all the events that had just taken place.

The marshal's name was Virgil Huggins and he introduced himself to me while I remained sitting on the floor holding Jon David in my arms.

"Son, your brother's gone," he said rather gently, "and you best stand up and allow me to cover him. The commotion of this many shots fired will draw a

A Hard Life

considerable crowd in a little while and it would be better they didn't see Jon David like this." I looked up at the man curiously.

"You speak as if you know Jon David, Marshal Huggins?" I questioned and the marshal nodded.

"You can call me Virgil, Branch," he began. "I knew your daddy and I remember you and Jon David from when you were youngsters. Your father and I did some business in times past when I still worked in my daddy's gristmill. That was before I took up law work here in Bloomfield after the war. Most folks around Bloomfield sorely regretted what happened to your family durin' the conflict and I can be counted among em'. Everyone knows you bought your old place back so's you could bury your mother beside your pa and we're proud of you for that, Son."

I gently placed Jon David's head on the floor and rose to my feet. I had already closed my brother's eyes and the marshal covered him with a sheet that one of the deputies handed him. The bartender had brought the sheets from the hotel's storage closet and the deputies used them to cover the other three bodies as well.

"Ed Saltsberry is the bartender yonder and he purty' much filled me in on what took place here, Branch. He even volunteered that he'd testify that you and Jon David acted in self-defense, if he needs to. My deputies or I don't recognize any of the three dead, so we know none of em' were from Stoddard County." Virgil Huggins hesitated and studied my face for a while before he continued.

"Branch," he said, "this is a bad thing to happen in a small town like Bloomfield. We don't have much killin' here'a'bouts and it's gonna' stir folks up some. I've gleaned enough information from Saltsberry to understand the trouble that started this battle seems to go back to what happened during the war. Who is this man, Logan Ryan, who killed Jon David and then run?" I met Virgil Huggins' eyes and held them as I replied to his question.

"He was the Union Sergeant who carried out the hanging of my papa, Virgil." I replied honestly. The marshal's eyes reflected some confusion.

"But why would he and his gang want to kill you boys, this far down the road from the end of the conflict?" I shook my head.

"I don't rightly know, Virgil." I replied. "I have as many questions to ask the man as you. Maybe more." I added. Virgil Huggins regarded the hard look in my eyes, which I tried to hide. I had something else to discuss with him.

"Virgil, Jon David is wanted over in Ripley County on a false charge. A complicated and bad one, but false just the same. Since he can't be called on that now, I'd kinda' appreciate you and me keeping it between us? I'll get his name cleared one day in the future, and I don't want folks around here holding bad thoughts about him or the rest of our family until that's done." The marshal studied on my request.

"You gonna' bury him here beside your ma and pa?" he asked and I nodded my head.

"No one around here will hear anything bad about Jon David from me, Branch." he said. "I'll talk to the bartender and make sure he keeps his mouth buttoned too."

"Thanks, Virgil." I replied. "I'll make you a deal if you're interested?"

A Hard Life

"I'm listenin'." he said.

"When I find Ryan and he tells me why he did what he did tonight, I'll come back to Bloomfield and tell you. Just to clear the record."

"I suppose that means you're leavin' town and takin' all this trouble with you? Kin' you promise me your business with Ryan won't involve Bloomfield or Stoddard County folks, Branch? If you can assure me of that then me or my deputies don't need to go lookin' for Ryan?" I nodded my head.

"I've come into a good deal of money in the last three years, Virgil." I said quietly. "I'll spend it all, if need be, to bring Ryan to justice, wherever he runs. You don't need to be spending any of the Stoddard County tax money on the chore."

"Your justice, or the law's justice, Branch?" he inquired.

"Does it matter to you, Virgil?" I asked and he met my eyes again.

"Not as long as me or my deputies can stay out of it and you don't do nothin' to bring any of this down on me." he replied.

"I won't involve you or your deputies, Virgil, and I promise if it's up to me, this will be taken care of in a way that won't bring any trouble to you." We exchanged knowing looks and he nodded to me. He started to turn away and I reached to touch his arm for one more query.

"Virgil, there's a young lady upstairs in a room who came to attend Mama's internment. Would you post one of your deputies outside her room for the night…just in case?"

"Just in case what, Branch?" he inquired.

"I'd like to know the answer to that question too!" Virgil and I both turned to look up to the head of the stairs. Rosa Kate was standing there wearing a thick white robe tied tightly around her slim waist with a belt of the same color. I noticed that her hair was down long, a little disheveled, and her feet were bare.

I wondered how much more of mine and Virgil's conversation she had overheard, and I hoped not much She appeared ready to burst into tears and she was obviously very frightened and upset

"Branch, where is… Jon David?" she inquired in a timid low voice. The expression on my face at her inquiry must have told her, for her eyes went directly to the sheet covered form on the floor beside me.

I surmised then that she must have just appeared at the head of the stairs and had not heard much before her name was mentioned. Rosa Kate burst into tears and she suddenly sat down on the stairs with her face covered by her hands.

I hurried up the stairway toward her and she rose back up to meet me. Tears continued to overflow her eyes and streak down her face, but she met my eyes with hers. She held my arms when I drew close and gazed into my face; her pretty eyes filled with anguish, compassion, and something else I dared not even try to interpret.

She stared at me like that for several moments, conveying an unspoken concern for me that touched me deeply, then she put her face into my chest and burst into tears again as she encircled my waist with her arms and held me fiercely!

"What in the world happened, Branch?" she asked when we separated a little and her sobs had subsided some. She arched her back to look up into my face again.

"I heard shots," she continued, "but they seemed to come from outside the building. I was awakened from a sound sleep and never dreamed you and Jon David were involved! I kept hearing voices so I came out of my room to see what was happening."

Virgil Huggins had followed me up the staircase, but at a much slower pace. He stood quietly aside on the steps below us with his hat in his hands waiting patiently. I stepped back a little from Rosa Kate.

"Marshal Huggins, this is Rosa Kate Asbury. She's...." I hesitated just for a moment before I continued. "She's a very good friend to me and she was a friend of my mama's." A touch of confusion registered in her eyes at my statement, but she recovered and reached her tiny hand out to the marshal.

"Pleased to meet you Miss Asbury." Virgil said as he took her offered hand, holding it like a delicate teacup he might break if he gripped it too hard.

"I'm just sorry about the circumstances, Ma'am." he continued.

"She doesn't know any of the men down there except for Jon David, Virgil, and she only met him yesterday afternoon. I'd rather she was not involved in this matter at all. I'm hoping you and I see can see eye to eye on this thing."

"We have a deal, Branch." he said. "You keep your end and you and me won't have any trouble." he stared into my face for a moment and then nodded courteously to Rosa Kate.

"Ma'am," he said, "there'll be a trusted man posted in the hallway outside your room. You don't need to fret about anyone botherin' you for the rest of the night.." Rosa Kate nodded solemnly to Virgil and he donned his hat and made his way back down the steps.

"Virgil, I need to talk to you about something else." The marshal stopped and looked back at me when I said his name. "Would you mind waiting until I can walk Rosa Kate back to her room and make sure she's locked in good and tight?"

"I'll be downstairs, Branch." he replied.

"Branch, who shot Jon David and why? What is going on?" Rosa Kate asked me while I was escorting her back to her room. I pulled my Colt and went inside her room first to make certain no one was inside then I turned to her.

"Rosie, I'm going to make arrangements to take you back to Colorado first thing in the morning. I know you have lots of questions and I promise to tell you everything I know when we have time, and I feel that you're safe. You're going to have to trust me until I can be guaranteed you're protected! I'll wire McCloud to meet us and then I'll sit down and try to figure this horrible mess out. When I have some answers I'll tell you everything."

"Why do you fear for me, Branch?" she asked. "Why would someone want to hurt me, or you for that matter?"

"I hope no one wants to hurt you Rosa Kate." I replied. "I hope I'm just being paranoid, but that's what I have to find out, and I don't want to assume that you're not in danger and regret it later. I've lost most everyone I've ever cared about and I can't stand to think of something bad happening to you too." Rosa Kate regarded me closely and thought about what I had said.

"I trust you, Branch," she said finally, "and I'll let you do what you think is right, but I want you to take care of yourself too. I don't want to lose you either."

CHAPTER TWENTY-EIGHT

Virgil was waiting for me in the bar after I left Rosa Kate. "Eddie show up to stand guard in Miss Asbury's hallway?" he asked as I approached.

"He's there and he appears dependable." I replied.

"He is." he replied. "What else did you want to discuss with me, Branch?"

"Would you make arrangements with the undertaker to take care of Jon David?" I asked. "I want him buried beside Mama."

"You ain't stayin' to take care of your brother?" Virgil inquired.

"I don't know what Ryan's real intentions were last night," I replied, "and I'm worried about Miss Asbury. Until I know different I'm going to assume he was after all three of us and since I don't know where he is, or how many more men he has, I'm not taking any chances. Jon David wouldn't care if it were me or someone else that planted him. I'll come back some day and make my peace

A Hard Life

with him over not staying. I'll be able then to tell him what this night was all about and what I did about it."

"You promised me the same favor, Branch." Virgil reminded me, with a sly look in his eyes.

"I'll keep my promise, Virgil," I replied, "that is, if I live over my next encounter with Ryan "

"The barkeep said he'd never seen anyone draw faster or shoot straighter than you and your brother." Virgil said. "I'm bettin' you'll be back in Bloomfield some day after you deal with Ryan. I'll take care of your brother for you till' then, Son."

I took a piece of blank paper from my shirt pocket and with a stub of a pencil from the same pocket I drew an outline on the paper, wrote down several lines of script, turned it over and wrote Reuben Rosenthal's name and address on it, and then handed the paper to Virgil.

"Have the undertaker carve the headstone like my drawing, Virgil." I said. "I wrote Jon David's full name, birth and today's date, and what I wanted carved beneath it on the note also. He can send the bill to the attorney in St. Louis; his name's there on the back. I guarantee the undertaker will be paid whatever he charges." Virgil studied the paper I handed him and reached up to scratch his head beneath his hat.

"This is what you want on Jon David's headstone, Branch?" he inquired and I nodded.

"Exactly that, Virgil." I replied. "Word for word."

I reached down then, picked up Jon David's black hat and put it on my own head, replacing the one I was wearing, which I pitched down and left on one of the barroom tables.

I rented a covered buggy and paid a driver to take Rosa Kate and me to Cape Girardeau. We left Bloomfield right after daylight and while Rosa Kate rode inside I sat up by the driver, a man named Frank Johnson who was recommended to me by Virgil Huggins. I had my ten-gauge and a Winchester rifle either beside me, or held at the ready in my hands, the entire trip from Bloomfield to Cape Girardeau.

We arrived in Cape Girardeau late in the day without incident or mishap and transferred to a private passenger car on a train heading west. A week later McCloud and three armed men met our train in Cheyenne Wells, Colorado.

McCloud positioned Samuel Workman, the black cowboy, and two Cherokee warriors, who had formerly been trackers with the U.S. Cavalry, at each end of the passenger car. They each carried a Winchester rifle, plus all three men had a sidearm holstered on cartridge-filled gun belts. McCloud took a good look at me while Rosa Kate hugged him.

"You don't look like you've had any rest in over a week, Ben Branch." he said. "Get some sleep while we keep watch. There will be time to talk when you have rested."

I nodded to him and promptly stretched out in the aisle, between seats, in the center of the car, and fell instantly into a deep sleep. The passenger car was equipped with a small stateroom, including a bed, but that was where Rosa Kate slept.

The sound of the clacking wheels on rails awakened me several hours later. It was sometime deep into the night and only moonlight through the windows and one

A Hard Life

small kerosene lamp illuminated the shadowy passenger car. I looked out both sides of the moving trail trying to determine where we might be.

"We'll arrive in Denver a couple of hours after daylight." McCloud said quietly from his position in the shadows a couple of seats behind me. The Cherokee leaned forward and his face materialized from the darkness. "Rosa Kate's asleep." he added. I moved back toward him and took a seat in the aisle across from McCloud.

"Everything been quiet?" I asked. I couldn't see his face in the shadows, but I saw his hat move as he nodded an affirmative response.

"I have some sandwiches and water." McCloud said, and handed me a paper sack containing either beef or fried eggs on thick sourdough bread, plus a large canteen. I chose a beef sandwich and devoured it, chasing it down with long pulls from the canteen.

"Your appetite appears intact, Ben Branch." the Cherokee said in quiet tones.

"I've been a mite preoccupied with staying alive and keeping Rosa Kate safe, so food wasn't so important until you and your men came on board." I replied.

"I assume you're still keeping a guard close to Katherine?" I asked.

"The two men you befriended, Lonny Mossberg and Curly Griffin, have turned out to be valuable in my eyes also, Ben Branch. I left Katherine's safety in their hands when I received your wire to meet you." I smiled some to myself. It made me feel good that McCloud agreed with my assessment of the two Missouri men.

"You did well in Missouri, Ben Branch." the Cherokee said. "I'm proud of you and I'm sincerely sorry for what happened to your brother. Rosa Kate told me about the shooting while you were sleeping."

McCloud had never said such a thing to me. Praise for anyone from the stoic Cherokee was rare indeed, but to hear it twice in the same conversation was momentous.

"My brother and I talked about you the day before he was killed." I said thoughtfully as I stared out the window and watched the shadowy, moonlighted prairie slide by the passenger car window. Jon David's image was clear in my mind and the pain and loss I felt anew was intense. I wondered if that pain would ever subside?

"Jon David said you sounded like a man he could get along with." I turned to look directly at the Cherokee. "I agreed with him at the time, McCloud. You would have liked one another, I'm quite sure." McCloud didn't respond so we rode in silence for several minutes, each of us wrapped in our own thoughts.

"Rosa Kate wasn't sure about the details of the gunfight, Ben Branch." McCloud finally broke the easy silence. "Did you take a man's life?"

The question was not asked in a judgmental way. I knew from his tone that McCloud would not have been offended if I had refused to answer him.

"I did, McCloud." I replied. "He was attempting to bring a shotgun to bear on me and I shot him three times. I don't regret what I had to do, but it's not something I'm taking any pride in."

"Do you know the man's name you killed, Ben Branch?" he asked, and I turned away from the window and looked at the Cherokee. His face was still mostly hidden in the shadows and I couldn't read his eyes. I shook my head.

A Hard Life

"No, I guess I don't." I admitted. "The marshal or his deputies in Bloomfield didn't recognize any of the three dead men and I surely don't remember seeing any of them before, except Ryan." I waited on a response from McCloud and it was a few moments coming.

"You should know the name of any man you kill, Ben Branch." he said quietly.

I thought about what McCloud had said and although I didn't quite understand his reasoning, for some reason I agreed with it.

"That's another question I can be asking Ryan some day, McCloud."

"So you intend to hunt Ryan down in retaliation for what he did to your brother?" McCloud asked.

"Yes I will." My words were innocent enough, but the underlying tone in my voice was unmistakable.

"When you find Ryan, will you turn him over to the authorities?" McCloud inquired.

"I doubt it." I replied. McCloud was silent for another several moments.

"A lot of men are looking for Ryan, Ben Branch." McCloud finally said. I turned my face to him in the darkness and waited for him to explain his statement.

"Harley LaMarr and Sheriff Kennard Young were both murdered right after you left Denver to take your mother back to Missouri. Ryan disappeared at the same time and Frank Albright has issued a double murder warrant for his capture. Wanted posters have gone all over the country and Grayson put up a five thousand dollar reward for Ryan's capture, dead or alive."

I was astounded at what McCloud told me for it didn't make much logical sense to me. What possible connection did Ryan have to Harley LaMarr, the Secretary-Treasurer of Asbury Industries? What possible reason would Ryan have for killing Sheriff Kennard Young? I was certain if McCloud had known the answers to these questions he would already have shared that information with me.

"Frank Albright is the Denver sheriff now?" I asked instead and McCloud nodded. I remembered that Albright was the deputy that seemed to be close friends to Grayson. Since that was the thought in my mind I asked McCloud another question.

"Did Grayson pull strings to get Albright appointed sheriff?"

"Probably," McCloud answered, "everyone knows Albright always took more orders from Grayson than he ever did from Kennard Young."

A HARD LIFE

CHAPTER TWENTY-NINE

We arrived in Denver about nine a.m., where we were met by Grayson, Katherine, Lonny Mossberg, Curly Griffin, and the newly appointed sheriff, Frank Albright. Katherine hugged Rosa Kate to her and nodded to me. Her look toward me was not accusatory, but it was serious and lacked any cordiality. Grayson barely acknowledged a grunt and a nod in my direction and Frank Albright didn't even look at me.

Grayson, Katherine, Albright, and McCloud ushered Rosa Kate into a waiting carriage and they whisked her away toward town leaving me standing on the siding with Curly Griffin and Lonny Mossberg. I saw Rosa Kate turn her head to look back at me from the fast-moving carriage, and then she turned away again.

"You boys lose your guard duty jobs?" I inquired with a touch of a grin to my two friends. I handed my shotgun to Curly and shouldered the Winchester while I slung my duffel bag over my other shoulder.

"Suppose so, until McCloud calls for us again." Lonny answered. "That Cherokee don't say much, but he makes it crystal clear what he expects." I nodded my agreement to his statement.

"If it means anything, he bragged on both of you." I told them. "First time I ever heard him brag about anybody before, so the two of you should take pride in it."

As we strolled the short distance to town the two men filled me in on what had happened while I had been gone. According to them the lumber business had been going smoothly and we had good stands of corn, wheat, and sugar beets in the fields.

"I guess you noticed that Frank Albright is the new sheriff?" Lonny asked and I nodded.

"McCloud told me about the two murders and that Grayson had played politics to get Albright appointed. They still pinnin' the killings on Logan Ryan?" I asked and both men nodded their heads.

"Ryan shot my brother back in Bloomfield, Missouri a week ago." I said and both their eyes flew open in surprise.

"Ryan followed you all the way back to Missouri?" Lonny asked in a confused tone.

"I suppose." I replied. "I can't tell you boys all of mine and Ryan's history, even though I trust both of you completely. I suspect there's things that have happened to both of you in the past that is none of my business, so I'd appreciate it if you wouldn't ask me much about Ryan." Both men nodded and looked questioningly at one another.

A Hard Life

"What?" I asked, knowing they wanted to tell me something related to what I had said. Curly was the first of the two to speak.

"Word around was that Ryan had himself a girlfriend for the short time he was in town. Her name's Lynne Black and she's one of the whores over at Mandy's."

I was aware that Mandy's was the only hotel in town not owned by Grayson Asbury. Big Mandy Mathison had moved from Kansas City to Denver during the gold rush of the sixties and made a good living selling her special services to the miners. She had used her profits to build herself a small hotel on Main Street, and now she mostly sat on a big overstuffed couch in the middle of her hotel lobby keeping track of her stable of young whores.

"Frank Albright went over there sayin' he wanted to question Lynn, supposedly to see if she might know Ryan's whereabouts. He musta' got a little too rough with her to suit Lynn's boss, because Mandy pulled a Smith & Wesson pistol on the new sheriff and ordered him clean out of her hotel! Told im' she'd shoot im' on sight if he ever came back! Whole damn town thought it was the funniest thing that's happened in Denver in months!" Curly added with a smile. I smiled myself at the thought of Frank Albright being kicked out of Mandy's funhouse by Big Mandy herself.

The next morning I went to my office and attacked the pile of forms and papers that seemed to have happily bred and multiplied in my absence. Around eleven, after I had surrounded and gut shot the most important ones in the stack, I decided to take a break and go check on the progress of Papa's ol' pig stickin' knife.

"Good Morning Mister Walker." Fritz Solingen greeted me when I entered his foundry and knife shop. "I would wager you're here to pick up your knife?"

"Yes sir, I am. That is, if it's ready?" I replied to the friendly Austrian native. He smiled and nodded as he reached beneath the counter and produced an antler-handled knife in a carved leather scabbard. The scabbard was richly polished and smelled of fresh dye and leather stain. I slid the old familiar-shaped blade from its new home and admired its newly polished finish and razor honed edges.

"Papa might not recognize his old blade." I commented as I turned the knife over in my hand admiring the professional finish work of the new antler handle plus the brightly polished brass hand guard Mister Solingen had crafted.

"All I did was add pretty ribbons to a beautiful lady, Mister Walker." Fritz Solingen replied. "The real beauty of that knife, to someone like me, is in the steel and I have never worked with any better. I can make steel comparable to that old blade, but I can't surpass it. I doubt that anyone can."

"You've far outdistanced my expectations Mister Solingen." I said. "Do I owe you more than our bargained price?" He smiled and shook his head.

"It was my pleasure to work for you, Mister Walker." he replied and then his smile left his face leaving a more serious expression. "I do have one request?" He waited for my reply and I nodded solemnly to him.

"Yes' sir'?" I inquired

"If you should ever dishonor that blade by doing something wrong with it, please, for my sake, Mister

A Hard Life

Walker, bury it in a place where it will never be found. I would hate for it to be traced back to me and my workmanship." He held my eyes with his and I nodded an affirmative to him.

"I can do that, Mister Solingen." I replied. "You can count on it."

The board meeting was held on May 28, the last Saturday of the month. The ones attending the meeting in the bank's boardroom was Katherine, Grayson, myself, Rosa Kate and McCloud.

A report of the company's fiscal year earnings was reported by John Huntington, an accountant that had worked under Harley Lamar. Huntington had been appointed the interim Secretary/Treasurer of Asbury Industries by Katherine after LaMarr's murder. The first agenda item of the board meeting was Katherine's motion to appoint Huntington the permanent position, without making him a voting member of the board of directors. Grayson seemed surprised at her motion and could have stopped it, since he and Katherine were the only voting members at the time. He refrained however, and then when Katherine made a motion to appoint Rosa Kate and me as voting members, again Grayson went along.

With mine and Rosa Kate's appointment as voting board members Grayson brought up the fact that the board of directors was even in number again and then Katherine pulled the ace from her sleeve, so to speak. Katherine made a motion to appoint McCloud as a voting board member and I watched as Grayson realized he had been trumped! With Rosa Kate and me already appointed, Grayson could not stop the motion, so McCloud became the fifth voting board member of Asbury Industries. Grayson could not hide his anger at Katherine's brilliant political maneuver and he left the boardroom in a huff immediately afterwards without saying anything to anyone.

Three nights later I walked into Mandy's Hotel about eight o'clock in the evening. I walked directly toward a big red couch sitting in the center of the lobby. A mahogany bar went around two sides of the brightly lit room to my right and behind the couch, and to my left was a red carpeted grand staircase leading up to three floors of rooms. A piano player was beating out tunes on a big upright piano in the front corner of the hotel lobby.

A large woman dressed all in white was sitting on the couch drinking wine from a fluted glass. What of her hair I could see, beneath an enormous white hat, was dyed a rich black and someone had artfully made up her face with rouge, lipstick and eye color. Overall, and from a distance, she was an attractive lady. However, when you drew close, as I was now, she wasn't so pretty, but she wasn't ugly either.

"Well, bless my Aunt Molly's roses, if it's not the handsome and rich, Mister Ben Branch Walker." She said in a voice as smooth as Kentucky bourbon and with an accent relative to the same state.

"I don't believe you've ever been in my establishment before." she continued. Would you care for a glass of champagne, Mister Walker? I have it imported from Paris, France." I smiled at her and shook my head.

"Thank you, no." I replied. "Please call me Branch, Ma'am. Would you mind if I sat and talked to you about something?" She didn't say yes immediately, but rather studied my face momentarily with big intelligent eyes.

"You're not here for what all the other men come for, are you, Branch?" She asked and then waved at the couch beside her. "Please sit down with me and you may call me Mandy. I'll have all my girls green with envy when they see you sitting and talking with me."

"I suspect they stay pretty envious of you most of the time, Mandy." I countered and she smiled as she took another sip of her wine.

"Are you sure you don't want something to drink, Branch. It's on the house, along with anything else you might think of." She added with a smile.

"A talk is all I'm requesting at the time, Mandy. You might change your mind about being so cordial when you hear me out." I said with a smile aimed at matching hers.

"Well, Branch Walker, I'm not much on beatin' around the bush, so to speak, so why don't you ask me what you came to ask me?" My smile got some broader at her remark and so did hers.

"I would like to make an employment offer to one of your ladies, Mandy," I said with a serious expression now, "and I didn't want to do it until I had asked you about it first." Mandy's smile evaporated and a hard glint entered her eyes.

"If you were Grayson Asbury, I'd already be throwin' you out on your cute behind right now! However, I've judged you to be cut from a different cloth than that slimy bastard, so I'll hear you out! What do you want one of my girls to do for you anyway? Be your damned secretary?" I looked away from Mandy and began to chuckle in spite of myself and soon she joined me with a merry laugh. I looked back at her and we both became serious again.

"I can't tell you, Mandy." I said. "You'll just have to trust that I have no bad intentions in store for her and I will pay her handsomely. If she decides to work for me, it will be her own free will decision and if she owes you anything I will clear her debt to you." Mandy stared into my eyes with a distrusting glare, but then her look changed.

"My girls don't owe me a damn thing, Branch! They're free to come and go as they please. I don't own slaves and I can't abide the ones in my type of business that do. If you make an offer to one of my girls and she accepts it, then she's free to be your employee, with my blessing, as long as it's a different line of work than mine. With those conditions, if you hire one of my girls, you won't owe me a red damn cent!"

"Done." I replied quickly. "Would you ask Lynne Black to come to see me in my office tomorrow, Mandy? Eleven o'clock would work well for me. After we've discussed my offer I'll take her to Grayson's best restaurant for lunch and then we'll return here so she can give both of us her answer."

"You're goin' to escort one of my girls to Grayson Asbury's restaurant to have lunch with you, Branch? In broad daylight!" She asked quite loudly. "What will Lady Katherine and her snooty daughter think about that?" I lowered my head a little and locked eyes with Mandy.

"Katherine's a lady, just like you, Mandy, and so is her daughter, Rosa Kate! Have you ever met or talked to either one of them?" Mandy's eyes went angry like mine for an instant and then she relented.

A Hard Life

"No I guess I haven't, Branch," she replied, "and it's not fair for me to make judgments like I just did. Most of all, me! Please forgive me for what I said? If you do take one of my girls out for lunch at a fancy Denver restaurant, I'll never say another bad thing about you, or your family, and you can bet I won't be allowin' it to be said around me neither!" I stood up and replaced Jon David's black hat on my head, then tipped it to Mandy.

"Persuade Lynne Black to come visit me tomorrow, Mandy." I said "If she decides to refuse my offer, at least she'll get to enjoy a very expensive free lunch, and then she can enjoy being the talk of Denver for weeks to come!"

A HARD LIFE

CHAPTER THIRTY

At ten minutes before eleven the next morning I heard a light knock on the door to my office. I went to the door and opened it to find an attractive young lady with darkish auburn hair and big green eyes. Those eyes appeared nervous, but she held her chin high and met my eyes with an air of confidence.

"Good day, Ma'am." I said to her. "Are you Miss Lynne Black?"

"Yes, Sir, I am, Mister Walker," she answered, "I understand you wanted to talk to me?"

"That's correct." I replied. "May I call you Lynne, and you can call me, Branch."

"Branch it is, and yes, you may call me, Lynne." she replied. I showed her to a chair. Lynne was dressed in a pretty summer dress that reached to the floor and she had a stylish little hat atop her hair that was brushed out long and reached nearly to her waist.

"Lynne," I said after I had taken a seat behind my desk, "I'm going to get directly to the point of why I've asked you to my office. Do you think of yourself as a

A Hard Life

courageous lady?" She studied me and my question for a while before answering, which demonstrated an intelligence I had hoped for.

"Why, yes, sir...I mean, yes, Branch. I do consider myself courageous." she replied. "I have been on my own since I was twelve and I have not had a good life, as most folks would consider good. There are few secrets in Denver and probably fewer between us, Branch. You know what I do for a living and you should know that it takes a special kind of courage to survive in my world." I nodded my head to her answer.

"You had a relationship with Logan Ryan?" I inquired and her green eyes became suspicious.

"Is that what this is about?" she said, her voice rising in volume some. "Denver's new sheriff came to talk to me about that and he didn't want to just talk. My face is still bruised under my make-up!"

"I'll be completely honest with you, Lynne." I replied. "I probably do want the same thing as the sheriff, but for different reasons, and with a completely different approach. I suspect if I was dumb enough, or crude enough, to hurt you like he did, Mandy Mathison would gut me with a dull knife, after she had shot me full of holes with her Smith & Wesson!" Lynne smiled at my remark and the anger disappeared from her eyes.

"Logan Ryan paid for me to spend time with him Branch, which I did, because that is how I make my living. We didn't talk much and I haven't a clue as to where he might be now."

"I didn't expect you to know that, Lynne, and now we're getting to the difference in mine and Sheriff Albright's intentions. Do you like to travel, Lynne?" She looked quite surprised at my question, and again she thought about it before she answered.

"I would like to, Branch." she replied. "I haven't done much of it. I'm barely twenty."

"That's what I'd like to hire you to do, Lynne. I'd like to pay all your expenses, plus a generous salary, for you to travel by train and stagecoach to several cities back in Illinois, Missouri, or maybe Kentucky and Tennessee." Lynne Black regarded me suspiciously at my offer, but I could see that the idea of my proposal appealed to her.

"Alone?" she inquired and when I nodded my head she continued. "What else would I have to do besides travel to those cities?" she asked cautiously.

"Ask questions in the right places and pretend that you're looking for a lost lover." I replied. I recognized it in her intelligent green eyes when she realized what I was after.

"You think that I can find Logan Ryan." She stated and I nodded again.

"I can practically guarantee it, Lynne." I replied. You see, most of we males are more vain than we would ever admit, even if you held a gun on us. Which means that if a pretty young lady came hundreds of miles searching for one of us, telling everyone that would listen that she can't live without us, we would most assuredly allow ourselves to be found."

"And when I find him, I turn him over to the nearest lawman? Is that what I would do, Branch?"

"Not if you're as smart as I think you are, Lynne." I replied. "Let's examine your options. If you turned him over to the law, he might escape, or pay his way out of trouble. You know how the law works most of the time.

Ryan wouldn't be happy with you, to say the least. One of his men may take offense at you turning in their friend to the law and exact recompense in various ways also, even if Ryan stayed in jail. You would receive Grayson Asbury's reward of five thousand dollars all right, and maybe that would make it worth the risk." I stopped and let her go over what I had said.

"Or?" she inquired with her big eyes wide.

"Or, you could simply wire me when you discover where Ryan is. You wouldn't have to confront him or take any chances. Within days, or a week or two at most, I would be there to take care of Ryan, and his men, and you could just disappear. You would still receive Grayson's five thousand dollar reward, but then you would also receive a five thousand dollar kicker from me. You could double your money for half the danger? You tell me which is the smarter move, Lynne?"

"Why do you hate him so, Branch?" Lynne asked and her eyes said that she was only curious. I wondered if it was safe to tell her my reasons, but I decided that it probably didn't make much difference anyway.

"I have evidence that he probably murdered my mother, and I watched him murder my only brother, and my father, with my own eyes, Lynne. You can bet I hate him, and if you don't help me find him, then I'll just find another way. I wouldn't blame you for being afraid of him, Lynne. What I'm asking you to do you will take all the courage you can muster. I won't try to hide the danger that might be awaiting you. However, this I know, Lynne. You're too smart and pretty to live out your life doing what you're doing and I could be offering you a gateway to a new life. If you decide to turn me down, I'm just as sure that one way or another I'll find Ryan some day. Will you help me?"

"Will you still take me to lunch if I refuse your offer?" she asked. Her green eyes were both challenging and lovely just then. Heck, she was a lovely woman all over; I had to admit it to myself!

"You bet I will, Lynne." I replied. "Whatever you want to eat, and we'll stay for as long as you want to stay, whether your answer to me is yes or no!" She regarded me for several moments as she thought about my proposal.

"Then it's yes!" she replied. "I'll do my best to find Logan Ryan for you, and only you, Branch."

We left my office and exited the bank building headed for the stable a few buildings down where I had already arranged for a buggy to be waiting for us. I took Lynne's left hand and placed it on my right forearm to escort her across the street. A carriage I recognized was coming down the street and I waited with Lynne holding to my arm until McCloud recognized me and pulled the buggy to a halt in front of us. Katherine and Rosa Kate were in the buggy seat staring at us when the carriage came to a stop.

'Katherine, Rosa Kate," I said, as I touched my hat brim. "I would like to introduce you to Miss Lynne Black. She's a young lady that I have just employed to work for me. Lynne, this is Katherine and Rosa Kate Asbury. The solemn fellow up in the driver's seat is McCloud." The Cherokee touched his hat brim and nodded to Lynne.

"We're pleased to meet you, Miss Black." Katherine said with a smile. "Your summery dress makes even Denver's drab streets prettier today."

A Hard Life

"Thank you, Ma'am." Lynne said in a low voice. She seemed reticent to say much more.

"I've invited Miss Black to Grayson's restaurant for lunch to celebrate her decision to accept my employment offer." I said. "Would the three of you care to join us?"

"No, we have a previous appointment, Branch." Rosa Kate said quickly. Her smile was there, but it lacked the warmth of her mother's, at least toward me. She turned a friendlier smile to Lynne.

"I'm sorry we can't have lunch with you, Lynne." she said sweetly to her. "I would like to get to know you better. I hope you order the most expensive dish Grayson's serves. Branch hardly ever invites anyone to lunch and you should take advantage of him when you have an opportunity."

Just then one of the blooded mares McCloud was driving flinched and the buggy lurched forward a little.

"Whoa!" McCloud said rather loudly and the mare quickly settled down.

"Horsefly." The Cherokee said as he stared hard at me.

"We must be on our way, Branch." Katherine said. "It was nice meeting you, Miss Black. I hope we can have a visit soon." Lynne nodded to her and McCloud clucked to the team and they went on down the street. I noticed Rosa Kate glancing back over the buggy seat as they disappeared around the corner in front of the bank.

While Lynne and I were waiting on our orders to be served I noticed she wasn't saying much and she seemed preoccupied.

"Is there anything wrong, Lynne?" I asked and she looked up at me with tear-filled eyes.

"I didn't expect for you, or Mrs. Asbury and her daughter, to treat me so nice, Branch." she replied. "It's something I've never experienced before." I really didn't know how to respond at first so I thought about it for a while before I said anything.

"Lynne, we're all just people trying to get through this life. I have money now, but before three years ago my mama and I were dirt poor. There were times when we weren't sure we would have enough to eat. My mother washed clothes for my uncle and his family to keep a roof over our heads. My brother and I worked sunup to sundown for my uncle for nothing except the right to farm a small parcel of land for our own food. I can't judge you for how you have chosen to get by and survive in your situation. Katherine and Rosa Kate haven't seen the other side of the world that you and I have seen, but that doesn't mean they're not aware that it is there. If either of them had been faced with your situation, and had your options, they may have ended up surviving the same way you have, and that is why they're nice to you and not judgmental."

"I'm so ashamed of what I do, Branch." she said quietly.

"Then now is the time for you to make a change, Lynne." I replied. "I'm not setting any time limits on this project. There's a ten thousand dollar prize waiting for you if you're successful in locating Ryan, but as long as you're looking for him and you don't give up I'll continue to pay all your expenses, and you can bank your salary if you choose. Either way this goes, you should have a nest egg at the end of this that you can use to change your life to something you won't be ashamed of. You can move where folks don't know your past if it bothers you." She

A Hard Life

nodded and I noticed that the tears had gone away now. There was something else that I worried about.

"Lynne, we have to find a way to communicate so that our arrangement is kept secret. Your safety depends on Ryan never knowing that you and I are associated in any way. I'm going to ask Mandy to be my broker for any communication between you and me. We'll have to use the telegraph to communicate so we'll work out a simple code so that telegraph operators won't recognize what we're really communicating, because I don't always trust them. For example we'll designate Logan Ryan as your Uncle Henry. You might wire Mandy and say this." I took a piece of paper out of my jacket pocket, wrote on it and handed it to Lynne.

"Mandy, I'm in Elgin, Illinois visiting my aunt Martha. Uncle Henry isn't here so I will probably leave for Chicago in a week to look for him there."

"Mandy will send me the telegram and from it I'll know where you are and where you're going next. Do you understand?" Lynne nodded her head and I could see the excitement building in her eyes.

"I'll open an account at Katherine's bank in your name, Lynne." I continued. "When you wire Mandy to let her know where you are, and where you're going next, you can ask her to deposit whatever your accumulated expenses are. I'll make a deposit here and then you can wire the bank and tell them to transfer funds to another bank where you will be for a few days."

Lynne was nodding her head as I talked and I could tell she understood how the arrangements would work.

The next day I escorted Lynne to the railroad depot and waved to her as she boarded the east train headed for Illinois. I had no idea if Ryan was there, but it would be a good place for Lynne to begin her search.

A HARD LIFE

CHAPTER THIRTY-ONE

Two days later McCloud was sitting his horse alongside the road in front of Katherine's, waiting for me. He stopped me as I rode past on my way to work.

"Ride with me, Ben Branch." he said and I pulled Rascal off the road and followed the Cherokee through the open woods. I was puzzled at the somber man's actions, but I had learned early on not to question McCloud or his motives. When we got to the river he turned right and we rode downstream for a mile or so. I remembered that just beyond a bend ahead of us the river widened and became shallower. We rounded the bend and I was astonished to see someone standing in the middle of the river in thigh-deep water casting toward the far shore with a long fly rod!

McCloud stopped, then turned his horse and gave me a stern look as he rode back past me in the direction we had come from. I was puzzled until the person in the river turned to look at us and I recognized Rosa Kate in a man's flannel shirt and a pair of trousers!

Her long dark hair was tied into a ponytail and hung down her back. The trousers were far too big for her and she had them snugged tightly around her waist with a wide leather belt. She waved to me and gestured to a spot on the bank downstream. I saw her saddled horse tied in the shade of a large ponderosa pine to my right.

I dismounted from Rascal and left him grazing with the reins over the saddle horn while I found a large flat rock near the edge of the rushing river. There I sat down to watch as Rosa Kate was making roll casts to the far side. She followed the floating fly with the rod parallel to the water until the lure suddenly disappeared beneath the surface. Rosa Kate raised the rod tip smartly and the rod bent sharply toward a struggling trout trying desperately to throw the offending hook from its upper jaw. She played the fish expertly until she could reach beneath its belly, holding it there until she gently plucked the small hook from its jaw, and placed the fish in a wicker basket she carried on a strap around her neck and over her shoulder.

I watched her catch two more trout in a similar fashion and smiled as I heard her excited laughter as she played the leaping trout in the fast current. She placed the last trout into her basket and then made her way carefully back across the river to where I was waiting.

She was smiling happily as she made her way toward me and I marveled at how beautiful she was, even in a baggy man's shirt and trousers that would have wrapped around her twice! Huge snow-capped mountains were framed beautifully behind her and the rushing river sounded wild and free.

A Hard Life

"I like your wading pants." I said as she sat on a flat rock and removed her boots to pour the water from them. She rolled the wet trouser cuffs higher until they came half way to her knees and then pitched her water-soaked boots to the grassy shore, leaving her feet bare.

"So do I." she replied with a little laugh. "I borrowed them from McCloud and I doubt he will ever ask for them back."

"The shirt too." I commented. "It goes well with the pants." The shirt was heavy cotton in a black and red checkerboard pattern. I had seen McCloud wear it before.

"Have you ever had trout for breakfast, Branch?" she asked. "I took fly fishing lessons in college, believe it or not! Did you notice I was using the fly rod you gave me our first Christmas together?" I nodded.

"You handle it like a professional, Rosie, if you can take the word of someone who has never seen a professional fly caster before." I replied and she smiled again.

"If you have dry matches, I have a frying pan and some cornmeal somewhere near here where McCloud left them." she said.

"Does your mother know where you are and what you're doing?" I asked. Rosa Kate stood in her bare feet and her fists on her hips.

"I'm not a little girl that has to tell her mother everywhere I go and everything I do all the time, Branch Walker!" she declared and then smiled brightly at me again. "I'm sure McCloud has blabbed it to her by now anyhow." she added.

Near where I had left Rascal we found a canvas bag containing a fry pan, a small sack of cornmeal, some bacon wrapped in brown paper, and a saltshaker. There were matches in the canvas bag also.

I gathered some dry driftwood and soon had a small fire blazing hotly. I removed my dress jacket and threw it over a nearby log while Rosa Kate started the bacon frying in the skillet. I looked down and frowned at my previously polished boots that now looked as if I had been riding herd for a week.

"If I had known we were going fishing I'd have worn my work boots, Rosie." I said and she looked down at my expensive hand sewn boots.

"You might as well take them off, Branch. I want to see if you can still catch trout with just your hands." I smiled at her as I remembered our first day together.

"That's been a long time ago, Rosie." I replied. "I might have forgotten how to do that."

"Have you forgotten how to do this?" she said, reaching her arms around my neck and pulling my lips to hers! Our kiss lasted for a long time and my ears were ringing when she released me. She smiled at my surprised expression and moved away from me and back to the fire to tend to the sizzling bacon in the skillet.

"What was that all about?" I said as I sat down beside my jacket. Rosie looked up from the frying bacon to stare at me.

"If you can't figure that out, Branch," she replied, "I'm wondering how you found your way out of bed this morning." She continued to stare at me as if there was something I was supposed to say in return, but I suppose my brain wasn't firing too clearly at the time, for I couldn't think of a thing to say.

A Hard Life

"Let's just say that I didn't enjoy seeing you in the company of another pretty girl, Branch Walker! That's enough of an explanation for the time being." I nodded but words still did not form in my mind.

"Do you have a knife?" she asked finally. "McCloud forgot to put one with the skillet and I need something to clean the trout." I nodded and reached behind me Her eyes widened as I withdrew the big blade from its scabbard.

"Holy Toledo!" she exclaimed, "I only need to cut a trout's throat, not skin a buffalo!"

It did not dawn on me what I had done until I watched Rosie pull one of the fish from her wicker basket to begin the simple cleaning operation of a trout. I hurried over to her and grabbed her right wrist before the first cut was made.

"Don't Rosie!" I said and she looked at me with alarm. I gently removed the big knife from her hand and held it as she stared at me with a confused expression.

"What's wrong, Branch?" she inquired. "I can handle a knife without cutting myself."

"I'm sure you can, Rosie." I replied. I tried to meet her questioning eyes, but I couldn't force myself. I realized suddenly this was a defining moment in my life. I could have made some lame excuse for taking the knife from her and one of the most wonderful mornings of my life could have continued. I realized my dishonesty with Rosa Kate had to end sometime and whether or not it was right or wrong, I decided to end it now.

"But not this knife." I said and I turned away from her and walked down to the river. Rosa Kate looked at the trout for a while and then replaced it into her basket and dropped it to the ground. She didn't say anything and I stood with my back to her for several moments. Somehow she knew I had something to tell her and she waited.

"Rosie, your father didn't die on a Missouri battlefield like the war record shows." I spoke without turning or looking at her.

"Jon David killed your father in his tent while he was sleeping, and he did it with this very knife. I was there and I watched him do it, Rosie!" I heard her gasp and I turned toward her. Her hand was covering her mouth and her eyes were filled with shock and horror at what I had just said. She stood staring at me as if I was a complete stranger to her.

"Rosie, Jon David was only fifteen and I was seven!" I continued in an anguished tone. "I didn't realize what my brother was going to do, but I couldn't have stopped him if I had known! Please try and understand what was going though Jon David's mind, and mine! We had watched our papa hung and murdered on your father's orders! Our Mama had to stand and watch it happen, Rosie!" I hesitated as the tears began to spill from her eyes and run down her flushed cheeks.

"Can you imagine what a horrible experience like that does to a boy?" I continued. "Having to stand and watch as your father is murdered, and maybe even worse to have to watch your mother watch it, and go through such a horror and not be able to do a single thing to stop it?" Rosie's hand had left her mouth and she was staring coldly at me.

"Jon David stood and watched your father break my right arm, and then try to apologize to my father for doing it only moments before he gave the order to execute him! Can you picture that in your mind, Rosie?"

I was practically shouting by now and she couldn't stand it any longer! She turned to run, but I caught her by the arm. She fought me hard, but I grabbed her other arm and held her, not allowing her to run away from me.

"I love you, Rosie!" I practically shouted into her face as she struggled to break free from me. "I've loved you from the first moment I saw you!" She stopped struggling with me then and glared at me with look of pure rage.

"You love me?" she exclaimed through clenched teeth. "You love me?" she repeated. "You tell me how you and your brother murdered my father and then you try to tell me you love me!" I dropped my head and my eyes from the rage and pure hatred reflected in her eyes now!

"Turn me loose, damn you!" she cried and jerked her arms free from me. Then Rosa Kate slapped me hard on the left cheek. It wasn't a gentle slap from an offended female either, it was a blow meant to inflict pain, if not injury. I took the blow and raised my eyes to her. She saw the hurt and sudden anger reflected in them, but she slapped me again, even harder this time.

"Get away from me, Branch!" she said, her voice more controlled and quieter now. There was a tone of finality in her words that chilled my heart in my chest.

"Get away and leave me alone while I think about what you've told me!" she continued.

"If you don't leave I will hit you again and you might be forced to hit me back, then I will hate you forever!" I recognized these were going to be Rosie's final words to me.

I nodded soberly to her, turned away and walked stiffly to my horse. I pulled Rascal's reins down free from the saddle horn and led him away up the path back toward the road.

I didn't go to Denver to work that day, nor the next day, nor for several days thereafter. I rode back to Grayson's house after leaving Rosa Kate standing alone by the river. I changed clothes, gathered together some supplies, and rode north into the mountains.

Maria Ortega tried to question me as I packed food, water, extra cartridges, a slicker, and a small bag of horse grain into a bedroll, tying it securely behind Rascal's saddle. I slid my Winchester into a scabbard on the right side of the saddle and stuck the ten-gauge into another on the left.

"Where are you going, Senor Branch?" she asked and when I didn't answer her, she asked, "When will you return?" I looked down at her after mounting Rascal.

"I won't be back, Maria." That was all I said and she appeared frightened as I rode away.

A HARD LIFE

CHAPTER THIRTY-TWO

I rode to the Cherokee village from which Aatonyah had been kidnapped by Clifton McCarty. I wanted to tell her people what had happened to her. The leader of the small group greeted me suspiciously at first, but when I told him why I had come, he invited me to stay and have meals with them.

The Chief and others were very somber when I relayed what had happened to Aatonyah. Her mother and father were grief-stricken, at first, but then regained their composure and thanked me for coming. The chief, a man named Rain-in-the-Face, thanked me also for bringing the word to them and inquired about McCloud. I told him that McCloud was fine, but I had not told him that I was riding to their village. The chief appeared curious why I came alone, but was polite enough not to ask. I stayed in the village as their guest for two more days before I left.

I made camp that night on a wild little stream a few miles south of the Cherokee village. I slept late and was eating breakfast the next morning when I detected movement on the ridge above me. I remained sitting on a large rock, but my hand was just above the Colt Peacemaker on my right side. I recognized the rider as soon as he materialized into a clearing above me. It was McCloud.

"Why did you come?" I asked after the Cherokee had poured himself a cup of my hot coffee without even asking. He drank from my only cup I had sat down beside the fire ring.

"You need to come back with me to Denver." he said as he sipped the hot coffee.

"Why." I asked sarcastically. "Didn't Rosa Kate tell you what I confessed to her?"

"Yes, she told us." he replied without any emotion.

"By us, I assume you mean yourself and Katherine?" I inquired and he nodded as he took another sip of the hot coffee. He had squatted on his heels with his rifle in his right hand across his bent legs.

"Did you come to settle with me, McCloud?" I asked and my hand was not far from the butt of my Colt. McCloud met my eyes with his dark ones. He had not missed my inference and his eyes took in the position of my right hand.

"That is the second time you have challenged me, Ben Branch." he said solemnly. His rifle was pointed away from me and he made no effort to move it.

"The first time was when I found you and Aatonyah together and you asked me if Grayson had sent me. I was insulted then because I thought I had shown you before that day that I was your friend. I dismissed that insult because of your age and experience, but now you doubt me again. Don't you realize that I care as much for you as I would if you were my younger brother, or maybe even

A Hard Life

my son?" I was both astounded at what McCloud had said and mortified that I had insulted a man that I respected above anyone I had ever known outside my own family.

"The confession that your brother was the man who killed James Asbury was not information new to me or Katherine." he continued as I stared at him almost in disbelief.

"Your mother told Katherine, the first month you and she had come to live in Colorado, what your brother had confided to her years before. Your mother was a brave and loyal ally to you to the end, Ben Branch. She didn't want for us to find out the truth later and for Katherine to take your inheritance from you after you had grown used to it. Katherine told me soon afterward what your brother had done and we both agreed at the time that it was not something Rosa Kate needed to know. Your confession to her now was somewhat understandable, but foolish."

"You've known all this time, McCloud, and you didn't hate me for it?" I asked incredulously. McCloud looked at me curiously.

"Katherine and I both understand war, Ben Branch." he replied. "War is a place where men go to kill other men and be killed in return in the name of honor and glory. Fact is there is usually not much honor, and very little glory, in war at all. Most wars are fought over gold, or horses, sometimes for property, or even women. Your brother, Jon David, did what I would have done if I had been in his place, and when I explained that to Katherine, she understood. We tried to keep facts hidden from Rosa Kate over the years that would only make her doubt her father's honor. Now she must face the real truth about her father's death and decide for herself if he died as an honorable man or not. That is a hard thing for any child to do. Since you are the one guilty of telling her the truth, you must be the one to console her and help her live with it."

"I doubt that can happen, McCloud." I told him. "If you came all the way out here just to tell me that, then you've wasted your time. Rosa Kate hates me and probably always will."

"Then why is she sitting by the bedside of your dying teacher, Hiram McDougall, Ben Branch?" McCloud replied. "That is the reason I came for you. McDougall sent for you and you were gone. Rosa Kate went to be with him in your place. That doesn't sound to me like someone who will hate you forever and never understand that you were only an injured boy, both physically and mentally, the night her father was killed."

We rode all day and most of the night to reach Denver. It was close to midnight when we tied our horses in front of Hiram's modest little house. Rosa Kate greeted us quietly at the door and only met my eyes briefly as she brought us up to date on McDougall's condition.

His physician had been there most of the evening and had left for a while to check on another of his patients, a young girl who had given birth the previous night.

"The doctor does not expect Hiram to live until morning." Rosa Kate told us. "He thinks Hiram is waiting to die until he sees you, Branch." she said directly to me. I couldn't meet her eyes, but I nodded to let her know I was listening. "He keeps asking when you will be here. You should be the one to go in to see him first. He told me he wanted to speak to you alone."

A Hard Life

I opened the door quietly and entered Hiram's small bedroom. A familiar odor struck me as I entered the room that made my nostrils flare. There is something about the smell of a dying person that you never forget. I went over to a window and raised it slightly. I saw Hiram's eyes flutter at the sound and then open wide when he recognized me.

"You took long enough to get here, Branch." he said weakly.

"I'm sorry, Hiram." I replied. "I've been off in the mountains feelin' sorry for myself." He managed a small smile, mostly with his eyes, for moving his swollen mouth seemed to cause him great pain.

"Doctor says I won't see another daylight, Branch? Do you believe that?" he asked.

"I'd say that depends on how bad you want to see another sunny day, Hiram." I replied as I sat down in a chair and pulled it close up to his bedside. He nodded slightly.

"I suspect the physician is right, Branch." he replied. "I'm just about ready to go for I don't pay much attention to sunny days any longer. I have something to give you and I wanted to tell you something, and then I want for McCloud to come in and pray for me." I must have looked surprised for he continued.

"McCloud has been visiting me lately and we've studied the bible together." he continued. "A week ago I asked him to baptize me and he took me to the river. It was very cold and the doctor said he was amazed it didn't kill me. McCloud told both of us it wouldn't heal me or cure my cancer, but neither would it make my sickness worse. He must have been right for I've lived practically another full week." Hiram reached for some papers lying on his nightstand.

"I had an attorney draw up and notarize my last will and testament, Branch. I'm leaving everything I have to you." He noticed my expression and raised his hand, palm out, toward me.

"I know you're going to tell me you don't need it," he continued, "but that's because you don't know how much it is. I invested all my life's savings, including a tidy sum my father had left me years ago, into railroad stock, Branch. You can tell Grayson Asbury to go jump off a cliff, or something similar if you're so inclined, because you don't need his money any longer." I started to reply, but he raised his hand to me again.

"Don't say anything for I had my mind made up to do this months ago. That's settled, but now I want to tell you something important. You have had a hard life, Branch and all the money I have given you, or the Asbury's have given you, will never make up for what you have lost. I think something bad has recently happened between you and Rosa Kate, but my instincts tell me there are deep feelings you have for one another that can overcome what has happened, if the two of you will allow it. You and she could build a life together that would erase all the disaster in both your young lives. Don't waste the opportunity, Branch! I want to look down on you from somewhere and watch you as you raise your children and play with your grandchildren some day! That is the only secret to a good life here on earth. McCloud can help you both find the pathway to Heaven, the same way he helped me. Please don't allow either life to slip away from the two of you, Ben Branch Walker! I want you to promise me?"

A Hard Life

"I'll try, Hiram." I promised.

"That's all anyone can do, Branch." he replied. "Now go get McCloud. I don't think I'm going to be here much longer." His voice was weakening and I hurried to fetch McCloud.

McCloud prayed a simple and short prayer, asking God to forgive any sins that might lurk in Hiram's life. He also prayed for Rosa Kate, myself, and for himself. Afterwards we sat in the semi-darkness of Hiram's bedroom listening while my teacher's breathing became shallower and shallower, until sometime in the hour just before sunup, it stopped altogether.

A HARD LIFE

CHAPTER THIRTY-THREE

Katherine Asbury was alone in the front of the church building when I arrived before Hiram's funeral service the next day. She greeted me with a sympathetic smile and asked me to sit with her to chat for a while. She said that we had not had much time lately just to talk.

"I'm so sorry you lost your teacher, Branch. I know how much you respected one another."

She spoke sincerely and she took my right hand to hold as we sat together quietly waiting for others to arrive. Hiram's coffin had been placed in the front of the church building earlier in the morning and it served as a focal point for my attention. I started to say something in return to Katherine's statement, but I really couldn't think of anything appropriate, so I kept silent. Katherine didn't seem to mind and we just sat there together with her hands wrapped tightly around mine.

A few minutes later McCloud came in the front door with the preacher, the same nice man who had conducted

A Hard Life

my mama's service, and the undertaker. Rosa Kate, who was dressed in a simple black dress very similar to her mother's, followed the three men into the small church building.

"Rosie will want to sit with you, Katherine." I said as I started to get up to join McCloud in the pew behind us.

"She can sit with the two of us, Branch." Katherine said. "I want you to sit with me during Hiram's service." I nodded to her, but I was some uncomfortable because I wasn't sure Rosa Kate would want to sit with me and it might make for an embarrassing situation.

Rosa Kate hesitated for a moment at the end of the pew and then came and sat down beside me, on the opposite side of her mother. I felt strange being so close to Rosie, for all I could think of was the horrible experience at the river the few days previous.

After the service McCloud, the preacher, the undertaker, and I, served as pallbearers to carry Hiram's coffin to an open grave in a small cemetery behind the little Church of Christ. We laid Hiram to rest and the undertaker stayed to finish filling the grave. We were walking back across the churchyard, headed for the horses and carriages, when Rosa Kate, who was walking between McCloud and me, looked up at me.

"Would you ride with us to the ranch, Branch?" she asked. "I would like to talk to you after we drop Mother and McCloud off at home." I noticed the Cherokee and Katherine exchange knowing glances that made me even more uncomfortable than I already was. I shook my head to her request

"I don't think so." I replied quietly. I wanted to call Rosie by name, but I wasn't comfortable in calling her that anymore. She had allowed me that privilege when we were friends, or whatever we were before the incident at the river. Now I didn't know what our relationship was. However, if I addressed her as Rosa Kate, or Miss Asbury, it would be too obvious, and it might sound petty or childish, so I decided not to say her name at all.

"I have something else I need to do." I said simply. Her color heightened some and her head tilted as she stared up at me. It seemed obvious I had offended her and I wanted desperately to apologize, but I was afraid that might make things even worse, so I just kept my mouth shut and kept on walking.

I went directly to Rascal and stepped up in the saddle. When I turned to ride away the three of them were standing beside Katherine's carriage watching me closely. I touched my hat brim and rode away toward downtown Denver. I wasn't ready to talk to Rosie right now. I wasn't absolutely sure when, or if, I would want to talk to her again. I was convinced that what I had told her had squelched any feelings she might have ever had for me and I was ashamed that I had told her I loved her. I had convinced myself afterwards that she probably got a big laugh out of that!

I really didn't know where I was going, for my plans for the day had not extended past Hiram's funeral service. I suppose I was headed back to my office, but when I passed in front of Mandy Mathison's Hotel a thought occurred to me and I turned Rascal to the hitching post, dismounted, and dropped his reins over it. When I entered the hotel Mandy was at her usual place on the red sofa, although it was barely past noon on a weekday.

A Hard Life

"Have you heard anything from our girl?" I inquired after I was sure no one else in the mostly deserted room could hear. Mandy smiled up at me before she shook her head in a negative fashion.

"You saw her last telegram when she arrived in Peoria." she replied, also in a lowered tone. "I don't expect to hear from her again until she decides where she will go from there." I nodded and felt foolish for asking such an obvious question that I already knew the answer for.

"Is there anything else, Branch?" Mandy asked. I hesitated, trying to determine why I was even there.

"Maybe I need a drink, Mandy." I replied. "We just buried Hiram McDougal. Do you have any Irish whiskey?" She nodded and waved at the bartender. He came over and Mandy told him to bring a bottle and two glasses. Mandy waved me to a seat beside her and the bartender pulled a table over nearer the big red couch.

We clinked our glasses together and I downed a huge swallow of the fiery stuff and felt it burn all the way down my throat.

"I never met Hiram McDougall." Mandy said to make conversation. "Mine is not the type of establishment he would have patronized, but I never heard a bad word about him from people who knew him."

"He was a good man and a great teacher." I replied. "I owe him more than I could repay, even if he hadn't died before I could even try." I downed the rest of my shot of whiskey, which didn't burn quite as bad this time. Mandy was refilling my glass when the front door swung open and Rosa Kate stepped into Mandy Mathison's Hotel.

Rosie waited for a moment for her eyes to adjust to the darker room and then walked directly over to where

Mandy and I were sitting. The expression on her face was one of determination, maybe some anger, and a whole passel of purposefulness. Mandy and I continued to remain seated, more or less dumbfounded, and waited for Rosa Kate to speak.

"You refused to meet with me privately for a talk, Ben Branch Walker, so I suppose that means I'll have to talk to you in public!" Rosie's voice was low but very distinct and she turned her attention to Mandy.

"I'm sorry I haven't been introduced to you before." She said in a frank but polite manner. "My name is Rosa Kate Asbury and I apologize for barging into your conversation with Mister Walker, but he and I have something very important to discuss and I suppose we'll have to do it right here in front of you, if you don't mind?"

"I'm Mandy Mathison, Miss Asbury, and I own this… hotel. I believe it would be best if I went up to my room and left the two of you alone to sort out your difficulties. Branch has recently become a friend of mine and the two of you can stay here and talk as long as you want. Bill, my bartender will not disturb either of you unless you want something." Mandy stood then and left the hotel lobby leaving Rosie and me alone, save for Bill the bartender, and he was busy washing glasses and wiping down the shiny bar. I motioned for Rosa Kate to sit on the couch and she complied.

"Rosie…!" I started to say, and she interrupted me.

"So you do remember my name?" she exclaimed. "I thought you had forgotten it over at the church this morning, and before we talk about anything else, could you explain to me what you're doing in this particular establishment? Everyone in Denver knows it's not just a hotel!"

"I remember your name, Rosie!" I replied back, my voice increasing just a tad. "I just wasn't sure what you wanted me to call you since your blow-up at the river the other day! And as far as having a talk with you, my face is still sore from our discussion that day! I wasn't sure I wanted a repeat of that experience! As for why I'm here talking to Mandy Mathison, I can tell you our discussion is strictly legitimate business and has nothing to do with what this place is known for. I'm not telling anyone the details of mine and Mandy's business right now, not even you." I held Rosie's eyes with mine for a moment before I continued.

"I might ask you the same question," I said, "because you being in here will raise more eyebrows than me, I can assure you!" Rosie regarded me closely and seemed to accept my explanation of why I was in Mandy's hotel.

"I'm sorry I slapped you the other day, Branch." she began. "I regretted it as soon as I did it and more so after you left. I followed you to Grayson's house to apologize, but Maria said you packed up and left, telling her you would never return?"

"She told you right. I don't plan on ever goin' back to live in his house, Rosie." I replied. "I know Grayson resents me for some reason and I believe he always has. I've had enough of feeling like I'm somewhere I don't belong."

"Did you mean what you told me, Branch?" Rosie asked. "Do you still love me?" It was the question I had been dreading to deal with.

"I don't know how to answer that question, Rosie." I said plainly. She stared at me with questioning eyes.

"Either you do, or you don't! Isn't it that simple?" she replied.

"No, love's not that simple." I said. "At least not with me, Rosie. I've already told you I don't want to be somewhere I'm not welcome. The same goes for any feelings I have for you. I've hidden my guilt ever since I've known you. Anytime we were together I was conscious of what had happened to your father and I've always believed if you knew the truth you would hate me. I suppose my intentions were to never let you know, but the other day at the river I realized I couldn't hide it from you any longer. I do love you, Rosie, with all my heart I love you, but I can live my life without you. I'll never love anyone else as much as you, but I won't waste my life loving someone who can never love me in return. When you reacted the way you did, and I felt from your anger how much you wanted to hurt me, your actions confirmed all my fears. I didn't kill your father, Rosie, but if I had been old enough, and man enough, I would have! You must realize that I hated him for what he did to my family that day, and I still do." Rosie looked away from me for a few moments after I stopped speaking. I saw tears welling up in her eyes.

"Do you know how hard it is for me to believe that my father did something so horrible, Branch?" she asked.

"Yes, I do, Rosie." I replied. "If anyone tried to convince me of something like that about my father I'd never believe it, and I'd probably hurt them bad, or make a concerted attempt! You and I are alike in our loyalty to our parents and that's why I have convinced myself that

A Hard Life

we can't have a future together. At least not the future I have been dreaming about." Rosie thought about what I had just said before she spoke again.

"That's not fair, Branch." She started to speak quietly, almost as if she were speaking only to herself.

"I suppose I don't really know how much you love me, just because you say you do. I believe that real love has to be proven by the test of time and the rigors of two people experiencing life together. Your mother helped me to learn that. She and I became close friends and I could talk about things with her that I didn't feel comfortable in discussing with my own mother. She was a wise woman, Branch, with a wisdom tempered by real life experiences. I realize that you know that too. I know why you loved her so much and I shared your love of her. She told me, and convinced me, that real love goes beyond emotion and the little heart-fluttering feelings we have at some points in time." Rosie hesitated again before she continued in the same low voice.

"I've believed for some time that I love you, Branch Walker, with every fiber in my being! I was going to tell you about my feelings the other day at the river. I was going to ask you if you felt the same way about me, and if you did, I was going to ask you if you were ready to begin the test of our love." Rosie brought her eyes to mine then.

"When you suddenly changed the subject that day and told me about my father's death, and your part in it, and Jon David's part in it, I was absolutely devastated! I wanted to hurt someone to relieve my own pain, and you were the one I chose to hurt. Was that the first test of our love, Branch?" she asked. We were still staring into each other's eyes.

"Maybe so, Rosie." I replied quietly. "If love can cut like a knife then we surely must have been in love that day. I felt like I had been gutted!" I looked around then.

"Rosie?" I asked with the most serious expression I could muster. "Do you really think it's appropriate for us to be having this conversation sitting in the lobby of the biggest whorehouse in Denver?"

Rosie was still gazing into my eyes, but suddenly they crinkled at the corners and she began to laugh. I joined her laughter, and we hugged each other and laughed until we both had tears in our eyes.

"Let's get out of here!" I said after our hilarity had calmed some. I took Rosie's hand and we left Mandy Mathison's whorehouse.

A HARD LIFE

CHAPTER THIRTY-FOUR

For the next two weeks Rosie and I were rarely apart from one another. I would leave her mother's house late at night and go alone to Hiram McDougall's little house, where I had stored my belongings and where I slept. Rosie and I went for long rides into the mountains, or out across the endless prairie east of Denver. We fished and Rosie fried trout for our lunches. We talked for hours at a time, telling one another about the dreams and fantasy's all young people experience, and sometimes never share with anyone else. Rosie and I shared our dreams, our feelings, our philosophies, our likes and dislikes, and fell deeper and deeper in love every day.

When we were alone and away from prying eyes, we kissed and held each other for hours that seemed as minutes at the time. We didn't allow our love making to evolve past that because we both seemed to realize that it would be sweeter and more fulfilling if we left those pleasures for a future time when it would happen for all the right reasons. We were deliriously happy and late one afternoon, after riding up to the crest of one of the mountains surrounding Denver, while we sat our horses and admired the grandeur of the wild country spreading out below us, I asked Rosie to marry me and she accepted. I felt I was the luckiest man on the face of the earth. Right then, I genuinely felt sorry for all the other men who lived, or had lived before me, without the love of a woman like Rosa Kate Asbury!

We were saddling horses one bright September morning to go for a ride in the mountains. We hoped to hear elk bugling in one of the meadows surrounded by yellowing aspens. It had frosted overnight and we could see our breaths in the early morning chill. I heard a rider coming and I stood erect to see who was visiting from town this early in the morning. I recognized Curly Griffin riding past Katherine's house when he saw Rosa Kate and me outside the barn.

"Good morning Curly." Rosa Kate said with her bright smile. Curly smiled back and touched his hat brim.

"Mornin' Curly." I followed. "Looks like you got up before breakfast?" He smiled back at me and nodded and then handed me a sealed white envelope with my name written in bold cursive on the outside.

"Mandy Mathison said to give you this as soon as possible, Branch." he said. I tore open the envelope and found it contained a telegram addressed to Mandy. I read it quickly with Rosa Kate watching me closely. She recognized the change in my demeanor as soon as I refolded the telegram and placed it in my shirt pocket.

"What is it, Branch?" she asked.

A Hard Life

"I have to be gone for a while, Rosie." I replied. "I'm afraid we can't go riding today." I looked up at Curly. "Will you and Lonny keep an eye on things around here until I get back, Curly?" My friend saw the seriousness in my expression and he nodded back to me.

"You bet, Branch" he replied, "as long as it takes."

"How long is a while, Branch?" Rosie asked with a worried look.

"Three weeks, maybe longer, Rosie." I replied. "I need to go find McCloud. He will be going with me."

"Where are you and McCloud going, Branch?" Rosie asked and I could see she was getting frustrated with my short answers that didn't tell her all she wanted to know. I thought about it and figured there was no reason not to tell her. She had to know sooner or later, and I might as well face her objections now and get it over with.

"This telegram tells me where Ryan is right now, Rosie. McCloud and I will be headed east on the next train." Rosie paled perceptibly and I noticed that Curly dropped his head for a moment and then looked at me with a serious expression.

"I'd like to go with you, Branch?" he asked, but I shook my head.

"I need you and Lonny here to watch over things, Curly." My look to him told him he needn't argue, so he nodded and turned his horse back the way he had come.

"Lonny and I will be back in a hour with shotguns and bedrolls, Branch." he said over his shoulder. I suspected Rosa Kate wasn't through arguing with me just yet.

"There are lawmen you can send to capture Logan Ryan, Branch. Men who are paid to carry guns, be shot at, and risk their lives. Why must you and McCloud risk yours?" I stared into her determined blue eyes.

"If you don't already know this much about me, Rosie, I probably can't explain it to you." I said it slowly and distinctly. "You must trust me and believe that this is something I have to do. It would make it much easier for me if I knew you supported me in this, but you have to know right now that I'm going to leave to find Ryan regardless."

The expression on my features must have also convinced her that arguing with me about this would be fruitless, for she dropped her eyes from mine and nodded slightly.

"I'll try, Branch." she said quietly. "That's all I can promise."

'That'll have to do, Rosie." I replied resolutely.

I paced the aisle of the slow-moving passenger car from one end to the other, adjusting my balance to the car's slow, back and forth, rocking motion.. McCloud sat near the front of the empty car with his dark hat pulled down low over his face. He appeared to be asleep and I envied his ability to seemingly put all cares aside and sleep whenever he wanted to. I had not enjoyed a good night's rest since we had started the long trek by train from Denver to Poplar Bluff, Missouri. Finally I slumped down in a seat near the middle of the car and gazed out at the Missouri farmland and timber on either side of the railroad track.

I reached inside my shirt pocket, retrieved the folded telegram and opened it to read it for what had to be the hundredth time.

A Hard Life

WESTERN UNION TELEGRAM

August 30, 1879
To Mandy Mathison
Denver Colorado STOP

On my way to Poplar Bluff, Missouri STOP
Uncle Henry there waiting for me STOP

Signed,
LYNNE BLACK

Today was September 11th . It lacked two days to be two full weeks since Lynne had posted that telegram from St. Louis. If she had left the same day, which I assumed she had, it would have taken her two days to reach Poplar Bluff, which meant she had been there for well over a week.

Questions flooded into my brain. Would they still be somewhere around Poplar Bluff? Would Lynne have been able to get word to me somehow if they left to go elsewhere? Was the pretty girl still alive? What if Ryan had found out somehow that Lynne was working for me? Would he kill her? I thought about that for a while and the obvious answer made me frown and caused a cold shiver to run up and down my spine. Why did this stupid train run so slow?

I was back up again pacing the aisle. According to the conductor, we should be in Poplar Bluff, tomorrow morning. I wished it could come faster. My attention was drawn to three hoses running in a field alongside the railroad tracks. One, a paint with brown splotches and a white face reminded me of Rosie's little paint mare.

Rosie had ridden to the train depot in Denver with McCloud and me. Curly Griffin had ridden along too, and would accompany her back to the ranch after McCloud and I had disembarked. I was riding Rascal and holding the lead rope on a tall, sleek, black mare that was mountain bred and trailwise. McCloud was leading another horse behind him also, just as fast, and just as experienced as the one he rode.

I stopped by the telegraph office and sent a wire to Brady Foreister in Doniphan. I asked Brady to meet McCloud and me in Poplar Bluff in a week, but I didn't tell him why. I hoped he would get the wire, plus I hoped he would respond to my request. I also stopped by Katherine's bank and made a substantial withdrawal from my account.

I kissed Rosa Kate hard on the lips and promised her that I would be careful and return as soon as possible. She had held me until I had to make her release her arms from around my neck. McCloud and I watched as she and Curly rode away back toward the ranch.

We loaded the four horses into a boxcar equipped with stalls. We made certain there was fresh straw in the stalls and we checked the sides of the boxcar ourselves for nails, or anything sharp that might injure the horses during the long trip.

McCloud had suggested we take our own horses with us on the trip. He anticipated we might have to chase Ryan and his men down, and he didn't want to depend on rented horses. I agreed with him.

A Hard Life

Every day when the train stopped to take on coal or water, we would go back and check on the four animals, water them, and feed them some grain.

I paced the aisle until late in the evening, and finally curled up in a seat with my heavy coat to keep me warm. Tomorrow we should be in Poplar Bluff. I finally went to sleep with only an assurance that tomorrow could bring much peril to both McCloud and me.

Poplar Bluff is the county seat of Butler County and is laid out along the banks of the Black River. West and north of Poplar Bluff the country is hilly and rocky with deep ravines and clear fast creeks and streams. Heavy stands of oak, hickory, ash, pine, and giant sweet gum trees cover the hillsides as far as you can see from an elevated ridge. The people that live in the Ozark hills mostly hunt and trap their food, with some sustenance gained from thin crops planted in the narrow valleys between tall ridges.

East and south of Poplar Bluff the country is comprised of a low swampy land interspersed with large tracts of cypress, sycamore, and tupelo gum forest with most of the trees covered in a thick heavy moss that drapes almost to the ground. This unique moss practically shuts out the sun to a large portion of the swampland below. Heavy bodied moccasin snakes glide in the dark swampy waters and wolves and panthers ambush deer in the thick timber.

People that live in the swamps eat the fish, turtles, and the varied waterfowl that migrate there every fall. Crops are planted, but floods are frequent and oftentimes the crops are lost to the rising swamp waters.

Poplar Bluff was established as a trading town where the hill people from the Ozarks came together with the flatlanders from the swamps to trade. Over the years two distinct cultures had developed separating the hill folks from the flatlanders. Feuds between factions of the two groups were frequent, bloody, and often lasted for generations from fathers down to their sons and beyond.

Poplar Bluff is known to be a rough and dangerous place to visit. The law that exists is mostly there to protect the businesses and upstanding Butler County citizens. Outsiders, not from Butler County, are often found in the streets shot dead, or with their throats cut, and their murders go mostly ignored by local lawmen. Dead bodies are simply rolled into the swift running Black River, where they drift downstream toward Arkansas.

Poplar Bluff is an ideal place for a man like Logan Ryan and the men who ride with him to gravitate to and stay for a while. As long as they leave the locals alone, they would be more or less sheltered from outside lawmen, who hardly ever ventured into Butler County.

I shared this information with McCloud before the train pulled into the Poplar Bluff railway depot.

"Did you come here as a boy?" he inquired, and I nodded.

"During daylight hours only, to buy or sell produce, always on Saturdays," I replied. "Saturdays are the only day of the week when outsiders are expected and accepted in Poplar Bluff. We always knew to leave town long before darkness set in."

"How will the two of us be viewed coming into such a town, Ben Branch? Especially if they find out why we're here?" The Cherokee asked.

A Hard Life

"Simple, McCloud." I replied. "We pay for the privilege. That's why I had to go by the bank before we left. I'm hopin' Brady Foreister will be waitin' for us at the depot. I suspect he'll know which lawman is the current big dog in Poplar Bluff. When we discover his identity, we'll tell the man why we're here and pay his price for permission to take Ryan." McCloud nodded his nominal understanding.

"What if he just happens to be a friend or relative of Ryan, and refuses to give us any information, or trumps up charges against us?" McCloud asked as I stared out the dirty railway car window at the early Missouri morning. I turned to look at the dark Cherokee before I answered his question.

"Then I'll kill him and make a deal with the man that steps up to take his place, McCloud!" The Cherokee frowned at me and turned to stare out the opposite window. I smiled a little to myself, but not for long. I had not been entirely joking. After all, this is Poplar Bluff.

A HARD LIFE

CHAPTER THIRTY-FIVE

Dawn brought a light rain and a sudden drop in temperatures in Poplar Bluff. The train pulled to a stop at the depot and I looked up and down the tracks from the passenger car window trying to see if Brady was there. The depot appeared deserted, which wasn't surprising at six o'clock in the morning. McCloud and I pulled rain slickers over our coats and stepped down from the passenger car. McCloud carried his ever-present Winchester carbine and I had the ten gauge over my left arm.

We made our way back to the boxcar where our horses were waiting. We put saddles on Rascal and McCloud's black stallion and led the two spare mounts on to a freight landing beside the track. We were headed up the street toward a livery stable when Brady Foreister emerged from out of a darkened alleyway and greeted me.

"Mornin' Branch." he said as he pulled his horse alongside mine and kept pace. Brady was also wearing a

A Hard Life

tan slicker and a wide-brimmed felt hat. Water ran from the brim of his hat as the light rain continued

Good Mornin' yourself, Brady." I replied, "It's been a long time." He nodded his agreement.

"Meet my friend, McCloud, from Colorado, Brady." I continued and Brady nodded to the somber Cherokee on the other side of me. The Ripley County deputy looked down at my shotgun and over at McCloud's rifle.

"I've been stayin' kinda' back in the shadows." Brady said. "I didn't want to draw anybody's attention to the fact that I was waitin' for the train. The local lawmen know me, and they'd been curious about what I was up to. You didn't tell me much in your telegram, Branch. What exactly are you doin' in Poplar Bluff?"

"I received a wire that Ryan is here." I replied. Brady had been a long time friend of Jon David's and when I had wired him to tell him about Jon David's murder he promised to keep an ear open for word about the killer. He had also wired me back to say that he would help in any way possible to bring Ryan to justice."

"I've had someone else searching for Ryan too, Brady." I explained. "Last week she wired me in Denver and told me he was here in Butler County."

"You just said, she wired you, Branch." he replied. "You've had a woman lookin' for Ryan?" There was a surprised tone in Brady's voice.

"That's right, I have" I replied. "Ryan took up with her in Denver and I figured she might be able to find him when no one else might."

"That was smart, Branch." Brady said. "Jon David always said you was the smartest one of the Walker brothers. What do you plan on doin' with Ryan, if and when we find him." I looked over at him closely, but didn't answer. Brady finally looked away and frowned..

"We have wanted posters on Ryan for murders in Colorado, Brady. I didn't figure they would mean much in Missouri, and probably less in Butler County. I was hopin' you might know who I might persuade here in Poplar Bluff to let us take him without any trouble?"

"You'd most likely have to back up your request with money. You planned on that didn't you, Branch?" I patted my jacket over my left chest.

"I came prepared, Brady." I replied.

We were in front of the livery by then and we stepped down from our horses and led them inside the lantern-lit barn. A young man with a limp greeted us and I told him we needed stalls for five horses and we wanted to leave our saddles on the three. He agreed and I paid him. After he had led the horses into individual stalls, Brady, McCloud, and I stood in the open doorway watching the rain begin to come down harder and harder.

"We might as well go see John Taylor, Branch." Brady said. "He's the current elected sheriff and he knows me. He won't take money from you direct, he's too smart for that, but he'll let you leave it in a place where he can find it later. Don't give him any more details about Ryan than necessary. Taylor fought with the Union in the conflict and he might be a tad prejudiced, if you know what I mean?" I nodded to Brady.

"Let's go see John Taylor then." I said and we stepped into the rain and started up the muddy street toward the Butler County courthouse.

John Taylor was alone in his office. He was sitting behind his desk reading a newspaper. The aroma of freshly brewed coffee was coming from a large pot steaming as it sat on a pot-bellied stove in the center of the room.

The sheriff looked up suspiciously as the three of us walked into his office. He folded the newspaper and laid it in front of him. I could see the barrels of a shotgun leaned against his desk, a few inches from his right hand.

"Early for you to be up and about, Brady." he said as his gaze swept over McCloud and me, resting for a moment on my ten gauge and McCloud's carbine.

"Sheriff, John Taylor, this is Branch Walker and his friend from Colorado named McCloud. I met them at the train depot this mornin'." John Taylor's sharp gaze went from me to McCloud.

"You boys are a far piece from home." he commented, and I nodded an agreement.

"We've got wanted posters on a man wanted for three murders in Denver, Sheriff. We got word he came to Poplar Bluff within the last two weeks. We were hopin' you might know of his whereabouts?" John Taylor stared at me.

"Are you lawmen, or is this personal?' he asked.

"We're not lawmen." I replied and left it at that. Taylor continued to stare at me.

"I guess that means it's personal then, unless you're bounty hunters?" he replied. "Are you bounty hunters?" I shook my head slightly.

"We're not bounty hunters either, Sheriff," I replied, "although there is a price for Ryan's capture." John Taylor's frown deepened at my answer.

"Just who is the man you call Ryan, Walker?"

"Logan Ryan is his name, Sheriff." I replied. "He's a tall man and he wears a blue Yankee officer's hat. He might be travelin' with two or three men and he probably just met up with a pretty woman here in Poplar Bluff." The Butler County sheriff studied what I had told him for a while before he answered.

"I'm guessin' the woman tipped you off about him bein' here?" he inquired and before I could answer he continued.

"Why should I let civilians take a man here in my county if he's wanted by the law?" I turned away and walked over to the window in the front of the sheriff's office to peek out at the muddy dirt street.

"Sheriff," I began speaking while I was still gazing out the window. "it wouldn't surprise me if there weren't times when you could fix a lot of Butler County problems if you had a little extra money that no one knew about. Maybe money that the county can't afford?"

I looked at John Taylor then and his expression remained the same, but after a moment he spoke up.

"Go on, Walker." he said quietly.

"Is that your horse tied up in front of the office?" I continued. "The black with two white stockings?" Sheriff Taylor nodded.

"If you happened to find some cash in one of the saddlebags on that horse." I went on, "Cash with no owner, or anyone to claim it, couldn't that come in awful handy to a man interested in helpin' out his county citizens and their problems?"

"How much cash, Walker?" Taylor asked guardedly.

"You tell me, Sheriff?" I replied. He looked down at his desk and then back up to me.

"Let me make certain I understand your drift?" he said. "If I let you capture Logan Ryan and allow you take

A Hard Life

him back to Colorado, without any help or interference from my department, I might come across…say, five hundred dollars lost in my saddlebags?"

"Could be six hundred, Sheriff," I replied, "If you tell me exactly where he can be found?" John Taylor thought about that for a while before he spoke again.

"What if he resists and you have to kill him, or one or more of the men with him?" he asked. "Killings can make things awful complicated around here with paperwork and such. I'm sure you can understand that?" I nodded.

"I'd make a reasonable effort to see that doesn't happen, Sheriff." I replied, returning to the window and staring out. "But, if it did, four hundred dollars more, to make an even thousand, would make its way into your other saddlebag a day or so later." John Taylor looked up at Brady then.

"You vouch for these men, Foreister?" he asked and Brady nodded.

"I've known Branch most of his life, John. I've never known him to lie about nothin'." Sheriff John Taylor nodded and hesitated for a while seemingly struggling with his decision. Finally he shrugged and began to speak.

"A week or so ago a young woman came in from the north on the stagecoach." he began. "A tall man wearin' a blue hat like you described met her. He'd rented an old farmhouse east of town a few days before. He told everyone he was lookin' for land to buy, and said his name was Metcalf, Alvin Metcalf. He loaded the woman up in a buggy and drove her to his rented house, and as best I know, they're still there."

"Would you give us directions, Sheriff?" I inquired.

A HARD LIFE

CHAPTER THIRTY-SIX

The rain had set in for the day and McCloud, Brady, and I held our slickers tight around our throats to keep the cold moisture from soaking through to our clothes. Our horse's hooves made sucking sounds in the muddy road as we approached the old farmstead where Ryan was supposed to be staying.

We turned off the road a quarter mile from the house and eased our horses through a woods lot letting an old barn shield us from view from the front of the house. We stopped back in the timber and tied up our horses to make our way on foot to the back of the barn. For several minutes we listened with our ears close to the siding for sounds of horses or men inside. Upon hearing no sounds from inside, I slipped around the side of the barn and opened a side door as quietly as I could. I held the ten gauge in my left hand with the hammers cocked.

The barn was quiet inside. The horse stalls were empty, but fresh manure smell told me there had been horses there only a short time before. I tapped on the back of the barn as a signal to McCloud and Brady that it was clear for them to follow me. I eased up to the closed front door of the barn and was peering though the cracks at the house when the two men joined me, one on either side

"The house is dark and quiet." I whispered. "I haven't seen any movement and it's obvious there's been horses here up to a few hours ago. I'm afraid they've got wind of us somehow and vamoosed, or they just decided they had been here long enough."

"I can't see Ryan takin' a woman on the trail with him, can you, Branch?" Brady whispered and a coldness gripped my insides.

"Cover me from here." I said and handed the shotgun to Brady. "I'm goin' to check out the house." McCloud climbed a ladder up to the loft and eased the upper hay door open to shove his rifle barrel a few inches outside. I removed my wet slicker and threw it over a stall door, then drew my peacemaker from its holster.

The rain was cold on my back as I made my way slowly toward the front door of the house. When I stepped up on the porch and the boards squeaked I cocked the gun's hammer and held it at waist level in front of me. The door handle turned and I stepped inside the darkened quiet room. The house smelled musty, like it had been deserted for a long time, but a faint smell of burnt kerosene told me the lamps had been burning only a short time before.

I made my way quietly from room to room. The house was empty except for a bedroom on the second floor. Lynne Black was lying naked on the bed covered in blood from her bruised face down to her waist.. Her once pretty, but now blood soaked auburn hair was spread out on the coverless mattress around her swollen face. Her eyes were closed and dried blood caked the right side of her face.

I put my ear down close to her lips and was amazed when I detected that she was still breathing. I felt her wrist and found a weak, but steady heartbeat.

The doctor from Poplar Bluff stayed in the room with Lynne for a long time. When he finally emerged from the bedroom he nodded to Brady and me.

"She's suffered a terrible beating, Gentlemen, but she's a strong young woman." he said to the two of us "He stabbed her too, but he missed her vitals. She should recover fully in a few weeks."

I breathed a sigh of relief and told the doctor that I would stand good for all of Lynne's medical expenses. I gave the man fifty dollars in advance. He told us he would keep her in his clinic until she had fully recovered.

"Could I speak with her?" I asked.

"Only for a few minutes," he replied, "and please don't excite her, Mister Walker. She will be weak for several days yet." I nodded and went to the door to let myself in.

Lynne was covered with a quilt and propped on pillows the doctor had found in another room. I could tell she recognized me and I saw tears gather in her eyes.

"Don't worry about anything, Lynne." I told her quietly as I stood beside the bed. "The doctor says you're going to be fine in a few days. He will take you to town when you're able to travel and keep you in his clinic. When you're up and about your money will be waiting for you at the bank."

She nodded to me and I could tell any movement caused her great pain. She looked up at me and began to speak, slowly and quietly, but I could understand her clearly.

A Hard Life

"Ryan knows you are coming for him, Branch." she practically whispered. "He found the note you wrote to me to tell me how to communicate with you by telegram. I know I shouldn't have kept it, but I didn't dream he would go through my things. I had written your name on the back of the note and when he found it he just went crazy!" Tears were flowing from her eyes now and I put my fingers to her mouth.

"Don't worry about me, Lynne." I said. "I just want you to be well again. I feel responsible for your pain and I'm really sorry. I never intended for anything like this to happen to you." She caught my hand in hers and held it.

"It was my fault, not yours, Branch." she whispered. "I would just like for you to do one thing for me?" I held her eyes and waited.

"Make Ryan hurt real bad and tell him it's for me?" Her big eyes were dead serious. I nodded soberly.

"Just before I send him to hell, Lynne." I replied. "I promise." She closed her eyes then and I slipped quietly from the room.

McCloud joined Brady and me on the front porch.

"There's three of them, Ben Branch." The Cherokee said. "They've headed northwest and I believe we should be able to catch up with them in a day or two. They don't appear to be well mounted."

"Northwest should take them toward Ripley County and put them in my neck of the woods, that is if they don't change directions." Brady said. "That'd be good. I'd just as soon get clear of Butler County and John Taylor's jurisdiction."

We caught up with Ryan and the two men the following afternoon. It was still raining steadily and

McCloud thought they gave up trying to run from us because they were hungry, tired, wet and cold, and just plain discouraged. They made a stand in an old abandoned barn with half the roof gone.

McCloud, Brady, and I surrounded the barn and laid down a steady barrage of bullets that ripped through the rotted timbers. Ryan had a rifle, but he must have been low on ammunition, for he only fired a few rounds with it in the first minutes of the fight. The other two with him were young derelicts barely past their teens, and all three were only armed with pistols now. Ryan enticed the youngsters to join up with him by promising them a lucrative life of bank and train robberies. This was after Jon David and I had killed his seasoned war buddies over in Bloomfield.

Ryan abandoned his new friends, jumped on his horse and made a dash to escape, but McCloud put a rifle bullet in his horse's side. We were confident the animal wouldn't go far so we held our positions and kept up our fire.

While McCloud and Brady kept the boys heads down with steady rifle fire, I slipped up close with the ten gauge. I blasted a hole in the side of the old barn large enough to walk through, and the two boys pitched out their pistols, raised their hands, and gave up. We bound them hand and foot and left them in the barn while the three of us went after Ryan.

Ryan fired his pistol at us when we were still a hundred yards away from where he had barricaded himself behind his now dead horse. He fired three shots and then threw the Army colt toward us as we advanced on him. I had reloaded the shotgun and I dismounted and walked ahead of Brady and McCloud.

A Hard Life

Ryan was yelling obscenities and making threats about what he would do to me if I came closer. At the last minute, when I was only a few feet away, he bolted and tried to run toward a nearby patch of timber. I led him with the shotgun and blew out his legs before he had gone twenty feet. I dropped the shotgun then and drew my peacemaker as Ryan screamed in pain and tried to get up.

I shot him in the right knee, whereupon he went down flat on his back with a blood-curdling scream. He rolled over to his belly then and began to crawl away from me, dragging his bleeding right leg. I shot him in the left knee this time and he collapsed in the mud, cursing me and moaning in agony.

McCloud and Brady had followed on their horses and were behind me a few feet now. I holstered my colt and reached behind me for my papa's knife. I held it in my right hand and began to advance toward Logan Ryan.

"McCloud, I think it's time you and Brady made yourselves scarce!" I said loud enough for them to hear me plainly. I sensed them pulling their horses to a stop, for I didn't look back.

"We'll gather up the two boys back at the barn and make camp on that little stream we crossed a mile or so back, Branch." Brady said from behind me. "When you're through here, you can meet us there."

I never turned around to look at either of them. I could hear them riding away as I reached down to take a handful of Logan Ryan's hair in my left hand.

A HARD LIFE

CHAPTER THIRTY-SEVEN

Brady Foreister said his goodbyes to McCloud and me and headed back toward Doniphan and his job as a Ripley County deputy. The Cherokee and I rode the St. Louis-San Francisco Railway line back across Missouri, Kansas, and into eastern Colorado. Before we left Missouri I sent a wire to Rosie to let her know my search for Ryan was over and McCloud and I were on our way beck to Denver.

Something had changed between McCloud and me since the gunfight with Logan Ryan. Maybe the uneasy feeling about our friendship had always just been in my mind, but now we both recognized that we were closer than just friends, and we each held a mutual strong respect for one another.

I kept going over the past in my mind trying to get it straightened out within myself. Why had there been times when I doubted McCloud? I thought that if I could explain it to myself, then maybe I could explain it to him, but I finally decided just to leave it alone. The important thing now was that we had developed a deep friendship. Maybe how we got there didn't really matter.

"What are your plans when we get back to Denver, Ben Branch?" McCloud asked, jarring me out of my meditation.

"I'm going to get things straight between myself and Grayson first, McCloud, and then I'm going to marry Rosa Kate." I replied. "That is, if she hasn't changed her mind since we've been gone." I added.

"I don't think there's much chance of that, Ben Branch." he said. "I know Rosa Kate as well as anyone and I've sensed for a long time that you were the one she had chosen to spend her life with. I believe she knew that from the very first." I stared hard at the Cherokee.

"Why didn't you tell me, McCloud?" I asked. "I would have gone back east to see her those years she stayed away from the ranch."

"My words would have been wasted on you then." he replied. "You weren't sure you could trust me, Ben Branch. Now you know you can." McCloud had put into words what I had been trying to say to him for two hundred miles.

"When you face Grayson, Ben Branch, I will be at your side." The Cherokee said.

"I would appreciate that, McCloud." I replied.

We didn't say much to one another for the rest of the ride back to Denver. We were comfortable with one another now.

The train arrived in Denver mid-morning on a Thursday. I was a little surprised that Rosa Kate was not there to greet us, but I reasoned she didn't know exactly which train we would arrive on. After unloading our horses and getting them settled in the livery we walked together to Grayson's Mountain Top Hotel, where he resided most of the time now.

We stepped into the lobby headed for the stairs when we met Katherine coming down from the second floor. She appeared worried about something and when she saw McCloud and me I recognized relief and real joy in her eyes to see us.

"Branch, and McCloud." She exclaimed and tried to hug both of us at the same time. "I am so happy to see the two of you. You can't imagine how relieved I am. I am so worried about Rosa Kate. She went riding early this morning and was supposed to be back to get dressed and have lunch with me. I have been waiting for more than two hours! How did the two of you know I was here?" McCloud and I exchanged glances.

"We didn't know, Katherine." I replied. "We came to see Grayson."

"Well, Grayson's not here, Branch." Katherine replied. "He left Denver yesterday on one of his trips west. He caught the train late in the afternoon with Frank Albright, the Denver sheriff."

"Where would Grayson and Frank Albright be going together?" I asked and Katherine shook her head.

"Who knows where they go." She replied. "They're nearly always together. People are talking and wondering about how Albright can be gone so much and still be an effective sheriff!"

I pushed Grayson and Frank Albright to the back of my mind. After all there was more urgent things to be thinking about.

"Do you know where Rosa Kate was riding this morning, Katherine?" I inquired, and she looked worried as she shook her head.

"She never tells me, Branch." she replied. "She did tell me that she was missing you and riding helped ease her mind. She might have said something about a place where the two of you had been riding before." I nodded to McCloud.

"I might know where she was going, McCloud." I said hurriedly. "Would you go to the livery to fetch our horses and meet me at Hiram's house?" The Cherokee nodded his agreement. "I'm tired of totin' the shotgun." I continued. "I would rather have my rifle and I have ammunition there."

The Cherokee nodded again and started down the street. I trotted in the opposite direction toward the house Hiram McDougall had left me.

McCloud met me in the street outside my new home. He had saddled his black stallion for himself and he was leading Rascal.

"Where's your rifle?" he inquired as I stuffed the shotgun into the saddle scabbard.

"It's gone." I replied. "Maybe Lonny or Curly borrowed it. They knew where I kept it under the bed." McCloud looked skeptical, but he never said anything.

We rode west toward the mountain where I had asked Rosa Kate to marry me. We had ridden there together several times and it was our favorite spot to be alone. McCloud and I pushed our horses and made the little aspen meadow at the top of the mountain in less than an hour.

We pulled our horses to a stop in the small empty clearing. Their flanks were covered in sweat and their breathing was labored. McCloud pointed into the timber and my heart skipped a beat when I saw Rosa Kate's riderless paint mare staring at us from the shelter of the pine forest. We turned our horses toward the mare.

I heard the bullet hit and actually saw it's impact as it struck McCloud high in his left chest, just before the crack of the rifle shot reached my ears. The Cherokee pitched backwards from his stallion and his rifle went flying from his hand!

I reached for my colt, but suddenly something hit my right arm, between the elbow and my shoulder, with the force of a falling boulder. I heard the second shot echoing as I was spun off Rascal's back and fell heavily to the ground.

My right arm was broken and collapsed inward toward me when I tried to use it to rise to my feet. The searing pain practically blinded me and I felt close to passing out. Rosa Kate's image in my mind, and what might be happening to her, forced me to concentrate on staying alert! If I went unconscious now I knew I could not be of any help to her!

I used my left arm to push myself to my knees and then struggled to my feet. My head was spinning and everything appeared somewhat hazy, but I saw three figures marching steadily toward me from the pine forest.

My eyes cleared then and I recognized Grayson Asbury holding a rifle in one hand and the other was clutching Rosa Kate by her left arm. Her right arm was held securely by Frank Albright on the other side of her.

A Hard Life

I could even see Albright's silver badge shining in the bright sunlight.

Rosa Kate was struggling with the two large men, trying to break free. She was screaming my name and sobbing hysterically!

I grabbed my numb right hand and forced it into my waistband. Taking the weight off my arm seemed to relieve some of the fiery pain and my vision cleared even more.

Grayson handed the rifle to Frank Albright and released his hold on Rosa Kate. Albright wrapped his arm around her and held her securely from behind. She was powerless to escape from the much stronger man. Rosie was still saying my name between sobs.

"I heard you caught up with Logan Ryan, Branch?" Grayson said. "Did he tell you everything you wanted to know?" I was dizzy and unsure of my footing, but I tried my best to stand up straight to face the man

"He told me everything, Grayson." I replied. "Now you've killed McCloud and I'm sure I'm next. Why don't you let Rosa Kate go? You don't want to hurt her and she doesn't need to see this."

"You're right, Branch!" he said bitterly. "I never wanted to hurt Rosa Kate, but because of you I have no choice now. I'll do it with your rifle however, Branch. It was foolish for you to leave it where I could find it so easily. They'll find you dead and they'll find McCloud and Rosa Kate both shot with your rifle. Everyone will think you and McCloud had a gun battle after you shot Rosa Kate. Some folks will have trouble believing it, but they can't tie me to it because Frank and I are supposedly on a train headed to California." Grayson smiled slightly then and I wanted badly to kill him.

"I've got it all figured out, Branch." he continued. After this is all over I'll come back all teary eyed and remorseful. Katherine will need my support then and the two of us will be back where we were before you came into our lives and ruined everything!" He stared at Rosa Kate then.

"However, Rosa Kate's going to watch me gun you down like the mangy Missouri dog you are! She doesn't know it, but I'm saving her from a horrible life with a loser such as you! You're no better than your murdering brother who killed her father and my only brother!"

"Is that it then, Grayson?" I replied. "Are you just going to shoot me down without a chance?" Grayson smiled then. A cruel malevolent smile.

"No, Branch." he replied and drew his colt from his holster.. "Stand real still and don't move a muscle, or I will shoot you down right now." Grayson approached me carefully holding his cocked revolver on my face. He reached to my right and withdrew my Colt and then stuck it under my waist belt on my left side, with the grip of the revolver toward my left hand. Then he stepped backward a few steps and re-holstered his Colt.

"Now you've got a fighting chance, Branch." he said mockingly. "Not much of a chance against me, but at least Rosa Kate can't accuse me of murdering you in cold blood, like I did that mangy Cherokee, McCloud! I enjoyed killing him, Branch. I should have done it years ago."

A Hard Life

I could feel the Colt at my left side and I looked down to check its angle and then I raised my eyes to Grayson's face again.

"Since you're going to kill both Rosa Kate and me, Grayson." I inquired. "Will you tell me if you were the one that murdered my mother?" Grayson smiled again.

"I thought Logan Ryan murdered your mother, Branch?" he replied mockingly. "Isn't that why you ran him down and killed him?"

"Logan Ryan denied it, Grayson," I said. "and when he did he had no reason to lie to me." Grayson studied me and nodded.

"He didn't lie." Grayson said. "But, I didn't kill your mother either. In fact, I killed the man who murdered her." I stared at him and he took his time in continuing.

"I don't guess it matters now if I tell you what really happened, Branch." he said. "Harley LaMarr, who was secretary-treasurer of Asbury enterprises decided he wasn't satisfied with just earning a salary from the company. He decided he wanted to control Asbury Industries. He and Kennard Young, the former sheriff of Denver, cooked up this scheme together. Somehow LaMarr found out about Logan Ryan. I suspect Ryan contacted him with a scheme to blackmail you once you were appointed a voting board member. LaMarr thought that if Katherine was out of the picture, and he could control your vote, then eventually he could swing things to push me aside and take over the company." Grayson hesitated then to make certain both Rosa Kate and I were listening and understanding.

"LaMarr convinced Kennard to murder Katherine and pin it on Logan Ryan by leaving evidence McCloud would find that would point to Ryan. The fool sheriff shot your mother by mistake! What LaMarr didn't count on was that Logan Ryan came to me and told me about his and LaMarr's original deal. I told Ryan that his only chance was to make a run for it, which he did. I set up a meeting with Harley LaMarr and Kennard Young and I took Frank Albright with me. We killed both of them and dropped their bodies in an old mine shaft where they will never be found."

"I know why Logan Ryan came to you, Grayson." I said when he had finished talking. "You knew Logan Ryan from before the war. Ryan told me about the deal he had made with you before your brother James joined the Union forces." Grayson's eyes widened in astonishment and them narrowed in fury.

"That's enough!" he said angrily. "We've shared enough old times! Now it's time for me to finish this business and put it all behind me."

I could see Grayson shift his weight forward and I knew he was getting ready to draw. I remembered something Jon David had told me years before when we had been discussing gunfights. Jon David had told me to watch a man's eyes. He said that the decision to draw a gun, or swing a fist, always showed in the eyes first. I watched Grayson's eyes closely and suddenly I recognized what Jon David had told me to watch for.

My left hand flashed and my colt peacemaker swung away from my belt as my thumb flicked back the hammer. I shot Grayson low in his chest when his gun had just cleared leather. Grayson was slammed backward with the impact of my bullet and his colt fell from his right hand. His eyes were wide with amazement. He never suspected I might beat him to the draw, especially with my left hand!

I swung the pistol barrel toward Frank Albright then, who had released Rosa Kate to try and bring his rifle to bear on me. He halted all his movement when my cocked peacemaker was aimed at his middle. He dropped the rifle to the ground and threw his arms in the air.

"Don't shoot, Walker!" he cried. "I ain't drawing on you!" Rosa Kate moved toward me when Albright released her. The sheriff turned his back to me then and began to walk away

"I'm a lawman, Walker!" he said loudly. "I'm droppin' my gun belt!" His left hand went to his gun belt buckle and it fell from his waist to the ground as he continued a slow walk toward where he and Grayson had left their horses.

"If you shoot me in the back they'll hang you sure!" he yelled and by then Rosa Kate had gotten to me and thrown her arms around my neck. Albright was about thirty feet away when I saw him begin to turn back toward me.

In his right hand was another pistol, which he had hidden under his vest! Rosa Kate was between us now and my gun was pointed to the ground with the hammer down! Albright had his pistol leveled at us when a shot rang out and a small blue hole suddenly appeared in the sheriff's forehead! He fell backwards to the ground dead as a stone!

Rosa Kate and I looked toward where the shot had come from. McCloud was standing beside his black stallion with his rifle across the saddle to steady his one-armed aim. Blue smoke was still curling from his rifle barrel. The Cherokee was holding his left hand to a bloody wound in his upper left chest as he began to walk toward us.

"I told both of you once before!" McCloud said as he stepped nearer. "When something needs killing, then don't hesitate. Kill it!"

"McCloud!" I was so surprised to see him alive I was stunned and only stared at him im disbelief for a moment.

"I was certain you were dead!" I finally said.

"Not quite yet, Ben Branch." he replied. "Grayson never was much of a shot with a rifle."

"Damn you, McCloud!" Asbury said from behind us. The man had sat back upright and was holding his middle with both hands. Dark red blood was leaking out between his fingers. McCloud walked up to Grayson and stood before him with his rifle in his right hand.

"That looks like liver blood leaking through your fingers, Grayson." the Cherokee said. "You'll likely be dead in a few minutes."

"I know that, McCloud." Grayson replied with a grimace "I've seen enough belly wounds to have already made that assessment." Grayson looked up at me then.

"How in the hell did you beat me to the draw with your left hand?" he asked. "You're not left handed!"

"No, I'm not, Grayson." I replied. "You're right about that., but when I was a little boy I had to learn to do lots of things with my left hand. When you taught me how to draw a gun I practiced alone with both hands. I just didn't tell anyone about it."

"Branch," Rosa Kate said. "I want to know how Grayson was acquainted with Logan Ryan before my father went off to fight in the war?" I looked down at Grayson's face that was becoming paler by the minute.

"Grayson paid Logan Ryan to kill your daddy and make it look like he had died in battle, Rosie." I replied. "Ryan took his time about it because he was stealing from Missouri folks under your daddy's command. He knew if he was put under another commander his war profits might be cut off. When Jon David killed your daddy for him, he made it look like a battle fatality so Grayson wouldn't want his money back." Grayson wouldn't look at Rosa Kate.

"Isn't that right, Grayson?" I said to the dying man "You wanted your brother killed so you could take his wife and his half of the empire? Problem was, Katherine wouldn't have you, would she?" Grayson raised his eyes to mine and they practically crackled with hatred.

"You're no better than me, Branch Walker." he said bitterly "You hunted down and murdered the man you only thought killed your mother."

"You're almost right, Grayson." I replied. "I shot Ryan in both legs and I carved him up some with Papa's old knife." my voice hesitated for a moment, "but I didn't kill him." Rosa Kate looked up at me with relief evident in her gaze.

"You didn't kill Logan Ryan?" she asked astounded.

"Nope," I replied, "McCloud, Brady Foreister, and I carried Ryan back to Bloomfield to stand trial. The bartender there says he's plumb anxious to testify that he saw Ryan shoot Jon David in the back! The Bloomfield sheriff told me they'd try Ryan in a fair court of law and when he had recovered enough to be propped up on a gallows, they'd hang him!"

A few minutes later Grayson Asbury began to spasm uncontrollably. Rosa Kate, McCloud, and I stood and watched as life drained from the once powerful man.

A HARD LIFE

CHAPTER THIRTY-EIGHT

Virgil Huggins, the Bloomfield sheriff rode beside the buggy carrying Rosa Kate and me to see Jon David's gravesite beside my parent's. My right arm was still in a sling and it pained me to move it much, but the bones had mended and I had been told my arm would return to normal in a few more weeks.

Rosa Kate and I had been married two weeks before in the little Church of Christ in Denver where Mama's and Hiram McDougall's funeral services had been held. Rosie had told me she wanted to honeymoon where there was warm water to swim in and lots of sunshine to burn our bare backs. Her bare back comment intrigued me so we were on our way to Florida to spend the winter and return to Denver in the spring.

We turned up the grassy lane that led us by the house where I had been born, and under the oak tree where my father had been hung. We passed the barn and tied up the horses to the corral fence to make our way up the hill to the gravesites.

I could see the granite headstones that had been placed since I had been there before. My papa and mama shared an ornately carved headstone that spelled out their names, birthdates, and the dates of their deaths.

I stepped over in front of Jon David's headstone with Rosa Kate holding to my good left arm. I had carried a box I had retrieved from the back of the buggy. I took off the lid and removed a blue union officer's hat. I placed the hat on the special notch that had been carved into the right side of Jon David's headstone. I stepped back then and Rosa Kate and I read the inscription together.

Jon David Walker
Born November 4, 1850
Passed from this world
April 18, 1880

"Life didn't turn out exactly the way I planned, but at least
I'm wearing the hat of the man who shot me, while mine's still out dancing with pretty women!"

"One pretty woman, Jon David." I said. "I'm afraid that's all I'm allotted now days." I hugged Rosa Kate to me with my good arm.

"Is that what you wanted carved on his stone, Branch?" Sheriff Huggins asked and I nodded to him.

"You did good, Sheriff." I replied quietly.

We returned to Bloomfield where we had taken a room for the night. We were scheduled to catch the stage

A Hard Life

the next morning to Poplar Bluff, and go by train from there to Florida.

About midnight I slipped from the big bed where Rosa Kate was sleeping peacefully. I had placed my clothes in the outer room and I dressed quietly and hurriedly. I found the saddled horse I had previously arranged to be left outside the hotel, and in another half hour I was turning back up the moonlighted lane of our old homestead. I rode to the little graveyard, dismounted beside Jon David's grave, and untied a small shovel secured behind the saddle

I dug a narrow trench a foot or so deep at the foot of Jon David's headstone. It took a while because of my nearly useless right arm. When it was deep enough to suit me I reached behind me with my left hand and removed Papa's knife from its scabbard. I held it in my hand for a while, and then dropped it into the trench and covered it up. I tamped down the dirt and smoothed it with the shovel.

"I know you don't need this old blade where you are now, Jon David," I said, "but. I believe it's served us Walker's enough in its day. I think it's better off here, where it can never draw blood again."

I reached down and put my left handprint in the soft soil. I stood then and surveyed what I had done and then I spoke to my brother one more time.

"You can ask Papa what the handprint in the dirt is all about, Jon David."

THE END

A HARD LIFE

EPILOGUE

A horn blared behind me and my eyes shot open. The traffic had begun to clear in front of me and the drivers behind me were impatient, to say the least. I sat upright, pulled the gear lever to drive position and sped down the boulevard behind the now-moving traffic.

I rubbed my eyes and looked at my watch to see that it was now 6:43. I had dozed for only a few minutes. The dream I had about Ben Branch Walker was still clear in my mind, but I imagined it would soon fade like all my dreams seem to do.

I felt different somehow. I reflected on the day's activities I had been thinking about when I dozed off and now they didn't seem nearly so important.

I looked up at an oncoming highway sign that read, Exit - Highways 40-61-64 to Wentzville and I-70 west I knew that Interstate 70 west was the way back home.

For some unfathomable reason I eased the SUV off the boulevard to the exit ramp that would take me toward Wentzville, instead of to my upstairs apartment. When I was fifteen miles up the highway headed west I realized I was going home.

I wondered what Cheryl would say when she saw me coming home on a Monday night? I smiled a little to myself. I knew exactly what she would say. She would say the same thing that Rosa Kate Asbury would say to Ben Branch Walker after he had been gone for a while.

"Hello, Sweetheart." she would say. "What took you so long to decide to come home?"

I smiled broadly and even laughed to myself as a thought crossed my mind.

"This is not such a hard life after all!"

LAW OF THE PROPHET
By: Ronald Wallace

It was early May, in the year of our Lord 1770, and four men had devoured about half of a deer ham when suddenly a sound from somewhere in the wilderness outside the light of the fire momentarily froze their every movement. I smiled to myself and then whispered to Reanna.

"Don't be afraid any longer." I whispered very quietly where only she could hear. "When I tell you to do so I want you to throw yourself to the ground face down and I will shield you with my body. Don't look up until I say you can." Reanna looked perplexed, but I gave her my most reassuring look and she held my eyes and nodded very slightly.

The strange sound emanating from the darkness was Prophet's song and it seemed to echo from all directions in the river valley. I'm rather certain it was difficult for the four men to judge where it was coming from, or how far away the singer actually might be, but I knew my father was very close

Before Prophet had finished his song the four men hurriedly fetched up their flintlocks and stood in a semicircle around the campfire facing the darkness. It was satisfying for me to see that my father's strange song had a dramatic effect on all four of the men. The two Frenchmen's hands were visibly shaking as they held their rifles hard to their shoulders. I noticed the two Fox warriors glance at each other with serious expressions on their dark features. The warriors held their rifles in a more appropriate posture than the Frenchmen, with the muzzles up, ready to turn and aim in any direction.

The first audible sound after my father's song had stopped was an almost gentle "splat" followed immediately by a rifle blast. The splat sound was a bullet hitting Henri Le Moyne square in the center of his extended belly.

"Now Reanna!" I said, and at my signal she dropped face down and I threw myself over her, shielding her from the carnage I anticipated.

Henri Le Moyne dropped his rifle and held his belly with both hands as a crimson fountain began to spurt through his woolen vest and out through his fingers. Henri was staring downward at his wound as if amazed and suddenly dropped to his knees wailing like a child!

The other three men were staring at Henri as he knelt on his knees transfixed by the sight of his own blood spurting out on the ground, when suddenly a figure launched itself from the darkness and with dizzying speed flew through the encampment. I momentarily caught a vision of my father's face and form outlined in the firelight. He had his long knife in his right hand and his tomahawk in his left. His long hair was flying around his head and the expression on his face was almost gleeful.

Prophet flew through the camp and then was gone, but before he had completely disappeared from sight Henri Le Moyne's son, Pierre, suddenly dropped his unfired rifle and clutched his throat with both hands, his face contorted in both pain and unspeakable fright. Blood spurted between his fingers from severed arteries in his neck and he pitched to his face, his entire body vibrating in death throes.

Likewise, the nearest Fox warrior fired his rifle harmlessly into the air and fell heavily, partly into the campfire, his forehead and face split and drenched in blood from Prophet's hatchet!

The remaining Fox warrior fired his rifle also, but into the darkness in the direction of my fleeing father, whom I was certain was nowhere near when the lead missile whizzed harmlessly through the brush. The warrior took one downward look at his fallen comrade and vaulted into the darkness in the opposite direction. Only seconds later I heard an agonized high-pitched scream from the same direction, which I was certain was the Fox's final death cry.

Henri Le Moyne still knelt on his knees holding his bleeding belly and wailing with pain. My father stepped back into the firelight still holding his bloody knife and hatchet. He leaned down to stare into Henri's face. The wailing stopped.

"What's ye name, Frenchie?" Henri appeared confused for a second before he replied.

"Henri Le Moyne, from New Orleans." he replied hoarsely.

"Do ye know who I be, Henri?" Prophet inquired and Le Moyne nodded without a verbal reply. Prophet continued to stare into the man's eyes.

"Then what would possess ye to treat my son in such an inhospitable manner?" Prophet asked.

"You murdered my eldest son, Jean Baptiste, a year ago. I deserve justice." Le Moyne answered weakly. His face contorted in sudden intense pain and he closed his eyes. Prophet waited patiently until the Frenchman recovered from the spasm and had reopened his eyes.

"Ye be right, Le Moyne, except I don't commit murder, and I'm the only designated one to administer justice in this territory." Prophet replied. "Ye son Jean Baptiste was a true murderer. He led a band of cutthroats given to pirating whiskey boats. Before I stopped im' he was credited with murdering over a dozen sailors." Henri Le Moyne's face contorted in agony again.

"Would ye want me to end ye sufferin', Le Moyne?" Prophet asked. I put my hand on Reanna's head so she would not lift it to see what I was certain was about to happen.

Henri Le Moyne raised his eyes to my father's again and nodded. Prophet's sharp knife made a slash across the Frenchman's throat and Henri fell to the ground on his face, his remaining lifeblood gushing from his body and soaking into the sandy soil. My father turned in my direction then.

"Ye be wounded, Shepherd?" Prophet inquired and I shook my head, rolled my body away from Reanna and spoke her name. She raised her face from the ground and stared in horror at the bloody knife and tomahawk in Prophet's big hands. He glanced down at them also and with a slight twitch of his shoulders, as if an apology, he reached down and wiped the blades clean on the back of Henri Le Moyne's woolen vest. Then he walked over to the fire pit, rolled the dead warrior out of the embers with his foot, and reached for the haunch of venison. Prophet carved off a slice of meat, then turned to face Reanna and me. He bit off a piece of the charred deer ham and chewed for a while.

"Fox warriors cook good venison." he commented thoughtfully.

Be watching for Ronald Wallace's next released novel "Law of the Prophet" to appear in print late in 2006

About the Author

Ronnie Wallace was born in a little four-room house on a forty acre sand farm in the southeast corner of Missouri that local residents oftentimes refer to as, "Swampeast Missouri."

The timing of Ronnie's birth was thirteen years before the last surviving Civil War soldier was laid to rest in Minnesota. Upon his birth Ronnie became a member of only the fourth generation since this southern Missouri delta country was part of the extreme western frontier of the United States!

Ronnie grew up listening to tales of the struggles of brave men and women that had struggled mightily to change this hostile river environment into the rich farming country that it is today. That heritage made an indelible impression on him and has resulted in several novels of a time in the early years of the western frontier.

CPSIA information can be obtained at www.ICGtesting.com
Printed in the USA
BVOW08s0701080114

341192BV00001B/3/P